The crew of th...
The Simiu were unexpected ...

Earth's first contact with an alien race turns to disaster when a friendly encounter erupts into inexplicable violence and the threat of interstellar war.

But two young individuals—Mahree Burroughs, an ordinary woman with a gift for friendship, and Dhurrrkk', a male Simiu with boundless curiosity—have forged a bond of understanding that bridges their many differences.

Along with a reluctant Robert Gable, brilliant young ship's physician, they make an astounding journey across the stars, to seek a way to save the future of the galaxy!

◆　　◆　　◆

Books by A. C. Crispin

V
YESTERDAY'S SON
TIME FOR YESTERDAY
GRYPHON'S EYRIE (with Andre Norton)
THE EYES OF THE BEHOLDERS

The StarBridge Series

STARBRIDGE
STARBRIDGE 2: SILENT DANCES (with Kathleen O'Malley)
STARBRIDGE 3: SHADOW WORLD (with Jannean Elliott)
STARBRIDGE 4: SERPENT'S GIFT (with Deborah A. Marshall)

A.C. CRISPIN

★★★★★★★★★★★★★★★★★ *Book One*

STARBRIDGE

ACE BOOKS, NEW YORK

This book is an Ace original edition,
and has never been previously published.

STARBRIDGE

An Ace Book/published by arrangement with
the author

PRINTING HISTORY
Ace edition/September 1989

ISBN: 0-441-78329-5

Ace Books are published by The Berkley Publishing Group,
200 Madison Avenue, New York, New York 10016.
The name "ACE" and the "A" logo are trademarks
belonging to Charter Communications, Inc.

PRINTED IN THE UNITED STATES OF AMERICA

10 9 8 7 6 5 4

ACKNOWLEDGMENTS

Some writers may produce books in an attic, or a vacuum, requiring no inspiration or assistance except that provided by their own inner voice.

I am not one of them.

I owe many people a debt of gratitude for their assistance in producing *StarBridge*. I, like many others, get by with a little help from my friends. Heartfelt appreciation is due the following people:

First and foremost, my collaborator in Book Three of the StarBridge series, *Silence Dances*, Kathleen O'Malley. O'Malley is my good friend and first-line editor, the person who keeps me on my toes and honest between book covers. Without her creativity, advice and editing ability, StarBridge would never have gotten off the ground. Thanks, Kathy.

Ginjer Buchanan, my excellent ACE editor, who improved *StarBridge* vastly by putting it on a diet. Ginjer, I'm grateful for your faith in me, in this book, and in the StarBridge series.

My agent, Merrilee Heifetz of Writer's House, who first suggested that the time was right for me to create my own series.

Deb, Teresa, Anne, Deborah and Faith, my Whileaway buddies, who provided (as always) encouragement, advice and moral support.

My mother, Hope Tickell, for proofreading the manuscript.

My friend, Paula Volsky, for her advice and encouragement.

I'm *not* a scientist, so I am dependent on people "in the know" for technical advice when putting the "science" into my science fiction. I'd like to thank the following people (with the *caveat* that any errors contained herein are exclusively my own):

Vonda N. McIntyre, my friend, who patiently listened (long-distance, yet) and gave advice on a variety of subjects;

Dr. Robert Harrington of the U.S. Naval Observatory, for help in figuring out orbits, interstellar distances, and the like;

Irene Kress, for reading the manuscript and making comments;

Ben Bova, for information on the effects of explosive decompression.

Also:

Hérica Kamer, for vetting my extremely rusty French;

J. Kalogridis, for information and advice on linguistics, both human and alien;

Harlan Ellison, for advice on writing during the Boca Raton writer's workshop of 1983, for inspiration gained throughout the years from his works, and in hopes that this will eliminate the last of the "frisson of unhappiness." Thanks also for arranging that suite with the maid and the aspic for me when I get to Heaven . . .

And last, but by no means least:

My husband, Randy, for child care, vacuuming, loading the dishwasher, and going out for pizza while I was parsecs from home.

This book is dedicated to Andre Norton, First Lady of science fiction and fantasy . . . and my friend.

When I was growing up, your stories, more than any others, filled me with a sense of wonder about the universe. A sense of wonder is one of the greatest gifts a writer can bestow . . . something to treasure always. Thank you, Andre.

CHAPTER I

✦

Sixteen Parsecs From Nowhere . . .

Dear Diary:

Nothing ever happens in space. Of course Uncle Raoul's happy about that—I suppose *Désirée* getting clipped by a chunk of comet or skidding into a black hole would be bad for business. And he *did* warn me that space travel would be boring. But I never dreamed *how* boring!

I think Maman must have remembered her trip from Earth to Jolie, because she gave me a handful of memory cassettes, suggesting that a diary might help pass the time. I'll try and make an entry each day—it may be the only thing that will keep me from losing my mind.

They only woke me up out of hibernation yesterday, and already I've explored this freighter five times—except for the cargo hold and that's off-limits for the remaining six months of our trip to Earth.

Six months!

In six months I'll be a raving lunatic. College can't possibly be worth it. The "cradle of humanity" can't possibly be worth it. Everyone says how wonderful Earth is, how I'll love it . . . then, in the same breath, they mention it's so overcrowded and noisy that they never regretted becoming colonists . . .

But if I want an education past U-prep level, I'm stuck being bored for the duration. Boring Mahree Burroughs, sixteen, almost seventeen, stuck on a boringly routine voyage on a boringly ordinary freighter—I may be the first person in history to *die* from boredom.

If only I were different! But I'm so damned average-looking . . . brown hair, brown eyes, medium-fair complexion, medium height, medium build (except for my chest measurement, which is definitely *sub*-normal, dammit!).

Medium . . . average . . . ordinary . . .

When I was little I used to worry that I'd disappear.

Dad always tells me I'll improve with age and experience. He says I look very much as he did at sixteen, and now, though he's not holo-vid handsome, he's considered quite attractive. Distinguished. Only trouble is, he's a man, and features that look good on a middle-aged man will probably look shitty on me when I'm his age. I feel disloyal admitting this, but I wish that I looked like Maman, instead, because she has gorgeous auburn hair and sapphire eyes.

(But of course there's nothing ordinary about my father—Dr. Stanley Burroughs, physician and researcher, the man who discovered the L-16 vaccine. Maman isn't ordinary either—she designed and built half the buildings in Nouvelle Marseille.)

Six months!

And to make it worse, *everyone* on this ship is *venerable*. At least forty.

With one exception. The ship's physician, Robert Gable. He's twenty-four, which makes him barely seven years older than I am. (My little brother could access the security files on this system.)

Dr. Gable was my father's righthand assistant and friend during the Lotis Plague, but, due to the early quarantine they imposed on North Continent, I've never met him.

(It was terrible . . . the Plague hit, and suddenly I couldn't go home. We had to stay at school. They thought we'd be safe in the mountains, but it reached us, eventually. Several of my teachers and two of my best friends died. I'd never seen anybody die before . . .)

Anyway, I got a look at Robert Gable when I bypassed security and called up his personnel interview vid-record. He's definitely attractive! And *smart*. Even in these days of accelerated degrees and hypno-teaching techniques, he's something of a phenomenon. Graduated from Earth's version of U-prep at *thirteen*, and from med school at twenty-one. Getting to know *him* would definitely be a big step in alleviating my boredom!

Only problem is . . . at the moment he's lying in a coffin, stiff as a rail. They aren't scheduled to wake him up until—

Oops! That was Uncle Raoul on the 'com, wanting to know whether I've finished today's assignments. The main reason they woke me up after three months was so I could put in some concentrated study time—our schools on Jolie are good, but they don't offer the range of subjects that Terran schools do. So I've got some catching up to do . . . especially in Earth history.

Maybe later I'll go look at the stars again. You'd think they'd make me feel smaller, more isolated, but for some reason I find myself comforted when I see them—they've been there for such a long time, and they'll be there when we're all gone. And even *they* aren't eternal . . .

Enough metaphysical musing. Back to history. (But, honestly, I don't see why I have to learn chapter and verse about stuff that happened hundreds of years ago. What difference can it possibly make? And the Second Martian Colony is *so* boring!)

Au revoir, diary.

Mahree Burroughs hit the "save" button on the computer link in her tiny cabin, frowning at the slowness of the system response. Then she called up her history textbook, and stared determinedly at it for several minutes, but couldn't concentrate. Finally she gave up and flung herself onto her bunk. *I'll never make it*, she thought dismally. *I can't stand this . . .*

Finally she rolled over again and sat up. Gathering fistfuls of her hair, Mahree reached for her brush, then faced the wall over her minuscule washstand. "Mirror," she commanded, and the surface shimmered, then went reflective. Squinting with concentration, she began braiding her waist-length hair, fingers moving with the deftness of long practice. *If only I weren't so ordinary. So unremarkable that I'm practically invisible.*

Finished, she flung the heavy braid back over her shoulder. "Wall," she commanded, and the mirror disappeared, fading into the powder blue of the softly padded plas-steel walls.

"And while you're at it, turn green. I'm tired of blue."

She watched for a moment as the walls, ceiling, and floor began to change their hue, but even playing with the color controls in her tiny cabin had lost its appeal.

Footsteps sounded faintly in the corridor, breaking into her brown study. "*Two* heartbeats?" demanded a voice Mahree recognized as her uncle's. "Are you sure his unit's got two heartbeats?"

"I'm sure," came the response. "I started him on the Vita-stim airmix this morning, because he's scheduled for revival tomorrow afternoon. But when I checked his progress just now, there were two heartbeats, Captain! One normal for a man his size, and the other, much smaller, coming from the abdomen."

Mahree put her ear against the narrow crack she'd left in her doorseal. "So what are you implying?" Raoul Lamont demanded sarcastically. "That the man is pregnant?"

"Of course not, Captain! I'm simply . . ."

The voices faded away as the footsteps continued on down the corridor.

Too intrigued to resist, Mahree opened her door and scurried down the tan-colored plas-steel corridor, her bare feet soundless on the resilient flooring. Her uncle's companion was *Désirée*'s Bio Officer, Simon Viorst. The two men never glanced behind them—both were concentrating too deeply on their problem as they continued toward the hibernation chamber, located just forward of the cargo holds.

"Why didn't you notice this before?" the Captain was demanding as Mahree dared to move within earshot again.

The Bio Officer sounded embarrassed. "I don't know, sir. I checked the readouts every day, as usual. For some reason the second one didn't register until today."

"Could you bring him out of it now?"

"Sure," Viorst replied confidently. "I'd just give him the rest of the Vita-stim in an injection. Is that what you want?"

"As soon as I take a look for myself."

As they keyed open the door to the hibernation chamber, Mahree ducked behind a support stanchion. When her uncle and the Bio Officer stepped into the hibernation chamber, she mentally counted twenty, then began strolling casually past the open door, pausing when she saw them inside. "Oh, hi, Uncle Raoul. What are you doing down here?"

"Simon was concerned about some fluctuations in the readings on the unit containing the ship's physician," Lamont told her, raking his fingers through his thinning brown hair in a habitual gesture of worry. "So we're waking him up to make sure nothing's wrong."

Mahree followed them into the chamber, glancing around with

studied indifference. The coffinlike hibernation units, ten of them, covered three sides of the area. Each had a bank of readouts studding its top cover and a small window so the person sleeping within could be identified. Both men were standing by one of the middle units, so she joined them. "Okay if I stay, Uncle Raoul? I've never seen anyone revived."

"I guess so, unless he experiences an adverse reaction when we open the unit," her uncle told her, busy with the external controls. "Vita-stim makes some people upchuck, and that would embarrass the man."

Mahree glanced down at the doctor. *Sleeping beauty,* she thought wryly, experiencing again the attraction she had felt when she had called up Robert Gable's image on the holo-screen.

The Medical Officer had very dark, curly hair; due to the hibernation it was quite long, but Mahree recalled from his interview vid that he wore it considerably longer than current male fashion decreed. His skin was fair, but not freckled; his regular, almost delicate features were rescued from prettiness by a wide mouth and a rather long nose.

Simon Viorst administered an injection via the intravenous hookup. A few minutes later, Gable began to stir slightly; then he blinked. Captain Lamont glanced over at the tall blond Bio Officer. "Here he goes, Simon. Stand by with that O_2 mask."

Mahree heard a hiss as the seals on the hibernation "coffin" released, then a faint puff of cold air made gooseflesh spring up on her bare arms. The lid swung up.

"What the hell—" Raoul Lamont stared down into the hibernation unit, amazement etched on his ruddy, moustached features. "It's a damned—"

"Cat!" exclaimed Mahree in delight as she crowded under his arm to see better. "A real Terran cat!"

The small black animal lay curled on top of the man in the unit. As Mahree watched, it opened eyes of palest green, emitting a tiny questioning sound.

"I've seen them on Earth," Raoul muttered, mostly to himself. "Where did he get this one? They were only cleared by the ecologists last year for shipment to Jolie."

"The Governor has three," Mahree said. "I saw one of them at that party at the mansion when she gave Dad his award for discovering the L-16 vaccine."

The man in the unit suddenly gasped, then began to struggle.

"Oxygen!" snapped Raoul, grabbing the cat and thrusting it unceremoniously into Mahree's arms as Viorst clamped the mask over the doctor's face. The gasping noises abruptly changed to retching ones.

"Hell, he's sick. Get his head up!" Raoul and Simon dragged at the doctor's shoulders.

Mahree hastily scuttled outside. Once safely in the corridor, she leaned against the bulkhead with a sigh of relief—and discovered she was still holding the cat.

"Hi!" she whispered, delighted. Gingerly she shifted the little animal to a more comfortable position, then stroked the plushy fur. After a moment it snuggled against her trustingly.

She was still petting the cat when Raoul and Simon reappeared. Each man held one of Robert Gable's arms, steadying the newly revived man. The doctor was pale, his eyes puffy, but he wore a fresh ship's jumpsuit and his hair hung in damp ringlets from his shower. From the interview vid-record, Mahree had gained little impression of his size; now she saw that he had a slender, athletic build. He was also short; both Raoul and Simon towered over him.

The doctor's expression brightened as he saw Mahree scrambling to her feet, his pet in her arms. "Is she all right?" he asked—croaked, rather, his voice harsh from long disuse.

"She's fine," Mahree reassured him. "What a beautiful animal, and so friendly. I never got to pet one before."

"Her name is Sekhmet," Gable said, stepping forward under his own power to rub the backs of his fingers beneath the creature's chin. After a moment the animal began making a buzzing, rasping noise.

"Respiratory difficulty?" Mahree gazed anxiously at the cat.

Gable chuckled. "No, she's just purring. They do that when they're happy."

"This is my niece, Mahree Burroughs," Raoul Lamont said. "Mahree, this is Dr. Gable."

The girl nodded, her ease vanishing with the formality of the introduction.

"Hello." Gable's smile was a little strained as he formally extended his hand. "So you're Stan Burroughs' daughter. I've heard a lot about you."

Mahree blushed as she tried to disentangle first one hand, then the other. She nearly dropped the cat, who abruptly stopped purring and gave all of them a dirty look.

Gable, with an embarrassed laugh, clasped her hand with the briefest of touches. "Here, I'd better take her. I wouldn't want you to get scratched."

Regretfully, Mahree handed over the cat.

Raoul Lamont cleared his throat loudly. "Well, Doctor," he said, his voice gruffly official. "You've got a lot of explaining to do."

Gable nodded dejectedly. "I know. Can I get a cup of coffee before I start?"

Simon Viorst nodded. "That and some food. We brought you out early, so you're going to feel like you've got a hangover for a couple of hours."

The younger man grimaced. "Tell me about it."

Minutes later, the two ship's officers faced the errant ship's physician in the common room and galley over cups of coffee and a plate of sweet rolls. Mahree sat in one of the booths across the compartment, eating a sandwich, her history text before her on the table's monitor. She was careful to keep advancing the pages, but her ears strained to catch every word.

Robert Gable took a cautious swig from the steaming mug Raoul Lamont handed him, then made a face. "I'm so far gone I can't even tell if that's bad or good. At least it's strong."

Viorst sipped his coffee and scowled. "It's bad, Doc. Your taste buds must still be asleep."

"All right, Gable, let's have that explanation," Raoul Lamont snapped. "Where'd you get the cat, and what do you mean sneaking it aboard my ship?"

"Right," the doctor said, and sighed. "Sekhmet was a gift from Governor Tumali. 'An informal award for your services to Jolie during the epidemic,' as she put it. I had been called to the Governor's mansion to treat her little girl when she fell out of a parachute tree. When I happened to mention that I was fond of cats, the Governor hands me this one! I was on the spot—how do you turn down a valuable gift from the Governor without seeming churlish?"

"You say, 'I'm terribly sorry, but I can't. Thank you anyway, Governor,' " Lamont said evenly.

"Uh, yeah." The doctor cleared his throat. "Anyway, that same afternoon you called, saying your ship's doctor had de-

cided to get married and stay on Jolie, and offering me the
chance to get home months before I thought I'd be able to . . .
as long as I could leave immediately.

"I knew that there wasn't time to get clearance for Sekhmet,
but the chance to leave early was too good to miss. I'd already
been on Jolie a year longer than I'd planned because of the
epidemic, so"—he turned his hands palm-up, smiling ruefully—
"so I rigged my unit, then smuggled her in with me. Half of my
allotted baggage weight consists of food and supplies for her.
She's housebroken, so she won't be any trouble, Captain."

"Why didn't you *ask* me?" Lamont growled.

Gable looked abashed, and very young. "I was afraid you'd
say no," he admitted. "I'm sorry, sir."

"She'll have to go through quarantine when we reach Earth,"
Viorst warned him.

"I know. But six weeks won't be so terrible. Sekhmet's
young, she'll adjust. They'll let me visit her."

"Well, I guess it's all right," Raoul said, pouring himself
another cup of coffee and clamping a lid over the steaming
liquid. "But I'm going to have to fine you for disobeying orders,
Doc."

"I figured you would," the younger man said resignedly,
stroking the cat. Sekhmet was asleep, relaxed trustingly into the
hollow of his lap.

Raoul grunted and picked up his coffee. "Simon, we have
work to do." He stood up, slanting a sardonic look down at
Gable. "Doctor, you have until tomorrow to officially report for
ship's duty. Welcome aboard *Désirée*."

"Thank you, sir."

With a brusque nod, Lamont left, Viorst close on his heels.

Mahree heard the doctor sigh with relief, then he softly addressed his cat. "I suppose that could have been worse, girl. At
least he didn't chuck us out the airlock."

She glanced covertly at him again, only to find Gable regarding her curiously. Mahree blushed as she turned back to her
history text. "Want a cup of coffee?" he called. "There's half a
pot of this mud left."

"All right," she said, surprised, and moved over to take the
mug he held out.

"Sit down," he said, waving her to the chair opposite him.
"Here you go, Sekhmet"—he passed the cat to Mahree—"say

'thanks' to Ms. Burroughs for rescuing you." He shook his head, smiling. His easy, boyish grin revealed very white, even teeth. "If you hadn't shown such an attachment to her, your uncle might have insisted she go right back into hibernation."

Mahree smiled shyly as she took the cat and began rubbing her chin, eliciting another purr. "I doubt it. Uncle Raoul is too softhearted for his own good. He probably will 'forget' to collect that fine from you unless you remind him. He just puts on that official-sounding tone because he's afraid people won't respect him if they find out what a nice guy he is."

Gable took a sip of coffee. "I'm glad to hear that. On the way out from Earth I had a captain who was a real martinet—saluting, formal ship's uniform, all that rigamarole." He fell silent, watching her as she sweetened her coffee. "You're what . . . sixteen? Seventeen? Stan told me, but I've forgotten. He talked about you all the time."

"I'm almost seventeen," Mahree said.

"Just my sister Linda's age," he told her. "She's the baby of the family."

"Do you have any brothers?"

He shook his head. "I'm the only male. Three sisters, all younger. You have a younger brother, right?"

"Stephen. He's twelve."

He grinned at her. "If memory serves, twelve-year-old boys are a real pain in the neck."

"Steve has his moments," Mahree said. "But he's not bad. He didn't have much opportunity to drive me crazy because I was away for two years, going to school on South Continent."

"During the Lotis Plague."

"Yes. First thing they did was quarantine North Continent, but then it spread down there anyway, during the second wave."

"The quarantine was only lifted a couple of months ago. You didn't have long to be home before leaving again."

"I was only there for six weeks before *Désirée* left. It wasn't long enough . . ."

He didn't miss the faint tremor in her voice. "Homesick? Me, too. That's the real reason I couldn't leave Sekhmet behind—she reminded me too much of Nefertiti, the cat I had when I left home. She seemed like a link back to Earth."

"What did you do with her?"

"My mother's keeping her for me. I hope she's all right. I've been gone a lot longer than I'd planned."

Mahree heard the regret in his voice, and recalled that he'd traveled to Jolie from Earth to intern in colonial medicine. He'd landed during the early stages of the epidemic's first wave—when the doctors were barely realizing that Lotis Fever had mutated into a planet-wide threat, no longer the flulike virus only dangerous to the very old and the very young.

She realized that her earlier awkwardness had vanished . . . she felt as though she'd talked with Robert Gable before, and often. "Well, if the Governor had given me Sekhmet, I wouldn't have been able to resist her, either," she said warmly. "She's beautiful, Dr. Gable."

He winced exaggeratedly, shaking his head. "Call me Rob, please! 'Dr. Gable' makes me think of my parents, not me."

"They're physicians?"

"Yeah . . . my father's a surgeon, my mother an abdominal specialist. They met over a patient during an emergency bowel re-section; isn't that romantic?"

Mahree giggled at the thought, then sobered. "Is that why you went into medicine?" She glanced down at the table and said, because she didn't want to betray her previous knowledge, "You seem awfully young to be a doctor."

He shrugged. "I'm twenty-four. I kind of grew up with it, so it's not as impressive as it might seem at first glance."

Yeah, sure, Mahree thought dryly. *My dad was plenty impressed, and he doesn't toss around words like "prodigy" and "brilliant" easily.* "This is my first trip to Earth," she said.

He nodded. "I know. Your dad told me all about you and your brother. He talked about his family all the time. If I hadn't been so groggy from the hibernation, I'd have recognized you, from all the holos on his desk. Your father used to read me excerpts from your letters—I particularly liked the one about how you masterminded the scheme to switch the food-preparation programs so the faculty ended up with the students' dinner menu, and the kids got the teachers' liquor allowance."

"I got in a lot of trouble over that," Mahree said, ducking her head in embarrassment. "It was a pretty juvenile stunt. Dad didn't think it was funny."

"Maybe he didn't admit his amusement to *you*," Rob told her, "but he went around the lab chuckling every time he thought about it. Life was grim around there, and your letters were the only things that weren't depressing. At least . . . until the Plague hit your school. Then it got rough, I know.''

"It was better for me than for the others," she said, not meeting his eyes. "At least I stayed healthy.''

"I don't know," he said grimly. "I think it's worse in some ways to be one of the ones who isn't sick. I remember that by the end of the epidemic, you wrote that you were pulling regular duty alongside the teachers and nurses.''

Mahree nodded, then changed the subject. "My dad talked about you in his letters," she said. "He said he couldn't have completed his research on the L-16 without you.''

"Bull. He'd have discovered it. Your father is a brilliant researcher, as well as an excellent physician.''

"He's a great father, too. Even during the worst of the first wave, he still found time to call me once a week; usually from the lab.''

"And now you're on your way to Earth for college?" Rob asked. "Where?''

"The Sorbonne in Paris.''

He whistled admiringly. "Good school. What are you planning to major in?''

Mahree frowned as she stroked the cat. "I don't know. I don't seem to have much aptitude for the things I'm interested in, and the things I'm good at, I don't care about doing. I've even considered medicine, but . . ." She shrugged.

"You ought to be sure before you spend four or five years of your life immersed in a subject," Rob warned. "It doesn't pay to pick something just because of your parents, because you want to make them proud, or admire the prestige and the money.'' He reached over to caress Sekhmet. Mahree saw that his hands were beautifully shaped—long-fingered and capable. His voice took on a bitter note. "I should know.''

"You?" Mahree was startled. "But you're a *doctor*. My dad says you're very good! Don't you like it?''

He sighed. "Yes and no. The whole time I was growing up, it was all I could imagine doing . . . my parents were so thrilled when I was accepted at Johns Hopkins, because that was where they both went . . .''

He took a sip of his coffee and made a face at the taste. "A lot of the time it's rewarding, but for some reason I've never seemed to get everything I want out of it. I also got a Ph.D. in psychology, and sometimes I think that's more my line. But . . .'' He shrugged. ''I don't know. I've always wanted to do something that would make a difference, that would be *unique*, that I could look back on at the end of my life and feel good about. Like your father, when he discovered the L-16 vaccine.''

''I know what you mean,'' Mahree said eagerly. ''I want to accomplish something special, too.'' Then her shoulders slumped. ''But . . . I don't know what that 'something' is.''

Rob smiled wistfully, nodding. ''I thought medicine would be my 'something special.' I thought that as a doctor I could really make a difference.''

''But you did! During the epidemic, you and the others saved lots of lives.''

''And lost nearly as many. Hundreds . . . *thousands* of people died, and we were helpless to stop it.'' For a second the dark eyes in the unlined face were old, filled with pain. ''I suppose I did make a difference, but . . . every time I think about the people we saved, I remember all the ones we lost, so it doesn't feel right, if you can understand that.'' He sighed bitterly. ''To me, it felt like failure.'' Rob shook his head, obviously frustrated. ''I sound like some kind of glory hound, don't I? That's not the way I mean it.''

Mahree cocked her head at him, forgetting her shyness as she considered his words. ''I understand. Like me, you want a challenge. Something *big*. But at the same time you're afraid that even if it came along, you couldn't handle it.''

His eyes met hers for a long moment, then he chuckled self-consciously. ''For two people who supposedly have most of our lives still in front of us, we're a gloomy pair, aren't we? And, as the person who supposedly keeps tabs on the mental health of everyone aboard, I'm hardly talking like a therapist. I'm supposed to make you feel better, not depress you.''

''Then let's talk about something else,'' Mahree suggested. ''Since *Désirée* is too small to need a full-time doctor or psychologist, you must have another shipboard job. What is it?''

''When Viorst goes into hibernation next week, I'll be in charge of the hydroponics,'' Rob replied. ''Checking the greenhouse and the algae tanks to make sure the ship's oxygen supply stays constant.''

"Can I help?" Mahree asked. "I had a garden back on Jolie."

"Sure." He grinned at her and lowered his voice confidentially. "The moment I met Simon Viorst I could just picture his hydroponics stock. Strictly by-the-book. Regulation algae strains, and maybe some neo-soy."

"Yuck."

"Exactly. So, before we left Jolie, I stocked up on some seeds. By the time Viorst wakes up, we'll have a variety that'll make his eyes pop. Flowers for the tables in the galley. Fresh vegetables."

Mahree smiled back at him. "Tomatoes? Zucchini?"

He chuckled. "Of course. They're the easiest of all."

"And if we don't eat all the zucchini"—Mahree began to giggle—"we can always implant them with transmitters and use them for space buoys."

The doctor shook his head ruefully. "Isn't it amazing that no matter how few you plant, you end up with a surplus?" Sekhmet mewed, butting her head against Rob's arm as she rose. After stretching herself to a seemingly impossible length, the cat jumped down and began cautiously exploring the galley. Mahree looked back at her companion. "What part of Earth are you from?"

"OldNorthAm, the Midwest. A place called Terre Haute."

"High Earth," Mahree translated, surprised. "That's French."

"You speak French?"

"That was my mother's first language. A lot of Jolie's colonists came from France. But tell me about Earth. What is it really like?"

"Well, when I left three years ago, it was about the same as it's been for the last two hundred years. Crowded. Even the colonies on NewAm, Jolie, and Novaya Rossiya haven't taken the overpopulation pressure off, because most people won't travel fifty klicks to work, let alone fifty parsecs to have a better life. You were lucky to grow up on a colony world."

"Are the cities everywhere?" Dismayed, Mahree thought of her long walks over Jolie's fields, of the hikes and camping trips she had taken in the mountains. How could she give that up for years?

"No, not in OldNorthAm. The government owned a lot of the land, and they hung onto it until the bitter end. So there are still big wildlife refuges and parks, and there are several huge areas belonging to the InterCouncil of Native American tribes. They call them living museums.''

"Can anyone visit these places?''

"Well, they screen visitors pretty carefully, but I'm sure you could get in on a student pass. You enjoy hiking?''

"I love it.''

"Sometime you'll have to catch the morning shuttle over and I'll take you out to the Blue Ridge Mountains, or the Rockies in Colorado. We'll take a picnic.''

"That would be great! But I wouldn't want to . . .'' Mahree trailed off.

"Impose?'' he guessed. "I remember vividly what it's like to be a stranger on a new world. Your father and mother made me feel as though I were a part of the family. It would be a pleasure to begin returning the favor. And I'd really enjoy hiking again.''

She smiled. "Too bad we can't put on spacesuits and hike around the outside of the ship. We'll be closed in for—''

"Attention,'' interrupted the ship's intercom. "First Mate Joan Atwood report to the communications station immediately.''

"Communications?'' Rob frowned. "We're in metaspace, aren't we? Too far from Jolie to be receiving any messages?''

"I know.'' Mahree jumped up excitedly. "That was Uncle Raoul. He sounded funny. Something strange must be going on . . . maybe we've crossed the path of another freighter.''

Rob shook his head. "The odds against that are—''

"Come *on*!'' She headed for the door, waving impatiently for Rob to follow her.

Fortunately, the galley was located forward of the work areas and crew quarters, because even as Mahree bolted toward the bridge, she heard the excited babble of the other crew members behind her. She and Rob were at the forefront of a living wave as it spilled through the entrance into the control cabin.

All of the watch crew plus the Captain and the Chief Engineer stood clustered around the communications console located on the left side of the bridge. A quick glance at the viewscreens showed Mahree normal stars, instead of the flickering, elongated violet trails indicating passage through metaspace. *That's strange, we're not due for a change of course,* she thought, remembering that she had asked her aunt about it that morning over breakfast. *Is something wrong?*

But the navigation console and pilot's control bank looked normal—no telltales flashed red.

"What's going on?" she whispered, tugging on the nearest man's sleeve. He was dark-skinned and wore a baggy ship's jumpsuit with the green shoulder patch of maintenance engineering. His ID strip identified him as Azam Quitubi.

"Don't know," he said, in strongly accented Standard English. "I was giving a report to the Captain when the emergency-frequency signal went off. Jerry checked and said that it was a radio source, but that it didn't sound like an E-beacon to him. He was pretty excited."

"Excited? *Jerry?*"

Azam shrugged. Mahree craned her neck, trying to see the communications board. *What's going on?*

Travel between Earth and its three colony worlds was still minimal; five or six freighters and one or two passenger ships each year. Even though ships could move at faster-than-light speeds, using the Stellar Velocity Drive, no method of making FTL transmissions had yet been discovered, so *Désirée* and vessels like her transported messages and mail, in addition to freight and passengers.

Even though the chances of another ship happening by in time to assist in an emergency were practically zero, all vessels were equipped with emergency beacons, and, by law, all ships kept their E-frequency channels open at all times.

By now the entire nonhibernating crew had jammed into the back of the little cabin. Mahree couldn't hear over the babble, and she could barely breathe, sandwiched as she was between taller people. Sweat trickled down the back of her neck. The ship's ventilation blowers were doing their best, but they weren't designed for such a concentrated crowd.

"Let me *through,* dammit!" Mahree heard her Aunt Joan bellow. "Raoul, I'm back here!"

"All *right!*" the Captain's voice roared suddenly. "I want all crew except myself, the Chief Engineer, the First Mate, and the Communications Chief to clear out! I'll let you know what's going on as soon as we know!"

Muttering reluctantly, the crowd shuffled backward, into the corridor. Joan Atwood finally emerged, a tall, raw-boned woman with pale, patrician features and a permanent frown line etched between her brows. Joan was an excellent pilot, hard-working and unimaginative by nature, and coldly intolerant of stupidity or incompetence. She was stronger than most men, and had once fractured the skull of a crewman who had attempted to smuggle drugs aboard *Désirée*. Mahree was a little afraid of her aunt.

As the crowd shuffled slowly out, Mahree stayed at the rear of the group. She paused within the entrance to glance back.

Joan Atwood was just seating herself at the communications console, beside Jerry Greendeer. The Communications Chief was a member of the OldNorthAm Winnebago tribe, and his features showed his ancestry clearly. Like most crew members when on duty, he wore a ship's-issue, blue-gray coverall with *Désirée*'s logo and his name above the breast pocket, but Greendeer had ripped the sleeves out and left the front fastening half-unsealed. Fetish necklaces of abalone shell swung against his broad chest, and turquoise studs winked from his earlobes between the lank strands of his shoulder-length black hair.

Still hesitating in the doorway, Mahree bit her lip, torn between obeying her uncle's orders and her overwhelming curiosity. Then she turned back into the control cabin. Since *she* wasn't crew, she decided not to move until specifically told to do so. Luckily, her uncle had already turned back toward the communications board and didn't notice her.

"What's going on, Raoul?" Joan demanded.

"Something activated the E-frequency," her husband told her. "Jerry's not sure what. First time I ever heard the thing go off—gave me a hell of a start."

"Do you scan any ships in the area?"

"It wasn't an E-beacon," Jerry told her, his eyes bright with excitement. "An SOS is impossible to mistake. This was just a wave on the same frequency."

"How long did we receive this . . . whatever it was?" Joan asked, raking an impatient hand through her cropped auburn curls.

"For about ninety seconds," Jerry told her, "but it was pretty weak. Then it began breaking up. Interstellar scintillation, maybe. Or our receiver isn't big enough. Or whatever was making those waves stopped making them."

"Well, which do you think it was?" Raoul demanded.

"No way to tell."

"Let's see it," Joan said. "And turn on the audio."

Jerry's short, squarish fingers skipped capably over the controls, and the central holo-tank display filled with a rainbow profusion of colored peaks and valleys, even as hissing, chattering bursts of static-ridden sound erupted from the audio speakers. "See it there?" he pointed. "The pale orange-colored wavelength."

"And what about how it sounds?" Raoul demanded.

"It's so faint, it's hard to make out."

Raoul gestured at the board. "Isn't there any way to eliminate all this other stuff and boost the signal so we can hear it better?"

"Yeah, I can fiddle with it, and probably do a little better. It's still going to be weak. Maybe if I can pick it up again, get a stronger reception, I can isolate it better . . . but to do that we'll have to stay sublight and search this area."

Mahree turned at a light touch on her arm to find Rob Gable standing beside her, Sekhmet draped over his shoulder. "You're not supposed to be here," she whispered, putting a finger to her lips.

He grinned recklessly at her. "Neither are you," he returned, his mouth only inches from her ear. "What have we picked up?"

"Electromagnetic radiation," Mahree told him, still in an undertone. "Long waves. Radio."

"Radio?" He looked startled. "You mean from *Earth*? But we're too far—"

Mahree was already shaking her head. "Shhhhh!" she reminded him. "No, it doesn't have to be from Earth. All kinds of things produce radio waves . . . anytime electrons move, you get them. Quasars, pulsars, Seyfert galaxies . . . even ordinary stars produce some, though they're not strong sources."

He gave her a look of surprised respect. "I took a semester of astronomy at U-prep, and I can't remember a damned thing about any of it."

"I just had it last year, two terms' worth," she explained, flushing with pleasure.

"So why did the E-beacon go off?" he asked.

"We picked up a wave that was on the same frequency," Mahree replied, then she waved him to silence in order to hear what her uncle was saying.

"You're telling me it definitely wasn't an E-beacon, Jerry." Raoul Lamont's voice was slow, heavy. "Then what was it?"

"Don't know, boss." Jerry had regained his usual equanimity. "I'd like to listen to it all by itself, and I'd also like to run both the visual and the audio through the computer for analysis—have it tell me whether those waves were totally random, or whether they contain any repetition of patterns or sounds.''

"What would that indicate?" Raoul asked.

"Maybe something other than a natural radio source."

Mahree's eyes widened. Rob jabbed her with his elbow. "Does what he just said imply what I think it implies?"

"Shhhhh!"

Raoul Lamont stared at his Communications Chief for nearly a minute in silence. "Jerry . . . we're still more than two hundred light-years from Earth. What are the chances we could be picking up old radio waves that originated there? Television, for example?"

"Slim. The frequencies don't fit. And that sure didn't sound like any human language or code I ever heard. I'll have the computer search its auxiliary files to make sure." Greendeer's broad, OldNorthAm Native features were still impassive, but his voice betrayed an undercurrent of excitement.

"Any other possible sources? Natural ones?"

"Maybe . . . if we've stumbled across something totally unknown."

"Couldn't it be a pulsar?"

Jerry shrugged. "Pulsars—neutron stars—are the strongest radio signals we *should* be receiving out here—but they all have well-documented frequencies. They're so regular that people used to speculate about setting clocks by them. And they've got a broad distribution of frequencies." He pushed his hair behind his ears. "This thing here falls roughly into the 200 to 400 megahertz range. That's *narrow*. Then it drops off abruptly on either side. Pulsars and quasars don't do that."

"So what are you saying? What do you think it is?"

The Communications Officer drummed his fingers thoughtfully. "I'm guessing we'll discover that this signal didn't originate on Earth, that it's not from one of our ships, and that it didn't come from any known natural source."

Greendeer paused, running his fingers through his long hair again, then fished a scrap of cloth out of his jumpsuit pocket and tied it back. Mahree saw that Jerry's hands trembled, belying his studied calmness.

"And?" Raoul prompted.

"And, since we're sixteen parsecs from nowhere, that leaves

only two other possibilities. One, that it's some kind of pre- viously unknown stellar phenomenon—which I doubt, because nothing natural has such a narrow frequency—or, two, that it was generated by an artificial, nonhuman transmitter.''

For the first time Paul Monteleon, *Désirée*'s Chief Engineer, spoke. "Jerry . . . you do know what you're saying, don't you?" His soft, tentative voice was in keeping with his gangly, spare body, his graying brown beard and wispy hair. "We've never discovered any evidence of sentient life-forms other than ourselves out here.''

The communications tech shrugged. "There's a first time for everything, Paul. I'll want to check it out further, of course, but I think we may have hit the jackpot this time.''

Silence enclosed the control cabin like a giant, invisible fist. Nobody moved.

Mahree's heart was pounding so hard that she could hear the blood throbbing in her ears. A strange mixture of fear and joy filled her, and she realized she was shaking, too.

Rob put a steadying hand on her shoulder. She glanced up, seeing that he was flushed with exhilaration. "I can't believe we're this lucky—talk about challenges—this is *great!*''

"An alien transmission," Mahree whispered, putting the idea into words, trying it on for size. Her mouth was dry and her lips felt stiff. "Oh, my God.''

CHAPTER 2

♦

The Phantom Frequency

Dear Diary:

I'm so excited! Jerry and Joan have searched every auxiliary file on board, and the strange signal we received *still* hasn't matched up! Whatever it is, it is *not* from Earth.

Joan refuses to believe that we've actually stumbled onto a transmission from an alien race, and keeps maintaining that it must be electromagnetic radiation from some kind of weird solar flare or black hole or something. She's being unreasonable, which is unlike her. Usually she's pragmatic to a fault. I have no idea why she finds the idea of a world occupied by people who aren't Terran so unsettling, but it's obvious that she does.

The reaction among the crew seems about seventy percent positive, thirty percent negative on hoping that we can pin down the signal as definitely artificial. Simon Viorst, for example, turned pale when he heard—I mean, the man was *scared*. But other people were breaking out hoarded bottles of the finest Jolian champagne and toasting one another.

To think that we are probably making *history*!

Uncle Raoul has a real dilemma: should he use our precious fuel reserves and search this area, hoping to pick up the signal again?—or just log our position, then continue on our original course and turn the coordinates over to officials Earthside?

I'm glad *I* don't have to make that decision.

Uncle Raoul has called an "all hands" meeting tonight in the galley.

I can't wait!

The galley, which had never been designed to host the full ship's complement at one time, was crowded past capacity. Raoul Lamont stood in the doorway, clapping his hands for attention over the buzz of conversation. "Okay! Pipe *down*!"

The galley quieted slowly. "Everyone knows why we're here," he began, "but to make sure we're all on the same wavelength" —everyone chuckled at the pun—"let me tell it the way *I* see it. Then we'll discuss the pros and cons."

He waited for dissension, but none came. "Yesterday we picked up a brief transmission, on a narrow frequency. It doesn't match anything we've seen before. We have no proof that it isn't some kind of natural—though unknown—phenomenon, but, on the other hand, it *might* mean we've stumbled onto a transmission in an alien language or code."

He nodded over at Jerry Greendeer. "Jerry and Joan have managed to amplify the audio portion, and screen out a lot of the background interference. I'd like all of you to listen to it."

Jerry flicked a switch and sounds emerged. They were still laden with static, but much clearer than Mahree had heard on the bridge. Sharp chattering sounds merged into guttural rumbles, then higher-pitched yips and squeals. They were not continuous— there were five or six short pauses, one of them lasting nearly three seconds before the sounds resumed.

The transmission faded into bursts of static.

Voices jumbled at Raoul Lamont in a cacophony of sound. Everyone had an opinion: "That sounded like a damn language to me!" ". . . just like a terrier I had when I was a kid." "Those pauses surely indicate speech!" "Pulsars have pauses, too." "With so much static, who can tell anything?" And, loudly, "But we've had interstellar travel for over a hundred years! If there was anybody out here, we'd have found them by now!"

"Everyone hold on," Raoul broke in hastily. "It's a big universe, remember! Anything could be out here. What we have to decide is how far to pursue this. As Captain, the ultimate decision is mine, but each of you has a stake in getting our cargo home, so I want to hear what you have to say."

"I say we keep going," a gray-haired woman from the engineering crew demanded loudly. "If we try and follow some now-you-hear-it-now-you-don't signal, we'll use up our fuel and be stranded out here until our food runs out. Then we'd be shit outta luck. We can't take the risk."

Simon raised his hand. "I agree, we should head for Earth to report this, Captain. Even if there are nonhumans out there, how do we know they'll be friendly? They might attack us!"

Jerry waved for attention. "I say we keep going so *we* don't endanger *them*. We might be carrying diseases they could catch."

Rob Gable broke in. "We could take precautions against that . . . everyone could stay suited. The computer will have to analyze their air anyway—maybe we don't even breathe the same kind. Anyway, we wouldn't unsuit or advise them to do so until we'd completed extensive testing."

"We have *no* proof"—Joan Atwood's voice was hard—"that we're not just talking ourselves into something here. Without additional transmissions, we wouldn't have a prayer of homing in on anything."

"So we stay in this area and cast around for a couple of million klicks!" yelled someone impatiently. "If we find anything, we'll be able to home in by cross-vectoring! We've got enough fuel for that!"

"But what if they're inhuman—" Simon broke in. Mahree saw that his forehead was beaded with sweat.

"Do you realize how *rich* we'd be when we got back to Earth after confirming a First Contact? Media contracts, advertising, interviews . . . we'd never have to work again!" The speaker was a portly, balding black man Mahree had never seen before. Raoul must have ordered the sleeping crew members awakened. "We *can't* ignore this! We'd be throwing away a bottomless credit balance!"

Mahree leaned over to Yuriko Masuto, the Cargo Chief, who was sitting next to her on top of one of the galley tables. "Who's that, Yoki?"

"Ray Drummond," the short, plump, almond-eyed woman with the waist-length ebony hair whispered back. "Paul Monteleon's assistant. This is his first trip with us."

"But we're just a freighter crew," Paul was protesting in his quiet voice. "We're not diplomats, or ambassadors. We're not qualified to handle this."

"If you leave it to the bureaucrats back on Earth, they'll *really* screw it up," Rob called out, his baritone carrying easily over the babble. "Besides, what if they don't believe us? Even if we decide not to pursue a contact"—he was fighting to sound calm—"we need more proof that we've actually found something."

"Who's the new kid, Raoul?" yelled the older woman.

For a moment Mahree thought the speaker was talking about *her*, but then she saw Rob's face reddening as he stiffened resentfully.

"With all the confusion, I forgot," Raoul said. "This is our new ship's physician, Dr. Robert Gable."

Gable nodded, formally, from his perch atop another table.

"That guy's a *doctor*?" Yoki whispered to Mahree.

"Yeah," Mahree returned. "He's only twenty-four, but my dad said he's really good."

"I'll bet," Yoki murmured, wiggling her eyebrows suggestively. "I can hardly wait for my next physical."

"I say we keep our noses out of what doesn't concern us!" It was Evelyn Maitland, the older woman from engineering again. "Let the proper authorities deal with this!"

"Hey!" yelled another woman from the back. "Where's your sense of adventure? Dammit, aren't you people *curious*?"

A chorus of "I am!"'s and "Let's go!"'s followed her words.

Raoul had to pound the bulkhead for order.

"Okay, I've heard some very good points both for and against. Does anyone have anything further to say before I make my decision?"

Mahree's hand shot up before she was aware that she'd made a decision to speak. Her uncle pointed at her. "This is my niece, Mahree Burroughs. Yes, Mahree?"

The girl wet her lips as she stood up on top of the table, clutching the two computer flimsies she'd brought. "Uh," she began, only to have it emerge as a squeak. She cleared her throat, trying to look only at her uncle, not at all those eyes. "I just wanted to say that I think we have a . . . responsibility, I guess, to investigate this. We can't just sail on by. Does anyone recognize these? I looked them up in my history files this afternoon."

She let the flimsies unroll and held them up, one in each hand. From the murmurs and head shakings, it was clear that nobody did. "Well, this one here, the golden plate with the picture of the naked man and woman on it, that's a picture of the plaque that was attached to the Pioneer 10 and 11 space probes. They were launched in 1970. This thing here"—she pointed—"that looks like a starburst is really a map showing the location of Earth in relation to a bunch of local pulsars."

She dropped that flimsy and pointed to the other. "This one, the golden circle, is a container. Inside is a disk they called a 'phonograph record' with music, pictures, sounds, and greetings from Earth recorded on it. It was attached to Voyager 1 and 2, which were launched in 1977. Yoki is going to read you one of the messages, which was recorded in Mandarin Chinese."

The Asian woman's voice was distinct in the silence as she haltingly spoke in liquid syllables. "That means," she translated, her voice not quite steady, " 'Hope everyone's well. We are thinking about you all. Please come here to visit us when you have time.' "

"Right now," Mahree said, as Yoki sat down, "we have a chance nobody's ever had before. Something our ancestors hoped would happen to them, but it never did. Can we turn our backs on it? Wouldn't that be letting them down, the people whose dreams and efforts made spaceflight possible in the beginning? If it hadn't been for them, none of us would be where we are now, that's for sure."

She cleared her throat again. "This is our chance to be *explorers*, not 'just a freighter crew.' If we don't check this signal out, I know I'll spend the rest of my life wondering what we missed."

There was silence for a moment when she finished, then Yoki and Rob began clapping furiously. Slowly, many of the other crew members joined in, until the room was filled with applause. When the noise finally died away, Raoul nodded agreement. "All right, folks. We'll stay sublight and search this area, trying to pick up any other transmissions"—an excited babble broke out and he raised a hand for quiet before he continued—"but *only* for thirty-six hours. That'll keep us well within our fuel reserve limits. If at the end of that time, we find nothing, we get back on course and report the incident when we reach Earth."

The Captain gave them all a searching look. "Jerry, please organize a roster of volunteers to staff a constant communications watch. Joan, I'll need you in navigation."

He turned and left, and the uproar broke out again as Joan Atwood high-stepped her way over feet and legs to follow him.

"Wow!" Rob Gable turned to grin at Mahree from his table-top. "You were positively eloquent! That little speech of yours turned the tide!"

Mahree blushed.

"Now, if we can just pick up some traces of that transmission within the next thirty-six hours!" Rob leaped down from the table, so excited that Mahree laughed.

"Take it easy, Rob, or you'll float right off the deck plates even with the gravity on!"

"I feel as though I could," he admitted, grinning and bouncing on his toes. Then his gaze fell on Yoki and he gave the younger woman a significant glance. "Mahree, I haven't been formally introduced to your friend yet."

"Oh, I keep forgetting that you came aboard after some of us were hibernating! Cargo Chief Yuriko Masuto, Dr. Robert Gable."

Yoki extended her hand. "Hi, Doc. It's a pleasure."

"Make it Rob, and the pleasure is all mine."

Mahree looked around at the crew members who still filled the galley, talking in small groups. "Now what?" she said. "I can't imagine just going off to bed after this. Anyone want to play cards?"

"I've got a better idea," Rob said, his dark eyes lighting up. He clambered up to stand on top of the nearest table, ducking his head to avoid hitting the ceiling, and waved his arms for attention. "Hey! Fellow explorers! If anyone here is too excited to sleep, you're welcome to watch some films with me. I've got a bunch of them."

"*Films?*" Yoki stared up at him. "You mean old ones? Where the hell did you get them?"

"It's my hobby," Gable explained, still grinning. "I collect them. I've got some goodies, too. All the Astaire and Rogers classics, Bogart, Errol Flynn . . . but tonight, in honor of our search, I'll show space movies."

"I'm game," Yoki said. "I couldn't sleep right now unless you stuck me in a hibernation capsule and gassed me."

Within minutes Rob, Yoki, and Mahree had lined up seats to make an impromptu theater. The doctor activated the viewscreen covering one wall, then hooked a small machine to it and slipped in a cassette. He dimmed the lights as introductory music began. "This is the prize of my collection . . . a real rarity."

Mahree began to laugh when she saw the title. "*Invaders

From Mars! Don't tell me they really believed that *Mars* had indigenous life?''

"Count your blessings." Rob grinned. "I'm sparing you the remake . . . this is the original. Believe me, you'll never walk over a sand dune again without remembering this film."

Yoki shook her head. "Don't forget, hon, this thing was probably made before they even had *computers*. At least a hundred years before the First Martian Colony."

Mahree settled down to watch, giggling. The tensions of the day made make-believe a refuge, and the audience eagerly plunged into the "movies" as Rob called them, hissing the villains, cheering the heroes, laughing uproariously at the comic elements. In addition, the films were rife with unintentional humor, since they contained so many anachronisms and scientific errors.

"I can't believe they were that *dumb*!" Mahree gasped, her stomach muscles sore from whooping. "They didn't even know sound doesn't carry in vacuum! And they thought you could pilot a spaceship by the seat of your pants in a fight, not to mention firing weapons using line-of-sight—'' Her voice failed her and she laughed till she choked.

"Hey, have a heart," Jerry said. "People had never been out in space when these were made. Pass the popcorn, please."

"Sure they had," Ray Drummond argued. "This was made at least a hundred years after the OldNorthAm Civil War, so they had begun early orbital flights. What year did Armstrong land on the Moon?"

"1970?" Yoki guessed.

"July 20, 1969," Mahree said.

"Shhhhh!" Rob admonished good-naturedly. "Now comes the scene where our heroes get their just deserts."

"Well, that was fun," Yoki said, a few minutes later. "Even though that presentation scene was pretty sappy. My favorite was the big hairy guy."

"You think *that* scene was sappy, you ought to see the one at the end of the third film," Rob said.

Yoki stood up and stretched. "Well, I'm still game . . . still wide awake. Got any more movies, Rob?"

"Sure," he said, sorting through his cassettes. "Make some more popcorn while I find one, will you? But in defense of my prizes, I've got to tell you that you're being too hard on them. Educated people during that time period knew that sound doesn't travel in a vacuum, but the filmmakers included those 'sound effects' because they felt they made the work more dramatic. Be fair, folks. How often do you catch modern holo-vid programs doing the same thing—sacrificing scientific accuracy for convenience or drama? All the time!''

"At least our spaceships *look* like spaceships," Ray insisted.

"That's because when holo-vid producers want to show a spaceship, they don't have to *build* one from scratch. They can just vid a real one doing whatever they want the audience to see," Rob said. "These early filmmakers had to *design* these ships, and then *construct* them—or at least models of them. And it's not as though they were astronomical engineers, either."

A moment later he pulled a cassette out of the file with an exclamation of triumph. "Ah, ha! Wait till you see what happens to the crew of *this* freighter! Try laughing through *this* one!''

He dimmed the lights and the credits began to roll.

Mahree found herself riveted, despite the *whoosh*ing noises the spaceship made. Her muscles tensed and jerked as she unconsciously tried to help the hapless crew, trapped aboard the doomed vessel. Adrenaline surged through her veins as she watched the heroine fling herself through the dark, dank passageways.

"No . . .'' someone groaned softly a few seats away. "Forget the damned cat, just get *out* of there!"

Mahree nervously caressed Sekhmet, who lay purring in her lap. She wasn't the only one to spill her popcorn during the film's climax.

"Hey, Simon," joked Ray Drummond when Rob finally activated the lights, "I wouldn't want to encounter one of those babies belowdecks, would you?"

Mahree glanced at the Bio Officer. Viorst's eyes looked glassy, and he didn't respond to the jibe, only licked his lips repeatedly.

All around them, people were silently getting up and leaving. "Hey," Rob protested, "wait a minute, guys! We've got to give the good aliens equal time. Here's *The Star Makers,* one of my favorites . . . and *The Day the Earth Stood Still*, arguably the best space film ever made . . . and the one about the cute little alien with the blue eyes who—"

"Some other time, Rob," Yoki interrupted gently. "I think everyone's tired."

• • •

The next morning Mahree stood her watch at the communications console. For two hours she monitored the holo-tank screen, her eyes searching for distinctive orange peaks and valleys, her ears straining for strange chattering noises.

Joan and Paul had hooked up a booster to the standard communications equipment, and *Désirée* was slowly sweeping across the spacial coordinates where the first signal had triggered the E-frequency.

At first Mahree sat tensely, willing a blip to cross the screen, poised to summon Joan and Jerry to track it down.

But the hours dragged by, and nothing happened. By the end of her watch, she was glad to relinquish her seat to Rob Gable. "See anything, Mahree?"

"Not a whisper, not an electronic hiccup. I've been sitting here wondering if we imagined it all."

"It was real, all right."

Her smile was grim. "Tell me that at the end of two hours staring at this screen. The line between reality and fantasy blurs fast."

"Psychologists specialize in what's real and what isn't."

"All the psychologists I ever met were doing their best to keep themselves afloat." Mahree slanted a look at him. "And not doing much better than the rest of us."

He pretended to wipe blood away. "Ouch! What's that French word . . . touché?"

Mahree smiled. *"Oui."*

"Right. I deserve that for such a snotty remark."

"It's all right, we're all a little on edge."

"I know I am." He yawned, finger-combing his tousled hair. "Maybe I should've gotten some sack time last night instead of playing Master of Ceremonies at the film festival."

"It was fun. Someday I'd like to see the rest of them."

He swiveled in his seat to gaze out the forward viewscreen, his expression sobering. "Do you think anyone's out there?"

"I don't know," she said slowly, her eyes never leaving the scanner holo-tank. "I'd like to think that they are."

"Me, too. How much time left on your uncle's deadline?"

"Only twenty hours," Mahree said gloomily.

Rob gave her a meaningful glance. "This could be our chance, you know."

Mahree stared at him, puzzled.

"You remember, what we were talking about before," he reminded her. "The chance to do something really different. Special. This could be it, for us."

Us? Mahree glanced down, feeling her cheeks grow hot. *Don't be silly, he didn't mean anything by that.* "After all," he continued, "our situation here is pretty unique."

Mahree grinned wryly. "It'll have to get 'uniquer' before we'll be able to count our pages in the history texts. Unless we turn up more signals, we won't even rate a footnote."

Rob grimaced. "Yeah, dammit." He pointed at the holo-tank. "Light up, I command you!"

The screen stayed obstinately dark.

That "night" Mahree went to bed despondently, knowing that in the early hours of the "morning," while she slept, the watch would be called off and *Désirée* would make the transition back to metaspace. *If only we could find something before the time runs out!* She lay there, wishing she could physically reach out, sense those strange frequencies, and drag them into range of *Désirée*'s receivers.

Finally sheer exhaustion made her fall into a deep, dreamless sleep.

Hours later she started awake, thinking that someone had called her. "Yes?" she said, into the darkness. "I'm here."

But her tiny cabin was dim, and her intercom remained silent. Mahree checked the chronometer, then lay down again, tossing and turning, eyes wide open in spite of her weariness. At last she decided to wander up to the control cabin and keep the last watch company.

Raoul was not in the control room, but Joan Atwood was there, at the navigation console. Yoki Masuto was standing the communications watch.

"Hi," Mahree said, sitting down beside the Cargo Chief. "Thought I'd keep you company, since I couldn't sleep."

Yoki yawned, revealing pearly little teeth, and brushed her black bangs off her forehead. "Bless you, sweetie. After staying up for most of two nights running, my eyes are closing no matter what I do. But if I drink any more coffee, I'll have to slosh my way to the head."

They had sat, exchanging desultory comments, for about forty-five minutes, when Joan Atwood approached. "How much longer till Uncle Raoul's limit?" Mahree asked anxiously.

"Five minutes," Joan said. "I'll be glad to put this craziness behind us and get back on course."

"Aren't you disappointed?" the girl asked, unable to fathom how her aunt could remain so unconcerned.

"Hell no. I thought this entire thing was a bunch of malarkey from the beginning, and I told Raoul so. We picked up the last hiccup of a dying star or something." She leaned over to flip off the automatic recording device. "Guess I might as well begin dismantling the long-range scanners."

"But the time's not up!" Mahree protested, knowing it was silly. *What difference can five minutes make?*—but she couldn't bear to let her aunt call off the search with even a minute left. This had been their chance to be special. Her *one* chance, probably—and it was slipping away even as she watched. Her throat tightened. "Please, Aunt Joan! *Don't!*"

"Four minutes is going to make a difference? Don't be silly, hon." The older woman switched off the audio receiver, then the flight recorder.

"Well . . ." Yoki got up from her station. "If you're going to take it apart, I'm going to make a run to the head. My kidneys are floating."

"Go ahead," Joan replied, walking back to her station to take down her tool kit. "You can bring me back a cup of—"

"*Look!*" Mahree shrieked, leaping up and pointing at the screen. "There it is! That orange wavelength!"

Both women bolted back to the console.

"*Where?*" they demanded.

"It was only there for a couple of seconds, this time, but I *swear* it was the same!" Mahree looked up at her aunt, and what she saw in the older woman's expression made her protest, half hysterically, "It *was* there, dammit! You have to believe me! I *saw* it! We *can't* stop searching now!"

CHAPTER 3

♦

Needle in a Spacestack

Dear Diary:

I cry when I get mad, and as I sit here keying this, tears are pouring down my face. I have *never* been so outraged!

Tonight I got up and sat out the last of Yoki's watch with her. And, while everyone's back was turned, I saw a transmission blip cross the screen! I *know* I did! But they don't believe me. Aunt Joan didn't exactly call me a liar, but I could tell she was thinking it. She *did* suggest that two nearly sleepless nights had made us all edgy and ripe for hallucinating things that weren't there.

Dammit, I *did* see that blip!

It's not that *nobody* believed me, exactly . . . Rob did. Of course, he's hardly impartial. I had to fight back the tears in the control room when Uncle Raoul, Jerry, Paul, then Rob came in. All of them looked at me so *gently*, so *sympathetically* . . .

At least Uncle Raoul ordered Jerry to program a search pattern around the coordinates I'd noted on the screen (when I thought to look for them, that is, which was a full second or two after the blip had already disappeared). *And*, even more important, he ordered the long-range watch extended until midnight tonight. I can tell he's really hoping we find something—not like Joan and Simon.

"I've got it!" Jerry announced. "Look at that!"

"What?" Every occupant of the control cabin rushed over to the communications console. Rob, who'd been dozing in the copilot's seat, swung down so abruptly that he banged his shin on the footrests. He swore as he limped over to join the others.

Across the darkness filling the holo-tank, orange zigzags crawled. Jerry switched on the audio and deep yips interspersed with static and electronic squeals filled the bridge. "Get a directional reading!" Rob demanded. "Can we cross-vector with the original one?"

"Give me a minute!" Jerry's fingers flew over the board.

"Is the recorder on? Are you getting it all?"

"You bet your ass, Doc," Jerry said fervently. "And this one has already lasted for more than a minute! If I can get enough so I can put the computer to work analyzing both transmissions for similar sounds and patterns . . . don't stop on me, signal . . . keep coming . . ."

Suddenly Rob remembered Mahree. *She ought to be here. If it weren't for her, Raoul would have given up the search . . .*

He keyed the intercom, drumming his fingers nervously as he glanced around the bridge at the viewscreens, fore, aft, port, and starboard. *Which one?* he wondered, eyeing the stars. Some were larger and brighter, others just faint pinpoints against the nightsatin of the void. Looking back along the Sagittarius Arm toward the center of the galaxy, they resembled a thick swath of multicolored fireflies. *Which one are you coming from? Who are we listening to?*

"Yes?" said a sleep-grainy voice.

"Get up here, Mahree. Jerry's got another transmission!"

An excited whoop was his only reply. Rob grinned as he closed the circuit, then reactivated it. "Yoki?"

"Huh? *Rob?* What's going on?"

"I'm up in the control cabin. Jerry's picked up the signal again. Get your rear up here."

"Great! Be right there."

Smiling, he walked back to the communications console, and saw that the signal was still marching across the holo-tank. "What are you doing now?" he asked Greendeer.

The communications specialist shook his head, absorbed. "He's trying to triangulate from our three recorded positions," Raoul told the doctor. "Like drawing invisible lines across space. Where they intersect is our goal."

"Theoretically, anyhow," muttered Jerry. "But gravity can

bend waves in space. So if we've got a star between us and their system . . .''

The sound of hurried feet made Rob turn, to find Mahree behind him. "We did it!" he said, scooping her into a quick, hard embrace. "Jerry is trying to trace them!"

Her eyes shone and her cheeks were flushed when he set her back on her feet. "Oh, Rob . . . that's great!"

This transmission lasted nearly twenty minutes, and by the time it was over, everyone in the crew had had a chance to see it. Even Joan had to admit that it must be artificial in nature—though she insisted that it must be some kind of robot beacon. "Guess you were't seeing things, Mahree," the older woman said awkwardly. "Sorry I gave you such a hard time."

"Hey, I was beginning to wonder myself!" Mahree smiled, touching her aunt's arm reassuringly. "But the question is, what do we do now?"

"We let the computer analyze and compare those little peaks and valleys," Jerry said. "And see whether it can cross-vector from our three positions—"

He broke off as a string of coordinates began marching across the screen. "It's got it! The system!"

"Where?" everyone demanded.

Jerry was speaking commands and didn't respond. As they watched, a three-dimensional view of their area of space appeared, with *Désirée*'s location indicated by a flashing red dot. One nearby system was highlighted on the screen.

"That's it! About five parsecs away"—Jerry's words were clipped and precise, but there was no disguising his excitement—"and, Captain, it's practically on our course! We'll hardly have to deviate at all."

Everyone turned to Raoul, who stood staring at the starmap with a bemused expression. "I'll be damned. I never thought we'd actually find it."

"Well, I don't know which *planet* it is," Jerry said, trying to look modest. "But we ought to be able to discover that when we get there."

"Raoul," Paul Monteleon said urgently, "everyone's assuming we're going. Are we?"

"How will a stop there leave our fuel reserves?" the Captain countered.

The lanky engineer's soft voice was flat. "I'll have to check it on the computer, of course, but my guess is, we'd be okay. It isn't far off-course, Jerry's right about that."

"We've come this far," Raoul said, "it seems stupid to turn back now."

Rob looked over at Mahree and Yoki and gave them a thumbs-up signal. They grinned back excitedly.

"How long will it take to reach the system?" Simon Viorst asked, no expression in his green eyes. *I need to have a talk with him,* Rob thought, studying the older man. Viorst's handsome features looked pinched beneath his shock of graying blond hair. *He's trying not to show it, but he's really scared.*

"About ten and a half days," Joan was saying. "Maximum Stellar Velocity, of course."

"We'd save fuel if we cruised at normal S.V.," Paul said. "That'd only add another two days."

"Yeah, that way we'll have more time to look over the computer analysis of these transmissions," Jerry said. "We may be able to figure out what we've been picking up."

"But how can the computer translate it?" Mahree asked, as Joan instructed *Désirée* to change course and speed.

"It can't," Jerry said, "but it *can* analyze the signals and determine like ones. That's the first step . . . trying to isolate just how many separate signals there are, and how frequently they occur. If it's a language as opposed to some kind of code, the distribution is probably very random. I mean, look at the old Morse Code. In that, things broke down to either dots or dashes. Spoken language has incredible variety in comparison."

"What if it *is* a language?" Yoki asked.

"Then we may be able to begin translating it. After all, archeologists were able to translate dead languages, like those Egyptian hieroglyphics and the Mayan symbols."

"Any chance that what we're seeing has a visual as well as an audio component?" Mahree asked. "Like holo-vids?"

"It certainly is possible," Jerry told her, "but without some idea of what visual images those transmissions are *supposed* to translate into, we're out of luck."

"I see," Rob admitted. "Maybe we're better off just trying to analyze the transmissions in terms of whether they're spoken language, machine-generated, or code."

"Yeah. In three days we may be able to get some sense of that," Jerry said.

Mahree sighed. "They made it look so easy in those movies . . ."

"Can I talk to you a moment, Simon?" Rob Gable said quietly to the man seated by himself in the booth in *Désirée*'s galley.

The older man hesitated. "Is it important?"

"Kind of. But if you're tied up, I can check back."

"How about later this evening?" Viorst asked.

"Depends," Rob said. "I'm meeting someone for dinner. If you're busy at the moment . . ." He knew very well that the Bio Officer was off-duty, but meeting with Simon was important enough that he'd be willing to call Yoki and cancel if that's what it took to get Viorst to talk with him; he knew she'd understand.

The other man grimaced. "Hell, I suppose now's as good a time as any. You want to talk here?"

"Let's go down to hydroponics. I need to check on those seeds I've got germinating down there."

Viorst nodded curtly, and the two men left the galley. They walked in silence down the padded plas-steel corridors (this week they were a pale rose), until they reached the ladder-well to belowdecks, where the hydroponics system and the lower cargo holds were located. The artificial gravity was set at one-sixth gee in the well; both men swung down effortlessly, using only their hands.

When they reached the hydroponics labs, Rob went first to his seeds. After adjusting the moisture level in the germination incubator, he pulled up a stool and gestured the Bio Officer to another. "Have a seat, Simon."

The other man did so, plainly nervous. "What's going on? Why did you want to see me?"

"I just wanted to talk for a moment," Rob said, his voice consciously taking on the calm, neutral tone he had used during therapy sessions in med school. "So much has been going on, these past couple of days, it's going to take all of us a while to get used to it. People tell me they're having trouble sleeping—so have I, matter of fact—so I'm trying to check on everyone. How about you, been experiencing any insomnia?"

Viorst shrugged. "I'm all right, I guess."

"Any nightmares?"

The Bio Officer's green eyes shifted for a second. "No, nothing of the kind."

"Uh huh. Well, it wouldn't surprise me if you did. The possibility of a First Contact is pretty stressful, don't you think? Meeting people completely different from ourselves."

"You mean aliens, not *people*," Viorst said. "Whatever they are, they won't look like *people*."

Rob shrugged. "You're almost certainly right that they won't physically resemble us. But they may well be 'people' mentally and emotionally."

Viorst's well-cut features tightened. "Maybe, maybe not."

"What's the worst thing you can imagine an alien looking like?"

The Bio Officer considered for a moment. "Invisible, I guess. They could sneak up on you and you'd never know."

Rob blinked. "But it's possible that even invisible beings might not be antagonistic, isn't it?"

"I suppose so," Simon said, reluctantly. He hesitated for a moment, then burst out, "That's what you think, isn't it, Doc? That they'll be glad to see us, that everything will be peachy, right? Well, suppose it's not?"

"I don't know," Rob admitted. "But we'll never know unless we introduce ourselves, will we? And if they *are* people we'd rather not encounter again, we'll be able to warn Earth and the colonies to steer clear."

"*If* we live to tell them."

"It might be a good idea to jettison an E-beacon with a copy of the ship's log, before we enter their system," Rob said thoughtfully. "That would serve as a warning to any other Terran ships, if we're never heard from again."

"I think our best course would be to head for Earth and send back a trained expeditionary force—and a squadron of troops to back it up." The Bio Officer's eyes were flat and hard. "We're asking for trouble, barging in this way."

"I admit you have a lot of good arguments," Rob acknowledged. "But instead of concentrating on everything going wrong, why not spend half your time thinking about the possibility that this may be a positive experience? That we may meet creatures who have a lot to share, that we can learn from?"

"I'd like to think that," the Bio Officer sounded almost

wistful. "But if their *outsides* are different, it makes sense to me that their *insides* will be, too."

"Makes sense to me, too," Rob said, studying Viorst's eyes, his face and hands, but careful to keep his glance casual. "But different doesn't invariably mean different in a negative sense. Who knows? They might be nicer than we are."

Viorst considered the idea. "I suppose it's possible," he admitted reluctantly.

Rob smiled reassuringly. "I think perhaps you're getting a little anxious over all this, Simon, which isn't surprising . . . but worrying about something that hasn't happened—and may never happen—isn't very productive."

Viorst glared. "Don't patronize me, Doc. It's hard enough having to report to someone who looks as though he isn't even shaving, yet."

Rob took a slow, deep breath, reminding himself not to let Viorst get to him. The man was frightened, and that was making him antagonistic. *I ought to be used to cracks like that by now*, he thought, with a trace of bitterness. "I'm sorry if it sounded like I was talking down to you," he said evenly. "I didn't intend that. Will you just promise me one thing?"

"What?"

"Think over what I said, okay? We'll talk again, soon. And, Simon, I want you to come to me if you don't get a good night's sleep tonight, and I'll give you a mild sedative to take tomorrow night. All right?"

"Okay, Doc."

Rob slid off the stool. "Thanks for talking."

Mahree groaned and rubbed her eyes. "I can't look at another orange squiggle without going blind. We've been at this for *hours*, and we're no closer to any answers than when we started!"

"She's right." Yoki stretched, her backbone creaking audibly. "Shit, maybe Joan's right, too. Maybe we've been getting signals from intelligent black holes."

"We haven't wasted our time. Some of the programming we've adapted will prove useful later, after we get there," Jerry said. "You've got a real feel for this kind of work, Mahree. How about helping me tomorrow when I try and set up a catalogue of universal constants?"

"Sure," Mahree said, pleased with the praise. Jerry never

said such things lightly. "I just hope we'll get further than we did with these transmissions."

"We will."

"But we *have* made progress," Rob pointed out. "We're almost certain that each transmission was made by a different voice. And the computer has recorded nearly five hundred perfect matches. Some of the matches represent sequences that are repeated many times within each transmission."

"So?" Yoki raised her eyebrows at him. "Tell me what good it's going to do us to be able to identify the alien equivalent of 'and,' 'the,' 'but,' and 'for.' Let's face it, Rob, these people are just going to have to remain an unknown quantity until we reach their world and contact them in person."

"Well, at least we're sure that we're dealing with a language instead of a machine-generated message or a code." Rob sighed, digging wearily at his own eyes. "Too much repetition and too much variety for it to be anything else."

"It is by any *human* standard," Jerry reminded him gloomily. "We don't have any way of knowing how sophisticated their machines are. We can only judge them in comparison to our own."

"Compared to this stuff, history and physics are wildly exciting. Maybe I ought to go study for a while to wake myself up," Mahree said. She tried unsuccessfully to smother a yawn, then burst into shrill giggles when the others reflexively copied her. "Sekhmet has the right idea," she added, stroking the cat, who lay sprawled over half the flimsies, asleep.

The animal began purring. *Wish I could be that relaxed,* Mahree thought confusedly, feeling tears suddenly threaten. She blinked furiously. *What's wrong with me? A moment ago I could barely stop laughing, and now I'm ready to cry.*

"We all need sleep," Rob admitted. "The tension is getting to everyone. Evelyn Maitland came to me yesterday and asked to be put back into hibernation. She said that if we screwed this up, she didn't want anyone blaming her!"

"I had a dream last night," Mahree said haltingly, not looking up as she rubbed Sekhmet's jawline. The purr grew louder, more rasping. "I dreamed we got there, and somehow we'd made a terrible error and recorded the transmissions *backward,* and that was why we hadn't recognized them. It was all a mistake and we'd just ended up on Earth. But there weren't any people there anymore. It was deserted . . . lifeless.''

Nobody said anything for nearly a minute. Mahree glanced up to find them all staring at her, but then none of them except Rob would meet her eyes. Her stomach turned over, and she bit her lip, reddening with embarrassment.

Yoki finally broke the silence. "Honey, why don't you get some sleep? We've all got the creeps, and that's natural enough in this situation, right, Rob?"

"Sure," he said, reaching over to drape Sekhmet over his shoulder. "I'll walk you back to your cabin."

When they reached the relative privacy of the corridor, Mahree burst out, "Dammit, I shouldn't have said that! Now everyone's going to think I can't take it, that I'm losing it!"

Rob slung his free arm over her rigid shoulders. "No, they're not. You've held up better than any of us." He chuckled ruefully. "Just this morning I forgot I'd left my mirror on and nearly panicked when I came out of the head and caught a glimpse of myself. For a second my heart felt like it was coming straight out of my chest—then I felt like a jackass."

Mahree smiled wanly. "You're only saying that to cheer me up, but thanks anyway."

"No, I'm not. Last night I'd probably have had nightmares too, but I self-prescribed a sedative, and slept like the dead. No wonder I'm so groggy today. Over half the crew has asked for them, at least once."

"Really?" Mahree began to feel better. She was suddenly conscious of the warm weight of Rob's arm across her shoulders, the closeness of his body. She felt herself blushing again.

"Here we are," he said a moment later, stopping before her little cabin. "Home again, home again, jiggety-jig. Now I want you to march yourself straight to bed. No studying, no nothing, understand?" He gave her a mock-severe glance.

"Yes, Doctor," she said meekly.

He put two fingers under her chin and tipped her face up, his dark eyes studying her intently. Mahree caught her breath as their gazes locked. *He's going to kiss me,* she thought for a dizzy moment, then her common sense reasserted itself like a dash of icy water. *No, of course he's not.*

"Your color isn't good," he said, studying her. "And I don't like the looks of those circles under your eyes. Seriously, do you need something to help you sleep?''

She swallowed. ''No, I'll be fine.'' Even after he dropped his hand, Mahree found that she couldn't look away, that her eyes seemed determined to memorize the details of his face. The roughness beginning to darken his chin and jaw, the new lines etched around his eyes and mouth, the finger-combed dark curls. She felt a sudden, nearly irresistible urge to raise her hand and smooth his hair into place.

Stop it, she ordered herself, turning away with a jerk, abruptly afraid that he'd noticed—but his voice was unchanged. ''Okay, if you're sure,'' he said. '' 'Night Mahree.''

''Good night,'' she said, letting the door slide shut behind her. She leaned against the wall until her heartbeat slowed and her stomach steadied, then took a deep breath, feeling drained. *The green beans*, she thought suddenly. *I forgot to remind him that we have to rig the climbing strings tomorrow.*

Quickly she left her cabin and headed back down the corridor toward his, her steps taking her along automatically. She was halfway there when she heard it: a woman's low, throaty murmuring, then a man's voice.

Rob's voice.

Mahree stopped in mid-stride, then cautiously tiptoed to the intersection and peered down the left corridor. She was just in time to see Yoki palm open the door to her cabin and disappear inside. Rob was only a half step behind her.

The door slid shut. Mahree heard the privacy lock activate with a small, distinct *snick*.

CHAPTER 4

♦

Tempest Fidgit

Dear Diary:
   I *hate* him. I *hate* her. I don't want to talk about it!!!

"Pi, of course," said Jerry decisively. The Communications Chief and Mahree sat hunched over a table in the galley, the terminal on, but nearly obscured by printout flimsies. "That's comparatively easy for the computer to render with a holo-sketch. We can carry it out to fifteen or twenty places, so they can use that to cross-check their translation of our numbers."

"Pi was certainly the first concept I came up with," Mahree said. "But then I thought of a couple of others. 'Star,' 'planet,' 'moon'—we can demonstrate all of them by presenting a schematic of their own solar system."

"Of course!" Jerry's broad features creased into a grin. "And, more than that, we can probably do 'asteroid,' 'comet,' and maybe 'ring.' "

"Right. And those lead to 'orbit,' and 'year.' They're more abstract, but the computer should be able to illustrate them using a sequence of images."

"Another constant is the speed of light. But first we'll have to figure out their units of measurement."

Mahree nodded. "That brings us back to numbers. But we can

illustrate them with dots. You know, one dot beside the numeral one, two dots beside the numeral two, and so forth.''

"I already thought of that," Jerry said, fumbling through flimsies to produce a sketch. "This what you meant?"

"Yeah, and we can just keep working our way up all the way to scientific notation."

"*Providing* their system has visual scanners."

"Ours does, so why shouldn't theirs?"

"Don't forget, Mahree, that all we've gotten from them so far are radio waves. On Earth they produced radio waves from television broadcasts that escaped into space long before they had computers that were past the punch-card stage."

"I never thought of that." Mahree tapped her pen against her front teeth. "Can we represent going from the very *large* to the very *small*? Show a star, then focus in on increasingly smaller portions of it until we depict a hydrogen atom? Then show the star converting that to helium?"

"Possible. I'll see what the computer can come up with as a representation. But probably before we do that, we ought to try the periodic table."

"We could do 'solar system' and 'galaxy,' " Mahree suggested a few minutes later. "Depending, of course, on how advanced their astronomical sciences are."

"They may know more about the universe than we do. We ought to think about chemical laws, also. Like $PV = nRT$ . . . the equation for the perfect-gas law."

"What's that?" asked Rob Gable. The doctor had entered the galley so quietly the two at the table hadn't noticed him. "Something that results after consuming too many helpings of Ramón's refried beans?"

Mahree felt her cheeks grow hot at the sight of him, and struggled to regain her composure. "Very funny, Rob."

Jerry snorted disgustedly. "We're trying to get some serious work done here, Doc, so unless you want to help, keep it zipped. Remember your basic chemistry? The perfect-gas law is the equation of state for an ideal gas. It combines Boyle's law, Charles' law, and Avogadro's principle. Or don't you medical geniuses have to study that anymore?"

Rob ignored the jibe as he bent over to study the list they'd been compiling. "Are these your constants?"

"So far," Jerry said. "You got any ideas?"

"Give me ten minutes with one of them using the 'scope in the infirmary, and I might be able to give you some. DNA, RNA, maybe. Amino acids . . ." He thought for a moment. "If they have physical bodies that are even remotely like ours, then we can use those similarities. 'Eyes,' or 'legs,' for instance."

"I sure as hell *hope* they have physical bodies," Jerry growled. "How could we discover any common frame of reference with beings made out of pure energy?"

"Good question," Rob admitted.

"How much longer?" Mahree asked. She didn't have to specify what she was asking about.

"We should be entering System X in about thirty-six hours. We'd better get busy and finish this," Jerry said, frowning down at their list. He stared at the scribbled figures and sketches for nearly a minute, swore under his breath, then dug at his eyes. "Damn. I can't even think anymore. If I could only get eight peaceful hours in the sack first, I *know* my brain would start functioning again!"

"No offense, Jerry, but I'm detecting unmistakable signs of exhaustion and stress in your behavior," Rob said dryly. "And the last thing we need when we meet these folks is a cranky communications expert, right?"

"Yeah," Jerry admitted reluctantly. "You're prescribing a dose of sleep?"

"Absolutely." Rob watched as the communications tech pushed himself up, then gave him a gentle shove toward the door. "Joan told me it will probably take at least forty-eight hours until we even know which world we're heading for. Get some rest."

"See you later, Jerry," Mahree called. "I'll try and come up with a few more concepts, then start some of the basic programming."

"Thanks, kid," Jerry told her. "You keep working your tail off like this, we'll have to make Raoul cut you in for a share of the profits."

Mahree didn't look up as Rob sank into the seat opposite her. Sekhmet, who had followed her master into the galley, meowed plaintively and the girl leaned over to pick her up. "How are *you* doing today, kiddo?" Rob asked, eyeing her worriedly.

"Fine," she said, hoping he wouldn't notice how puffy her eyes were.

"How did you sleep?"

"Okay," she lied.

"You sure? I sense that something's wrong."

"I'm fine, honest. Just jumpy because we're almost there, I guess." Steeling herself, she met his gaze. When she saw the genuine concern on his face, she had to struggle not to blurt out her feelings. She gave herself a stern mental shake. "Are we still receiving many transmissions?"

"No, they seem to have peaked last night. Now they're slacking off. Joan told me there were only two this past hour." He frowned. "I hope these people are still there when we reach them. We got that first signal pretty far out . . . they've had decades to destroy themselves, or be swept by a planet-wide plague."

"Jerry predicted this," Mahree said. "Or at least he mentioned that it might happen, if their technological development followed a similar path to Earth's."

"How so?"

"Well, the first radio waves strong enough to escape from Earth and head out into space were generated in the mid-1900s. They've been traveling for about 300 years now."

"Yeah, which means they're now nearly a hundred parsecs— approximately 300 light-years—from Earth's solar system. I follow you."

"Good. The thing to remember, though, is that if we were on a ship heading to Earth and set our frequencies to pick up those old broadcasts, we'd receive the maximum number of transmissions at a distance of about 250 light-years from Earth. Then, the closer to the planet we got, the fewer we'd receive."

Rob frowned. "That doesn't make sense."

"Yeah, it does, the way Jerry explained it. It's because Earth's technology kept getting more sophisticated. Before the millennium, Earth was the 'dirtiest' radio source in its solar system. It put out far more radio waves than Sol or Jupiter. But as human technology improved, it got 'cleaner,' although a fair amount of stuff still escapes."

"What do you mean, improved?"

"Their aim at satellites grew more precise, and they began using technology like buried cables. When they reached that level, they didn't 'lose' nearly so many radio waves by beaming them out into the ionosphere—unintentionally, of course."

"I see." Rob was impressed. "So the reduction in transmissions we're experiencing might mean that 'System X's' technology and ours have something in common.''

"It's possible. The closer we get, the 'cleaner' this planet appears as a radio source. Seems to me there's a good chance that's the result of recent technological advances.''

The doctor ran a hand through his hair, making it stand on end. "Wait a minute. That first signal we received was 57 light-years away from System X. If what Jerry's guessing is true, then their technology has advanced much faster than ours did, comparatively.''

"Maybe they're smarter than we are.''

Rob grimaced. " 'Maybe,' 'perhaps,' 'possibly'—dammit, I want to *know*!''

"We'll find out soon enough,'' Mahree said, looking down at Sekhmet, who was butting her arm and buzzing for attention.

"Yeah, and being impatient won't make the hours pass any faster. As long as they're still there, I guess I can wait,'' Rob conceded. "But it would be terrible to find that we'd missed these people by as little as fifty years.''

"Have you talked to Uncle Raoul about how we're going to handle this? I mean, if we do find somebody.''

"He asked my advice. I don't know whether he'll follow it.''

"What did you tell him?''

"I recommended that we jettison an E-beacon with a copy of *Désirée*'s log just before we enter the system. After all, we have to get out of metaspace before we enter the star's gravity field anyway.''

"Makes sense to me. What else?''

"I also suggested that we have one of their own broadcasts ready to play back to them, so they'd know what brought us here.''

"I don't think that's a good idea,'' Mahree objected. "Suppose that particular transmission turned out to be somebody's declaration of war? Mirroring what they sent when we don't understand it might be dangerous.''

"Raoul pointed that out, so I retracted that suggestion.''

"What else?''

"I said that if we see any signs of them, it'd be best for us to just sit there and let them make the first move. And that if we meet them physically, we should do it unarmed.''

"What did he say to that last proposition?''

"I could tell he was having trouble with that one."

Mahree sighed. "I'm not surprised, although I agree with you. It might not matter whether we're armed or not, since they may not even recognize our weapons for what they are."

"And vice versa, I suppose." Rob leaned his head in his hands. "God, I'm so tired. I can't remember when I last slept well. This waiting is wearing us all down. You could take a laser and slice up the tension in this ship, then stack it in the cargo hold, it's so tangible."

"I know. I heard that Uncle Raoul and Joan had a terrible fight last night. They hardly ever fight," Mahree said, shaking her head sadly.

Rob indicated the stack of computer flimsies. "Can I help you with this, or should I go below and check the zucchini?"

He looked so worn and haggard that Mahree's heart lurched, and she couldn't trust her eyes to meet his. "You go on," she said. "I'd rather work alone for a while. This stuff requires total concentration."

"Right." He stood up. "You *sure* everything's okay?"

She forced herself to smile brightly. "Positive. Don't worry so much."

"There goes the E-beacon," one of the engineering techs said as *Désirée* lurched slightly.

So Raoul decided to follow my advice, Rob thought. *I hope that E-beacon won't turn out to be the only trace of us anyone ever finds.* He brought himself up short. *Stop it. Those talks with Simon must be getting to you.*

He glanced up at the viewscreen as he sat in the booth in the crowded galley. The stars shone in unwinking glory, for *Désirée* had emerged into realspace several minutes ago.

Ahead of them lay System X. From this distance, farther than from Sol to Pluto, the central star was only marginally brighter and larger than the surrounding stellar profusion.

"Yellow-white," Joan Atwood's voice reached the listeners in the galley. "Younger and a little larger than Sol."

"Sixteen planets," Paul Monteleon said. "Three ringed gas giants, plus five ice-and-rock chunks out here at the farthest reaches . . . barely bigger than moons."

"Can you pinpoint the source of the transmissions?" Raoul asked, his voice coming through strained and hoarse.

"Not yet," said Jerry, sounding abstracted. "But they're not from these eight worlds. They're from deeper in . . . which makes sense."

Rob watched tensely as they passed within visual range of one of the frozen worldlets. Sunlight glittered off ammonia snowbanks and methane lakes. "How many hours will it take us to reach those warmer worlds?" he asked Mahree, who was sitting in the next booth. "They're our best candidates."

"At this speed, about three hours to reach a distance of about two Astronomical Units," she answered. "That's a little more than the distance from Sol to Mars."

"Past the gas giants," Rob said. "By then we should be able to get some data on those eight inner worlds."

Mahree mumbled a monosyllabic agreement.

Rob glanced over at the girl, noting the dark shadows that still lay beneath her eyes. And those eyes . . . there was something haunted about them, a sadness that he'd only seen before when she'd avoided talking about the deaths of her friends from Lotis Fever. Mahree had aged in the days since they'd received the first transmission. Her previously rounded, unmarked features appeared fined-down, more mature. *She'll be an attractive woman someday,* Rob found himself thinking.

She turned to glance at him, blushing, and he realized with a start that he'd been staring. He colored, too. "Sorry. I seem to be fading in and out of consciousness."

"That's all right," she said, but she didn't meet his eyes.

Rob wondered whether Mahree was still upset about her nightmare. But he'd asked her if anything was wrong and she'd said "no," so there was nothing more he could do.

As they sat watching the viewscreen, Yoki came in and crowded into the seat beside Rob. "How's it going?"

"Nothing so far," he told her, giving her hand a quick, unobtrusive squeeze. "Just more hurry up and wait."

"We all must be masochists," Yoki said, glancing around the galley at the pale, tense faces surrounding them. "What we ought to do is just put on one of your films and let the bridge crew tell us whether anyone pops up to say 'hi,' instead of sitting here sweating it out."

"We could always go view one privately," Rob said, his voice pitched for her hearing alone. "Something romantic, maybe. You haven't seen *Casablanca* yet."

She smiled ruefully. "I probably couldn't concentrate . . . on anything, including films. Could you?"

"No," he admitted, truthfully.

Désirée penetrated deeper into the alien solar system. The star finally began to look like a sun, and Joan reported an asteroid belt, much thinner than the one that lay between Mars and Jupiter. They passed one gas giant, a dark-ringed orange behemoth slightly larger than Saturn.

At some point Rob dozed off, only to awaken an hour or so later with a stiff neck and back, his mouth dry and tasting of ancient coffee. Yoki was shaking his elbow. "Huhhh?"

"Shhhh! Listen, Rob!"

Jerry Greendeer's voice was saying: " . . . sure. It's located about one and a half A.U.'s out. Nearly twice the size of Earth, but the gravity is only about one and a half gee . . . fewer heavy elements, maybe. Four moons, little ones."

Rob tried to unstick his tongue from the roof of his mouth. "He found it?"

"Yes." Yoki never took her eyes off the viewscreen. It showed only the sun, which now appeared nearly the size of Sol as seen from Earth.

"Where is it?"

"The sixth planet," Mahree said. "We've slowed down our approach. Uncle Raoul didn't want to barge in like we owned the place."

"Good idea," Rob allowed. He stretched, yawned, then got up to get something to drink. By the time he came back, the planet was visible as a tiny, green-and-white disk.

"We still receiving transmissions?" he asked Mahree.

"I don't know."

The disk grew larger. Rob leaned forward in his seat, his heart hammering, his mouth dry again. Glancing over at Mahree, he saw that she was chewing furiously on her lower lip. Yoki alone sat without betraying excitement, her dark eyes fixed intently on the viewscreen.

"Hey," Jerry's voice reached them, "I'm getting something. Transmissions. They're not from the planet."

"Then where are they coming from?"

Nobody answered. *Désirée* continued to glide forward, slowing even more. Ahead of them the planet turned, and Rob thought he could make out the blue shimmer of water.

"Captain." Jerry's voice was flat, but something about it made the hairs at the back of Rob's neck stir. "I've found the source of the transmissions. They're ships, sir."

"Holy shit, they sure are," Raoul muttered.

Rob was on his feet by then, barely aware that Yoki had grabbed his hand, that her nails were digging into his palm. He gaped, frozen, at the small vessels drifting into visual range. *Four, five . . . seven, no, eight.*

Désirée was surrounded.

CHAPTER 5

✦

The Face of the Unknown

Dear Diary:

I'm up in the control cabin, lounging in the copilot's seat and looking up at the central viewscreen. They're still there, the alien ships, all eight of them, shining amber against the blackness. They're shaped very differently than *Désirée* (which vaguely resembles a pregnant blimp).

These craft are narrow and streamlined . . . as though they could also navigate through atmosphere. Rob said they reminded him of an Earth predator called a hammerhead shark. On either side they have narrow, swept-back projections that don't really look like wings, but probably serve the same function. They're all the same golden orange color, with small black lines appearing amidships.

It's been nearly an hour and a half since they moved into position surrounding *Désirée*, but that was the last move they made. They're just pacing us out there, about twenty kilometers away, waiting, waiting for . . . who knows?

Uncle Raoul is sitting down in the galley, drinking Simon's horrible coffee, and from his expression I'd say he's having second thoughts about this whole venture.

When the eight craft first arrived, Joan slowed *Désirée* to a crawl, and our escorts decreased speed correspondingly. The question is, are they an honor guard, or are we prisoners?

In the beginning we were flooded with transmissions, but of

course we couldn't reply, and they soon stopped. We're still approaching the planet, but at this rate it'll take us half a day to get there.

There are four of us here on the bridge: Jerry, Paul, Joan, and me. A few of the crew members are still watching the screen in the galley, but most have gone back to work.

I don't know where Rob is at the moment, and, frankly, that's a relief. He's beginning to suspect something is wrong.

I wish I could get over the way I feel toward him! But no matter how hard I try, each time I see him it's like a jolt of electricity. Painful, but it makes me feel so *alive*.

I keep telling myself that what I'm feeling isn't love, that I'm too young for that . . . but it feels like love. Is it possible to *really* love someone when you're almost-seventeen?

How do you know when it's really—

Mahree stopped keying abruptly, her brown eyes widening. Only force of long habit made her hit the "save" button before she spoke. "Aunt Joan! One of the ships is moving closer!"

The First Mate looked up even as she keyed the intercom. "Captain to the bridge, on the double!"

Mahree and the others watched, mesmerized, as the little craft drifted closer . . . closer to them.

"Range, 750 meters," Jerry finally announced. "I'm going to take a better look at those black marks." He adjusted the magnification factor on the forward viewscreen to focus in on the small black lines Mahree had noted earlier.

Close up, the "lines" were actually strings of alien symbols. "At least we can be sure of one thing, now," Jerry said. "They have visual sensing organs, or they wouldn't have any reason to put external markings on their ships."

The little vessel moved toward *Désirée*, stopping about 500 meters away. Mahree narrowed her eyes, straining to see whether it had viewports of any kind, but the flared nose of the craft appeared completely featureless. Behind her she could hear the babble of excited voices as crew members jammed onto the bridge.

"It's moving again!" Paul Monteleon said, a moment later.

As they watched, tracking its progress on the viewscreen, the alien vessel began a spiraling course, circling *Désirée* from bow to stern. Then, as it began a second circuit, a bright light splashed out from its bow, to shine on the bigger ship.

Joan gasped. "Are they aiming some kind of weapon?"

Paul glanced at an instrument reading, then shook his head. "Just a light beam. They want a better look at us."

As it drifted past on its second survey, the little ship paused four times, the first time at *Désirée*'s bow; the next just forward of the galley, near the emergency suit lockers; a third time amidships, opposite the lifeboat hatch; and, finally, "below" the freighter's belly, opposite the cargo loading port.

"Why are they stopping?" Raoul asked. Mahree stole a quick glance and saw him standing beside her aunt, his hand gripping his wife's shoulder, either for comfort or support, Mahree couldn't tell which.

"They halted for nearly five seconds opposite each of our airlocks," Jerry muttered thoughtfully.

"Do you think they're planning to *board* us?" Mahree barely recognized Simon Viorst's voice, shrill with fear. She glanced back at the crowd, but could not see the Bio Officer.

"I doubt it," Raoul said sharply. "If they were hostile, surely they'd have fired on us by now."

"They were probably measuring the size and shape of our airlocks," Mahree said. "If they intend to meet us face to face, they'll have to connect one of their ships to ours."

As they watched, the little craft, indistinguishable from its companions, again took its place among those escorting *Désirée*. "Show's over, folks!" barked Raoul. "Let's clear out and free up the air in here. We'll inform you by intercom if anything else happens, okay?"

Mahree realized she was hungry. With all the excitement, she'd skipped breakfast and forgotten lunch. Now, her stomach seemed as empty as vacuum, and she felt weak and disoriented.

"I'm going to get a sandwich," she announced, sitting up. "Anyone want one?"

Moments later, she was making a list.

Once in the galley, Mahree began programming the servo. *Let's see . . . two ham and swiss on rye, one curried chicken salad, one tuna-melt in a pita, a roast beef with cheddar, and, what do I want . . . a nice turkey club. Too bad the real tomatoes and lettuce aren't ready to eat yet . . .*

Of course foodstuffs the servo produced were ersatz, formed and flavored to reproduce the sight and smells of the real article.

Désirée was a freighter, and lacked the luxuries of the huge, expensive passenger liners.

Mahree wolfed her sandwich while she waited for the system to produce the others, and, still hungry, ordered up a plate of nachos. "Can I steal one?" said a voice in her ear as the nachos slid out of the servo.

She turned around to see Yoki behind her. "Sure, take some. How's it going?"

"All right. I've been in the cargo hold, trying to see if we've got anything that might be universally appealing to another species." The older woman took a nacho, dipped it liberally with hot sauce, then popped it into her mouth. She grimaced.

"Too hot?"

"Not the sauce," Yoki said thickly. "Cheese is hot."

Mahree sampled one herself. "So, did you find anything?"

Yoki shook her head. "Impossible to say for sure . . . but I doubt it."

Mahree began collecting sandwiches, stacking them on a tray.

"It's funny how you can get used to anything," Yoki mused. "A couple of days ago we were all beside ourselves with excitement over the *possibility* that we might be intercepting an alien message, and now, here we are, eight alien ships pacing us and we're thinking about food."

"I think people reach a point where their excitement quota just shorts out," Mahree observed, pouring coffee.

"Need help carrying those?"

"Thanks," the girl said, picking up the sandwiches.

Yoki gave the younger woman a searching glance. "And how about you, honey? Rob mentioned last night that you were looking a little strained."

"No, I've been fine," Mahree mumbled, picking up the tray. *Dammit, I like Yoki, it's not fair! Why can't things ever be black and white, instead of all these shades of gray?*

The Cargo Chief sighed, and Mahree wondered guiltily if the older woman had read her thoughts. "What's wrong?" she asked.

"I just hope to hell we don't screw this up," Yoki muttered as she maneuvered the tray out the door. "All of a sudden I've got a bad feeling about this."

"Well, Simon," Rob Gable began, carefully measuring nutrient solution into a beaker, "they've been escorting us for hours now, and nothing bad has happened. If they were hostile, surely they'd have tipped their intentions by now."

The Bio Officer shook his head stubbornly as he fastened up a trailing beanstalk. "They'd be fools to attack us on the fringes of their territory, when we might be able to get away and make a run for it. It makes a lot more sense to get us where they want us, and *then* make their move."

Rob sighed. "Simon, if you try really hard, you can put a negative connotation on even the most innocent actions!" His mouth tightened and he sternly reminded himself that he couldn't afford to allow Viorst to exasperate him. The Bio Officer was stubborn and opinionated, granted, but he was also genuinely scared, and getting mad at him wouldn't help the man conquer—or at least control—his fears.

"They've given us no reason to think we couldn't just turn *Désirée* around and head back the way we came," Rob said, after a moment's thought. "Those ships are so small they couldn't possibly stop us."

"How do you know?" Viorst demanded. "Now you're doing what you always accuse me of doing, Doc—generalizing from what humans do. Any ships *we* built that were that size couldn't have S.V. drive or much weaponry, but how do we know they don't have a drive that would fit into that box there? Or weapons the size of that beaker that could blast us into next week?"

Rob blinked, taken aback. Finally he nodded. "You're right, Simon, I was generalizing. But that kind of thinking is just as distorted as what you're doing when you put a negative connotation on everything, don't you see?"

"Maybe." Viorst's sullen tone was back. "That's what you keep telling me, anyway."

Rob measured the depth of the algae in a tank, then made a minor adjustment in the lighting. "All I'm saying is, don't jump to conclusions. Try to adopt a 'wait and see' attitude, okay?"

Simon considered the suggestion, then sighed. "Okay, Doc," he agreed, but he still sounded troubled.

"I'm getting a blip," Jerry announced tensely, "it's big, and it's dead ahead."

"One of those small moons?" Joan asked.

"Nope, it's artificial."

"A space station!" Mahree exclaimed, her voice squeaky with excitement. She flushed. *Why do I always have to sound like I'm twelve?*

"Not like any I've ever seen before, but that's not surprising," Jerry was agreeing.

"When will we be close enough for visual contact?" Yoki asked, after hastily swallowing the last nacho.

"In about five minutes. It's on the dayside of the planet, so we ought to be able to see it pretty well," Jerry said.

Raoul made a general announcement over the intercom, warning the crew that there would be something worth seeing on the viewscreen in the galley in a few minutes.

"Think that's our destination?" Paul Monteleon asked Jerry.

"Makes sense," the Communications Chief said, "because they've probably concluded from their observations that *Désirée* can't make a planetary landing . . . also, it's likely that they'll want to keep us in some form of isolation."

Mahree, who had been staring at the viewscreen, trying so hard not to blink that her eyes nearly crossed, suddenly gasped. "I saw a flash at about ten o'clock!"

"That's it," Jerry confirmed.

Mahree and the others sat watching, wide-eyed, as the object grew in the viewscreen. It was vaguely rectangular, with rounded-off corners, and it seemed small until they saw one of the little amber ships dart past it, and realized the scale. "The damned thing's nearly ten kilometers across, and fourteen high!" Jerry breathed, awed.

"It looks like something I've seen before," Mahree said.

"An abacus," Yoki said. "That silvery blue and black rectangular frame, and then all those round pods strung across, like beads."

"Different colored beads," Jerry said. "Another indication that they have eyes of some kind. Different colors may indicate different functions. Orange for engineering, green for communications, yellow for living quarters—like that, maybe."

"The violet hurts my eyes," complained Joan.

"It probably looks gorgeous to them," Yoki said. "Their eyes don't see the same color ranges we do."

"But they're close," Jerry said, his voice taut with excitement. "Pretty damn close. I don't think we're dealing with energy beings, folks."

By now they were near enough to the planet to make out large areas of deep green vegetation, plus the ochre of deserts. "Not much in the way of seas," Paul reported, studying a monitor. "Only that one we noticed earlier. Lots of lakes, several the size of Superior or bigger. Some really high mountain ranges. Temperature averages a couple degrees warmer than Earth's."

"Equatorial rain forests?" Joan asked.

"Yeah, and a lot of savannah."

"Any signs of cities?"

"Still too far away to tell."

With an effort, Mahree looked away from the planet and found that *Désirée* was nearing the space station rapidly. "Check the left viewer," she said. Jerry immediately switched the main viewscreen back to the massive structure.

They watched the station drift closer, and now they could see circular openings in the "frame" that were apparently docking bays for assorted sizes of spacecraft. One by one, the eight ships escorting them drifted away.

"Will any of those cradles fit us, Paul?" Raoul asked his Chief Engineer.

"Negative. All the ones in visual range are made for vessels with those flared-out bows, Captain," Monteleon replied.

"So what do we do now?" Raoul wondered. "We can't dock. How do we meet them?"

"I'd say our next move is to kill our speed so we don't ram into their station," Jerry said mildly, and, indeed, the huge frame was looming closer at an alarming pace.

Joan swore under her breath as she hastily activated the forward maneuvering jets. *Désirée* slowed even further, then the freighter was stationary. "That stations's big enough to exert enough gravitational force to gradually pull us closer," she said. "I'm telling the computer to check position and correct when necessary."

Raoul nodded absently. "*Now* what?"

Mahree and the others stared at him. Nobody ventured an answer to the Captain's question.

"Stalemate," Rob said, gazing at the galley's viewscreen. "How long has it been?"

"Nearly twelve hours," Mahree answered. "Maybe they're waiting for *us* to make the first move."

"Damn." Rob took a final swig from the mug of beer in his hand, then keyed the servo for another, his fifth. Mahree couldn't recall ever seeing him drink more than one before. She found it disturbing. *Why?* a sarcastic little voice inside her head asked. *Because drinking too much under stress is a failing, and the man you love isn't allowed to have any human weaknesses?*

Her mouth twisted as she ordered up a beer for herself. "Hey," Rob protested, "you shouldn't be drinking that!"

"Says who?" Mahree said, then deliberately took a gulp.

"You're too young."

"No, I'm not." She gave him an annoyed glance. "Jolie isn't Earth, remember. I've been a legal adult since I turned sixteen." She grinned wickedly. "We colonists mature more quickly than you Terran earthworms."

Rob winced exaggeratedly, but his answering grin was a little forced. "You don't have to get nasty about it."

"Sorry," she said, taking another sip of her beer. "It's just the waiting, getting to me. I wonder how long Uncle Raoul will just sit here."

The doctor drained the last of his beer, then peered at her owlishly. "Well, only thing I know for sure is that I'm *tired*, and at the moment I don't give a shit what those guys"—he jerked his chin at the viewscreen—"choose to do or not do. Screw 'em. *I'm* going to bed."

He put his mug down and walked out of the galley with commendable steadiness. Mahree sighed. *This is making all of us crazy. Maybe coming here was a mistake.*

Then, because she could think of nothing further to do, she finished her drink, then went to bed, too.

She was jerked from sleep several hours later by her cabin intercom. "Mahree! Are you awake? Answer!"

"Huh?" She had been sleeping so heavily and was still so tired that for long seconds she was completely disoriented.

"Mahree Burroughs, wake up! Are you awake?"

She struggled to sit up, then things clicked into place. Mahree thumbed the intercom. "I'm awake now, Jerry. This had better be something more than a request for sandwiches."

The Communication Chief's usually laconic tones were clipped with excitement. "Get up here, kid. I want you to see this."

The connection went dead.

Mahree dragged on pants and a sleeveless top; she braided her hair loosely as she jogged down the corridors, arriving in the control cabin panting and breathless. "What's going on?"

"Watch. I've got the main viewscreen focused on our bow."

Mahree steadied herself on the arm of the pilot's seat as she caught her breath. They and the planet beneath them had turned (the station was in a synchronous orbit) and it was now night "below," but the space station was lit up brilliantly. Then, as she took in the view, she realized that one of the small alien craft was directly before them, perhaps 500 meters out. As she watched, a blue light flashed at the nose of the little ship. One flash . . . two flashes . . . three flashes.

She waited, counting seconds in her mind, and when she reached twelve, the entire sequence repeated. Then the little craft turned away, moving slowly, and accelerated until it was several kilometers distant.

"Now"—Jerry's voice broke her absorption—"it'll come back and do the whole thing over again. This is the fourth time."

"They want us to follow them!" Mahree whispered. "I'm sure that's it!"

"That's what I think, too. Okay, I'm going to call Raoul."

Minutes later, Raoul, Joan, and Paul had joined them on the bridge. This time, when the little ship signaled, then moved away, Joan nudged *Désirée* after it.

The alien craft led them around the frame of the giant "abacus" until they were on the other side. Then it killed its motion, and Joan also halted *Désirée*. "Now what?"

Ahead of them another blue light flashed, within a spidery cradle extending outward from one of the dark openings. "They've built us a docking bay!" exclaimed the Chief Engineer. "That's why they surveyed our hull!"

"Now let's hope I can get us in there," Joan said. "It looks like a tight squeeze."

Désirée drifted forward, with Joan positioning the freighter with tiny touches on the steering jets. The First Mate's eyes never left her instruments and the schematic of the docking bay that showed on her control console. Slowly, gently, the big freighter poked its nose into the makeshift docking bay. "I'm in," announced Joan. "Now if our docking grapples will just work . . ."

She triggered them, then relaxed. "That's it, folks!"

Everyone stared at one another, grinning, then the bridge was filled with triumphant whoops. Mahree threw her arms around her aunt's neck and kissed her cheek. "You did it, Aunt Joan! We're the first ship to dock in an alien port!"

Her aunt returned her hug. "Does that mean I'm famous?"

"We're *all* famous!"

Their celebration attracted the attention of the night crew, and the next thing Mahree knew, the day shift was awake and demanding to know what had happened. Jerry played the holovid of the entire incident over again, and the party was on. Most of the crew seemed to be crowded into the bridge and the corridor leading to the galley, with the servos working full-time.

Mahree found herself on the outskirts of the crowd, after a long succession of toasts and congratulations and having to relate over and over again how she and Jerry had "seen the light." Azam Quitubi whirled her around until she was dizzy, then set her down. Mahree stumbled back, giggling, only to bump hard into someone else and nearly fall. She turned and froze when she saw Rob's face, eyes dark and shadowed beneath tousled hair. He had half slid an arm around her shoulders to steady her; with a jerk she pulled away. "Rob!"

He put a hand up imploringly. "Do you all have to *yell* so loud? Just what the hell is going on?"

Mahree's mouth twitched. "Forgot to take something for the hangover before you went to sleep, huh? You need something to eat. I could scramble you some nice ersatz eggs."

He gulped. "Sadist. C'mon, what's happening?"

Mahree explained.

When she was finished, Rob began cursing under his breath. ". . . and like a jackass I missed it all! *Damn!*" He shook his head fiercely. The motion was obviously a mistake, for the next second he was groaning and clutching his temples. Sekhmet, who was sitting at his feet, meowed plaintively.

"Come in here," Mahree said, grabbing his arm. She led him down the corridor and into her cabin, dimmed the lights, then pushed him onto the bunk. The cat jumped up beside him and sat like an ebony statue, tail curled around her tiny forefeet.

Rob made an abortive effort to sit up, then subsided with another groan. "What an asshole."

"I agree. Stay still," Mahree ordered, and went to get a cold compress for his forehead. "Where'll I find the hangover medicine? In your office? Or in the infirmary?'' She smoothed the damp towel into place.

"In the infirmary, but it's locked, of course," he muttered, relaxing with a resigned sigh. "Aspirin'll do."

Mahree produced two, and, after a minute, a cup. "Here, it's orange juice. Potassium, right?"

"Yeah." He gulped them, then sank back onto the pillow. "Be better soon. Thanks, kiddo."

Moments later, Mahree heard a distinct snore. She sat gazing down at him in the dimness, and her heart lurched within her. Hesitantly, she reached down and touched his hand.

"You watch him, Sekhmet," she told the cat.

By the time Mahree reached the control room again, she was weary but completely composed . . . or so she thought. Jerry took one look at her and drew her over to the pilot's section. "What's wrong, honey?"

"Nothing," she said. "I've missed out on another night's sleep, that's all."

Greendeer eyed her measuringly. "Whatever you say. Myself, I—" He broke off, staring intently over her shoulder at the rightmost viewscreen, which currently showed what was directly in front of the ship.

Mahree wheeled around to follow his gaze. *Désirée* was lodged bow-first in the docking cradle; the silvery blue wall of the alien station was approximately ten meters from the tip of her nose. On that wall a blue light was flashing—*one, one-two, one-two-three* . . .

"They're signaling again!"

She turned back to see that Jerry had already activated the recorders; he switched the image onto the main viewscreen. A bright white light, like the one they'd seen earlier, splashed out onto the station's wall, just below the flashing blue signal.

"*Now* what?" muttered the Captain. He switched on the intercom. "All hands, you might want to watch the viewscreen in the galley."

After a few minutes the white light was replaced by a picture. Star-studded blackness, with tiny spheres revolving around a large, blazing one. Mahree began counting planets.

"It's their solar system!" Paul Monteleon exclaimed.

The system representation held steady for several minutes. "They're orienting us," Jerry said. Even as he spoke the picture altered, began to close in on the sixth planet. Finally the picture duplicated the scene outside . . . the monstrous space station, the slowly turning world "beneath."

The picture stayed the same again for several minutes, then they were descending through the upper ionosphere toward the planet. "Is that what they want us to do?" Joan wondered. "Land? But we can't!"

"No, I think they know that," Raoul said. "They built this docking cradle, didn't they? They're just showing us where the presentation is taking us."

The atmosphere thickened as the picture plunged deeper, heading for the planet's surface. "Blue sky, almost like Earth's," Yoki observed.

"Bit of a turquoise tint," Paul said, "but pretty."

Mahree stared, fascinated. Any blue sky appeared odd to her; Jolie's was a soft rose-violet.

They were through the clouds now, floating gently downward. They passed over one of the huge lakes, glimmering aquamarine, and one of the savannahs. "Look, a herd of animals!" Jerry cried, and they could all make out dark specks that must have been grazing beasts.

Then the scene was filled with the improbably dark green vegetation. "Those trees are *huge*," Paul said, awed. "Bigger than sequoias back on Earth."

The picture moved closer to the ground, and now they saw something else located on the fringes of the forest. "Artificial structures?" Joan asked.

"Looks like," Raoul murmured.

They rose from the ground perhaps two or three hundred meters into the air, pyramid-shaped structures with flattened tops, some gleaming white, others the same silvery blue of the space station, still others rose, pale green, and yellow. All had black rooftops. "Solar collectors?" guessed Jerry.

"I'd put money on it," Paul said.

Each of the four sides of the pyramid buildings was covered with a spidery lattice of curved interlinking shapes. "You think those overlaying trellis things are decorations?" Yoki asked.

"They could be anything," Paul said.

"There are footpaths down there," Mahree said excitedly. "But I don't see any roads."

"Isn't that a park in the center of that group of buildings?"

Yoki asked. "Look, there's a stream running through, with an arch made of those interlocking curliques over it."

"A bridge?" Raoul asked.

"Not one that we could use," Joan said.

The picture made a slow circuit of the entire city, giving them ample opportunity to study the buildings, courtyards with accompanying gardens, and many parks. "It's pretty," Yoki said. "Reminds me in some ways of Japan."

"It's more like Mexico City," Ramón Garcia's voice came over the intercom. "All those flat-top pyramids are like the old city of Teotihuacan."

"Don't see any slums," Raoul said.

"If *you* were preparing a travelogue to introduce aliens to your world, would you show slums?" Jerry asked dryly.

"Maybe they don't have any," Mahree said hopefully.

The picture descended until it was only a few meters above the pale rose paving in the courtyard next to the largest of the blue-silver buildings, then it stopped moving, giving them a nearly ground-level view. "Now what?" Joan wondered.

"They've shown us their world and their homes," Jerry said. "Now I suspect they're going to show us themselves."

Mahree and the others watched, scarcely daring to blink. After a minute or two a being came into view.

They had no way to judge scale . . . the creature could have been tiny or huge. It moved toward them on four legs, with a swinging, somehow bold stride. Two piercing violet eyes gazed directly at them. It wore no clothing, and needed none, for it was covered with fur the color of flame. A heavy mane rose into an upstanding crest on its head and cascaded down over powerful shoulders, reaching to the middle of the almost-level back. A short, top-knotted tail was held straight up as it moved.

"A lion!" Paul Monteleon muttered. "Sort of."

"More like a monkey," Jerry whispered. "Two eyes, one nose, four limbs . . . no matter how different it looks, it's obviously evolved along the same lines as we have. It's a primate."

"But look at the way it walks!" Joan pointed out. "Like a big dog!"

Mahree had never seen any of those animals except in holo-vids, and to her the creature resembled nothing she'd ever seen before.

Its face, beneath the upstanding crest of hair, had an outthrust muzzle with powerfully muscled jaws. The nose was broad and flat, the mouth almost lipless. The cheeks and forehead were covered with short fur, but the pale orange muzzle was smooth-skinned. The ears were small and triangular, close-set to the sides of the creature's head.

As they watched, the being walked up and down, presenting them with frontal, rear, and sideways views of its body. Its fore and hind feet had long, mobile-looking digits. "Six," breathed Jerry. "I counted six, front and back."

There were no recognizable sex organs evident, but the area between the alien's hind legs was shadowed as well as furred. In contrast, the hair over the buttocks was so thin that they could discern the orange-colored skin beneath it. Dapples of a deeper chestnut color marked the being's back and haunches.

Finally it paused and sat up on its hind legs, exactly as a human would squat. It made a complicated but graceful gesture with its right forelimb, touching its eyelids, muzzle, chest, then holding out its paw (hand?) toward the camera, fingers curled in. At the same time it ducked its head, eyes lowered.

"What's that supposed to mean?" Raoul asked.

" 'Greetings,' " Jerry guessed, trying the gesture on for size, then repeating it, trying to capture some of the alien's flowing grace.

The first alien was now joined by others, some much smaller, only two-thirds the size of the others. "Females?" Joan wondered.

"That would be true if they were dogs, lions, or monkeys," agreed Yoki. "But they could also be a slightly different race, like pygmies."

All the creatures faced the camera and made the gesture. " 'Greetings,' it's got to be!" Jerry cried.

The scene shifted abruptly back to the space station, and they saw eight small ships escorting a bigger ship whose outlines were only too familiar. *"Désirée!"* Raoul exclaimed.

They followed the image of their own docking maneuver, then, suddenly, the photographic image of *Désirée* was replaced by a simple line drawing of the freighter's outline. "Huh? Why the change?" Paul asked.

"I don't know." Jerry sounded mystified.

Mahree sat straight up with excitement, and for once didn't care that her voice went squeaky. "I've got it! Up to now they've shown us past events. What we're seeing here is the *future*, so they couldn't photograph it, they had to draw it!''

From the wall of the space station a blackness suddenly yawned, then there were spacesuited figures swarming around it. Slowly, a flexible-looking rectangular extrusion was constructed, reaching from the space station toward the outline of the Terran freighter. *Like a tube with squared-off sides,* Mahree thought.

The next view showed the forward airlock drawn onto the line sketch of *Désirée*. The "tube" was clearly aiming toward it.

"They had all this waiting," Jerry said, sounding awed.

"Yeah, but why?" Joan said tersely. "If you were starving, you'd couldn't wait to encounter a herd of nice juicy rabbits."

"My, aren't we cynical," Raoul said lightly, but there was a warning note underneath. Mahree stole a quick glance at her aunt and saw her flush, then clamp her lips tightly together.

As they watched, the tube extension reached the opening of the freighter's airlock, and the workers sealed it tightly. The scene then shifted to a corridor, lit so brilliantly it dazzled human eyes. *The view inside the tube,* Mahree realized.

A silvery blue, spacesuited figure appeared in that too-bright white expanse, moving three-legged, carrying some kind of orange bag or satchel. The figure reached the drawn-in outline of *Désirée*'s airlock, then tapped. One . . . one-two . . . one-two-three . . .

The airlock door vanished, and a small cubicle was drawn in beyond. It looked nothing like a human-built airlock, but naturally the alien artist had no idea what was inside *Désirée*.

The spacesuited figure moved inside the "airlock," then rummaged in its satchel for several instruments. It moved them around, then held each up to its helmet, appearing to study them as the outer airlock door reappeared on the image.

The spacesuited alien made the "greetings" gesture again—then abruptly the picture winked out.

"What was that all about?" Joan asked.

"I think they'd like us to let them into our airlock to test our air," Jerry said. "Determining whether we can breathe each other's air would be the first order of business, seems to me."

"Yeah, Rob said something like that," Yoki said.

Rob! Oh, my God, he'll never forgive me for letting him sleep through all this! Mahree thought, jumping up in confusion.

Fortunately everyone was still too intent on their discussion of the alien presentation to notice.

She elbowed her way through the crowded corridor leading from the bridge to the galley, then, abruptly, she was alone again. Racing down the hall to her cabin, she keyed the door open. As she stepped inside, she ordered up the light level, and the doctor raised himself up on his elbow, blinking. "Huh?" he mumbled. "Mahree? What're you doing here?"

"You're in my bunk," she explained tersely. "You fell asleep after I brought you the aspirin. You okay now?"

He sat up, rubbing the back of his neck gingerly. "Better."

"In that case, on your feet. We just watched a film the aliens made to introduce themselves."

He leaped up so suddenly that Sekhmet landed on the floor with an offended squawk. "You *saw* them?"

"Don't worry, Jerry recorded it all. Come on!"

"That's the fourth time you've watched that thing, Doc," Jerry said.

Rob stretched until his back creaked, then rubbed his eyes gingerly. "Are they still showing it over and over on the wall of the space station?"

"Yeah. We're lucky we could see it the first time they ran it. Since then, they've altered it so it would be visible to people having everything from ultraviolet- to infrared-based vision."

"Maybe they showed it first in their own vision range."

"Makes sense. Their sun and Sol aren't all that different."

"I can't *believe* how similar these people are!" Rob shook his head. "After all the wild possibilities I imagined, this is almost like finding human beings out here."

"They may be more alien *inside* than they are outside," Jerry cautioned, watching Rob stand up. "Where are you going?"

"Down to my lab. I'd started on an atmosphere-analysis kit of my own, and I'd better get it together. I don't think it'll be long before we hear that knock on the airlock door."

Jerry glanced at the left viewscreen. "Yeah, they're coming right along on that airlock extension they're building."

Spacesuited figures swarmed over the flexible-appearing extrusion, just as they had in the alien "film."

Rob yawned so widely his jaw hurt. "I wonder if I'll ever get eight hours in the sack again?"

"We'll have months to sleep on our way home," Jerry said. "I'll call you if anything happens."

"Thanks." The doctor turned to leave, then glanced over at the copilot's seat, where Mahree lay, curled up. "Poor kid, she's out like a light. Should I carry her down to her cabin?"

"No, she'll probably wake up if you do," Jerry said. "I'll just dim the lights in the forward section."

Rob stood for a moment looking down at the girl's shadowed face; she had turned on her side, her cheek cuddled into the bend of her arm. Her long hair had come loose from its braid and spilled over her shoulders, hanging off the armrest. The doctor experienced a sudden rush of tenderness that surprised him. "She's a good kid," he said softly, remembering the matter-of-fact way she'd produced the aspirin and orange juice. "She's holding up better than most of us."

"She's a *smart* kid," Jerry said respectfully. "She seems to intuitively grasp things about these aliens."

"You're pretty good at that yourself," Rob said. "How does that greeting gesture go?"

Jerry demonstrated. "I just hope we're reading it right."

"Well, at least we know that they can see, and that their vision is fairly close to our own. That's likely to mean their computers have optical scanners, like ours."

"Which reminds me, I've got to finish up the last of the programming and set up a portable terminal with a scanner," Jerry said. "I just hope we can get our computers to interface with whatever they've got."

"Sounds like a tall order," Rob said.

"I'm not so sure." Jerry pushed his hair back behind his ears, a sure sign that he was thinking hard. "When you break human computers down to their most elemental level, binary boils down to two possibilities . . . 'on' or 'off,' right?"

Rob nodded, and the Communications Chief continued, "Well, that's such a simple concept—so simple that it seems to me that aliens might well utilize it, also. And if they do, we should be able to develop a mapping algorithm that will allow us to interface."

"Makes sense to me," Rob said. "Guess I'd better get busy in the lab. See you later."

After he'd been in the lab for an hour or so, Simon came down and offered his help. Rob, pleased that the Bio Officer seemed to be adjusting to their situation, accepted gratefully, and after that the work went twice as fast.

Two hours later, Raoul's voice emerged from the intercom. "Doc? You finished yet?"

"Just a few more minutes," Rob said.

"Well, hustle." The Captain's voice was taut with repressed excitement. "It looks like they're sealing that tube around our airlock."

"Look!" Paul's voice reached the doctor faintly. "Before it looked as flexible as thin plastic or cloth, but now it's stiffening!"

"They must be in the final stages," Viorst said. "Won't be long now."

Rob finished up hastily, then packed the equipment into a small duffel bag that resembled the one the alien had carried. He looked up at the Bio Officer. "Thanks for the help, Simon. I'd have never finished in time without it."

The other man made a dismissive gesture. "You about had it sewed up when I came down. I only hope it works right."

"Yeah, I wish we were as well prepared as they are," Rob said, then added, "They seem very welcoming."

Viorst shrugged. "Yeah, they do. Maybe it's going to turn out all right."

Rob smiled at him. "Sure it is."

When the doctor reached the control cabin with his equipment, he found Raoul, Jerry, Joan, and Mahree waiting for him. "You all set, Doc?" the Captain asked.

"It's ready." He glanced at each of them. "Who'll be doing the testing? I'll have to show you how."

"You are, Doc," Raoul said. "We're going, you, Joan, and I."

Rob's mouth went dry, even as he felt it widening into a huge, silly grin. "Me?" He glanced at Jerry and Mahree, saw the disappointment in their eyes, and felt a brief stab of guilt. *They're the ones who worked so hard on the programming . . . especially Mahree.* "You sure you want me?"

"Yeah. Joan and I'll carry the computer hook-up, and I want you to handle the atmosphere testing personally. I only wish we had some kind of film about us to show to them."

"Uncle Raoul?" Mahree tugged at her uncle's sleeve. "I thought about that, and I had the computer run off these flimsies and fastened them into a sort of book.'' She held out a sheaf of what appeared to be photographs.

''Huh?'' Raoul flipped through them. Rob caught a quick flash of scenes from Earth, some in color, many in black and white, plus diagrams of the Sol system. ''This is the kind of stuff I meant. Where'd you come up with this?''

''My history text, the same place where I found the Pioneer and Voyager pictures.'' She managed to smile, though it was a bit shaky. ''These are the images they sent out on the Voyager disks. They're terribly dated, I know, but better than nothing. And each scene was carefully chosen by experts to tell the maximum number of things about Earth.''

Raoul gave her a warm smile and a quick hug. ''I think it's entirely fitting that part of the message those folks sent out to the stars will finally get there, honey. This is *great*.''

''You did good, kiddo,'' Rob said. He gave her a thumbs-up sign and grinned.

She tried to smile, but this time it didn't quite come off. Rob leaned over and whispered, ''Stay up here on the bridge. I'll call you on the security channel. It'll be almost like you're there with us. Okay?''

She nodded, biting her lip.

Raoul took a deep breath. ''Okay, I guess that covers everything. We'd better get suited up.''

''Why the rush?'' Rob asked.

For an answer Raoul flicked on the intercom, and Rob read the location ID above it. The forward airlock.

A hollow thump reverberated, then two more, then three more.

Then it came again. *One . . . one-two . . . one-two-three . . .*

''They've been knocking for nearly five minutes,'' Raoul said. ''It'd be rude to keep them waiting.''

CHAPTER 6

◆

The Simiu

Dear Diary:

I'm sitting here in the control room all by myself. It was nice of Rob to promise to call me, but . . . but, dammit, I'm *tired* of him treating me like his kid sister! I mean, he doesn't have to fall in love with me, but I'm *not* twelve!

I get the feeling that he's sensitive about his own comparative youth, and that treating me like a little kid is one way of widening the gap between us . . .

I'm also pissed because I'm not going with them. Jerry and I developed those programs. One of *us* should be there, not Joan.

This is it, this is really *it* . . . the something special, the thing nobody else has done. If only my—

Wait a minute! The vid-cams just came on, presenting me with a view of three spacesuited figures in the airlock!

As the inner airlock door hissed closed behind him, Rob pulled on the gloves to his spacesuit, then sealed them. Taps sounded against the outer airlock door. *One . . . one-two . . . one-two-three . . .* Quickly he reached over and returned the signal. "Just hold on a minute, and then we'll open it," he muttered. He glanced over at Lamont, who was clamping his helmet into place, then hastily donned his own. Joan, too, was ready.

"Radio check," Raoul said.

"Receiving you loud and clear," Joan responded in clipped tones that betrayed her excitement.

"Me, too," Rob said. He glanced over at the weapon the First Mate was sliding into the tool sheath located on the hip of her spacesuit. "Do you really think that's necessary?"

She glanced at him, and he watched her mouth tighten. "Just following orders," she said shortly.

"I thought over what we talked about, Doc," Raoul explained. "But one of us should be armed. I can count on Joan to keep her head in an emergency. I wish I felt comfortable enough to walk out there completely unarmed, but I don't."

"It's set on 'shock,' Rob, not 'disrupt,' " Joan said. "And believe me, I wouldn't use it unless I had a damned good reason."

"All right," Rob said. "Just promise me one thing, Raoul."

"What?"

"If there's ever a time when we meet them en masse, *don't* issue one of those to Simon. We've made progress, but he's still xenophobic. I encouraged him to join Evelyn Maitland in hibernation, but he refused."

"Do you mean that he's dangerous?" Raoul demanded sharply. "I can order him to be frozen, if you have evidence that he's mentally unstable."

"No . . . I don't think that's necessary. He's definitely making progress."

Joan nodded. "Simon will be all right, Raoul," she said. "Rob, don't forget your suit camera." She reached up to activate her own helmet's vid-cam. Then she switched on the ship's recording units, and verified that they were working properly.

"Cycle the airlock, Joan," Raoul directed when she finished. "Leave the gravity on. Everyone remember that their gravity's higher than Earth-normal."

Rob picked up his testing equipment, clutching it like a security blanket. He was sweating so profusely that the suit's extra cooling unit cut in; he tried consciously to relax.

"Vacuum" flashed on the control panel. Raoul checked another indicator. "Okay, we've got vacuum outside," he said. "You two ready?"

"Ready, Raoul," Joan said. Rob gave a thumbs-up signal.

The Captain pressed the "airlock open" switch.

The doors split apart to reveal a glare of white light. A spacesuited figure stood there on all fours.

It looked up at them, and Rob saw that the being's shoulders nearly reached his waist. *If it stood up on its hind legs,* he thought, *we'd be about the same height.* It wore a suit that was iridescent blue, with a dark blue helmet. The faceplate must have been polarized, for Rob could barely make out the alien's furred face and violet eyes through the transparency.

It seemed rude to tower over the creature, so Rob clumsily knelt and, after a second, Raoul and Joan did the same. The alien rose until it was squatting on its heels, bringing it to eye level with the humans. Very slowly, the being made the ceremonial gesture they had seen in the film sequence.

"Think we ought to imitate it, Doc?" Raoul asked.

"Yes," Rob said.

Carefully, the three humans did their best to reproduce the flowing motions. The alien's eyes widened behind its faceplate, and they could see its mouth moving.

"I'll bet it's reporting back to its people," Joan remarked.

Shit! Rob thought, remembering his promise. Hastily he activated the security channel. "Mahree? You there?"

"I'm here, Rob," her voice reached him, breathless with excitement.

"Can you people see and hear everything?"

"Yes. I'm still up on the bridge with Jerry, but everyone else is watching and listening down in the galley. We can hear you, but only Jerry's allowed to respond. Which I can understand . . . it'd be too confusing if everyone tried to talk."

"Okay, if I need to speak privately, I'll use this channel."

The alien took a cautious step forward, then held up the orange bag it had brought. It moved its head to the right, its right hand turning palm upward. The doctor watched its lips move again. "I think our friend is asking whether it can come in and do the atmosphere testing," he told his companions.

"How do we say 'okay, go ahead'?" Raoul asked.

Rob thought for a moment, then he rose and backed up, motioning Joan and Raoul to do likewise. He began beckoning exaggeratedly with one hand, while pointing to the clear space in the middle of the airlock with the other. "Come on," he said, nodding hard so their visitor could see his helmet move.

The alien took another step forward, then glanced at Rob. The doctor repeated his motions. Then, with a sudden air of decision, the being strode over to the spot the human had vacated. It squatted there, gazing around curiously.

"I'm going to have to close the airlock doors," Raoul said. "I hope that won't alarm it."

"I don't think so," Rob said. "After all, it knows why it came here."

"Here goes. Joan, don't take your eyes off it." Raoul carefully made the widest possible detour around the squatting alien. He triggered the airlock to pressurize.

The doors began sliding together, but the alien did not move, only watched everything that went on with a bright, nearly unblinking gaze.

Finally the airlock was again filled with air. Rob cautiously went over to the green light that was flashing. He tapped it with his gloved forefinger, nodded vigorously at the being, then returned to pick up his own duffel bag. He took out the first of his instruments and peered intently at the calibrations. "Earth-normal," he said, then nodded again.

The creature obviously figured out his intended message, for it immediately took out its testing equipment.

Rob saw that the alien's six-fingered hands moved with greater speed and dexterity than a human's, despite the heavy spacesuit gloves. In just a few minutes, the being was done with its tests and had stowed its equipment away.

"I wonder if they'll let me do the same thing?" Rob asked his companions, as Raoul triggered the depressurization sequence.

When the doors opened, the doctor held up *his* bag and pointed toward the aliens' airlock. Their visitor watched him intently, then, with great deliberation, nodded its head. "We're making progress!" Rob cried, jubilant.

The being turned to lead them out into the tube. Rob saw that the corridor was at least fifteen meters long. As he stepped over the threshold, he suddenly felt as though his boots had acquired lead soles.

"Watch it," he warned. "That higher gravity." He glanced at his sensing equipment. "One-point-five Earth gee."

Raoul grunted; he and Joan were carrying the vid-cam and computer link. "How are we going to get the idea across of what *this* stuff does?" the Captain wondered.

"One thing at a time," Rob said. "Let me get these atmosphere readings first. Where's Mahree's picture book?"

"I have it," Joan said.

Rob activated the security channel. "Mahree, will that equipment you and Jerry cobbled together play back an image of what's standing in front of the camera? Simultaneously, I mean?"

"Sure," she replied. "Just set it on 'record' with the red switch, and 'play' with the blue one. Then whatever's in front of the camera will show on the holo-tank."

The humans followed their host to the aliens' airlock, then halted as the creature manipulated the controls. The portal before them was the same flat-topped pyramid shape as the buildings they'd seen.

The doors opened, and the humans followed the creature into the airlock, standing shoulder to shoulder in the center of the cubicle, because the walls sloped inward, like the interior of a pyramid.

"Cramped," Raoul muttered. His head nearly brushed the ceiling.

"But the design makes sense," Rob pointed out, kneeling again. "They don't need space vertically, they need it horizontally." When the alien closed the doors and nodded, the doctor busied himself with his equipment. Finally, he stowed the last of his gear away. "That's it."

"Can we breathe it?" Joan asked.

"Yes, the mix itself is eminently breathable. Oxygen a little higher than we're used to, nitrogen a little lower, carbon dioxide still lower . . . some of the trace elements are different, but nothing that's harmful to us. I'll need to complete an in-depth microbial analysis, of course."

Their host opened the airlock doors, then preceded the humans back into the tube.

"Let's set up the computer link and vid-cam here," Rob said, stopping near the middle of the connecting tunnel.

Raoul began setting up the equipment.

The alien squatted down to watch, violet eyes intent. Rob knelt down beside it, and carefully spread Mahree's book out on the floor in front of the being. He demonstrated turning the pages. "See this? This'll help you learn things about us. I'm sorry we don't have a film like you did, but we weren't expecting to meet anybody out here." Though he knew the alien could not hear him, he spoke aloud so the listeners aboard *Désirée* could follow everything that was going on.

The alien regarded the pictures for a long moment, then

cautiously reached out a gloved finger toward them. As it did so, it glanced up at Rob. "Yes," he said, nodding vigorously. "It's for you. Go ahead."

After a quick touch and another sideways glance—Rob just kept nodding determinedly—the creature picked it up and began turning the pages.

A few minutes later the alien looked up. The doctor saw that it had several digits inserted between pages, as if marking them. The being tapped one of the pictures, pointed at Rob and made the same interrogatory gesture he had noticed earlier. Rob leaned over to glance at the picture, which showed a color photo of an astronaut floating above Earth, wearing a spacesuit.

The doctor was surprised to realize how little the basic design of spacesuits had changed in three centuries. The pictured suit was much less streamlined in design than the one he was wearing, but to alien eyes they must appear virtually identical. He nodded. "Yes, that's a picture of a man in a suit like I'm wearing. He's floating above our home planet, Earth."

The alien then deliberately turned to another color photo, which showed a man seated on a stool, painting. Its gloved forefinger tapped the picture and again it made the questioning gesture. "Yes," Rob said, nodding. "That's right. I look very much like that without my suit."

Finally, the being turned to the last marked page, which bore a series of black-and-white anatomical drawings. It made the gesture again, pointing at Rob. "Yes," the doctor said, nodding, "that's how I'm made inside."

He had no idea whether that was what the alien was actually asking, but that's what he *thought* the creature meant.

Rob had caught a glimpse of another picture as the alien flipped through, and he quickly put a finger on it. He pointed at the silhouette of a man, then patted his own chest. "Man," he said. Then he pointed at a similar silhouette of a woman, except that an inset in the figure's midsection showed a fetus, and pointed to Joan. "Woman," he intoned, feeling rather like Tarzan of the Apes. He repeated the words and the motions.

Solemnly and silently, the alien copied his pointing gestures from book to humans. "That's right!" Rob exclaimed.

The doctor heard Joan chuckle. "When you give them the lecture on the birds and the bees, Doc, I want to be there."

Rob looked over at the First Mate and laughed. "Only if you promise to get pregnant, so you'll match this illustration."

"Heaven forbid," Raoul muttered abstractedly. "That's all I need." After another moment, he announced, "I'm done."

Rob climbed to his feet and went over to the computer link. "Set it to record and playback simultaneously. Does this thing have an audio hookup?"

"Yeah, that was Mahree's idea," Raoul said proudly. "In addition to simply recording sounds, it vocalizes words and sounds as it displays them on the holo-tank. *Assuming* they pressurize this tube so sound will carry, it'll be a big help."

"Great!" Rob exclaimed, knowing Mahree was listening.

The Captain switched on the vid-cam and holo-tank. Rob walked over to the alien, who glanced up from the picture book inquiringly. The doctor beckoned, and the creature followed him.

Raoul made an adjustment in the angle of the vid-cam, and in the holo-tank, the doctor's and the alien's images suddenly appeared. The alien peered closely at the image. Rob pointed to the vid-cam, then to the holo-tank, and moved his arms up and down so the alien could see that the optical device was indeed "seeing" what was before it.

After a moment, the alien nodded, then peered into the vid-cam. Its image loomed at them from the holo-tank, distorted by proximity. Raoul turned on the unit's prerecorded program, and Jerry's first image, that of the alien solar system, coalesced.

The alien studied the picture, then began to nod.

"Think we got our meaning across?" Raoul asked.

"I hope so. It's reporting in again," Rob said.

After the being finished its conversation, it pointed at Joan, at Raoul, at Rob, then at itself, then it patted one gloved hand on the floor of the tube, and, after settling back into a sitting position, picked up the book of pictures again.

"Was he—it—asking us to stay here?" Raoul wondered.

"Looked like it to me," Joan said.

"I agree," Rob said.

The two men stood beside the computer link, arms dangling, feeling awkward, while Joan stayed where she was, against the wall opposite the alien. Several minutes passed, then their host glanced over at its airlock.

When Rob turned, the portal was opening. Two more aliens emerged. One was carrying equipment, and the other was empty-

handed. The third alien was much smaller, making Rob wonder
again whether the smaller ones were females.

Working swiftly, the two larger aliens began setting up the
instruments the second creature carried. Though very different in
design, materials, and workmanship, the resulting artifact possessed a recognizable monitor. The alien pressed a colored spot
on the casing, and it filled with images. "Bingo!" cried Rob
happily. He chinned the security channel. "Mahree, it looks like
we've hit the jackpot!"

"Great! *Now* we're getting somewhere!"

The two aliens adjusted their unit so it faced the humans'
computer link. Then all three of the beings made the greeting
gesture. The humans echoed it, more confidently this time. The
aliens watched the two machines interact for a moment, then
they abruptly turned away and headed for their own airlock.

"What now?" Raoul wondered. "Do we just walk away?"

Rob shrugged. "Apparently greetings are ceremonial and formal, but not farewells."

The humans began trudging back to *Désirée*'s airlock, and
decontamination. Rob suddenly realized that he was hungry,
thirsty, and exhausted. His leg muscles were in knots from all
the walking and standing in the higher gravity.

He also realized that none of the discomforts mattered; he'd
never felt better. He grinned to himself. *You wanted something
special? I'd say this past hour definitely qualifies . . .*

During the next two days the human and alien computer tie-ins
flashed images, symbols, and words at each other. Midway
through the first day, the aliens pressurized the connecting tunnel, so Jerry also triggered the audio portion of the presentation.
At the same time he put out a call to the crew of the *Désirée* for
assistance in collecting and organizing more data for the linkup.

As the Communications Chief had hoped, the alien computers
also functioned on an "on-off" basis, one that could be translated into binary. Steadily, as the two computers built up a
backlog of mutually comprehensible concepts and terms, the
systems began developing a mapping algorithm. This interface
would be the first step toward a translation program.

Morale aboard *Désirée* ran high; the petty bickering and tensions evaporated. The stress level was still considerable, but it

was a healthier stress. Curiosity about their hosts grew as their knowledge about them increased.

Ray Drummond dubbed the aliens "the Simiu," and, despite Rob's protests that the name might encourage the crew to think of them as animals, the designation stuck. As Raoul pointed out, they had to call them *something*.

The smaller Simiu were indeed females. The aliens' internal makeup proved amazingly similar to that of Earth primates, including humans, though there were, of course, differences—the heart, for example, was pear-shaped and located in the center of the chest. The beings also possessed *two* fully opposable thumbs—one where human thumbs were located, and one on the opposite side of their hands.

The aliens' own data, confirmed by *Désirée*'s orbital scans, indicated that their world did not suffer the population crunch that continued to plague Earth. All of the Simiu dwellings were located in small cities like the one they had been shown, with sizable tracts of land surrounding each. There were no networks of roads—all shipping seemed to be done by air or river transport. All traffic within the cities was pedestrian, with Simiu strolling leisurely from place to place, or loping on all fours as fast as a terrestrial horse could trot.

"They're big and muscular enough to have considerable strength," Raoul said. "Not to mention that their species evolved under higher gravity."

The aliens used the latticed overlays on their buildings to swarm effortlessly up and down the pyramids, using both hands and feet to grasp.

"Handy in case of fire," Paul observed. "It'd be hard to trap people who don't need stairs or elevators to go up or down."

The humans as yet had little grasp of their hosts' social, governmental, or familial organization—except that none of these seemed to resemble those on Earth. Their society appeared remarkably homogenous—there were no discernible racial differences between the people, and they all spoke the same language.

One thing seemed reassuringly clear—Simiu were not a warlike people. None of *Désirée*'s scans revealed anything that looked like military bases; nothing even resembled a weapon in any of their pictures.

Even Simon was mollified by this, though he pointed out that none of the information the humans had given the Simiu had included pictures or drawings of weapons, much less descriptions of war or the existence of military organizations. "They're built like predators," Viorst pointed out, "just as we are. But maybe they've evolved past that." He smiled thinly. "Matter of fact, Jerry says they're vegetarians."

When Rob started to grin, he shook his head. "Don't give me that I-told-you-so look, Doc. I said, 'maybe,' remember."

The Bio Officer assisted the doctor in the lab, culturing the microbes contained in the alien atmosphere. As soon as Raoul had declared his decision to detour to System X, Rob had grown tissue samples from cells in his medical banks—skin, blood, organ, and bone samples, among others. He and Simon used these lumps of organic material to test the alien atmosphere, exposing them, then monitoring the effects.

As far as the doctor could determine, there were none. "But it's still a risk," he told Simon. "We have no way of knowing that some bug of theirs isn't going to catch up with us in a year—or five—or fifty."

"Or that one of their microbes might not mutate in our systems and eventually become dangerous, like the one that caused Lotis Fever," Viorst agreed soberly.

"Still, we can't seal ourselves inside a bell jar. Somebody's got to breathe that air . . . I'll try it tomorrow."

"No, we need you in case somebody gets hurt or sick. I'll do it," Simon volunteered. "But what about contact with the Simiu themselves? To test *their* bugs, we need a blood sample—at least."

"I'll have to think about how to accomplish that," Rob said with a frown.

The next morning, Rob and Jerry put on suits, while Simon, unsuited, stood by. When they were ready, Jerry triggered the opening sequence, and they stepped out into the aliens' tunnel between *Désirée* and the Simiu airlock.

The Bio Officer took several deep breaths, while Rob and Jerry watched him anxiously. He smiled, giving them a thumbs-up sign. "How is it?" Rob asked.

"I feel a little high because of the extra oxygen, but otherwise, fine," Simon reported, speaking into a radio link he wore. "There's a faint odor . . . kind of musky-spicy. Not objectionable, though."

"Let me know immediately if you have any trouble," Rob

said. He continued to observe Viorst while Jerry busied himself with minute adjustments to the computer link. The Bio Officer wandered over to study the design of the aliens' airlock.

"What kind of metal is this?" Simon asked, eyeing the station's silvery blue skin thoughtfully.

"I don't know," Jerry answered, glancing up from the keyboard. "Some kind of alloy? Maybe Paul could tell you."

The Bio Officer moved to touch the frame around the door with cautious fingers, but just as he did, the door slid open. Even in the higher gravity, Simon jumped noticeably.

Two spacesuited Simiu males were standing inside. As they saw their visitors, the aliens made the customary greeting gesture the humans had come to expect. Rob, Jerry, and, finally, Simon echoed it.

"Now what?" Viorst stammered, backing away. The aliens followed him out into the tunnel, gazing up curiously at the Bio Officer. They circled him slowly, chattering to each other. One of them was carrying a satchel similar to the first one Rob had seen. Simon backed up until he bumped into the wall of the tunnel and could go no farther. His voice was edged with panic. "Do . . . d'you think they're mad to find us here?"

"No. They're just curious, Simon. It's their first look at an unsuited human," Rob said, hoping fervently that the aliens would make no sudden moves. Sweat was beading on Viorst's upper lip, running in greasy tracks down his cheeks. He walked over to stand beside the Bio Officer, signaling furtively behind his back for Jerry to stand on Simon's other side. "Okay, let's just walk back to our airlock."

The humans turned and headed for their ship, three abreast, and the Simiu followed them. When they reached the open airlock door, the first alien pointed to the interior of the chamber, then touched its own helmet. Then the creature made the interrogatory gesture.

"He wants to come into the airlock with us," Rob said. *Oh, shit, why'd they have to pick **now**? I don't want to leave Simon outside with the other alien, and I don't want the two of them in close quarters inside, either! Damn!*

He glanced over at Jerry and realized that the Communications Chief fully realized his dilemma. "That's fine," Greendeer said. "You take both of them into the airlock with you, while Simon and I will wait out here. They probably just need to do some more atmosphere testing."

"Right," Rob said gratefully. He began beckoning, and this time the aliens responded immediately to the gesture. They squatted inside the airlock, the second male gazing around curiously as Rob closed the outer door and signaled the compartment to empty and repressurize.

When the green light came on, he repeated his original motions of pointing to the indicators and announcing "Earth-normal," whereupon the first Simiu, the one carrying the bag, spoke to his comrade. The second alien put both hands to his helmet and lifted it off. The first alien watched tensely, much as Jerry and Rob had observed Simon.

Rounded nostrils within the Simiu's narrow, squarish muzzle widened noticeably as the alien drew deep breaths. After several minutes, the being stirred, then chattered emphatically at his companion. *The oxygen's thin, and this air sure smells funny, but so far, no ill effects!* Rob mentally translated.

The unhelmeted alien turned back to the human, and, reaching into the bag, withdrew a greenish ovoid. The object had a metallic sheen and a hole at each of the narrow ends. The Simiu held the ovoid up at Rob, chattering away (the doctor could hear the alien's voice faintly through his suit helmet); then, with grave deliberation, removed the glove from his right hand. The being inserted his forefinger into one of the holes.

The alien gestured with his other hand at Rob, beckoning. The helmeted companion tapped the other opening, then, with unmistakable meaning, pointed at Rob's hand.

The doctor hesitated for a moment. *Some kind of analysis instrument. Since the Simiu is keeping his digit in the other end, that must mean that some comparison of our respective body chemistries will occur. Will there be actual physical contact? Fluid exchange? What about the risk of infection?*

He knew that Raoul would probably turn thumbs-down on such a risk, but . . . *Now's my chance to put my credit where my mouth is.*

Taking a deep breath, Rob unsealed his suit glove, then knelt down on the airlock floor and cautiously pushed his forefinger into the opening.

As he'd suspected, he felt a cold stinging sensation that meant blood was being drawn.

Symbols flickered across the surface of the ovoid. The two Simiu anxiously scanned them, then seemed to relax. They chattered at Rob, then both exaggeratedly nodded. The second alien ceremoniously removed his helmet.

"So your machine says we can't make each other sick," the doctor interpreted. "Wonder what my equipment would say?"

The Simiu motioned for him to withdraw his hand. There was a tiny, tingling cold patch on the ball of his finger, but not even a drop of blood marred the skin.

As the doctor curiously eyed his finger, one of the aliens reached into the satchel and withdrew a small, padded rectangular container. He handed it to Rob, then showed the doctor how a nearly invisible seam in its side split open when a small red symbol was pressed. There was a stoppered vial inside, half-full of a thick, reddish purple liquid. Rob reached in and pulled it out. The vial lay in his ungloved palm, cold.

The Simiu chattered at the doctor, pointing first at Rob's finger, then at himself. The alien pantomimed squeezing the finger and holding it over the vial.

"I've got it," Rob said, nodding. "This is a sample of your blood, so I can use it for my analysis. You guys think of everything, don't you?"

Carefully Rob returned the vial to its insulated holder. He cycled the airlock, opened it, and waved at Jerry and Simon. Then, because it seemed the right thing to do, the doctor slowly reached up and removed his own helmet. His first breath of alien air tasted like musk and cloves.

Rob's tests during the next twenty-four hours confirmed the Simiu conclusion, and the doctor informed Raoul Lamont that he now considered unsuited contact between the two peoples to be safe—at least, as safe as he could determine, barring years of tests.

The Captain shrugged. "I know. Risks come with this business."

Jerry reported that the two computer systems had completed their mapping algorithm. He, Paul, Ray, and Mahree were busy working on designing voders that would allow spoken words to be flashed onto a screen. "If we were better equipped, we could hook it all together so that you could hear a spoken translation," the communications tech said regretfully. "But, as Raoul put it, none of us knew that we'd be tapped to play Marco Polo on this trip."

"How big will the monitor be?"

"You'll be able to hold it in your hand, or strap it on your wrist," Jerry said. "And everyone's going to have to carry a portable computer link, so they can enable the translation program when they need it."

"You mean we'll have to actually *key* for translations?" Rob said, dismayed. "That's pretty awkward."

"Best we can do with the equipment we've got," Jerry said, a bit defensively. "Pisses me off, too, but we're stuck."

"Hey," Rob demurred, "don't get me wrong. You guys have done a terrific job, you really have."

Jerry shrugged and changed the subject, mentioning that he and Mahree had made strides in deciphering several of the original transmissions *Désirée* had received. "Really? What were they?" Rob asked.

"One was a report on some kind of competition, giving scores and names of individuals."

Rob grinned. "The Superbowl or the World Series, you mean?"

"Something like that. The others were apparently news reports or speeches—can't tell the difference yet between fact and opinion."

"No holo-vid daily dramas?"

Jerry chuckled wryly. "No. And that lack probably constitutes the single best argument for Simiu superiority as a species."

It was on the morning of the sixth day after they had docked that Raoul's voice on the intercom summoned Rob from the laboratory. "They're knocking on the airlock again, Doc."

"I'll be right up."

When he reached the airlock, Rob quickly pushed his way through the crowd to reach Raoul's side. The Captain handed him one of the newly completed translating voders and computer links, then grasped the doctor's arm and drew him a few steps down the corridor so they could speak in relative privacy. "What are you going to do?" Gable asked quietly.

"I'm going to invite them in," Lamont said, sotto voce. "There's no reason not to, right?"

"Give them a tour of the ship, that kind of thing?"

"Guess so. Put that voder on, Doc. I want you and Jerry with me, since you two have a flair for this sort of thing."

"We ought to have Mahree, too. She's responsible for at least half of that translation program," Rob pointed out.

"Okay, she can wait outside the airlock, and join us when we begin the tour. Otherwise, it'll be crowded as hell in there."

"What about the rest of the crew?" Rob glanced around at all the eager faces—and his eyes met Yoki's. He felt a stab of guilt. He'd been so busy with all the testing that he'd barely had a chance to say hello to Yoki in passing—much less spend any time alone with her.

As their gazes locked, she smiled and gave him a small, reassuring nod that told him she understood.

Raoul raised his voice. "Mahree and Jerry, please stay here. The rest of you, beat it. You can follow along on the viewscreen in the galley. I don't think it's wise to overwhelm these people the first time by sheer force of numbers. We can gradually allow more interaction during future visits."

A disappointed mutter arose, but Raoul's order was just common sense; nobody argued as they dispersed.

"Get yourself a linkup, *chérie*, then wait for us here," Raoul told Mahree. "You're going to be one of the tour guides."

His niece, who had been smiling uncertainly ever since the Captain had ordered her to remain, lit up like a torch. "Oh, Uncle Raoul!" she gasped, flinging her arms around his neck and giving him several resounding kisses. "Thank you! *Thank* you!"

Lamont was flushed with pleasure as he firmly set her back on her feet. "You should thank Doc, here," he said, a little gruffly, but his smile belied his tone. "Rob insisted you should be included."

Mahree gave her benefactor a heartfelt smile.

The doctor shook his head in mock disappointment. "You mean I don't rate hugs and kisses? My heart is broken."

She colored violently. "I have to get my linkup," she mumbled, and, turning, raced off down the corridor.

The three men opened the airlock and went in. Rob felt oddly naked standing there without his spacesuit. He watched Jerry strap the tiny monitor to his left wrist. Feeling awkward, the doctor copied his actions, just as Raoul was doing.

"When they talk, you'll read out what they're saying on the screen, in English," Jerry told them. "If a word comes across the screen in Simiu characters, then I'll key in a request for the system to search for, and, if possible, define that word. Our system is hooked into theirs, so the more we talk to them, the better our working vocabulary is going to get."

"What do you call a working vocabulary?" Rob asked.

Jerry grimaced. "One that allows us to communicate on a basic level. The mapping algorithm is complete, and I *think* it's going to be all right . . . unless we've still got bugs in the program. I hope we're not way off-orbit."

"Let's find out," Raoul said. The Captain signaled the airlock to open. Rob saw four unsuited Simiu, three males and a female, squatting outside. Humans and aliens made the greeting gesture formally, then the female, who wore a device on a collar around her neck, plus something that looked like a tiny greenish fan clipped to one ear, spoke. .

"Greetings," Rob read on his screen. "We the"—an alien word flitted across, probably their name for their species— "welcome you to our world. Our people gain much honor from your presence. Mutual benefit will follow from our association, is our best . . ." another Simiu word followed. Jerry hastily keyed for a translation. The alien's equipment must have signaled her that a translation had been requested, because she paused and stood waiting until the word was defined for them. "Aspiration," Rob's screen read, finally.

Jerry frowned. "I'm sorry, Captain. I know system response is slow when it's got to search for translations."

"That's okay," Raoul reassured him, then addressed the female Simiu directly. "We humans are honored to be your guests, and we also aspire for mutual benefit to our peoples."

The female Simiu nodded, seemingly pleased by the Captain's response. She turned and spoke to her people, then all the aliens were nodding at once.

She spoke again. Rob read: "If possible for you at this"—a Simiu symbol that the doctor guessed to be a time measurement crossed the screen—"will you honor us with talking? We have much to discuss."

"I'd say that's the understatement of the century," Rob muttered.

"Yes, it will please us very much to talk," Raoul said, making a formal ushering gesture toward the inner airlock door. "Would you care to come inside?"

CHAPTER 7

♦

The Honor-Bond

Dear Diary:

It's been a busy week since the Simiu boarded *Désirée* for their first visit. We're learning a lot.

While most Simiu technology seems on a par with our own, they have two VERY IMPORTANT advances we don't: the first is an FTL drive that's *twice* as fast as ours; the second is that they have a way of making FTL *transmissions*.

The translation program is working better than we expected, but it's far from perfect, especially as regards technical words.

Everyone else seems resigned to the fact that we won't be able to speak directly to the Simiu. They're content to rely on the voders. But reading translations off those little screens drives me crazy; I like watching people's faces when they speak. So I keep going over and over our holo-vids of them talking, trying to understand what they're saying, even if I can't pronounce it. It's tough going, but it's slowly paying off.

Simiu features are very mobile, though in a different way than ours. They never smile, and when Uncle Raoul grinned broadly at them, I noticed that it distressed them, as though he'd done something rude. They don't mind if our mouths turn up when we smile—just if we display our teeth when we do it. I told Uncle Raoul what I'd seen, and he warned everyone.

We try hard not to offend them, but it seems unavoidable. We keep running into taboos; for example, Jerry asked how far they had explored this area of the Orion Arm, only to be met with polite evasions. They are graciously tolerant of our unintentional transgressions, and we try to avoid repeating them.

I've spoken with the First Ambassador a few times. We exchanged polite greetings and a few cautious questions about each other's society. The last time we spoke, the F.A., Rhrrrkkeet' (her name sounds like a low breathy growl, ending with a soft squeal and a strange *click* at the end), asked me how old I am. I wonder why?

The connecting tunnel between *Désirée* and the Simiu space station was no longer a bare white expanse; it was scattered with portable tables and chairs the humans had brought, as well as the low, ottomanlike lounges Simiu used. The lights had been dimmed to be more comfortable to Terran eyes. Mahree sat on one of the chairs, watching seven humans and twenty-odd Simiu mingle.

She saw her aunt and Paul Monteleon leaning over the chessboard, engrossed in their game. Six Simiu squatted in a circle around them, intent on the moves, obviously fascinated. Mahree smiled, thinking how relaxed her aunt had become around the aliens. Then a glimmer of blue-gray metal protruding from the tool sheath on the hip of her aunt's coverall caught her eye, and she sighed, her smile fading. *If only Joan could quit toting that damned gun.*

Mahree had argued the point with Raoul several times, but her uncle remained adamant; one crew member must be armed whenever the humans were in contact with the aliens.

The girl turned as she heard her name called. "Mahree! Come over here!" Raoul beckoned. "The First Ambassador wants to talk to you."

Quickly she hurried over to the female alien. "Greetings, Honored First Ambassador," she said, making the formal gesture automatically to the Simiu leader.

Rhrrrkkeet' returned the greeting. "Greetings, Honored Mahree. Your uncle relates how you are traveling with him to be educated in a famous place of learning on Earth."

"That is correct, Honored Rhrrrkkeet'," Mahree said, trying to keep one eye on the alien's face, as well as on her voder's screen. She was pleased that she'd understood several of the spoken words.

"Why does education demand that you voyage so far?"

"My world has schools for the teaching of young humans, but not for the teaching of those who are about to be adult humans," Mahree replied, choosing her words carefully. "So I must travel to the homeworld of our species to receive an adult's education."

"I understand," Rhrrrkkeet' said. "Our people do not have to travel to be educated, though."

"Honored Rhrrrkkeet'," the girl ventured, "how many of your people are there?" The humans had no idea of the population of Simiu, and she thought she saw an opportunity to find out.

The First Ambassador hesitated for nearly a minute. *Uh, oh,* Mahree thought, *is this another taboo subject?*

"There are many of us," the F.A. said, finally. "I do not know exact number."

Mahree nodded. "Forgive me, I did not mean to offend."

"You did not offend, child." Rhrrrkkeet' glanced around at the crowd of milling Simiu, and emitted a breathy growl. One of them, a male with a sorrel-colored coat, looked up, then came swiftly toward them.

When he arrived, the First Ambassador said, formally, "My"—alien symbols marched across Mahree's screen—"you would say, cousin-son, accompanied me to your most-excellent vessel in hope you would honor him by making his acquaintance. He is being much the same age as you, Honored Mahree. May I introduce you?"

Mahree glanced over at the young Simiu, who wore one of the Simiu voder-collars and ear-clips. "I would be honored to meet him," she said.

"Excellent!" the First Ambassador yipped. She turned to the young male. "Dhurrrkk', this is Honored MahreeBurroughs, also a student. She voyages far so that she may study at a Terran place of adult learning. Honored MahreeBurroughs, this is"—the alien symbols again—"cousin-son Dhurrrkk'."

Mahree repeated the greeting gesture, saying, "I am pleased and honored to meet you, Honored Dhurrrkk'."

The humans had learned early that Simiu measured things not as good or evil, moral or immoral, but as honorable or dishonorable. Individual honor, clan honor, planetary honor—even their system of exchange was based on honor.

"The honor is mine," the young alien responded, after his formal greeting gesture. He stole glances at Mahree's face with barely concealed curiosity.

Raoul put a hand on Mahree's shoulder. "*Chérie*, why don't you take Dhurrrkk' here on a tour of *Désirée*?"

Mahree nodded. "I'd be happy to." She nodded at the new-comer. "Honored Dhurrrkk', would you like to visit our vessel? It would be an honor for me to guide you."

Dhurrrkk' nodded, and Mahree beckoned him to follow her.

Once inside *Désirée*, she escorted the Simiu through the ship, identifying the various sections for him. He gazed around with avid curiosity, though Mahree noticed that he seldom made eye contact with her. She decided that was out of politeness, not shyness—Dhurrrkk's bold strides certainly held nothing diffident about them.

"Do you like school, Honored Dhurrrkk'?" she asked, sitting on her bunk as he squatted in the middle of her cabin, gazing around him with bright-eyed interest.

The Simiu nodded. "Yes, I enjoy learning."

"Honored Rhrrrkkeet' mentioned that we are almost the same age. I'll be seventeen soon. If I may ask, how old are you?"

"I am being nine of my planet's years old," Dhurrrkk' said. "One more year and I will be mature for mating, should some-one honor me with her selection. One more year, and I will be working each day, instead of studying."

That's right, Simiu females have only temporary sexual liaisons, Mahree remembered. The basic family unit consisted of several related females, living with their children (of all ages, including adults), plus the females' male "friends"—who might or might not be the fathers of any of their children.

Courtship was nonexistent. A female selected a male, then intercourse ensued immediately, lasting only a minute or two. The aliens apparently attached no more importance to mating in public than humans would to sharing an ice cream cone; several of their holo-vid travelogues had panned past mating couples.

Mahree beckoned and Dhurrrkk' followed her out of her cabin. In the corridor she glanced down at him as they walked. "What are you studying to be?"

"Pardon?" Simiu were invariably polite.

She tried again. "When you finish going to school, what job will you be prepared to do?"

"I have not yet made final selection. My studying has been to allow me to work in space." He thought for a moment. "Perhaps I will be a pilot. I am good at that."

"Then I know you'll want to see our bridge."

Dhurrrkk' was obviously fascinated by Joan's piloting and navigation station. Mahree described the controls as best she could. "And, finally, over here"—she patted an instrument panel—"is the communications console. This is where we first received the radio waves from your world." She sat down on Jerry's seat, then asked, "Have your people explored other planets, Honored Dhurrrkk'?"

The Simiu looked away, his crest hair flattening until it was lying between his ears. Mahree knew instantly that she had touched on a taboo subject again.

Before she could apologize, he said, "I am not . . . I must not . . . that is not something I can—"

Mahree interrupted hastily. "I am sorry, Honored Dhurrrkk'. Please forgive me. I did not mean to offend."

"I am not offended," he said, but he was silent as they left the control room.

Mahree kept quiet during the remainder of the tour, except to describe what they were seeing. She didn't want to chance upsetting the first Simiu she'd really had a chance to *talk* with.

When they reached the medical lab, Dhurrrkk' froze, standing mesmerized by an inky shape curled neatly into the cushion of Rob's chair. "That?" he said, gesturing so excitedly that his double-thumbed hand was a blur Mahree's eyes could hardly follow. "Please, that is what? Animal?"

"Yes, animal," she agreed. "It is a pet."

"Pet?" His formality had vanished. "Please, what means 'pet'?" *He's really interested in the cat,* Mahree thought, realizing that here might be a chance to recoup from her faux pas in the control room.

"Pet . . ." She keyed the English word into her computer link, so he would be able to see it translated into Simiu as she spoke: "Pets are animals who live with humans. They are our friends. 'Friends,' " she repeated slowly, articulating the word for him, when she saw how intently he was watching her mouth. "This particular species of pet is a 'cat.' "

"We have pets, too," Dhurrrkk' told her. "If Honored" —several alien symbols raced by—"Rhrrrkkeet' will permit my return, I will bring image of mine. We learn from pets . . . how to get along with family, be considerate, kind . . . to treat with honor those who are weaker and more vulnerable."

Sekhmet chose that moment to wake up. She blinked trustingly at Mahree, but then she saw the alien. Her ears flattened against her skull, and she snarled loudly. "Easy, girl!" Mahree protested, but the cat was not reassured.

"I am frightening her," Dhurrrkk' observed, his crest visibly drooping again. "Better I withdraw."

"No," she responded, "wait a moment. She's a young cat, she may be able to adjust. Just make yourself appear small, and be quiet while I talk to her."

The Simiu squatted down, moving slowly.

Mahree made soothing sounds. Finally Sekhmet's growls lessened, and her ears lifted a little. The girl hesitantly began stroking her, and, long minutes later, the cat relaxed enough to bump its black head caressingly against her hand. "That's it, that's it, Sekhmet," Mahree encouraged. "Now, this is Derrk"—she gave a swift glance of apology to the Simiu for the way her pronunciation butchered his name, but he did not seem affronted—"and he wants to be your friend, too."

Sekhmet glared distrustfully at the newcomer.

"Give me your hand," Mahree said, holding out her own. After a moment, strong, leathery fingers with softly furred backs slid across her palm and closed over her fingers. It was a shock to feel their warmth, and, Mahree realized suddenly, she was the first person to actually *touch* one of the aliens. She forced her voice to remain steady and comforting.

"Now, Sekhmet, take it easy," she said, holding the Simiu's fingers firmly in her own, so the cat could catch both their scents. Sekhmet hissed, but gradually, as Mahree reassured her, she finally relaxed enough to sniff Dhurrrkk's hand.

"That's it, girl! Good, Sekhmet!"

Mahree let go of the alien's hand, and sat back on her heels, remembering just in time not to grin. Dhurrrkk' appeared pleased; his crest stood straight up. He made a low, crooning sound to the cat. "Much gratitude to you, Honored Mahree," he said. "Your 'pet' is a creature of much beauty."

"Her name is Sekhmet." Mahree keyed in the name. "Sekmet," she repeated.

"Thhhheekkmeet," Dhurrrkk' tried. He lisped terribly.

"No, with the front teeth together," Mahree corrected. "Like this. Sssss."

"Thhhh . . ." he tried again. "Thssss."

"Better, much better!"

"Ssseekkmeet."

"That's terrific!"

"It is unfortunate that we cannot make each other's speech sounds easily," Dhurrrkk' observed. "It would be much improvement if we could converse without computer aid. I dislike not speaking directly."

"I feel the same way," Mahree said. "You know, if we practiced together, I bet we could learn to speak to each other."

"That is possible."

"To begin with, I would like to be able to say your name properly. Will you help me?"

"I would be honored."

"Dherrk," Mahree said slowly, trying to lower her voice for the initial sound. It was difficult; human mouths and vocal cords just weren't designed to produce such a guttural growl. And that final *click*—!

"Much better!" he encouraged. Hesitantly, she tried the name several more times. She finally learned to reproduce the low, breathy initial growl, but the *click* following the "kk" sound remained beyond her. Still, Dhurrrkk' praised her efforts.

"What is your name for your world?"

Dhurrrkk' produced a series of panting grunts. Mahree glanced at the translation, saw that the name literally meant "land-air-water."

She tried pitching her voice deep in her chest. "*Hhurrr*-ee-haah," she managed.

"Correct!"

"What about the word for your space station?"

Dhurrrkk' pushed his lips out exaggeratedly so she could watch him. "Tchh'ooo-kk'. That means 'Station One,' " he added.

Mahree tried copying him, without much success. "I'm going to have to practice that," she said. "Why is your station called 'Station One'? Do you have more than one space station?"

Dhurrrkk's crest sagged. "I . . . I explain poorly," he said. "Forgive, please, that I have confused you."

Uh, oh, another taboo, Mahree thought.

"Would you like to see our station?" Dhurrrkk' asked quickly, "I would be most honored to escort you."

"*Would* I? Oh, I mean, yes, yes, I would! Thank you! I'd be honored!"

"Then let us ask permission for you to accompany me."

Mahree hastily grabbed a vid-cam unit, after asking whether it would be permitted for her to record her expedition to show to her people. Dhurrrkk' nodded, and they set out, stopping first at the gathering in the tube to ask Rhrrrkkeet' and Raoul for permission. The Captain was obviously delighted that someone aboard *Désirée* was going to get to see their hosts' station.

"Station One" proved to be a fascinating warren of brightly colored three- and four-sided pyramid-shaped rooms, with ramps and grid lattices instead of elevators or escalators. Dhurrrkk' took her through several "rows" of the abacus, pointing out offices and shops. In a store that sold fruits and vegetables, Mahree was interested to note currency being used—small green disks.

That's odd, she thought. *I thought they conducted financial transactions with "honor-debts."* She knew that the Simiu system was a sophisticated form of barter that employed "honor debts" as a form of credit. Intrigued, she pointed to the currency. "What are those, Honored Dhurrrkk'?"

Her escort froze, crest drooping. "I . . ." he hesitated, obviously flustered. "I cannot discuss those items, Honored Mahree. It is not permitted."

Another taboo! "I am sorry I asked, Honored Dhurrrkk'," she said quickly. "Please excuse me."

"There is nothing to excuse," Dhurrrkk' said graciously, but he still seemed disturbed. "We have seen enough shops," he said. "Would you care to observe the docking bays for our ships?"

"I would like that very much."

Fortunately, Mahree possessed a good head for heights, so she was able to follow her escort when it came to scaling the lattice surrounding the largest of the Simiu docking bays.

As she panned the vid-cam down over the hammerheaded Simiu ships, some in docking cradles, others in repair bays, with maintenance technicians swarming over them, Mahree tried to get as many close-ups of their power assemblies as possible. *Paul is going to go crazy over these films,* she thought. *He's been in a panic to find out more about how they manage that super-fast FTL drive of theirs.*

After a half hour of walking and climbing in the higher gravity, Mahree was tired, her head spinning with alien sights, sounds, and scents. Simiu architecture, with its odd angles and parabolas, was actually painful to her vision, used to human-engineered right angles and straight lines. And the shade of violet the aliens were so fond of made her eyes water if she looked directly at it.

When Dhurrrkk' announced that it was time for them to return to the tube, she didn't argue. "It was wonderful, seeing your station, Honored Dhurrrkk'. I only wish that I could visit your planet," she said as they walked back to the airlock.

"I would like to show you my world, my home," Dhurrrkk' replied, "but our leaders have decreed it is not possible until our scientists have completed more tests to make sure your microbes cannot harm us."

"I understand," she said. "We would do the same thing, I'm sure, in your place." She hesitated. "Forgive my curiosity, but we know so little about your social structure. Is it permitted to ask how your government functions?"

"Each of our clans appoints a leader, and she represents us in the Under-Council, which governs each province. The Under-Council members who have . . ." he hesitated, "proved themselves the worthiest also serve in the High Council, making decisions of planetary importance."

" 'She'?" Mahree echoed. "Your Council members are female?"

"Of course," Dhurrrkk' said. "Females govern the clans; they own the land. Who else should rule?"

So, their culture is a matriarchy, Mahree thought. *That's interesting.* "But up to now," she said, "almost all of your people that we have met are male."

Dhurrrkk' nodded. "Naturally. We males are the ones who have the time to explore, to risk ourselves in space. Females have the young to teach, a task requiring the greatest wisdom. They also administer our society, and govern our people. Is it so on your world?"

"No, on our worlds both males and females work in space. Males as well as females own property and serve as government officials."

He gave her a sidelong glance from his violet eyes, and Mahree realized that, even when he was intent upon their conversation, Dhurrrkk' tended to avoid prolonged eye contact. *Must remember to mention that to Uncle Raoul,* she thought. *Tell him to warn everyone not to stare.*

"That is most interesting, Honored Mahree," the Simiu said. "In our world, males do the work in space. Females only travel into space when they must do so in order to administer, or, as in the case of Rhrrrkkeet', when they must meet with—" he broke off abruptly.

With whom? Mahree wondered, but she had the feeling that she'd tripped over another taboo, so she did not voice the question aloud. By this time, they had reached the airlock. Dhurrrkk' busied himself with the controls, and did not speak again until they stepped out into the tube, only to see that it was deserted. "We have been gone much time," he said.

Mahree glanced at her watch. "It's been over two hours! Everyone will be wondering where we are."

"Yes, we must each return to our people," he said with regret. "It has been most instructive. It is too much to hope that you would honor me thus again, but I wish that it could be so."

"Of course I can," she said. "And don't feel you have to be so formal about asking! After all, we're friends, correct?"

His expression was solemn, but his violet eyes danced. "Friends, yes. I am honored." Then he made an obvious effort. "Ffrreenndz," he said aloud, in English.

"Ahrreekk'shh," she agreed, in Simiu. "Friends."

Dhurrrkk' did indeed return the next day—and the next. Their meetings became the high point of Mahree's day. Each encounter began with a language lesson, and her new friend proved to be a careful and patient teacher. By the time the girl could say, "Greetings, Dhurrrkk', I am honored to see you again," Sekhmet had grown so accustomed to the young Simiu's presence that she allowed him to pet her.

During their teaching sessions, Mahree grew used to phrasing every question on a new topic with extreme caution. As the humans had already discovered, many subjects were proscribed, but there seemed to be no consistency in what the Simiu avoided discussing. For example, while Dhurrrkk' had displayed no uneasiness in telling Mahree that their leaders were female, her tentative question concerning *how* top Simiu leaders were chosen was met with yet another polite evasion.

The same was true of any reference to their judicial system. Mahree became adept at backing off immediately whenever she encountered a sensitive subject.

"Now, it is my turn," Dhurrrkk' said, after several lessons. "I wish also to speak your language. Please, I would like to say your name, first." He wrinkled his muzzle, obviously trying hard. "Hhhahhhrree."

"Mah-ree," she said, exaggerating the initial sound.

"Hhmmahhhree."

"Good!" She nodded enthusiastically at him. "Just bring your mouth together a little bit more for the 'm' sound." She demonstrated.

"Mahhrreee," Dhurrrkk' said.

"You've got it!"

"This," Dhurrrkk' announced, a few minutes later as he stroked Sekhmet gently, "is *my* pet."

Mahree looked down at her computer link's tiny holo-screen as an image formed. It showed Dhurrrkk'—it was amazing how quickly she'd learned to identify his features even in a group of other Simiu—with an animal perched on his back, holding to his mane with tiny clawed paws. It had short, sleek black fur, with a white-ringed tail. Long, thick whiskers below a white bandit-mask gave its short-muzzled face a mischievous look. It had big, dark liquid eyes. To Mahree it looked vaguely like a cross between a lemur and a seal.

"Oh, it's adorable!" she exclaimed.

"Her name is Rrazzkk'll."

Mahree smiled, carefully keeping her lips together. "She looks like a 'rascal,' " she said, amused.

"Please, what is 'rascal'?"

"Someone who is mischievous, who enjoys making people go to a lot of trouble for his or her sake . . ." Mahree said, thinking as she spoke. "Someone who likes to play jokes."

"Jokes?"

She sighed. "Jokes," she began, "are hard to explain. I will try, but you must stop me if I speak of something I should not. Will you promise to do that?"

He nodded solemnly. *Good,* she thought. *That way I won't get myself in trouble with their taboos. Okay, here goes.* "Honored Dhurrrkk', how do you feel when you see or do something that should happen one way, but instead happens another way? An awkward way, but not so that it causes hurt?"

"You mean when I try to do a thing the right way, but it goes wrong and I am left to feel foolish? It depends on who is present and whether my honor is compromised.''

''Well, what about when you see that sort of thing happen to somebody else, does it make you feel amused?''

''Amused?''

Mahree waved her hands helplessly. ''Let me show you.'' Waking the dozing Sekhmet, she hastily found the cat's play mouse on its string and dangled it. Dhurrrkk' watched as the cat lazily batted it; then, as Sekhmet got into the play, Mahree began swinging the mouse. The little black animal nearly turned herself inside out as she leaped and pounced, finally rolling over on her back and grabbing her toy with a mock-fierce expression on her face. She bit the mouse, ''disemboweled'' it with her hind claws, then, when she had thoroughly ''killed'' it, strode away with an erect tail and a disdainful expression.

Mahree glanced at Dhurrrkk'. ''How did that make you feel?''

''Good,'' he responded. ''Feel warm inside. Sekhmet is being so silly, looking so fierce, when she is really so small. She wants us to think she could have easily defeated a far more powerful opponent.''

''Well,'' Mahree told him, ''that's feeling 'amused.' Sekhmet's actions amused you. You found them humorous. And a joke is a humorous little story or action that's told or done deliberately to make you feel amused.''

Dhurrrkk' thought that one over for a minute. ''I believe I understand,'' he said, finally. ''Do your people have many jokes?''

''Many,'' she answered.

''Tell me one, please.''

Mahree shook her head. ''It wouldn't be humorous—amusing—to you.''

''I understand that this is cultural, in the most part. But I am curious.''

She screwed up her forehead in thought. ''It's no use,'' she told him, after a long moment. ''I can't think of any clean ones. And Uncle Raoul would never forgive me for telling you a dirty one.''

''Clean? Dirty?'' He touched his own computer link, obviously puzzled. ''My translation gives these terms as measurements of personal hygiene and of one's interior environment, especially concerning items such as dust, earth, grease, and assorted individual effluvia due to lack of grooming. What have these things to do with jokes?''

Mahree began to giggle, hiding her teeth behind her hand. "Oh, dear! I just *can't* figure out a way to explain dirty jokes! If I can ever think of a way to do it, I promise I will, but right now, it's just impossible!"

"Impossible? Really?" His violet eyes held disappointment.

"Really," she assured him. "Trust me."

"Trust?" He was suddenly solemn again. "You are speaking of an honor-bond? Most people would say we have not known each other long enough for that . . . but I feel that you are a friend who is worthy of it. Perhaps even of being honor-bound."

"What is honor-bound?" she asked, suddenly alerted. Somehow she knew that Dhurrrkk' had just revealed a vital piece in the puzzle of how Simiu society was structured.

The alien hesitated, then said, "Among my people, to be honor-bound is the strongest tie possible between Those-Who-Are-Not-Family. When two individuals swear that they are honor-bound, it means they pledge to defend each other's name, each other's honor . . . even unto the Arena-of-Honor."

"You mean *fight*?" Mahree held her breath. There had been no indication of violence in the films the Simiu had shown them, and none of their information had included this "Arena-of-Honor."

Dhurrrkk's crest flattened suddenly and the girl's heart sank. *Oh, no. Another taboo.* But after a moment, her new friend said slowly, "I am not supposed to be conversing of these things, but I forgot that you were not one of us. It is good to just . . . talk . . . without constraint."

"I am honored that you feel you can talk to me," Mahree said. She hesitated, then continued, "Honored Dhurrrkk' . . . I promise I won't speak of any of this to my people unless you give me permission. Does that make it all right?"

"I am grateful," Dhurrrkk' said, with evident relief. He hesitated. "My people are not sure how you humans will respond to knowledge that we battle for our honor. Not as a *people*, you understand, but when two individuals, or two clans, challenge each other, yes, their difficulty is settled in the Arena-of-Honor. When we select our leaders, each must be judged by the people after her performance in the Arena, as well as on her personal merit as a leader. The Council did not think you would like knowing that we can be violent."

Mahree's jaw dropped, then, abruptly, she was fighting the urge to dissolve into hysterical laughter. Hastily, she put both hands over her mouth so her teeth would not show. She saw Dhurrrkk's crest flatten abruptly. "No, no," she said, sobering instantly. "I am *not* laughing at you! I'm laughing at both our peoples—each worrying that the other would be distressed to find that they were capable of violence!"

He gazed at her wonderingly. "Your people fight, also?"

"Not quite in the same way," she said. "We don't have challenges or duels anymore. But until a couple of hundred years ago, your people would have had a hard time finding any people *more* prone to violence than the human race. And we are still capable of doing terrible things to one another. Now *I'm* telling *you* something my people wouldn't want me to admit, so I will ask you for your silence, in return."

Dhurrrkk' made a small chirping, bubbling noise, the Simiu equivalent of a chuckle. "I see," he said. "This is, I think, a good joke on both of us, is it not?"

"It certainly is," she agreed. "These fights . . . are they to the death?"

"Not often. Most are conducted as 'ritual hence.' The combatants do not attempt to injure or draw blood. When they give the ritual bite, they do not tear the skin. Ritual-hence encounters are like . . ." he paused, signaled his computer link, then listened intently for the translation, "the word translates best as 'wrestling.' You know of that?"

"Yes, I understand. So you don't use weapons—sharp or blunt objects you hold in your hand to strike blows with—things like knives, clubs, or guns?"

"I have seen 'knives' that you use to eat. What are 'clubs'? And 'guns'?"

She sighed. "A club is a long, heavy piece of material that can be used to injure by striking blows. A gun is an instrument that projects a beam that knocks people out, or disrupts living cells, or even rearranges the molecular structure of matter so it's vaporized instantly."

"Oh, no." Her words had shocked him, Mahree could tell. "Do you mean to tell me that your people actually *use* these 'weapons'?"

"Yes," she admitted, feeling uncomfortable. "Mostly to protect ourselves. Don't your people use weapons?"

Dhurrrkk' drew himself up. "That would be ultimate dishonor. Even in a death-duel, all we need are these"—he flexed powerful, thick-nailed hands—"and these. Your pardon, Honored Mahree, I do this only to show." So saying, he opened his mouth wide, lips pulling back.

Mahree recoiled, startled. She'd never seen a Simiu's teeth before, except for glimpses of the short, squared-off incisors. Dhurrrkk's curved canines gleamed ivory, strong and sharp, and so long she could see where they fitted into grooves in the bottom teeth.

Now she knew why baring one's teeth was threatening to a Simiu! "I can see why you wouldn't need guns to kill somebody," Mahree said feebly.

"Oh, killing is a most unusual happening, even as the result of a death-challenge," he replied equably. "The winner is usually satisfied by the loser's humiliation and dishonor and does not inflict death. But sometimes death results when the loser proves his complete loss of honor by taking his own life." He shook his head. "That is *very* bad. Then the loser has dishonored his entire clan."

"I understand," Mahree said. "Tell me, Honored Dhurrrkk', are you honor-bound to anyone?"

"No." The Simiu was uncomfortable; his crest drooped. "At home I am regarded as being one who likes to think his own thoughts, go his own way, and thus am not one others desire to know very well. That is why Rhrrrkkeet' brought me here, I think . . . she hoped to improve the way I am regarded by my peers. There is much honor, much status, to be gained by being chosen to meet you humans."

"You know," Mahree said, smiling, "I was thinking the same thing about myself the other day. I hope for both our sakes it works!"

"So," the young Simiu said, after a long pause, "we have now trusted each other to keep a confidence of grave consequence, were it to be revealed to our elders, correct?"

"Yes," Mahree said. "At least for the time being, until our peoples know each other better, and we decide together to tell them what we've learned from each other."

"Correct," he said. "So, in addition to naming each other friend, we have now taken an honor-bond."

"Does that mean we have to fight to defend each other?" Mahree asked uneasily.

"No, we are not honor-*bound* to each other. That is for two people who have many honor-bonds between them. No, but we must be prepared to do whatever is necessary rather than betray each other's trust. Do you agree?''

"Yes, I do," she said, after a moment's consideration. "But I think that soon there will have to be complete truth between our peoples.''

"I do, too. I know that Rhrrrkkeet' believes so, too. She is arguing for the Council to agree.''

"Do you think they will?''

"Eventually. They are often slow to decide, because they must envision every possibility that could result from their actions. It can be frustrating, waiting for them.''

Mahree sighed and nodded. "I know *just* what you mean.''

"Human governments are like that, too?''

"Oh, yes. Our people are much more alike than I would ever have dreamed.''

Dhurrrkk' was puzzled. "But we are very different. Look.'' He reached over and took her hand, held it up and splayed his own fingers beside hers. "See?''

She glanced quickly at him, careful not to stare, and smiled. By this time keeping her lips together was almost automatic. "Are we really, Dhurrrkk'? You're too intelligent to think only of what's on the surface. I know you are.''

He considered, and Mahree could tell he was amused. "You are right. How could we have an honor-bond if we were as different as we appear outwardly? It is strange, but I am now realizing that I think of you as more of a friend than most of my classmates.''

She nodded, and said in his language, "I think same, Honored Dhurrrkk' my friend.''

The violet eyes widened. "You have been practicing! That was almost perfect!''

Mahree grinned. "Damn right.''

"Damn? Please, what is that word mean?''

She got to her feet. "I'll tell you on the way over to your place. I want you to ask Rhrrrkkeet' if you can show me around your station again, all right?''

He nodded vigorously. "Oh-kkay!''

CHAPTER 8

✦

Checkmate

Dear Diary:

Do you believe in inter-species marriage?

JUST KIDDING!

Seriously, after some of the human boys I've known, Dhurrrkk' would be a *big* improvement. Of course, I'd be robbing the cradle . . . he's only ten Sol-Standard years old. Even though Simiu mature faster than we do, he's still relatively younger than I.

It's been over two weeks since we met, and we've both been working hard during our language lessons. Soon I'll feel confident enough to walk up to the First Ambassador and say in understandable Simiu, "Greetings, Honored Rhrrrkkeet'. How are you today?"

Won't that be *great*? Especially if Dhurrrkk' is standing beside me and greeting Uncle Raoul in English!

The honor-bond Dhurrrkk' and I swore is becoming an awkward burden. Jerry and Rob suspect that the Simiu are hiding something, and last night they asked me if I had any ideas on what it might be. Of course I told them "no," but I felt guilty saying it.

During our talk, Jerry pointed out something that I'd missed, which is that the Simiu technology we've seen so far is on a par with ours—in some ways it's less advanced. So how come they've forged ahead of us in just *two* areas—the faster S.V.

drive and the FTL transmissions? It could be coincidence, but Jerry doesn't think so. Rhrrrkkeet' took the bridge crew on a tour of the space station, and Paul finally got a good look at the S.V. drive on one of the Simiu vessels.

Parts of that drive, Jerry said, bore only a superficial resemblance to the rest of the aliens' technology. He compared it to finding a cryo-crystal memory hooked up to an antique punch-card computer.

What's going on here? And *why?*

I was tempted to ask Dhurrrkk', but he'd only tell me under another honor-bond, and that would just be one more thing I couldn't tell anyone else. It's hard enough not letting on that I can understand Simiu without my voder.

The "social hours" continue to be a success, and Uncle Raoul said yesterday that everyone can go from now on. Joan is teaching several Simiu to play chess. They're crazy about it.

Uncle Raoul still won't relax that damned rule about one crew member remaining armed whenever the Simiu are around. I tried again to talk to him about it; he listened politely, then ignored me. Of course, due to the honor-bond, I couldn't explain how disastrous it would be for the Simiu to realize that all along we humans have been wearing *weapons.* We'd be forever dishonored in their eyes.

Lately, Rob and I have been spending a *lot* of time together. He's with me more often than he is with Yoki, how's that for irony? The bastard still teases me and treats me like his kid sister, damn him.

It's hell working with him. I have to control my reactions when he smiles at me, or tells me I look nice, or gives me a compliment. Once or twice he casually put an arm around my shoulders, and that was the hardest of all. When he touches me I either want to lean against him and feel all my bones dissolve, or I have to fight not to stiffen up and yank away. Either reaction would give me away, and that would be so humiliating I can't bear the thought.

There I go again, running on about my angst, and I promised myself not to do that, because it just makes me depressed. I've been depressed a lot lately. Possibly it's the letdown from working so hard on the translation interface . . . or maybe physical weariness from spending several hours each day in the connecting tube, with its hot, moist air and its higher-than-Earth geefield

(Jolie's gravity is slightly less than one gee, so I probably feel it more than the native-born Terrans) . . . or perhaps it's just that my period is almost due.

At least I'll get to see Dhurrrkk' in about an hour.

The "social hour" was in full swing. For the first time, *Désirée*'s entire crew complement was present, along with twenty Simiu. The two species mingled, chatting via voder, and the connecting tube was noisy and crowded. Dhurrrkk' and Mahree stood by the wall, watching the First Mate give a chess lesson to a young Simiu named Khrekk'.

"No, no! The bishop moves *this* way—diagonally. Like this, see?" Joan demonstrated with the chess piece, her opponent watching every move with wide violet eyes. After a moment, he re-moved the piece to a more orthodox location.

"Yes, that's right," she told him. "Though that move leaves your bishop in a bad spot. Watch what happens to it when I move my rook."

The alien watched with visible distress as the First Mate captured the errant bishop.

"Okay, now it's your move again," Joan announced. Khrekk' shot a glare in her direction, but she was studying the board and didn't see. Quickly, at random, the Simiu grabbed a chess piece. His teacher held up a warning hand. "*Wait*, Khrekk'. Before you move, you'd better *think* about whether that piece is really the one you want to move, and what the consequences of that move will have on all the other pieces on the board."

Slowly, the Simiu replaced the piece and surveyed the board. He evidently found Joan's advice difficult to follow. He fidgeted, fingering the elegant hand-carved wooden pieces, his crest drooping with frustration.

"Khrekk' is not accustomed to losing," Dhurrrkk' said quietly to Mahree, in accented but comprehensible English. He changed to his own language. "His mother is in the High Council, and he has not had to endure much adversity in his life."

"I can tell that," Mahree said softly in Simiu. "He is getting angry. I wish Aunt Joan had taken a different student for today."

With a growl, Khrekk' dropped his Queen on the floor, then, as he bent to pick it up, the Simiu deliberately jostled the chess board with his elbow, sending the pieces sliding around.

"Hey!" Joan protested. "Be careful! This set has been in my family for two hundred years!"

Khrekk' sat up, glaring defiantly at Joan, who, with a visible effort, managed to keep her temper, saying, "I know that was an accident, but *please* be careful. This chess set is very precious to me." With a few quick motions, she restored the pieces to their positions. "Now, it's still your move."

Khrekk' angrily picked up his white Queen and slammed it down in front of Joan's black King, then knocked the carved ebony piece over in the traditional manner that indicated defeat.

"No, *no!*" Joan's voice rose impatiently. "You can't checkmate like that! And even if I were in checkmate, *I'm* the one who's supposed to concede if I've lost. *You* can't go knocking over somebody else's King!"

Khrekk' responded with an emphatic, wordless growl that clearly translated to, "I can so!"

"No, you can't! That's against the rules!" Joan was furious, and no longer trying to hide it.

Concerned, Mahree tried to catch her uncle's eye, but Raoul was deep in conversation with the First Ambassador. The girl frowned, wondering whether she should try to intervene.

As Mahree hesitated, Khrekk' lunged forward and angrily scooped up the ebony King, then, with a single twist of his powerful fingers, snapped it in two.

The First Mate let out a yell and leaped out of her seat. She leaned over the chess board, glaring down at her opponent. "How *dare* you! Talk about poor losers!" She gave a harsh, angry laugh. "They told me you people had a code of honor. Well, *you* sure don't!"

"Aunt Joan!" Mahree called, trying to distract her aunt. *Don't laugh! Don't show your teeth! And don't stare!* she cried silently. Both she and Dhurrrkk' started toward the enraged chess players.

Khrekk' pushed himself up until he and Joan were nearly nose-to-nose—then he snarled, jaws opening wide, lips pulling back to reveal his enormous fighting fangs. "You dare to challenge me?" he roared.

Suddenly confronted by those gleaming ivory canines, Joan yelped and flinched back. *"Shit!* Get *away* from me!"

"Aunt Joan." Mahree grabbed the terrified woman's elbow, steadying her. "Just take it eas—"

A heavy body slammed into Mahree from behind, sending both women staggering. The girl tripped and fell, landing hard in the higher gravity. "It's Simon! *Grab him!*" she heard Rob yelling frantically.

Viorst stumbled over Mahree as the Bio Officer flung himself forward, grabbing Joan, clawing at her hip. The First Mate struggled, trying to push the berserk crewman away. "Stop it! Simon, that's an order!"

"They're going to kill us all!" Viorst shrieked at her. "I'm the only one who can see them—I have to stop them!"

"Watch out!" Paul Monteleon yelled. "He's got her gun!"

"Stop him!" "Oh, my God!" Humans milled in panic. Many broke and ran for the airlock.

Mahree gasped, trying to get her wind back. Ray Drummond made a grab for the Bio Officer's arm, but Simon lashed out with a hard left, sending the Assistant Engineer staggering back. Dhurrrkk' flung himself forward, only to have Viorst kick him in the shoulder.

Growling, Khrekk' leaped into the melee, and he, the First Mate, and the Bio Officer slammed into the table, overturning it and the chairs. Then they all went down in a thrashing welter of clothed and furred arms and legs. Mahree heard a sound like dry wood snapping, then Joan's agonized screams.

As Mahree rose, wavering, Simon rolled away and was on his feet, Joan's sidearm in his hand. Khrekk' and Dhurrrkk', not realizing the significance of the weapon, advanced on him steadily. "I'll kill you, I swear! You'll never get me!" Simon panted, backing away. Mahree watched, horrified, as the Bio Officer deliberately released the safety and thumbed the gun's intensity level all the way up.

Joan's screams dwindled into gasping moans.

"Simon, no! Stop!" Raoul ordered, waving Jerry and Paul back. "We're in the *tube*, for God's sake! Fire that thing and you'll breach the wall! We'll all be killed!" He glanced around at his crew. "Stay back, everybody! Don't move!"

Dhurrrkk' and Khrekk' continued to glide forward on all fours.

Simon bumped into the wall of the tube, waving the gun wildly. "Stop! I'll shoot, I will! Stay back, Ray! Don't try it, Jerry! I can't let you stop me! You can't see them, but I can!" He was deadly pale, his eyes glittering feverishly, as the nose of the gun moved back and forth between the Simiu and Drummond, who was closest. Poised to leap, Ray, Jerry and Paul hesitated, restrained by Raoul's order.

Waving Dhurrrkk' back, Mahree walked around one of the overturned chairs, and came at Simon from the side. "Simon, it's Mahree," she said softly, moving with slow, unhurried steps. She held out her hand. "Give me the gun. They don't even know what it *is*. You don't want to make a terrible mistake!"

"They'll kill us," he insisted. "I have to stop them!" But for a moment he wavered, uncertain.

"Why is he behaving like this?" Dhurrrkk' asked, in Simiu.

Hearing the soft, slurred growl of the alien's words, words that he could not understand, Simon screamed, "No!" His finger tightened inexorably on the trigger.

"*Simon!*" Mahree flung herself at Viorst's arm, shoving it just as he fired. The bolt of ionized power whined over Khrekk's shoulder, then swung wildly past Mahree and into the wall. There was a thunderous *shump* as the tube material was breached, then the shrill, maniacal screaming of air being sucked into vacuum.

As the weapon's bolt nearly grazed Mahree's head, she felt as though each individual cell in her brain had been wrenched and twisted. Gasping, she collapsed.

In the following seconds, she was dimly aware of a rush of panicky bodies, and terrified screaming. Mahree would have screamed, too, but she couldn't muster the strength. Pain seared through her head, blurring her vision.

Dazed and sick, she fought to stay conscious as the force of the atmosphere rushing into the vacuum outside through the fist-sized hole began pulling her helpless body along the floor. The air was filled with a wild barrage of debris: computer flimsies, Joan's gun, chessmen, and chair cushions. The hole grew larger as objects were sucked through it. Soon the tube was bound to give way altogether.

The artificial gale tore at Mahree's lungs, hurting her as she struggled to breathe. She made a grab for one of the chairs as she was pulled past it, but it was not heavy enough to anchor her; she let it go.

As Ray Drummond skidded by on hands and knees, Mahree saw him snatch up something, then he let himself be pulled forward again. When he reached the wall, the Assistant Engineer struggled to his feet and manhandled the stiff, flat object against the unbreached side of the tube. Fighting with all his strength to keep from being sucked through, he slid the square shape over the now head-sized hole. The screeching wail abruptly ceased, reduced to a muffled hissing.

Mahree blinked, finally focusing her eyes. The object covering the hole was Joan's treasured marble chessboard.

She heard her aunt moan. Joan was sprawled close by, her arm at a sickening angle, something moist and red protruding from a joint that shouldn't have been there. Blood spurted into the air in a sanguine jet.

"Get my medical kit! There's arterial bleeding!" Rob yelled, scrambling to the injured woman's side. "Yoki, see if Mahree got hit!"

Simon lay buried beneath Yoki, Paul, Raoul, Ray, and Azam Quitubi. The Cargo Chief began wriggling out of the pile at Rob's order, leaving the men to guard Viorst. The Bio Officer whimpered and sobbed as they pulled him into a sitting position and held him, twisting his arms behind his back. Raoul abruptly let go of him and sank down onto the floor, dazed. He began cursing softly in a mixture of French and English.

"FriendMahree? Are you hurt?" Furred hands gently rolled her onto her back, and she saw Dhurrrkk' peering anxiously at her. At first Mahree didn't understand what he'd said, then she realized that, for the first time, he had addressed her using the "familiar" form, reserved for family and the closest of friends.

"Honey, are you okay?" a voice asked. Mahree slowly turned her head, seeing Yoki kneeling beside her. She managed to nod.

"Oh, Mahree . . . thank God! I thought that bastard had killed you!"

"I'm all right," Mahree mumbled, wondering if it were true. She felt very odd—as though her head simultaneously weighed a ton and was about to float off her shoulders. Every breath hurt. Feebly, she reached out to pat Dhurrrkk's arm. "Go see how Khrekk' is doing," she said. "Please . . ."

The alien nodded. "I will do so. You displayed great courage, FriendMahree. Unlike some of your people"—he shot a vicious glance at Simon—"you have behaved with honor this day."

Then Dhurrrkk' was gone.

"He said that you were very brave, honey. He said that you

behaved with honor," Yoki said, unaware, of course, that the girl had understood the Simiu words without her voder.

Mahree nodded, biting her lip to hold back a moan. An inner voice was shrieking that Simon had actually *shot* Khrekk' with a *weapon*, in full sight of a score of Simiu. The voice wailed that it was all ruined, but Mahree refused to listen; refused to let the tears she could feel behind her eyelids begin to fall—she was afraid that if she gave in, even for a second, she'd never be able to stop crying.

Instead, she sat up, shutting her eyes as the tube spun around in a dizzy blur of white splotched with red. "What about Khrekk'? Did Simon kill him?"

"I don't think so. He was moaning, so he's breathing. They've helped him up. He's walking."

Mahree opened her eyes and slowly her surroundings steadied. She saw that the Simiu contingent, supporting a staggering, furred shape, was just disappearing into the station's airlock. "Oh, God," she whispered. "This can't be happening."

"Raoul?" Both women turned to see Paul Monteleon carefully pushing aside overturned furniture. Someone was lying there, nearly buried beneath computer flimsies, a Simiu lounge, and a human table and chair. The Chief Engineer's face blanched. *"Mon Dieu!"*

Lamont scrambled toward Monteleon, calling "Doc! *Doc*!"

"One second," Rob said tightly, working over his now-unconscious patient. Droplets of blood had spattered his face in a ghastly parody of freckles. "I've almost got this bleeder fused."

A heartbeat later he snapped, "Yoki! Stay with Joan!" Grabbing his bag, the doctor darted over to Paul and Raoul. Mahree saw his back stiffen. "Oh, God," he muttered. "It's too late. He's dead."

Raoul looked up incredulously. "Doc, you've got to help him! Begin resuscitation!"

"It's no good, Captain," Rob said softly. "There's nothing I can do." Fishing in his bag, he took out a sensor patch, pressed it into place. "No brain activity, see? He's dead . . . his neck's broken."

"For the love of God, who *is* it?" Yoki cried.

Rob swallowed. "It's Jerry."

Raoul put his palms over his eyes, grinding them viciously

against the sockets. His voice dropped to a broken mutter. *"Mon Dieu, il est mort . . . Seigneur . . . il est mort . . ."*

Tears flooded Mahree's eyes. *Jerry! Oh, God, not **Jerry!** Please, not Jerry*. Memories of the Communications Chief flashed through her mind. In the weeks since they'd received the Simiu signal, they had become friends, and knowing that he was gone hurt worse than the disruptor bolt.

"How?" Yoki said, raising her voice. "Did anyone see how it happened?"

"I caught a glimpse of him," Azam Quitubi said. "When the tube went and we were all flailing around. He and one of the Simiu seemed to be struggling to hold onto each other. But . . ." he hesitated, then said reluctantly, "but they could have been fighting, too. Things were moving so fast, I couldn't . . ."

"Don't make this worse than it is." Rob's voice was tight as he examined the body. "In this gravity, simple falls can be disastrous . . . yes, that's what happened. He slammed into this overturned chair. Death was . . . was . . . instantaneous." His voice cracked, and he fought to steady it. "He never felt a thing."

The doctor climbed unsteadily to his feet, then went back to Joan. "We need stretchers," he called to several of *Désirée's* crew who had emerged from the shelter of the airlock.

Mahree began to weep.

"Chérie . . ." Raoul said, coming over to gather her into his arms, "are you sure you're not hurt? From where I was standing, it looked as though Viorst couldn't have missed blowing half your head off."

"I'm all right," Mahree said dully, wiping her eyes. "Honest I am."

"Raoul," Rob said, "take Mahree to the infirmary. I want to examine her as soon as I finish with Joan."

Rob's words seemed to galvanize Raoul, because the Captain wavered to his feet and stood looking down at his wife.

"She'll be okay, Raoul," Rob said. He finished inflating a temporary cast. "Compound fracture of the radius and ulna, but she'll be all right." Rob activated the emergency stretcher, and he and Raoul lifted Joan onto it. Only then did the doctor take out a sheet and gently cover Jerry Greendeer's body. He knelt beside his dead friend for a moment, head bowed.

Raoul turned away from the doctor. His gaze fell on Simon,

still sobbing in the grip of his captors. The Captain's face darkened with a terrible rage. Grabbing the Bio Officer by the collar of his coverall, Lamont jerked him to his feet. *"Debout, espèce d'enfant de salaud! Look* at what you did! You sorry sonofabitch! Jerry's *dead,* and it's *your* fault!"

Viorst took one glance at the shrouded corpse and the pool of blood congealing on the floor of the tube, then vomited.

Mahree turned her head away, but not quickly enough. The smell hit her, and she, too, was wretchedly sick, tears of pain, grief, and embarrassment streaming down her face as she heaved. She felt hands holding her head, and heard Yoki's voice: "You poor thing . . ."

" 'm sorry—" she gasped, gagging. "Can't help—"

"Of course you can't," Yoki soothed, supporting her through another spasm. "You've been so brave, honey . . . you're a hero . . . if it weren't for you, that Simiu would've been killed . . ."

Finally, the girl collapsed onto the floor of the tube. Dimly, she was aware that crew members were carrying Joan's stretcher and Jerry's body into the airlock. Her head whirled and she felt faint.

Strong arms scooped her up, lifting and cradling her against a broad chest. Mahree opened her eyes to see her uncle's face. "I'm taking you to the infirmary," he said.

"I can walk," she protested.

"No, you can't," he said, striding toward the airlock. "Just lie still, *chérie.*"

"Raoul!" Yoki's voice reached them.

Lamont stopped and turned around, facing back down the tube. Mahree raised her head to see two Simiu males in vacuum suits emerging from the aliens' airlock. One of them carried a plate large enough to repair the tube. As Mahree watched, they walked over to where Paul Monteleon and Ray Drummond still stood, keeping watch over the chessboard-patched hole. The pull of the vacuum outside was enough to hold the marble square against the wall, but the engineers weren't taking any chances.

"I—we—are very sorry," Paul said brokenly, as the aliens approached. "We deeply regret what happened."

The Simiu did not respond to the apology—they ignored both humans completely, working around them as though they were inanimate objects placed in their path. Working with smooth efficiency, one slid the chessboard off the hole, even as the other slid the plate over it. The Simiu then propped the board against the wall of the tunnel, and Drummond picked it up.

"Please, how is the person who was injured?" Ray begged. "We are so sorry—"

The Assistant Engineer broke off as the two Simiu deliberately turned their backs on him and began working on the patch.

"Leave them alone, Paul," Raoul ordered bitterly. "You two come on. It's no use."

"C'mon, Mahree," Yoki said, helping her sit up on the infirmary examining couch. "Let's get you out of those messy clothes, honey. Rob'll be here in a moment."

Mahree winced as she sat up enough for the Cargo Chief to pull the stained garments off. Yoki gave her a concerned glance. "Does your head still hurt?"

"Like someone's swinging a hammer inside it," Mahree said, lying back down with a sigh. "And Simon isn't helping."

Both of them could hear the Bio Officer where he was confined under guard in the quarantine section of the infirmary. Viorst was alternating between fits of sobbing, wailing that he was sorry, and hysterical shrieks that the Simiu were coming after him.

Yoki's little rosebud mouth thinned. "If Rob doesn't give him something to shut him up, I'm going to go in there and *kill* that sonofabitch."

Mahree stared at her, startled at her vehemence. "But . . . but . . . Yoki, he's not responsible for his actions!" she protested. "He sounds like he's gone completely round the bend."

"So?" the Cargo Chief retorted, wringing out a towel in cold water and gently wiping her patient's face. "So what if he's cleared his jets? It's his fault Jerry's dead and we're in a terrible mess—he ought to pay for what he's done. But because he's conveniently gone crazy, he never will. Screw him!"

Mahree didn't know what to say; this was a new Yoki, one she had never seen before, implacable and hard. "Here, honey, slip this on," the Cargo Chief said, holding out a clean patient's gown.

A few minutes later, Simon's howls abruptly ceased.

When Rob Gable finally walked into the room, he had the

look of a man who has seen his most cherished dream destroyed before his eyes, but as he came toward Mahree he mustered a reassuring smile. "Hey . . ." he said gently. "How you feeling, hero?"

Taking her hand, he held it in both of his, his fingers sliding down to her wrist to feel her pulse.

"I'm fine," Mahree said, trying to pull her hand away. "All I need is some rest, Rob. You don't have to—"

"Let me be the judge of that, okay?" he said absently, his gaze intent on her face. He ran his fingers gently over her head, sliding them through her hair. "Hmmmmm."

"I'm fine!" Mahree protested as he began passing a portable bioscanner quickly over her head and torso. She colored deeply as his fingers brushed against one breast, but the doctor didn't notice—he was too intent on shining a light in her eyes so he could check her pupil response. "Tell me when you see two fingers," he ordered, holding up his forefinger, then moving it toward her nose.

"Now," Mahree said immediately. "I told you, I'm fine."

"Bullshit. You're seeing double," he corrected her without rancor. "Are your ears ringing?"

"No. Well . . . just a little. Honest, I'm *okay*!"

"Breathe," he said, ignoring her, moving the scanner slowly over her chest and back again. "Deeply, now."

Mahree took a couple of breaths, then began to cough weakly. The pain in her head made her whimper despite herself.

"Hmmmmmm . . ." He checked her pupil response again. "You're a very lucky kid. By rights, your brain ought to be scrambled, but you've only got a touch of concussion." He gazed at her intently. "Bet you've got one hell of a headache, don't you?"

"Yes."

"I want you to rest here in the infirmary for the next couple of days, where I can keep an eye on you." He turned away to rummage in a cabinet. "Here, this should help the pain."

Mahree meekly downed the medication, then took a drink from the cup Yoki held out. Swallowing triggered another coughing spell.

"You're coughing because of the decompression," Rob explained.

"Can I have some more water?" She sipped gratefully. "Thanks. How's my aunt?"

"Resting comfortably. Raoul is with her. She'll be fine in a few weeks, after a couple of hours a day on the regen unit."

"And Simon?" Mahree asked.

Rob shook his head grimly. "Sedated. Raoul's ordered me to freeze him as soon as possible. He appears to be experiencing a full-blown psychotic episode. He's paranoid and delusional."

"That asshole's wrecked *everything*," Yoki said viciously. "Too bad he didn't shoot himself. We're going to go down in history as the people who screwed up the First Contact, and it's all Viorst's fault. Damn him to bloody hell." Yoki's voice was so cold and flat that Mahree knew she meant the curse literally.

The doctor sank down onto the edge of Mahree's couch, his whole body sagging. "Take it easy, Yoki. Simon's not responsible for his actions." He ran his hands through his hair, biting his lip. "*Shit*. It's really *my* fault. I should've advised Raoul to order Simon into hibernation before we ever entered this system."

Mahree's heart went out to him. "You couldn't have known he'd react like that, Rob."

"I should never have taken the chance," the doctor insisted angrily. He clenched his fists impotently. "But I could've *sworn* he was getting better! Adjusting! I never *dreamed* he'd react the way he did!"

"What's done is done," Yoki snapped. "Sitting here beating yourself up about it isn't very useful. Pull yourself together."

Mahree glanced up at the older woman, shocked by her brusque tone of voice. *How can she talk to him like that if she loves him?* She realized suddenly that Yoki was *not* in love with Rob Gable, and never had been. "Nobody could've predicted this, Rob," she said, touching his arm comfortingly.

He shook his head fiercely, not looking up. "That's not the point, Mahree. The point is that I *knew* Simon was xenophobic and had paranoid tendencies, and I should *never* have allowed him anywhere near the Simiu. I'm to blame for this . . . for Jerry's death, too."

Yoki sighed, and made an effort to be conciliatory. She put a hand on her lover's shoulder and gave it a slight shake. "C'mon, you're being too hard on yourself, honey. You told me yourself you haven't had any actual psychiatric counseling experience outside what you did in school. You're young. You made a mistake. It's something we've all done.''

Rob jerked his head up as though he'd been slapped. "What the *hell* does my age have to do with it?" he demanded, furious.

Yoki took a step back, her mouth tightening. "Sorry. I didn't mean that the way it sounded.''

"Yeah, you did," Rob said, his voice deadly quiet. "And, damn it, you're probably right. But you shouldn't have said it.''

The Cargo Chief shook her head, her eyes no longer meeting his. "Uhhhhh . . . listen, we're all upset, right now. I'll talk to you later, okay?''

Rob said nothing as she walked out. *Whatever was between them,* Mahree thought, *it's over now.* She supposed she ought to feel selfishly glad, but she didn't. She just felt numb.

After a moment, the doctor drew a deep, shuddering breath, then raised his head. "Excuse me," he muttered. "I . . . uh . . . I'd better . . . check on Joan.''

Mahree put a hand on his arm, holding him back. "You okay?''

He swallowed. "Yeah. I'm . . . sorry. You shouldn't have had to witness that. Yoki and I . . . well . . ." He shrugged. "The worst thing about it is that she's right. I *am* young, and I didn't have the experience to make a judgment in this case. I should've admitted that to myself, and to Raoul, and insisted Simon be frozen, just in case.''

Tears were glistening in his eyes as he finished, "And now, because of me, Jerry is *dead*. This thing with the Simiu, it's all *ruined*. I'll never forgive myself." He gulped, blinking, and a tear slid down his cheek. He wiped it away, embarrassed and angry. "Excuse me.''

"Rob," Mahree said gently, through her own tears, "you *have* to forgive yourself. You made a mistake, yes. But Jerry's death was an accident. And Yoki may not have expressed herself very tactfully, but she was right. You've got to accept what happened, you've got to get past this, or you're not going to be any good at all to us in the coming days. And we're going to *need* you, we're going to need you badly. Understand?''

He nodded. The motion caused another tear to fall.

Mahree reached over and picked up his hand. The clenched fingers slowly relaxed, then curved until they gripped hers tightly. "I thought I was so smart," he said bitterly. "I thought I could cure Simon, but I couldn't, any more than I could cure so many of those people during the Plague.''

He gave a short, ugly-sounding laugh. "So much for the Boy Wonder. Talk about hubris . . .'' He wiped his eyes on his sleeve, still clinging to Mahree's hand like a lifeline. They sat there silently for a while, then Rob turned to look at her. "You know, that was the bravest thing I ever saw, what you did today.''

She gave him a shaky smile as she brushed her own tears away. "I didn't think about what I was doing," she said. "I believe it only counts as courage if you have time to think about it before you do it.''

He looked down at their clasped hands. "Bullshit. That Simiu owes you his life. And I owe you something, too. If you hadn't been here just now, I—'' He shook his head and took a deep, shuddering breath. "I don't know what I would have done.''

Mahree gripped his hand, hard. "Bullshit," she said, deliberately copying his own words. "You don't owe me anything. We're *friends*, and friends help each other out, don't they?''

Rob nodded, then reached over to hug her. Mahree rested her head on his shoulder, closing her eyes with a sigh.

After a moment he stirred, then gently let her go. "I'd better check on Joan, and I've got to prep Simon for hibernation. I'll be right next door, so if you need me, buzz me, okay?''

She nodded. "Okay.''

"It's been over a week," Raoul Lamont said heavily, "and they still aren't speaking to us. I'm beginning to wonder whether we shouldn't just disengage our moorings and get the hell out of here.''

Rob sighed. He'd been forced to wonder the same thing as the days crept by. *Dammit, there must be something we can do. Some way to make them listen to us.*

He glanced around the circle, seeing the strained faces of Joan, Paul, and Mahree as they all sat huddled around the largest table in the galley. "Maybe Paul and I should make another attempt to talk to the guards at their airlock," the doctor suggested. "If we could only speak to Rhrrrkkeet' personally—''

"You've tried that twice, Rob," Joan Atwood pointed out. "Those guards aren't wearing voders, so you can't ask to see anyone." The First Mate's face still showed the marks of pain and stress, and her arm was in a repressor-field sling. "They've cut us off, face it. We definitely ought to get out of here while the getting's good.''

Rob sighed and slumped down on the base of his spine, turning his hands palm upward in a gesture of surrender. ''I don't agree, but, frankly, I'm out of suggestions as to what we *should* do.''

''I think we ought to wait a few more days,'' Paul Monteleon said. ''They'll *have* to talk to us again, even if it's only just to tell us to beat it.'' In the overhead light, his face bore new lines, and his faded red hair looked even thinner. The star sapphire he wore in his left earlobe winked dully. ''Besides,'' he continued, ''Mahree's working on a message we can transmit to their communications center at the station, and it ought to be completed soon.''

''What does it say?'' Joan demanded.

Paul shrugged. ''Ask Mahree.''

All eyes fastened on the girl, who sat twisting her hands together in her lap, obviously uncomfortable. ''I . . . uh . . . it's complicated,'' she said slowly. ''Getting the right wording is pretty delicate. It . . . it's kind of a cross between an explanation and an apology. I don't want to discuss it until it's finished.''

''Do you think we might be able to transmit it tomorrow?'' Raoul asked.

She shook her head, looking trapped. ''I . . . well, for various reasons, I won't be able to send it unless I can speak to my friend Dhurrrkk', first. Maybe they'd let *me* in if I went.''

Lamont shook his head again. ''No. I don't think that would be wise. I think we'll just have to wait until *they* make the next move.'' He narrowed his eyes as he took in her dark-shadowed eyes, her fined-down features. ''You don't look well, *chérie*.'' He turned to Rob. ''You sure she's recovered?''

The doctor nodded. ''Physically, at least. I released her from the infirmary day before yesterday, so she could attend Jerry's memorial service. She's under orders to take it easy for a while,'' he added, then looked around the table at his comrades. ''Truth to tell, none of us is looking real perky.''

Raoul shrugged. ''Yeah. Well, I think we should—''

''Captain!'' Azam Quitubi interrupted from the door of the galley. ''The First Ambassador is in our airlock, requesting to be allowed to speak to you.''

Raoul's bushy eyebrows rose nearly to his receding hairline. "She *is*? Well, bring her to the galley immediately!"

Moments later, the Simiu official entered, attended by two other aliens Rob thought he recognized. Raoul hastily knelt so that he was eye-to-eye with the First Ambassador, then made the greeting gesture, as did all the other humans present. "Honored Rhrrrkkeet'," the Captain said, and paused, obviously at a loss.

Slowly, reluctantly, it seemed to Rob, the Simiu contingent returned the greeting. It was a moment before Rhrrrkkeet' spoke. "Honored CaptainLamont," the First Ambassador began. "It is unfortunate that we must now converse upon distasteful topics, but there is no remedy for it."

"I understand," Raoul said. "I want you to know that we deeply regret what happened."

The Simiu envoy nodded. "We also regret. But 'regret' is useless unless it provides incentive to reparation and the restoration of honor. Both our peoples have been dishonored by the ill-considered actions of our subordinates."

"Uh, yes," Raoul agreed. "How is Honored Khrekk' doing?"

The F.A. looked distinctly uncomfortable. "There is no honor to attach to Khrekk's name until suitable reparations can be decided upon and enacted."

"You mean, Khrekk' has dishonored himself?" Raoul asked. "Then he *is* alive?"

Rhrrrkkeet' nodded. "Naturally, he has dishonored himself! The aggression display and property damage performed by Khrekk' was utterly forbidden—an act of utmost thoughtlessness. As to his physical body, it is completely recovered from the effects of your"—she glanced away and seemed almost ready to gag—"your . . . weapon."

Raoul glanced over at Rob, who was closest to him. He turned off his voder. "What now?" he whispered.

"Leave the subject of Khrekk' alone. It's obviously a sore spot," Rob said. "We need to find out what these 'reparations' are that she mentioned."

"How should I phrase that?"

The doctor thought for a moment. "Say that you hope that both our peoples may regain our mutual honor, so we may continue to grow in friendship for each other."

Raoul turned his voder back on and voiced the suggested sentiments. As he spoke, Rob thought he detected a gleam of satisfaction growing in the F.A.'s eyes. The Simiu leader nodded enthusiastically. "Then you will be willing to work with us to erase these stains on our mutual honor?"

"Yes," said Raoul, without hesitation.

Rhrrrkkeet's crest stood straight up. "I knew we could depend upon your honor! Do you prefer to select champions, or will those whose honor must be cleansed engage for themselves? I must tell you that Khrekk' aspires to personally restore the honor of his clan and sept, as well as his own, so he requested me to urge against the choosing of honor-vessels."

Raoul blinked as the torrent of words raced across his screen. "Uh, oh . . . ." he whispered to the doctor, "Does it sound to you like she's talking about what I think she's talking about? Trial by combat, or something?"

Rob's heart sank. "It certainly sounds like it."

Frowning, Raoul said, "Please explain to me the method by which you are proposing this honor-cleansing, Honored Rhrrrk-keet'."

The Simiu said slowly, "Despite the serious nature of this trespass, despite the fact that a . . . weapon . . . was employed, I do not feel honor will be best served by a death-meeting. I believe instead that a strength-meeting will suffice, ending at first blooding. We will arrange an Arena-of-Honor here, aboard the station, since the quarantine our health officials have decreed for your people still holds."

Lamont's glance at the doctor was bleak. "If I understand you," he began, "you are saying that the one among your people that Simon Viorst injured—Khrekk'—wishes to engage in physical combat with one of my people, in order to regain his honor. Is that stating it correctly?"

"Yes, that is correct. Khrekk' wishes most to engage Simon-Viorst, so he will have the greatest chance to regain his honor."

"Well, in the first place, we do not settle our problems by combat, Honored Rhrrrkkeet'," Raoul said. "And in the second, Simon Viorst is a sick man. He was not responsible for his actions that day."

The First Ambassador's crest flattened. "He was not injured. I saw him, and there was no mark upon him!" Her nostrils flared with indignation. "How can you say that he was not responsible? Did he not hold the dishonorable instrument in his hand? Did he not discharge it at my people?"

Raoul turned off his voder. "She's really pissed," he murmured. "Sounds like we've broken one of their most sacred taboos by simply having guns on our persons."

I warned you about that, Rob thought, but he held his tongue, remembering that Raoul hadn't voiced a single word of blame to him, for failing to correctly evaluate Simon's mental condition. He spoke up. "Honored Rhrrrkkeet', may I speak?"

She inclined her head, graciously. "Do so, Honored Healer-Gable."

"In the first place, I would like to explain that Simon Viorst's illness is not a sickness of the body, it is an illness of the mind. Such illnesses make the victim not responsible for his or her own actions. They are fully as debilitating as any physical wounding or sickness."

Rhrrrkkeet' considered his words. "We have seen cases of such nonrationality before, in our own people," she said, finally, "but only when the center-of-thinking is physically damaged. I have never heard of the sort of intangible illness you speak of. It must be peculiar to your people." She paused. "Is it caused by a microbial agent?"

"We still don't know everything about the causes of mental illness," Rob temporized, "but if you are worrying about whether such diseases are communicable, and might possibly infect your people, the answer to that is 'no.' "

"I see. Well, then, an honor-vessel will have to be chosen for the combat."

"Absolutely not," Raoul said. "My people don't settle problems in that manner."

Her eyes flashed with anger. "Then how do you settle them, Honored CaptainLamont?"

"We apologize. We say we're sorry. In this case, Simon is incapable of speaking for himself, so we are speaking for him."

"Words!" she said, her muzzle wrinkling with scorn. "Only words? What reparation can they make?"

"One of my people is dead," Raoul said tightly. "I am not risking another just to appease your concept of honor! Surely you must be able to see that we are not your physical equals! None of my people could hope to match yours in physical combat—not unless he or she were armed."

She drew herself up. "Are you speaking of that . . . weapon? A thing such as the one that wounded Khrekk'?" She continued without waiting for Lamont's answer. "Perhaps honor is served differently on your world. But we cannot countenance the use of a weapon! Such a transgression would stain our Arena forever!"

"You have no weapons at all?" Rob asked, finding that hard to visualize.

Rhrrrkkeet's crest lifted proudly. "We"—the symbol for the Simiu name for their species flashed across his screen—"need no 'weapons.' We have no such instruments, beyond the stun rays used—rarely—to control crowds during natural disasters. We *are* weapons—the only weapons needed or permitted in the Arena-of-Honor."

Rob visualized the fighting fangs of the males, and the strength of the aliens' thick-nailed hands and feet, and knew that an unarmed human would last only seconds against an adult Simiu.

He had a sudden impulse just to get up and leave. *There's not going to be any way out of this mess. It only keeps getting worse . . . what the hell are we going to do?*

The F.A. had evidently been thinking, too, because she said, "You speak the truth about the physical inequities between our species. It may be possible to persuade Khrekk' that his honor can be restored by a mere ritual-hence meeting."

"What's 'ritual hence'?" Raoul asked.

"I will show you," Rhrrrkkeet' said. "I will direct the images to appear upon your screens."

Mahree tugged on her uncle's sleeve. "I think you should say 'yes,' Uncle Raoul!" she whispered. Her uncle gave her a look that reduced her to silence. All those present in the room turned to look up at the big computer screen in the galley.

It filled with the image of two Simiu, both big, powerful males, approaching each other in a large outdoor enclosure. Each of them squatted down on his haunches, crests rigid with anticipation, teeth bared in the ritual threat-display. Each of them then made a formal speech to the assembled Simiu who watched from the tiered stands. The whole thing reminded Rob eerily of *Spartacus*, one of his favorite historical films.

Without warning, both Simiu leaped, their movements blurringly fast. They grappled, then rolled over and over, snarling, like a cross between humans wrestling and cats fighting. Then, suddenly, as if by a prearranged signal, the fighters' powerful jaws opened, and they fastened their teeth in the thick fur at each other's throats—

"That's *enough,*" Raoul said, in a deadly quiet voice. "Turn it off, please."

The First Ambassador stopped the holo-vid. "That is a ritual-hence engagement," she said. "As you can see, there is no danger to the participants."

"I don't see anything of the damn kind!" Raoul growled. "No way will I permit one of my people to walk into your Arena and face something like that!"

"Uncle Raoul, *please!*" Mahree broke in, jumping up. Hastily, she made the greeting gesture to the F.A. "Tell her yes, please! I'm volunteering to be the honor-vessel! Dhurrrkk' can be the other. He'd never hurt me . . . don't you see? It's all stylized, like—like a combat in a ballet!"

Raoul turned to look at his niece. Rob could not see his expression, but whatever she saw on his face made Mahree shrink into herself. "No," said Lamont quietly. "Doc, escort her to her quarters, please."

"Come on, Mahree," Rob said, taking the girl's arm and tugging her toward the door.

As they reached it, he heard the F.A. speak again, and checked his voder for the translation. "Honored CaptainLamont, due to your dependence on weapons for fighting, your people have already lost much honor in the eyes of mine. This refusal, I believe, will complete the disintegration of their respect for humans. Will you not reconsider?"

Rob looked back, only to see Raoul shake his head, his face stern and implacable. "I will not."

Rhrrrkkeet' sat back on her haunches, in the most formal of Simiu stances. "Then, CaptainLamont"—Rob noticed that she had dropped the "Honored"—"I fear we have no more to say to each other."

Rob started down the corridor, towing Mahree behind him, though she resisted and he knew his grip must be hurting her. "Rob, stop!" she pleaded. "I can fix this, I know I can! I won't be in any danger, honestly!"

At the doorway to her cabin, he turned to face her, so angry that he had to restrain himself from shaking her. "Shut up, you little idiot! Do you honestly think I'd let you do anything like that, even if Raoul would? My God, Mahree, they bit each other's *throats*, didn't you see that?"

"Yes!" she shouted back, "but I could wear something thick

around my neck so that Dhurrrkk' could give me the ritual bite, and not hurt me. They don't break the skin!''

"So you say," Rob snapped. "Mahree, I'd walk into that damned Arena myself before I'd let you do it—Raoul is right. The entire notion is barbaric!''

"They think *we're* the barbarians," she cried passionately. Tears of frustration welled up in her eyes. "Because we use weapons, don't you see? Nobody's right and nobody's wrong, we're both just *different*. We have no right to judge each other!''

"Well, if the only thing that will satisfy the Simiu is ripping up one of us for public edification, then I think we have every damned right to refuse. We've bent over backward to apologize, and we're the ones who lost one of our people!''

"*You* don't understand!" she whispered. A tear broke free and coursed down her face. "The way they look at it, the *Simiu* are bending over backward to accommodate *us*!''

"You're right," he said tightly. "I *don't* understand. I'm not a goddamned barbarian, and if understanding means I have to start thinking like one, you can just forget it!'' He paused, breathing hard, then, seeing how she was crying, his expression softened. "Mahree . . . kiddo, I'm sorry, I didn't mean to yell at you. Why don't you go lie down? I'll get you something to help you relax. You're overwrought.''

"And *you*," she spat furiously, her voice breaking despite all her efforts, "are an *asshole*, Rob Gable! You go to *hell*!''

Mahree stormed into her cabin. Rob stood in the corridor, hearing the lock activate with a final-sounding *click*.

CHAPTER 9

♦

Revelations

Dear Diary:

Things are awful. I miss Jerry so much . . . and now the situation with the Simiu has gone from bad to worse. I thought I'd die of frustration when Rhrrrkkeet' suggested a ritual-hence meeting and Uncle Raoul wouldn't even listen. He's acting like a closed-minded idiot . . . and so is Rob!

I can't understand why everyone is being so stubborn. We're in danger of losing this entire First Contact, and nobody seems to care! Uncle Raoul thinks Simiu are barbarians because they solve problems by unarmed combat, and Rhrrrkkeet' thinks humans are barbarians because we use weapons . . .

I don't see any way out of this mess . . . it just keeps getting worse. I feel desperate, watching everything crumble around me. I've been having terrible nightmares.

If only I didn't have that honor-bond with Dhurrrkk', so I could tell what I know! Presuming, of course, that Uncle Raoul would listen to me—which he wouldn't, judging by the way he behaved today . . .

Shit!

What's going to happen? What should I do?

"Captain," Yoki said urgently, "the First Ambassador has returned. She's alone, sir, and she's asking to see you."

Raoul raised his eyebrows as he glanced at his officers. "Well, show her in. Maybe she'll have something to say that will help us make our decision."

The moment Rhrrrkkeet' entered the Captain's small conference room, Rob was alerted by her drooping crest, her downcast eyes. He recalled that their liaison was nearly forty-five Simiu years old—elderly, as her people reckoned age. Today, for the first time, she *looked* old as she dispiritedly made the greeting gesture.

"Honored Ambassador," Raoul said, returning her greeting. "I must say that I am surprised to see you."

"Honored Captain"—her translated words marched across Rob's voder screen—"there is no longer any question of Khrekk' regaining his honor. He is dead. Now reparation must be made so that the honor of Khrekk's entire clan can be cleansed."

"Khrekk' is *dead*?" Raoul shot an I-don't-think-I-want-to-hear-this glance at his officers. "We are very sorry to hear that. Please convey our sympathy to his family. I wish there was something we could do to help . . ."

Rhrrrkkeet's crest drooped even more. "There is no grief to be attached to the demise of one who was so without-honor as to do what Khrekk' has done. And *only* you and your people, Honored Captain, can aid his unfortunate family, by allowing them to regain their honor."

Rob took a deep breath. "Honored Rhrrrkkeet' . . ." he said, "may I speak?"

She inclined her head, still gracious despite her anxiety. "Please do so, Honored Healer."

"You said 'what Khrekk' has done' . . . does that mean that he took his own life? He *killed* himself?" Rob could not conceal his distress at the thought.

She nodded. "That is so. Khrekk' committed the ultimate personal and familial dishonor—when he received the news that CaptainLamont would not allow him to regain his honor by a meeting in our Arena, he entered an airlock on this station, then cycled it. What remained of him was discovered this morning."

Oh, my God . . . Rob felt his stomach turn over. Death by decompression conjured a hideous image. "That's terrible," he mumbled. "We are very sorry."

Rhrrrkkeet's violet eyes were shards of amethyst in her expressionless countenance. "Do not waste sorrow on one-without-honor. Sorrow, rather, for his family, who are now also without-honor. And, unless I may convey your choice of an honor-vessel to my superiors, sorrow for me, and for yourselves, for I know that you humans truly wished for beneficial contact between our peoples."

Rob wet his lips. *Oh, shit.* "Honored Rhrrrkkeet'," he said, "doesn't Khrekk's death end this problem? He's gone, so he can't demand an Arena meeting anymore. If his family needs satisfaction, remind his family that a human is dead, too." *An eye for an eye,* he thought. *That ought to appease them.*

The F.A.'s crest dropped even farther. "You do not understand. Khrekk's family is very powerful. His mother is a member of our High Council. She has authority over me. Because Khrekk' killed himself, his dishonor is magnified, and transfers to his family. Their honor must now be cleansed. If you humans do not grant them the chance to redeem their honor . . . things will be very bad."

Raoul hesitated. "Honored Rhrrrkkeet', you know that I honor you. I consider you a . . . friend. You have been honest with us, even when the truth brought you discomfort, so I ask you to be honest with us once more. What effect has Khrekk's untimely death and his family's dishonor had on the relations between your people and mine?"

The Simiu fixed them with her enormous violet eyes. "The High Council is divided," she said, dispensing with the polite, formal phrasing for once. "Many argue that you are not citizens of our world, therefore for you to honor our ways is not something we have a right to expect."

Rob felt a quick surge of excitement. *So, we do have some supporters!*

"They say that your refusal to enter our Arena is not dishonorable cowardice, merely proof that other worlds have other customs."

Raoul nodded. "They are wise, those leaders. They reason excellently."

"So do I think, Honored CaptainLamont. But I am only a diplomat. And the leaders I just spoke of are only slightly more than half, which in our Council is not enough to decide matters of this importance."

"What does the other faction say?"

Rhrrrkkeet' had to ask her computer link for a translation for the word "faction." When it came through, she nodded thoughtfully.

That's something we've taught them, Rob found himself thinking. *Nodding to express agreement . . .*

"The other faction," the First Ambassador began, "is repre-
sented by several Councillors who have always decried involvement with—that is, our hoped-for involvement with—other worlds.
They say that our own world is wide, that we have enough to do
solving problems on our planet without seeking trouble in the
form of aliens from another world."

"Sounds familiar," Raoul muttered grimly, under his breath.
"We can understand their point of view, also, Honored Rhrrrkkeet'—it is one that is still prevalent on our world, despite the
fact that we have had star travel for over one hundred years." He
hesitated, then continued, "Suppose this second faction prevails,
Honored Rhrrrkkeet'. What will happen then?"

"I do not know, Honored CaptainLamont," the F.A. re-
sponded. "I am doing everything I can to convince the High
Council to continue to accept your people as worthy-of-honor.
But I do not know whether they will listen to me."

She knows more than she's saying, Rob thought. He glanced
at Raoul and whispered: "Don't give up. Push her."

"We realize, Honored Rhrrrkkeet', that you cannot be certain
of what the future will hold any more than we can," Raoul said.
"But surely you must have an opinion, and it would honor us
greatly if you would express it."

A few exchanges were necessary before the F.A. understood
"opinion"—or was she stalling? Rob couldn't be sure.

Finally, she said, "It honors me greatly that you wish to hear
my private viewing of what will come. It saddens me to say that,
in my opinion, if the second faction is able to sway even a few
more Councillors to its view—and the death of Khrekk' may aid
them in doing this—then honorable contacts and relations between our peoples will cease, because humans will no longer be
regarded as worthy-of-honor."

"Shit," Rob whispered, reading his screen. Impulsively he
asked, "In that case, we humans would have no alternative
except to leave and not return, is that correct, Honored
Rhrrrkkeet'?"

The Simiu hesitated for a split second too long before replying, "I have not had time to fully consider the alternatives,
Honored HealerGable."

Rob felt the blood leave his face; cold sweat broke out on his
forehead. *Rhrrrkkeet's too damned honorable to lie outright to
us,* he thought, experiencing a sudden flash of insight. *But she's*

not telling the truth. The truth is that if this second faction has its way, we won't be permitted to leave.

He *knew* in his bones that his hunch was right. *What could they do to us? Keep us prisoner? Rip us apart in their damned Arena?*

Raoul's good-natured features were drawn; his mouth tightened grimly. "Honored Rhrrrkkeet', my friend . . . would you, as my friend, advise me to take my vessel and depart before your Council can decide to act?"

The First Ambassador's crest lay absolutely flat against her head and neck. "Honored CaptainLamont—my friend—I truly do not know whether that option is still possible." She paused, then continued, "I came here today without speaking of my visit to anyone. If you depart, it would become known that I had told you as much as I have, and I would then be required to defend my honor in a death-duel against a professional honor-vessel chosen to represent the Council. But you must do as you must."

Without another word, the Simiu representative turned and left them.

Mahree thrashed impotently as she felt herself drawn irresistibly toward the huge hole in the tunnel wall . . . toward the silent, black void lying beyond it. With a final gasp, she was sucked out into space. She tried to scream, even as she felt herself ballooning outward, ready to explode in a gush of quick-frozen blood and mangled tissue—

"Ahhhhhh—" she managed to gurgle, and, in so doing, woke herself up.

Oh, God, ohgod . . . just a dream, just a dream, calm down . . . She sat bolt upright in bed, afraid to blink, terrified that closing her eyes would plunge her back into the nightmare.

Mahree shivered. *You can't be cold,* her mind told her. *Ship's temperature is constant.* But still she shivered.

Pulling on a robe, she went over to her computer link and signaled the bridge. *I'll try talking to Uncle Raoul again. Maybe this time he'll listen.*

Azam Quitubi's voice, with its distinctive accent, emerged. "Yes, Mahree?"

"Azam, what are you doing standing watch?"

"After the Ambassador left, your uncle called a meeting with the whole bridge crew and all department heads. So I'm on watch. What can I do for you?''

"Uh . . . nothing. I just wanted to tell him that I had that message translated and ready.''

"Well, he told me he didn't want to be disturbed, but I'll let him know as soon as they're done, okay?''

"Don't worry about it, I'll tell him myself, tomorrow.'' She yawned audibly. "Right now, I'm going to bed. Thanks, Azam.''

"Good night, Mahree.''

She switched off.

A big meeting, in the middle of night shift? And I'm not invited? Her mouth tightened. *We'll see about that.*

She pulled on her clothes, then sat back down at the computer link. Five minutes later, Mahree had bypassed the security codes and activated the intercom unit in the conference room. A babble of voices burst out:

"—can you *say* that? The damned F.A. as good as told Raoul we're prisoners!'" The voice was Joan's.

Raoul's voice: "Rhrrrkkeet' said herself she doesn't know how their voting is going to go. We can't jump the gun and act out of panic. They may decide not to hold us responsible for Khrekk's suicide.''

Mahree's fingers tightened on the edge of the table. *Khrekk' committed suicide? Oh, no!*

Ray's voice: "But if they do decide to do that, we'll be S.O.L., Captain. We can't afford to take the chance! We should get out *now*, while we still can!''

Joan: "Ray is right, Raoul. This time your damned wishy-washy 'wait and see' bullshit is apt to get us all *killed*!''

Mahree bit her lip. *What the hell is going on?*

Raoul's voice was coldly formal: "Do you have a better plan, First Mate?''

"Yes, I do, Captain,'' Joan said, matching her husband's tone. "I checked before we came down here, and they've got magnetic grapples on *Désirée*. They think that's enough to keep us here—but it's not. We can pull free. I can get us out of this cradle, and then we can head at top speed for the edge of their solar system.''

Yoki spoke up, sounding shocked: "Without warning them? Pulling loose would cause a huge breach in this station's hull! We'd kill dozens—maybe hundreds—of Simiu!''

Joan: "So? We've got to look out for ourselves. We can't let them take us prisoner."

Paul Monteleon spoke up: "But their ships are faster than ours. What if they come after us?"

Joan: "If we have to, we cut in the S.V. and haul ass out of here."

Mahree gasped, and so did several of the participants at the meeting. Raoul sounded shocked: "You know what happens to a star if a metaspace field is generated within its gravitational field! How can you even suggest such a thing, Joan? That'd be murder! Hell, it'd be *genocide*!"

She sounded a bit subdued, but still defiant, as she replied: "Maybe we won't have to do that. Maybe we can get away before they get themselves together enough to notice we've gone."

Raoul: "Breaching the station's hull would be murder, too! These are *people* we're talking about."

Ray: "People, yeah, but not *humans*. We all saw the look on the Ambassador's face. She just as well told us we're screwed, insofar as being allowed to leave peacefully. If they force the issue, we've got a right to save ourselves, don't we?"

Yoki: "Maybe we can broadcast a message ten minutes before we pull free—give them time to get everybody out of this area."

Ray: "Yeah! That way nobody'd get hurt!"

Paul: "That sounds like the best suggestion yet."

Joan: "I don't think we should warn them—maybe they can increase the strength of those grapples, so we couldn't get free."

Raoul: "Wait a minute. Warning or not, that's still guaranteed to make enemies of the Simiu. I think we ought to wait and see if Rhrrrkkeet' can convince the High Council that—"

Joan cut him off: "Goddammit, Raoul, that's playing right into their hands! You've been kissing their furry asses for days and it hasn't done one bit of good! Get this through your head, *Captain*, your precious Rhrrrkkeet' isn't going to pull a miracle out of thin air. We've screwed this up, and all we can do is cut our losses and run."

Paul: "I think we should go with Yoki's suggestion."

Ray: "I agree."

Raoul: "Everybody shut up. I need to think for a second."

Mahree realized her heart was pounding wildly. *Oh, God*, she thought, *this is terrible. I can't believe what they're talking*

*about doing to the Simiu! Uncle Raoul sounds like he's wavering
. . . Joan sounds like she's on the verge of mutiny! I have to find
Rob, tell him what's happening. Uncle Raoul will listen to Rob!*

Raoul spoke again, heavily: "There's one thing nobody has
mentioned. Have you forgotten that we've shown the Simiu our
star charts? They know the location of Earth—and the colonies.
If we make enemies of them, what's to prevent them from
coming to Earth and demanding satisfaction under their admittedly barbaric code of honor?" He laughed softly, with no
amusement. "I can see that none of you tactical geniuses ever
considered that. And, as Paul reminded us, they have a faster
drive than we do."

Joan's voice was hard: "Then maybe we should do what I said
before, so they *can't* come after us. Paul and Ray can override the
gravity-sensor failsafes while I pilot us out of here."

Raoul sighed: "You haven't said a word, Doc. What do you
think we should do?"

Rob? Oh no!

Rob's voice was soft and full of regret: "I'm disappointed that
the Simiu are being so adamant about us adhering to their
customs . . . but I'm not surprised. If one of them came to Earth
and broke the law, we'd probably demand extradition." He
paused. "Raoul, I can't countenance any plan that would involve
hurting any Simiu. But if we warned them we were leaving,
maybe that's the best course. It might be our only chance to—"

Mahree slapped the "off" button, not waiting to hear any
more. Rising, she paced her tiny cabin, thinking furiously. *What
should I do? What **can** I do?*

Her mind conjured up an image of Dhurrrkk' and Rhrrrkkeet'
dying from explosive decompression, as *Désirée* tore free from
Station One.

I won't let that happen, she decided, quite coldly. *I will stop
it. I will **stop** it.*

But how?

If only there were someone I could talk to . . . she thought.
Someone who would understand . . .

Mahree stopped pacing. *Dhurrrkk'. Dhurrrkk' can talk to
Rhrrrkkeet'—help me persuade her to have the Simiu grapples
disconnected. Then we can leave peacefully!*

She refused to consider what losing this First Contact would mean to all of them. Her top priority now had to be survival—survival for both species.

Locating her computer link and voder, she strapped them on. Soft-footed, she stole out of her cabin. When she reached the airlock, it took her a minute to read the cycling instructions, then she ordered it to open.

Resolutely, she marched into the tunnel's bare expanse, swallowing as she saw the brownish bloodstains discoloring its floor. The echoing white tube seemed full of silent echoes—Joan's moans, Khrekk's snarls, Simon's berserk shrieks. As she passed the spot where Jerry had died, she fought back tears.

Fortunately, Mahree had viewed the holo-tapes of the "social hours" often enough that she knew how to trigger the outer door of the Simiu airlock. She stepped into the airlock, wondering how to open the inner door.

Even as she frowned at the controls, slowly translating the Simiu characters, the airlock's inner door slid open. Two Simiu entered, their crests flattened with anger and unease. As Raoul had mentioned, the guards wore no voders.

Mahree hastily made the greeting gesture, but it was not returned. Instead, one of the guards gestured peremptorily at the outer door. His message couldn't have been clearer if he'd spoken to her in French or English—"Leave! Now!"

Frantically Mahree struggled to speak clearly, knowing that, unlike Dhurrrkk', these Simiu would make no allowances for a human. "Honored Ones," she said, "please listen. I speak on an important matter. You must listen!"

They glanced at each other, their crests rising, plainly surprised to hear her speaking. Mahree thought that, despite her rendering of their language, they'd understood what she'd said. "Please!" she cried again. "I"—she thumped her own chest—"I *must* speak with Honored Dhurrrkk'! It is most urgent!"

The Simiu exchanged another look, then their crests began flattening against their heads again. It was obvious they weren't going to help her. Mahree wrung her hands, her throat aching with anxiety and the effort of speaking their tongue.

"Please, I am Mahree Burroughs. Honored Dhurrrkk' and I have an honor-bond"—she couldn't remember the word for between, so she pantomimed—"Dhurrrkk' and I . . . share an honor-bond. I must speak to him! His honor . . . my honor . . . demands that we speak!"

As Mahree identified herself, both of the Simiu guards' crests lifted nearly halfway. They began speaking together so softly and rapidly that Mahree could not catch what they were saying, then one of them left.

Several minutes later, the guard came back, this time equipped with a voder. The alien made the greeting gesture, and said, "Honored MahreeBurroughs, please accompany us. Honored Dhurrrkk' has been summoned, but he is planetside, and it will take time for him to come here. Please come with us. We will take you to a place of greater comfort than is to be found here."

Gulping with relief, Mahree followed them.

After a long walk in the higher gravity, they reached a room located deep inside the station, somewhere close, Mahree judged, to the center of the "abacus." Her guides motioned her to a seat on one of the piles of thick, puffy woven mats that served the Simiu as sleeping places. They also squatted down, though they did not relax, nor did they speak.

Mahree's watch showed that she had been waiting for nearly ninety minutes before the door opened and Dhurrrkk' entered.

"Honored Dhurrrkk'!" Mahree exclaimed. Hastily she remembered her manners and made the greeting gesture, though she was so glad to see him that she could have hugged him.

Her friend returned her greeting a little stiffly, his crest barely half-erect. "Honored Mahree," he said, his pronunciation of her name hesitant from lack of practice. "I am glad to see that you are well again."

"Dhurrrkk'," Mahree said. "I must talk to you. It is very important. A matter of honor. But please, must *they* be here, also?" She indicated the guards.

Her Simiu friend hesitated, then glanced over at the other two. He barked out a sentence that was too quick for Mahree to follow, though she did catch the word "alone." The guards conferred in soft yips and growls, then, in typical Simiu fashion, rose and left without fanfare.

Mahree hesitated. What if the aliens could listen to their conversation by tapping her friend's voder? She turned off her own, beckoning Dhurrrkk' close. Eyeing her wonderingly, he came. She leaned over to growl softly into the ear that did not bear the translation ear-cuff. "Turn off your voder."

Dhurrrkk' was obviously puzzled, but silently complied. He

was accustomed to her often mangled pronunciation, and understood her far better than the guards had. "Why?" he asked.

"There is danger for both of us," Mahree said slowly. "I cannot tell you of this danger, unless I am sure no others can read our words on their screens."

Dhurrrkk's violet eyes suddenly filled with comprehension. He touched his computer link necklet for a few seconds, then motioned to her to turn her own unit back on. "Safe now," his words marched across her screen. "I have sealed this conversation with an honor-code. Why have you come?"

Mahree took a deep breath. *I've got no choice but to believe he knows what he's doing. I have to trust him, or this venture is doomed from the start.* "Honored Dhurrrkk'," she began. "Several hours ago First Ambassador Rhrrrkkeet' came again to see Captain Lamont, and they talked. Did you know that?"

"No, I was not aware."

"Well, did you know that our ship may not be permitted to leave this place? That we may be detained here against our wishes? At least, that is what Rhrrrkkeet' implied when she spoke to my uncle."

" 'Implied'?" Dhurrrkk' keyed for a translation, but one was apparently not forthcoming.

"To imply is to tell somebody something while not saying it directly," Mahree hastily defined. "It can be discerned by a glance, a hesitation—nonverbal communication."

"Understood." Dhurrrkk's crest drooped even more. "I have heard that this may be so. There is debate in the Council about it, even now."

"To keep us here would be wrong, a dishonorable thing to do," Mahree told him. "We are sorry for what Simon did, please believe me, my friend. And we regret very much that Khrekk' died. I offered to be the honor-vessel, but my elders would not allow me. I tried to behave honorably, to tell them what honor demanded, but they would not listen."

Dhurrrkk's violet eyes softened. "Rhrrrkkeet' told me of your offer—and that you asked for me as the other honor-vessel. I am honored. That was a doubly honorable action on your part, seeing that you were the one who had caused Khrekk's life to be spared from Simon's weapon in the first place. I am truly honored to be your friend, Honored FriendMahree."

"Thank you, Honored FriendDhurrkk'," Mahree said. "But

my volunteering did no good. My uncle refused to allow me to be the honor-vessel. He would not listen when I tried to explain that 'ritual hence' meant no danger. You know how adults can be.''

He gave her a glance that she interpreted as rueful. ''I do know,'' he agreed. ''Matters would be greatly improved if your people had listened to you. But whether you enter the Arena or not, I believe that you humans should be allowed to leave without protest.'' He sighed, a very human-sounding sigh. ''But I am not the High Council. They may decide otherwise.''

Mahree took a deep breath. ''Now I must come to the hardest thing of all to tell you, my honored friend,'' she said. ''It is not just for *our* sakes that you must help me. It is also for your own.''

Dhurrrkk's eyes were puzzled.

She nodded emphatically. ''It is true. Listen well. Tonight I listened to Joan Atwood saying that *Désirée* should leave immediately, even if leaving meant tearing our ship loose from its moorings and ripping a hole in Station One! And, if your people tried to pursue, she proposed that we destroy your world! Your entire solar system!'' Her voice choked and failed her, as she took in Dhurrrkk's horrified gaze.

''I told you we were violent!'' she cried, hardly able to see him through gathering tears. ''You thought that because we are physically weak in comparison to yourselves, and have no Arena-of-Honor, no natural weapons in comparison to your people, that we were *harmless*?''

Mahree fought the urge to giggle hysterically, struggling to regain control of herself. ''My friend, learn this, and learn it well. Humans can be ruthless.''

''Please define 'ruthless'?''

''Someone who is ruthless is determined to have their own way, no matter what harm to others they may cause in gaining it,'' Mahree translated hastily. ''I had to warn you! Please help me!''

Dhurrrkk' made the questioning gesture. ''How could *Désirée* harm my world?''

''Honored Dhurrrkk','' Mahree said grimly, ''you have studied physics, haven't you? What would happen if *Désirée* were to generate a metaspace field within your sun's gravitational pull?''

Dhurrrkk' stared at her, his violet eyes wide. Then he nodded, slowly. "My people have never considered such an application of the S.V. drive."

"So now you know why I had to speak with you," Mahree told him. "Together we must think of some way to convince the Council to allow my people to depart in peace."

Dhurrrkk's crest drooped lower and lower, until it lay flat on his massive shoulders as he considered what she'd said. Finally, he spoke. "FriendMahree, this situation is even more serious than you realize. If your ship were to take such an action, bring destruction to the world we are now orbiting, that would plunge our species into a full-scale death-combat."

Mahree stared at him, baffled. "How could that be, if this planet was destroyed?"

Again Dhurrrkk' hesitated for a long time before replying, "We have not been completely honest with your people, my friend."

Mahree remembered the evasions, the things that didn't add up about the Simiu society. "We suspected that," she told him. "Will you be honest with me now?"

"Yes," Dhurrrkk' said. "We have six colony worlds in other star systems, FriendMahree. The mother world below us holds barely one-quarter of our total population."

"Oh, *shit* . . ." Mahree muttered, feeling as though she'd been punched in the stomach.

"Beg pardon?" Dhurrrkk' looked puzzled. "What, please, means 'shit'? My link lists no definition."

"Never mind, it's not important," Mahree whispered. "Dhurrrkk', *why* didn't your people tell us?"

"There are two main reasons: initially, it was decided not to reveal the locations of our colonies until we understood your people better and were sure they were not the forefront of an invasionary force."

"That's understandable," Mahree murmured.

"Yes, but soon we knew that your vessel was no threat. And still my people kept silent. There is much competition between the colonies and the mother planet . . . most of it is honorable and beneficial, but in this case, it may well have served us ill. We hoped to . . . establish firm relations between our world and yours, before revealing your presence to the colony worlds. We only did so ten days ago."

"Then . . . if we leave Station One forcibly, your people

would have a blood-debt—a *death*-debt—against Earth and all the human-inhabited worlds,'' Mahree said, feeling sick.

''Yes.''

If it came to war, she thought, *it would be seven worlds with superior S.V. drive against our four. Oh, God, this is worse than I ever imagined!* ''We have to stop this!'' she cried passionately. ''Dhurrrkk', we can't let this happen!''

''Perhaps if you talked to your uncle . . .''

''I tried! He won't listen!'' She glanced at her watch. ''I can't stay much longer—soon it'll be day shift, and somebody will notice I'm gone! What if *you* talked to Rhrrrkkeet'? Couldn't she talk to the Council?''

''FriendMahree, you are forgetting that Rhrrrkkeet' is already 'on your side,' as I think the idiom goes. She can do little more than she is already doing. The Council will decide today whether to continue honorable relations with your people—and, if not, whether to release your vessel.''

''What do you think they'll decide?''

''I do not know. The way the situation appears now, the decision may go against us. Then you will not be allowed to leave.''

''They've already put magnetic grapples on our ship.''

Dhurrrkk' cocked his head. ''We did that as soon as you docked. That is standard procedure.''

''We never checked before. We never thought we might have to get away fast until today.'' Mahree put her head in her hands. ''This is awful! We have to do something!''

Dhurrrkk' nodded silent agreement.

''Aren't there any neutral factions we could sway to the pro-human side?'' she said, hopelessly.

''Neutral? Factions?''

When she had finished translating the unfamiliar terms, Dhurrrkk' was silent for a long time, head bent. Again his crest flattened to his skull. Finally, he stirred. ''Your question suggests a possible solution,'' he admitted miserably. ''But if I relate it to you, I will dishonor myself for all time in the eyes of my people. I will have committed—what is the word?—crimes against the government?''

''You mean 'treason.' ''

Dhurrrkk' nodded. ''Yes. Treason against my entire world.''

Mahree sighed. ''Oh, FriendDhurrkk', I'm so *sorry*! What a

thing to ask of you! But I'm sure that many of the people aboard *Désirée* would say that is what I've done, coming here today. But it was the only thing I could do.''

Dhurrrkk' hesitated for several seconds longer, then, abruptly, said, ''You are right. The preservation of both our peoples is vital—and, if we are successful, I will know within me that I have acted honorably, no matter how those outside my flesh judge me.'' He eyed her measuringly. ''Here is the last, greatest secret, Honored FriendMahree: *You humans are **not** our First Contact.*''

Mahree stared at him, stunned and speechless.

''There are at least ten other sentient races in this part of the galaxy. We belong to an organization that such races may join. In our language, it is called''—Dhurrrkk' voiced several guttural grunts, as a series of Simiu characters flashed across the screen.

Mahree hastily enabled a definition search. The closest the program could come was ''The Amiable/Helpful/Cooperative Cluster/Group/League/Union of (Planetary/Star) Systems.'' She picked terms nearly at random, and ventured, ''The Cooperative League of Systems?''

''Yes, that is how it would translate into your language,'' Dhurrrkk' told her. ''There are many races. They set trade rules; they maintain peace in the dealings of one member with another. Ordinarily, they do not interfere in the internal runnings of planetary governments, unless they threaten League peace.'' He looked thoughtful. ''Threats to the peace are very rare, since global peace is one of the requirements to become even a provisionary member—which is what my world is.''

''Why aren't you full members?''

''We have not yet initiated a successful First Contact with another sentient, non-League world,'' Dhurrrkk' told her, bleakly. ''And the way the situation appears now, it seems we are not going to succeed with that in the near future, either.''

''Oh . . .'' breathed Mahree, as several things suddenly became clear. ''That's why you didn't tell us about the CLS—you were afraid we'd bypass you and go directly to the full members, and we were your chance at a full membership!''

''Yes,'' Dhurrrkk' confirmed. ''Our world has been close to full membership for years, though our internal territorial disputes are not regarded favorably . . . but, since they tend to be relatively bloodless, the League overlooks them. And our honor-code is regarded as something sacred to our people, so it does not come under League . . ." he paused for a translation, "League jurisdiction," he finished.

"Ever since we were contacted by the League, there has been competition between Hurrreeah—my world—and its colonies to see which world would fulfill the final requirement for full League membership.

"*That* is why we did not inform our colonies of your arrival until recently. *That*—in addition to the health quarantine, of course—is why you have been kept in this station, and never permitted to even suspect the presence of our other two stations. Interstellar trade with various worlds has been continuing there as usual, but we closed Station One to them, until we could reach a formal agreement with you humans."

Pieces of the Simiu puzzle were falling into place now with dizzying speed. "So your FTL communications ability and your super-fast S.V. drive weren't your own invention?" she guessed. *No wonder they seemed "grafted on" to existing Simiu technology!*

"That is correct."

"And those funny green disks that you were so secretive about?"

"League currency."

Mahree swallowed. "*Ten* other sentient species?"

Dhurrrkk' thought for a moment. "Perhaps it is eleven. Yes, I believe another new species was discovered last year."

She took a deep breath. *Back to the business at hand.* "What did you mean when you said there might be a neutral third party that could help us?"

"There is none on my world," Dhurrrkk' said. "But we could appeal directly to the League, at Shassiszss . . ." he hesitated, "at the place where they hold their gatherings of members . . ."

"Their headquarters," Mahree supplied.

"Yes. Since this is a matter threatening interstellar peace, it falls under their jurisdiction. We could rightfully ask them for their aid. But to do so would mean that my people could never count you humans as a successful First Contact. Do you see what I mean, FriendMahree?"

"Yes, I do," Mahree said. "But if there's the slightest chance that there might be war . . ."

"Yes, we cannot afford to take such a chance. We must contact the League directly, you and I." Dhurrrkk' straightened in sudden decision, his crest rising with excitement. "We must go immediately."

"Go?" Mahree said blankly. "You mean *travel* to their headquarters *ourselves*?"

"It is the only way," Dhurrrkk' told her solemnly. "The League communications channels are strictly monitored. I could not get through them, and I have nowhere near enough honor-credits to finance such a communication, even if I did."

"But," she stammered, "but . . . but . . . Dhurrrkk', *how*? You mean, just *leave*, without telling anyone? We'd need a ship! Who would pilot it? *I* can't!"

"I am a certified pilot," Dhurrrkk' reminded her. "I have a ship in mind . . . small, but fast. Ordinarily, it would be difficult to get to this vessel, but, since I am a member of the"—he yipped his clan-name—"I can get aboard. I will invent a suitable excuse for removing the ship from where it is docked. Rhrrrkkeet' will not be pleased, since it is her ship, but that cannot be helped."

"You mean . . ." Mahree gasped. "You mean we're going to *steal* the First Ambassador's' vessel?"

Dhurrrkk' nodded. "How else can we get there?" His violet eyes sparkled with a touch of wry humor. "The headquarters world is nearly thirty of your parsecs away. Or would you prefer to walk there, FriendMahree?"

Mahree could only stare at him, dazed. "You appear distressed." Dhurrrkk' peered at her, concerned. "I was not serious about walking, FriendMahree. I was making a joke."

Helplessly, Mahree began to laugh. It took her a while to stop. Shaking with hysterical giggles, she wiped tears away.

Dhurrrkk' was looking decidedly smug. "I am pleased that my first joke was so successful," he told her. "But now, I am afraid, we must return to practicalities. We have a great deal of planning to do, and not much time."

Mahree nodded, squaring her shoulders. "Then by all means, let us begin."

CHAPTER 10

♦

The Naked Stars

Am I doing the right thing? I could be making the worst mistake of my life. I could be betraying my people, maybe even condemning them to death.

My stomach is in knots. I keep fighting nausea. If only I could change my mind . . . but I promised Dhurrrkk'. He's risking his neck and, what's more, he's risking his honor. Can I do less?

At least I'm all packed, and the security system on the cargo deck now thinks I'm Yoki. The "airlock open" indicator on the bridge won't give me away. Fortunately, my period is over, so I won't have to worry about that . . . unless we're gone for a month, that is. Oh, God, we could be. I'd better prepare for that possibility . . .

Back again.

I keyed a message to Uncle Raoul, programmed to flag him several hours after we're safely away. I explained what Dhurrrkk' told me about the Simiu colonies, and the CLS. I warned him to not let the Simiu know that he's aware of their secrets. I'm trying to protect Dhurrrkk' as much as possible.

Dhurrrkk' is leaving an equivalent message for Rhrrrkkeet'.

Our destination is a small, yellow-white star "next door" (as stellar distances go) to the pair of double stars we call Mizar. In my head I've already begun calling those people the "Mizari." I wonder what they and the other CLS members are like. *Eleven* different kinds of aliens—!!

Sitting right on top of my bag of food, clothing, and other necessities is a gun. I sneaked into Uncle Raoul's cabin and swiped it from the arms locker. I doubt I could actually shoot anyone, even using the lowest setting, but maybe I could use it in a last-ditch bluff . . .

I just wish I could be sure I'm doing the right thing . . .

Mahree had to force herself not to tiptoe on her way through the corridors, carrying her supply bag, the weapon shoved into the waistband of her shorts. It made a lumpy bulge over her navel, its outline only too apparent beneath her shirt.

With all her being she wanted to hurry, but she made herself walk at a normal pace.

The only crew member she passed on the way down to the cargo deck was Ray Drummond, and the Assistant Engineer barely glanced up from the flimsy he was scanning. Limp with relief, Mahree mumbled a monosyllabic reply to his abstracted, "How's it goin'?"

The corridors seemed endless, but her watch showed that only two minutes had passed since she had left her cabin. She halted outside the entrance to the cargo bay and entered the access code she had prepared. The door slid open.

Mahree had one foot over the threshold when a pleasant baritone came from behind her: "Hey, kiddo, is Yoki in there?"

The girl froze, her heart pounding so hard that for a second she was afraid she might faint. *Of all the people to catch me, it had to be Rob! Shit!*

She took a slow, deep breath, pulled the gun out of her shorts, then swung around to face him, concealing the weapon behind her back as she did so. *Maybe I can talk my way past him. Please, God . . .*

"Hi," she said, surprised that her voice emerged without a squeak. "Yoki and I came down to check on the cargo, but she forgot something. She told me to wait here. She only left a minute ago—you can probably catch her if you hurry, Rob." Smiling, Mahree pointed back up the left-hand corridor leading to the ladder-well.

"Okay." He smiled, nodded, and turned away.

Mahree let out her breath in a soundless paean of gratitude.

"Wait a minute." Rob stopped abruptly and turned back to

face her. "Yoki wouldn't leave that hatchway un—'' he broke off, eyes widening as he saw the weapon in Mahree's hand.

"Don't move, Rob. I promise you I can hit what I aim at. I don't want to stun you, but I will if you make me."

He gaped at her, speechless. Finally, he grinned weakly. "You're kidding, right?"

"Wrong," she replied flatly. "Don't say anything else. And don't even *think* about yelling. Just step in here while I decide what to do with you." She beckoned him to move past her, through the open hatchway.

Mahree watched her prisoner narrowly as she followed him into the cargo-storage area. The scent of Jolian wool filled her nostrils, and the low temperature made gooseflesh pop out on her skin. "Stop. Turn around," she ordered.

Obediently, Rob halted and swung slowly to face her. His expression was a study in stunned bewilderment, but as she watched, it changed. Now she read a mixture of indignation and hurt in his eyes.

Her hand was steady as she held the weapon, but her thoughts verged on panic. *What am I going to do with him? I can't tie him up down here—it's too cold.*

"Mahree . . . kiddo . . ." he spoke soothingly, "want to tell me what's going on? Why are you doing this? I'm sure we can solve whatever's bothering you, without telling anyone about this."

He thinks I've completely cleared my jets, Mahree thought, both angry and amused. "Want to bet?" she retorted. "I'm perfectly sane, Rob. I've got good reasons for what I'm doing. What I *don't* have is time." She frowned at him, thoughtfully. "I think I'll have to take you back into the corridor leading to the engine room and stun you. I just saw Ray Drummond leaving there, after his systems check, so there won't be anybody down there for a couple of hours. Long enough to let me get away."

He stared at her uncomprehendingly, as though she had been addressing him in Simiu instead of English. "Leave?" he blinked. *"Leave? How? Where? Why?"*

"The 'why' is too complicated to explain quickly. As to 'where,' I'm going with Dhurrrkk' on the F.A.'s ship. This whole situation has gotten out of hand, Rob. If somebody doesn't do something, we're going to wind up at war with the Simiu—a war *they'll* win. But Dhurrrkk' and I are going to stop it, before it starts. We're going to bring in some outside help."

"Outside help?" He gave her a sharp, penetrating glance. "What kind of outside help?"

"I told you, I don't have time to explain!" Mahree hesitated, then squared her shoulders and beckoned with the weapon. "Okay, back into the corridor. Take the righthand branch. You ought to be undisturbed until you wake up, in an hour or so." She bit her lip anxiously, studying him. "It's a good thing you're young and healthy. You *are* healthy, aren't you? You don't have a weak heart, or anything? I mean, you'd know, being a doctor, wouldn't you?"

"Wait a minute," Rob said, holding out both hands in a gesture of heartfelt appeal. "*Wait* a minute. *Listen* to me for a second. How do you know this isn't some kind of trick? Maybe the Simiu are doing this to get you into their Arena without Raoul knowing, did you ever think of that?" He took a deep breath. "They're holding us prisoner here. We've just discovered that they've got a magnetic field on our grapples."

"They've *always* had magnetic grapples on the ship!" she snapped, exasperated. "Magnetic grapples are S.O.P. for Simiu docking cradles. Dhurrrkk' told me."

"Listen to me, Mahree. You think he's your friend, but I think he's setting you up—on Rhrrrkkeet's orders. They want you to fight in their Arena so their honor-code can be fulfilled. Or as a hostage to guarantee that we'll stay here peacefully, and not try to get away."

That makes a certain kind of sense . . . Mahree thought, then her mouth tightened. "No," she said. "You're wrong. Dhurrrkk's my friend. In the first place, *I* went to *him*. And in the second, I know he wouldn't betray me."

"Maybe he wouldn't," Rob said amiably. He moved one foot forward a tiny bit. "But maybe Rhrrrkkeet's using him unwittingly to get to you. Ever think of that?" He slid his other foot toward her, slightly.

"Rob, I'd hate to shoot you in here, where it's so cold," Mahree said quietly. "I'm not sure I could carry you out. If I left you here, your ass might freeze before you woke up. So just forget about jumping me and grabbing the gun, okay?"

He stopped, studying her face intently. Whatever he saw there made him swallow nervously. "Okay," he said. "Just tell me one more thing . . . *what* outside help?"

"There are other races the Simiu know," Mahree said. "Ten,

at least. One of them, the Mizari, are sort of . . . negotiators and peace-keepers. They'll make the Simiu let us leave peacefully. We're going to their homeworld, where the CLS headquarters are."

Rob's expression brightened in spite of himself. "*Ten* different species of aliens? An interstellar governing body?"

"I don't have time! Out into the corridor, now, dammit, or I pull this trigger!"

"*Wait* a minute, *please*," Rob said hastily. "*Please*, honey. I still think they're bullshitting you, but either way, I can't let you go alone. Take me with you."

"Hell, no," Mahree said. "You'll try and stop me."

"I swear to God I won't."

She eyed him suspiciously. "You don't believe me about the CLS, so why do you want to go along?"

He shook his head. "You're right, I think they're lying. I think the Simiu are setting a trap for you. But the First Ambassador respects me. If I'm there, maybe I can talk her into letting us go."

"And if I'm not walking into a trap? If Dhurrrkk' is telling the truth?"

"Then Raoul will sleep easier nights, knowing that another human is with you on that Simiu ship."

Mahree considered. She really wasn't sure she could pull that trigger in cold blood and watch someone she loved crumple up and fall to the deck. *You're being a fool to let him talk you into this,* she told herself savagely, but she nodded, gesturing with the gun. "Okay. Out of here. We'll head for your cabin. You'll need supplies. And, remember, you gave your word."

They met no one on the way to Rob's cabin, and Mahree breathed a silent "thank you." She had no illusions about Rob's oath.

"Okay," she snapped when they reached his quarters, "pack for an extended trip. Use a vacuum-proof bag."

Rob nodded silently, and moved around his cabin, collecting things. "What about food?" he said.

"I've got food," she said.

"Enough for two?"

"It'll have to be. Now, write a note to tell them you're coming with me."

Hastily he complied. "I'm asking Yoki to feed Sekhmet," he said, scribbling.

Mahree glanced at what he'd written and nodded curtly. "Come on. And remember, if we meet anyone in the corridor, I'm going to stun them first, then you, if you so much as let out a loud breath."

They were halfway to the door when Rob stopped abruptly. "Wait a second!"

Mahree's finger tensed on the trigger. "What?"

"My medical bag."

She relaxed. "Okay. Will it fit inside your other bag?"

"If . . . I . . . shove . . . There! That's got it."

"We've got to hurry, Rob. Don't forget what I said."

"I remember."

They were halfway there when they heard voices, and with a sinking heart Mahree recognized them as Joan's and Paul's. Tensing, she moved closer to Rob, almost treading on his heels as they walked. She poked the barrel of the gun between his arm and his back, concealing it, and whispered, "Rob, if you open your mouth, I swear I'll stun *all* of you. Remember how old Paul is . . . it might hurt him. *Please* don't make me have to do that!"

She could feel the clamminess of his coverall against her fingers, the tenseness of his body. He made no sound.

Joan and Paul were in sight now, arguing about the fuel reserves. Neither paid any attention to the approaching pair. Mahree held her breath as they moved past the Chief Engineer and the First Mate. *Keep walking, don't stop,* she ordered herself. *For God's sake, don't look back!*

Not looking back was the hardest thing of all to do.

As the First Mate's and Chief Engineer's footsteps faded into the distance, Mahree gave a heartfelt sigh of relief. "Thanks, Rob."

When she reached the suit locker on the cargo deck, Mahree glanced quickly at her watch, frowning. "I'll get into my suit first. You lie on the deck, facedown."

"But—"

"*Do* it!"

Trying to keep her eyes on Rob, and the weapon close to hand, Mahree quickly measured her arm against a small suit's, then pulled it out of the rack. Quickly she climbed into the spacesuit. Once Rob started to raise his head, levering himself up, but she immediately grabbed the gun and fired it over his head. The charge spat blue-violet, and she smelled ozone. Her prisoner gasped, then lay still.

"I can't believe you're doing this," the doctor's muffled voice reached her as she sealed up the front of the suit and reached for the helmet.

"I can't believe I'm doing it either," Mahree admitted.

A moment later, she had the helmet locked on, then she slid the gloves over her hands and sealed them. Mahree tapped the gun against the cargo hatch to get Rob's attention, then gestured brusquely at the other suits.

He got up a little stiffly, then selected a suit, donning it far more quickly than Mahree had, due to his recent practice. As he fastened his helmet, he spoke up: "Radio check."

"I hear you," Mahree said. "And I'll also hear you if you open a channel to the bridge, understand?"

"Yes."

"Now be quiet, I've got to concentrate."

Still keeping the weapon centered on the helmet of his suit, she keyed open the inner door to the big cargo airlock. She stopped short of the last entry. "All that," she muttered, "and I've got two minutes to spare." She glanced around her, frowning. "We may need these suits when we meet the Mizari. Rob, strap all the charged breathing paks together, so we can take them with us."

He obeyed quickly. They made a bulky bundle as he dragged them over to the airlock. "What do the Mizari look like?" he asked.

"That's not their real name," Mahree admitted. "I just made it up. And I haven't the faintest idea what they look like. Dhurrrkk' didn't have time to tell me."

Before he could say anything more, she keyed in the final sequence, and the airlock door slid open. "All right, inside," she said, motioning. "You carry in the bags, and then come back for the breathing paks. Don't forget that I've still got this gun, and that I'm watching you."

"Don't worry," he said, with an attempt at lightness, "you've got me thoroughly convinced that you'll shoot. I'm too cowed to do anything rash."

Mahree muttered an imprecation under her breath, then snapped, "Just *do* it!"

She was right behind him as he stepped through the doors, then she signaled the lock to depressurize. "Grab something, Rob. I'm going to turn off the gravity. How are you in no-weight?"

She could see him shake his head through the clear material of his faceplate. "I don't know," he said. "I've never experienced zero gee. How are *you*?"

"I'll be all right," she said. "I've got a cast-iron stomach . . . unless, that is, you get sick. If you do, you're on your own."

"Okay," Rob said dryly. "I'm warned."

Mahree slowly moved the switch that controlled the gravity in the airlock. She decreased it by one-half, then paused. "So far so good?"

"Yup," Rob answered cheerfully. "*Ten* different kinds of aliens, you say?"

"At least." She decreased the gravity again, until they were at one-sixth gee. "Still okay? This is lunar gravity."

"Fine," Rob said.

"Okay, I'm going for a tenth, now." She decreased the gravity again.

Even at one-sixth gee, there had been enough gravity to keep her feet on the deck. But now they had a disturbing tendency to lose contact with the flooring—a hard push with her toes would have been enough to send her bumping against the ceiling. But there was still a sense that the deck was "down" and the ceiling was "up." Mahree knew that sense would disappear as soon as she turned off the gravity altogether. "How's that?" she asked Rob.

"Feels funny," he said, cautiously clinging with both hands to the handrail that ran around the inside of the airlock.

"Experiencing any vertigo?"

"Not yet," he said nervously. "But the perilymph and endolymph are beginning to slosh around in my inner ear."

"Move *slowly*. Take it easy . . . very . . . easy . . ." As she finished speaking, she slid the switch up the final notch, until the gravity was gone.

At first it felt like dropping in a high-speed elevator. Then, as she looked around the airlock, Mahree realized that "up" and "down" had indeed become meaningless terms. She found that she could force herself to think of the deck as "down" *intellectually,* but that the designation had no credibility, because all her senses told her that *every* direction was "down." Or "up." Or just *away.*

"You okay?" she asked Rob.

"So far, so good," he said, sounding a little grim.

"Just keep thinking about seeing more aliens than you can shake a stick at," she encouraged him. "Now, move over into that far corner, away from the airlock controls, and stay there. I'm going to open the hatch. Don't jump me, or we'll both wind up out there without a lifeline, understand?"

"Don't worry," Rob said grimly, shuffling his magnetic soles along the deck, clutching the handrail, "moving fast is the last thing I want to try right now."

Mahree checked her suit's chrono display as she pulled herself over to the control panel. *Damn, I'm seventy seconds late! Is he still there?*

Feeling as though she were moving underwater, Mahree triggered the sequence to open the outer lock. A minute later, the panels slid aside. The girl could feel the rumbling vibration of their movement through her hands, but she could no longer hear any sounds except Rob's breathing—and her own—through the suit radio.

Mahree kept one hand clamped on the rail, the magnetized soles of her boots firmly pressed against the deck, as she leaned over to peer out, into space.

The cargo airlock lay in a patch of shadow, so she could see the stars—they looked like minuscule gemmed nailheads, sharp and unwinking. Mahree gripped the handrail tightly, because for a moment she seemed to be falling into a black well that surrounded her—and everywhere she looked was "down."

After a moment, her disorientation eased, and she was able to look "up," to a point opposite *Désirée.* Nothing hampered her view of the stars . . . no Simiu vessel, nothing.

He's not here, she thought, feeling her heart contract. *Either I missed him, or he couldn't get the ship . . .*

As she watched, something amber glided toward her, lit by the station's lights. Soon it blotted out the stars as it moved into a position alongside *Désirée.* It was one of the hammerheaded Simiu craft, a vessel not much larger than the cruisers that had escorted the freighter to the station.

Mahree laughed in sheer relief, bouncing on her toes in excitement. Her motion pulled the magnetized strips on her bootsoles free of the deck, and she had to grab the handrail with both hands. "He's here!" she cried, regaining her equilibrium, then cautiously turning back to Rob. "He got the ship!"

The alien craft's amidships airlock slid open, and a single spacesuited Simiu figure waved one arm, then beckoned. "I knew he'd come!" Mahree exclaimed triumphantly.

"Yeah, but how can you be sure that it's your friend in there?" Rob asked. "That we're not walking into a trap?"

"We're not walking," Mahree said abstractedly, leaning over the edge of the hull to look out again. "We're going to jump."

"*Jump!* The length of a football field, almost? It must be twenty-five meters across!"

Mahree ran a calculating eye over the void between the two now-motionless vessels. "At least that. But we'll be okay." She began programming the cargo cable for launch sequence, then waved the Simiu figure to get back into the shelter of his airlock. Dhurrrkk' moved out of sight.

At her signal, the cargo cable went sailing out into space like a silvery umbilicus. The trajectory was perfect—the magnetic end of the cable thudded against the bulkhead of the Simiu craft, and clung. Mahree gave it an experimental tug, finding it safely anchored.

"What are we going to do?" Rob asked nervously, watching as she unclipped several "skyhooks."

"We're going to hook these cargo skyhooks onto our suits, then push ourselves away from the airlock," she said. "We'll just slide over on the cable. They do it all the time during ship-to-ship transfers of cargo. Just be sure not to push off too hard, and not to thrash around. You could start spinning, and that would be dangerous. Remember your laws of inertia."

"Uh, yeah," Rob said dubiously, venturing to the edge of the airlock and looking "down" into the void, then glancing at the slender cable overhead. "That wire doesn't look strong enough. It's just a thread."

"It's strong enough, Rob," Mahree said, with eroding patience. "There's no gravity, remember? It doesn't have to support your weight, it's just going to control the path of your jump. Just take it slow. You'll keep drifting at whatever speed you start out with. Watch."

Moving cautiously in the zero gravity, Mahree picked up the bundle of breathing paks, clipped a skyhook to them, then fastened the other end over the cable. She gave the awkward bundle a push, careful to apply equal strength to both sides.

The bundle moved away, sailing across the intervening space in a slow-motion glide. Despite Mahree's caution, it began to spin, but it reached its destination without mishap. The spacesuited Simiu grabbed the bundle and detached it.

Mahree turned to Rob, motioning with the gun. "Your turn."

He gulped audibly. "Mahree . . . I don't know if I can . . ."

She glared at him through the faceplate. "Then clip your skyhook to one of these handrails so you won't float out when I stun you! I'm going, with you or without you!"

Rob sucked in a deep breath, then he clipped his skyhook to the cable, and launched himself into space.

Mahree realized immediately that he'd pushed off entirely too hard. He began spinning helplessly, and then he began to struggle, which made it worse. Gasps of fear mingled with curses emanated from the radio. "Rob!" she cried. "Stop thrashing! You might pull loose!"

As she watched helplessly, his spinning form reached the Simiu airlock. If it hadn't been for the quick reaction of the alien in the lock, he might have crashed into the edge with bone-breaking force.

"Rob!" Mahree called anxiously. "Are you all right?"

"Yeah," he answered, after a moment, gulping. "Trying not to be sick."

Quickly, Mahree tossed the gun back into the airlock, then she clipped her own skyhook. Grasping the handles of both bags in her right hand, she steadied herself on the edge of the airlock, legs bent. Trying for one smooth motion, she straightened her knees and pushed off.

She was free of *Désirée* . . . floating along effortlessly toward the Simiu figure that stood waiting for her. Mahree swallowed as she stared out at the stars, realizing for the first time that there was virtually *nothing* between her and them—only the material of her spacesuit, and a tiny layer of air.

She nearly panicked as the "everywhere is down" sensation filled her mind again. Resolutely, she squeezed her eyes shut, until she felt hands grabbing her, halting her. Her magnetized soles clung, then she was in the airlock of the Simiu ship, safe.

Dhurrrkk' detached her skyhook, and she grabbed for the nearest handhold, watching as her alien friend released the cargo cable, pushing it away from his ship. Then he closed the airlock. Gravity returned a moment later.

After triggering the air and pressure controls, the Simiu opened his helmet, and she heard his voice, faintly: "This is Honored HealerGable, is it not? Why is he here?"

Mahree took off her own helmet and nodded. "Yes. He found me leaving, so I had to bring him with me. But I believe that he will make no trouble, now that he has been convinced of the importance of our mission."

Rob had also removed his helmet, and was staring at her, his eyes wide. "You're . . . you're *talking* to him!" he sputtered. "You can speak their language!"

"After a fashion," she said. "My accent is terrible."

Rob turned to the Simiu. "Honored Dhurrrkk'," he said, in English, "I am very grateful to you for saving me. I consider it an honor to be allowed to accompany you on such a noble and vital mission."

"Honored Healer Gable," Dhurrrkk' said, aloud, formally, also in English, "your presence honors this vessel." Mahree could not tell whether or not the Simiu was being ironic. "FriendMahree, I must get us away from here," he continued, in his own language. "Any moment now they will miss this ship and start after us."

Mahree nodded, and the Simiu left.

She stood up and began pulling off her spacesuit, grateful that she had fresh air to breathe again, even if it was hot and sticky. Moments later, the Simiu ship began vibrating nearly imperceptibly. They were underway.

Rob took off his suit, then sat down on the deck with a sigh. "To think that you actually *speak* Simiu. Is that how you found out about these other races?"

"Partly," Mahree said. "It's a long story."

He patted the deck next to him. "At the moment, honey, time is all we have. Start at the beginning."

Taking a deep breath of the humid air, Mahree launched into the entire story.

When she finished, her mouth was dry. Rob was staring at her with a strange expression; it seemed to be composed of equal parts of exasperation and awe. Slowly, he shook his head. "No wonder you were in such a panic to reach these Mizari. But you might have trusted me enough to come to me and explain. I'd have helped you willingly, then.''

"I was afraid you wouldn't believe me, after I heard you saying we should rip *Désirée* loose. Everyone in that meeting sounded so . . . so hostile.''

"How long will the trip take?''

"I'm not sure,'' she admitted. "Dhurrrkk' said he was going to program us for a roundabout course, so we wouldn't run any chance of being intercepted before we can make Stellar Velocity. Several weeks each way, I suppose.''

Rob wiped his sweaty forehead with his hand, pushing back his damp, matted hair. "Several weeks?'' He sighed. "In this heat? Well, at least I'll get a chance to try and learn the language. How did you—''

He broke off at a noise from the entranceway, and they both turned to find Dhurrrkk' there. The Simiu was wearing his computer link and voder, and both humans hurriedly dug through their bags for theirs.

"We are underway,'' the alien said. "I believe I have set a course that makes it look as though we are heading for one of our colony worlds.''

"How long before we go S.V.?'' Mahree asked.

"Several more hours,'' Dhurrrkk' answered. "But I believe our escape had not been detected at the time we left, so they will have difficulty tracing us.''

"How did you manage to get the ship?'' Mahree asked.

Dhurrrkk's crest flattened, and his violet eyes dropped. "I told an untruth,'' he admitted. "A very reprehensible action on my part. Most dishonorable . . .''

"What did you tell them?''

"I said that Rhrrrkkeet' had instructed me to move this vessel to the other side of the station, so it would be ready to transport her down to the next Council meeting.''

Rob gave Mahree a skeptical glance. She nodded. "This society isn't nearly as suspicious as ours,'' she explained, aloud. "The Simiu assume you're telling the truth until it's proved that you're lying. Falsehood is very rare.''

"They managed to lie to us effectively enough,'' Rob muttered grimly.

"But, Honored HealerGable, it was early decided that equivocation would be allowed in our dealings with you, because you were outsiders, and therefore not to be trusted until you proved yourselves to be beings capable of honor," Dhurrrkk' said. Mahree thought that she detected embarrassment in his manner. "Such a decision was not very honorable, I admit, but my people soothed their consciences with the knowledge that, if you humans proved to be worthy-of-honor, the truth would then be revealed to you."

"After all," Mahree pointed out, "we were only risking ourselves. They were risking seven entire worlds, if we proved to be the vanguard of an invasionary force."

"I understand," Rob said thoughtfully.

Dhurrrkk' busied himself hanging up their spacesuits, then picked up the two bags. "Let me show you my vessel," he invited.

"Does it have a name?" Rob asked.

Mahree shook her head. "They don't name things the way we do. It just has a code."

Rob glanced around him as they followed the alien into the corridor. "We ought to give it a name, then," he mused. "Something appropriate to the occasion . . ."

"Be my guest," Mahree said, smiling, as they ducked beneath an arching overhead stanchion.

Rob was silent as they followed Dhurrrkk' along the brightly colored passageway. Finally he snapped his fingers. "Got it!"

"What?" Absorbed in her first glimpses into the hydroponics area (where dark emerald, olive green, and aqua vegetation grew lushly), she'd lost the thread of their conversation.

"The name. How about *Rosinante*?"

"What?"

"Not what, who. Rosinante was Don Quixote's dauntless steed, who carried him when he rode off on his crazy quests," Rob said, smiling. "Quests nearly as crazy as this one, it seems to me. They included tilting at windmills in lieu of giants."

Mahree laughed.

Dhurrrkk' led them on a complete tour of the small ship, from bow to stern. Mahree was fascinated by the control cabin, and the alien promised to teach her how to interface her linkup with the main computer so she could trade watches with him—although she'd have to take them sitting on the floor. Simiu "seats" were all wrong for human body contours.

Rosinante was lavishly outfitted, but very small—it possessed only two sleeping cabins and a small dormitory off the tiny cargo area. Dhurrrkk' led them up to the entrance to one of the cabins, then activated the portal with a flourish.

Obviously pleased with himself, he waved the humans inside. Mahree and Rob stepped into a small cubicle with bright orange and blue walls, and a scarlet heap of bedding/lounging cushions in its middle. It contained little else, only a few storage cabinets and shelves. "Do you notice the difference?" Dhurrrkk' asked. Both humans clearly sensed his anticipation.

Mahree glanced around, biting her lip, wondering what could possibly be different. But Rob, in his long-sleeved ship's coveralls, was quick to realize. "It's cooler in here!"

Dhurrrkk' nodded enthusiastically. "I have instructed the life-support system to maintain your quarters in this manner. Is it to your liking? Do you find it comfortable?"

"*Our* quarters?" Mahree repeated blankly. "But we can't—"

She broke off when Rob gave her a meaningful nudge with his elbow. The doctor nodded vigorously. "That is very thoughtful and kind of you, Honored Dhurrrkk'!" he said. "This cabin will be very comfortable indeed."

"Yes, it will," Mahree agreed, trying to sound enthusiastic. It *was* thoughtful of Dhurrrkk' to remember that the environment they were used to was at least ten degrees cooler than his own. The room was considerably less humid, also. She tried not to stare at the single mound of bedding. "Thank you very much."

Her Simiu friend appeared touchingly pleased. "I am glad that you like it." He turned back to the door. "Remember to keep the portal closed, so the cooler atmosphere will not be dissipated. Right now, I must check our course. Rest now, honored friends. You have had a wearying time of it this day."

He dimmed the overhead lights, then the Simiu was gone, the portal sliding shut behind him. Mahree turned to Rob. "Thanks for saving me from blurting out something churlish," she said.

Rob grinned cheerfully as he stuck his hand out. "Hiya, roomie. Won't this be fun? Just like camping out!"

She returned his smile feebly, as she shook the offered hand. "Yeah. Camping out."

"Don't look so dismayed," he said. "I only snore when I'm drunk, or so I've been told. I won't keep you awake."

"Right now not even a gun at my head could keep me

awake," Mahree said, yawning. "We can divide up those comforters into two piles . . . there are plenty of them."

Her yawn was contagious, and Mahree giggled as Rob also yawned suddenly, widely. "I don't know," he said, casting her a sardonic glance as they began wrestling with the pile of bedding, each dragging half of it to opposite corners of the little cabin, "having a gun pointed at you gives a helluva adrenaline rush." He sat down and unsealed his shoes. "Sure woke *me* up."

Miserably self-conscious, Mahree pulled off her own shoes and lay down. "G'night . . ." she mumbled, feeling exhaustion engulf her like a warm wave.

"Good night . . ." he murmured, then, after a moment, she heard his voice again. "Hey, kiddo . . . would you *really* have shot me?"

Mahree rolled over and lay staring up at the low, inward-slanting ceiling of the little cabin. She did not speak for a long time, but, finally, she replied, "Yes. I'd have felt terrible for doing it, but I would have."

"I figured," he said gently. "Go to sleep, kiddo."

Mahree listened to his soft, regular breathing as he fell asleep, and thought that she might cry, but sleep took her before any tears could fall.

CHAPTER 11

♦

Breathing Space

Nothing ever happens in space.

Where have I heard that complaint before? Well, it's truer than ever.

We've been underway for over a week, and I've already read all my books, viewed all my holo-vids, and watched all the films Rob brought—twice. It's amazing how many hours there are in each day to fill up. (It doesn't help that the Simiu "day" is longer than ours. The time is still the same, but, psychologically, the hours *seem* longer.)

Dhurrrkk' and Rob and I spend *hours* each day talking, and still there are times I end up staring at the four inward-slanting walls. Wish I'd thought to toss in my textbook cassettes. Right now, I'd love to peruse the history of the Martian Colonies.

(Rob told me some of his ancestors were settlers in the First Martian Colony, that grand and glorious failure. I asked him if there were any espers in his family. He said that one of his maternal great-aunts was a telepath—as well as a cranky old terror . . . so much for the notion that complete understanding promotes serenity and kindness . . .)

Sheer physical discomfort adds to the tedium. I'm hot and sticky all the time, and there's no way to bathe. We have to take turns washing at the cold-water fountain, using a minimum amount of water. Bathing is low priority compared to drinking or irrigating the plants in hydroponics. Used water gets recycled, true, but a certain percentage is always irretrievable.

(Simiu do not bathe; they groom, which is why *Rosinante*'s water supply seems small. Dhurrrkk' spends an hour or so each day licking himself, then he combs his fur with his nails. Simiu have some kind of secretion beneath their fingertips that leaves the hair soft and shiny. That secretion is the source of their slightly spicy, musky scent.)

Speaking of hair, mine is getting to be a nuisance. Yesterday I took it down and poured a cup of water over my scalp, then rubbed it hard with a towel, which made me feel better. I really ought to cut it, I suppose.

The food is worse than I thought it would be. Since it's unprocessed, it's impervious to spoilage, but the texture is grainy and the taste is awful. Both of us have lost weight.

(And, trust me, you've never lived until you've used Simiu sanitary facilities. The way they're *shaped* makes me feel like a contortionist. I won't depress you with the details.)

My language skills continue to improve, though I wouldn't call myself fluent. For that, I'd have to be able to *think* in it, and I'm still mentally translating everything Dhurrrkk' says to me into English or French, then translating my reply into Simiu before giving it.

We've definitely eluded pursuit. Dhurrrkk' listened for any mention of our escapade on *Rosinante*'s radio, but there was none. The High Council must be keeping the entire thing quiet— probably because they're embarrassed to admit that the Simiu chance to attain full membership in the CLS has gone so sour.

However, Dhurrrkk' *did* pick up a broadcast aimed at us—at least, he caught the tail-end of an ID code that matched *Rosinante*'s. The message was very neutrally worded—any other ship who intercepted it wouldn't tumble to what it was about. Dhurrrkk' thought he recognized the speaker as Rhrrrkkeet', though he couldn't be sure due to interference. She said, in essence, "Come home and all will be forgiven."

But we've gone too far to turn back, so Dhurrrkk' just turned off the radio without replying.

Rob and I have tried reading and viewing some holo-vid programs aboard *Rosinante*, but with limited success. Oh, they were fascinating to study as a reflection of Simiu society, but a bust as entertainment. It's hard to get emotionally involved in a story where the protagonist's sole conflict consists of figuring out obscure and clever ways to accrue honor-debts (which doesn't equate to getting rich, though that's what I thought at first), or the protagonist spends the entire program in an attempt to redeem his/her own, or a sibling's or friend's, honor. Sad endings are preferable to happy ones . . . as long as the protagonist's death is excessively honorable. Most Simiu stories are concluded by an honor-duel.

They're strangely beautiful to watch—the ritual-hence ones are as orchestrated, in their way, as ballet. But they don't touch me emotionally, and, during the blood-duels, I can't help remembering that this is a representation of a real event, and that people *die*.

Mahree sat cross-legged before the main holo-tank, watching a Simiu holo-vid. She shifted uncomfortably in the Earth-plus gravity, and discreetly rubbed her tailbone.

On the screen, the Simiu protagonist, Arrrkk'u, finished his final speech to his assembled kin, then stepped through the archway into the Arena-of-Honor. He squatted down on powerful haunches, his crest rigid with anticipation, teeth bared in the ritual threat-display. Waiting.

It reminded Mahree of stories about ancient Rome, and the gladiatorial combats, except that all the Simiu were silent; it was dishonorable bad manners to cry out during an honor-duel.

As the challenger entered the fifty-meter-wide Arena, Mahree saw Dhurrrkk's crest begin to sag. His gaze shifted away from the holo-screen. She had noticed before that he seemed uncomfortable watching honor-duels, and it bothered her. Several times she'd been tempted to ask him what was wrong, but she didn't want to bring up a sensitive subject unless they were alone. Which they were now; Rob was taking a nap.

"FriendDhurrrkk'," she began, "I do not wish to cause you pain, or dishonor myself by asking unwelcome questions. But I cannot help sensing your discomfort when you see one of these honor-duels on the screen."

Dhurrrkk's powerful shoulders stiffened, and Mahree knew by the expression in his eyes, the infinitesimal wrinkling of his muzzle, that he was angry. She hastily cast about for a way to take back her implied question.

Then her friend's violet eyes softened, and he nodded. "It is true, FriendMahree," he admitted. "I can barely stand to watch the events in the Arena-of-Honor, even when they are part of a fictional tale. You see, I have fought only two honor-duels in my life—far less than most of my peers—and during both of them, *I* was the one who declared ritual hence. In your language, you would say that I lost, and that my loss was not a particularly honorable one. What is your phrase?" The Simiu keyed for a translation. " 'Lost by default.' "

"You mean you quit? Or ran away?" Mahree didn't believe it.

Dhurrrkk's eyes flashed indignantly. "No, if I had done either of those things, I would no longer be a son of my mother!" Then his shoulders slumped, his crest drooped. "But in neither case did I battle even so far as the first blooding—mine or his. I declared ritual hence far too early, and my actions made me an outcast among my associates at school."

Mahree glanced up at the screen. "You fought in that Arena?" she breathed. "Oh, Dhurrrkk' . . . you told me you hadn't!"

"I told no untruths," her friend insisted, rather indignantly. "I have been in two honor-duels, but neither was in the Arena-of-Honor, nothing as major as that. These were what you might term 'schoolyard fights.' "

"I understand," Mahree said. "And I know how important these honor-duels are to you. But speaking as a human, I would have to say that it was smart of you not to let yourself be wounded—possibly seriously."

"You do not understand, FriendMahree. My peers now regard me as one without courage. To us bravery is basic—not merely an admirable trait, but an essential one."

"Well . . ." she considered, "couldn't you pick a fight with someone else after we get home, then stick it out until blood is drawn? Wouldn't that fix the situation?"

"Perhaps," Dhurrrkk' said gloomily, his crest absolutely flat against his neck, "but to do so I would have to choose a younger, weaker opponent, because none of my peers would consider me a worthy challenger. And I do not like the idea of using my age and size against another who is less experienced."

"You mean you *do* know how to fight?"

"After my second disgrace, Rhrrrkkeet' saw to it that I was coached by one of the foremost champions of his day—the Honorable K't'eerrr. But . . . FriendMahree . . . and this also is something I have never told another . . . my will-to-battle is weak. That is a shameful thing. I hope that I do not shock you too greatly in admitting it.''

"No, Dhurrrkk', my friend," Mahree said gently, "I am not shocked. And I truly feel that in helping to prevent a possible war, you have demonstrated a great deal of courage. More courage than it would take to fight an honor-duel.''

Dhurrrkk' brightened. "I felt that was so, inside me," he confided. "But it is gratifying to have someone else say it.''

Mahree pointed at the screen. "Why don't you turn that off? I don't like watching Arrrkk'u die.''

Her friend nodded. "Very well." He glanced over at the program. "It is not something that I enjoy watching, either, because my teacher, the Honorable K't'eerrr, is playing the role of Arrrkk'u.''

"Really? Wait a moment. *That's* K't'eerrr?''

"Yes.''

Onscreen, another Simiu had entered the Arena, a huge, heavily maned chestnut and salmon-dappled gladiator. "Why does it make you sad to see your former teacher?''

"Because Arrrkk'u's opponent in this challenge is played by Hekkk'eesh, the champion who, a year after this program was made, bit off K't'eerrr's left hand when they were selected to represent different clans in a blood-duel over a border dispute. K't'eerrr had acquitted himself well in the duel, but he is much older than Hekkk'eesh. For a crucial second, he was too slow." Dhurrrkk' switched off the pictured honor-duel with a saddened expression.

"How awful!" Mahree cried. "You said that permanent injury or death almost never happened.''

"I spoke the truth. But there was bad feeling between the two champions, and Hekkk'eesh took full advantage of it.''

"Wasn't his action considered dishonorable?''

"Yes, and Hekkk'eesh has been trying to redeem himself ever since, without much success. He is no longer retained for the most honorable challenges—only for the ones the other honor-vessels consider beneath them.''

Mahree frowned. "What kind of challenges are those?''

Dhurrrkk' sighed, a very human-sounding sigh. "Unfounded or illicit challenges against unwilling, unable, or smaller opponents," he explained. "Little more than killings-for-profit—" he keyed in a translation request, then added, " 'assassinations,' or 'executions,' you would call them."

"Do they happen often?"

"Not as often as wars, murders, and crimes appear to happen in human society."

She shook her head and said quickly, "The holo-vids that you have viewed are as distorted for the sake of drama as your own, FriendDhurrrkk'. Crimes are frequent in human society, yes, but not nearly as frequent as they appear in holo-vids. Just as in your programs honor-duels are almost all blood-duels and death-duels, involving the death of one of the combatants, which you tell me is not the case in reality."

"I understand. I should have guessed as much."

The Simiu slid off his lounge with fluid ease. "I must check our course. You will excuse me?"

"I'll come with you," Mahree said. "I want to work on that program I'm trying to develop to translate Mizari into Simiu, then into my language."

"How has your progress been?"

"Slow." Mahree made a face. "It's hard enough programming for translation from one language to another, but for *two* alien languages—! And the database and vocabulary you have aboard are pretty basic."

"I wish that I spoke the language better myself. Then I might be able to help you more—although they tell us Simiu tongues are poorly constructed to produce the sibilants the Mizari language requires. Human tongues may do better."

She smiled wryly, careful not to show her teeth. "Don't bet on it, my friend. I spit all over the navigation console this morning during my language lesson. Even if I learn to reproduce those sounds, I may have to keep my mouth shut! It would never do to spray saliva all over the founders of the CLS!"

Dhurrrkk' nodded, his violet eyes twinkling. "Sound diplomatic reasoning, FriendMahree. Your caution does you credit."

"Did . . . you . . . have . . . a . . . happy . . . childhood?" Rob gasped as they jogged in place in their quarters the next morning.

"Why d'you . . . ask?" Mahree countered, forcing herself not to break stride. She glanced at her watch. *Sixty seconds to go . . .*

Rob did not reply until they had sunk down onto the padded floor, and their breathing was returning to normal. He sat up, slowly. "Getting old," he grumbled, still puffing. "This gravity makes me feel about ninety."

Mahree, who had grown up in Jolie's slightly less than one-gee gravity field, could only nod.

"I asked because I want to know," Rob said, a minute later, in response to her previous question. "Sometimes, your eyes look . . . well, I get the impression that it's been a long time since you were happy, kiddo."

Mahree stiffened, hardly daring to breathe.

Rob mopped sweat off his forehead with a towel, then gave her a sidelong glance. "Tell me to go to hell and M.Y.O.B. if you want. I deserve it."

"No, that's all right." Mahree didn't look at him. "I guess the only answer has to be an equivocal one . . . yes and no. I was never the kind of kid that's popular, the kind that you just *know* is happy. The girl who has the cutest boys dying to go out with her, whose clothes are always perfect, whose grades are top of the class. The one who's Class President, Valedictorian, winner of the Creative Writing contest and the Westing-Dupont Science Search, whose biggest problem is choosing which two of a possible six terrific careers she'll decide to pursue. You know the kind I mean. There's one in every class."

He nodded.

"But I had friends . . . I wasn't lonely all the time. Besides, I had a wonderful dad and *maman* . . . they loved me, even if I wasn't pretty or popular. That's important." She kneaded her calf muscle, eyes downcast. "And I had other friends who were always there, just a glance away . . ."

"What do you mean?"

"You may know them . . . Tarzan of the Apes, Jirel of Joiry, and Kim, and Jo March, and King Arthur. Cirocco Jones, Raz of Padseniro . . . D'Artagnan . . . Aslan the Lion, the Crystal Crusader and Frodo and Jane Eyre. Lots more. Sidney Carton . . . the Scarlet Pimpernel, and Kaththea of Estcarp. Even Dracula and Dr. Frankenstein's poor misunderstood creation."

Rob grinned, nodding with recognition. "Yeah, I know a lot of them. I had a collection of adventure stories that filled an entire cassette file. Most of them you couldn't call classics, but they were *fun!* Ever read *The Prisoner of Zenda*?"

"No, I never did."

"I'll lend it to you. Great stuff. Lookalike cousins and royal impersonations and swordfights and noble sacrifice. Pure melodrama, but a hell of a lot of fun. I have the movie, too."

Mahree grinned back at him. "Did you ever read Twain's *The Prince and the Pauper*?"

"Sure. Ever read *Cyrano de Bergerac*? Talk about swordsmen!"

"Mais oui—en français, naturellement."

"Snob."

She laughed. "You're just jealous."

He sobered. "I am, a bit."

Mahree was startled. "I was kidding! What could possibly make someone like *you* jealous of *me*?"

Rob's dark eyes held hers. "You can talk to the Simiu, and try as I might, I can't even begin to catch up to you."

Mahree's cheeks grew hot, and she looked away. "I just practiced every day."

"So did I. I really tried. I'm not bad at languages, either. I speak and read Spanish and Russian, and I read German and Latin. But I'm not in your league. You've got a real gift."

"I only speak English and French," she protested. "And some Simiu. I may sound good to you, but half the reason Dhurrrkk' and I understand each other is that we're just used to our mangled pronunciation."

"Ah, but you're *bilingual*—you grew up speaking both languages, right?"

"Yes."

"The brains of bilingual people are configured differently than those of non-bilingual people." Mahree gave him a skeptical glance. "It's true."

"But on Jolie, most everyone is bilingual. Uncle Raoul and Paul are, too."

"But they're not young. The older you are when you try to learn a language, generally speaking, the less successfully you're going to master it. The brain gets less flexible, the older you get." He nodded thoughtfully. "That may be why you alone, out of all of us, really learned to communicate in Simiu."

She was silent for nearly a minute, then glanced back up, diffidently. "You mean that at least in that respect, I'm not ordinary?"

Rob raked a hand impatiently through his hair. "There's no

'least' about it, Mahree! You're an extraordinary person, and if you haven't realized it by now, you should. You're smart—Jerry said once that you've got better programming sense than most people who do it for a living. And now this ability to speak Simiu—'' He turned his hands palms upward, and shrugged. "Where in hell did you get the idea that you're ordinary?"

She shrugged. "Until this whole thing started, I was."

He studied her so closely that she blushed.

They were silent for a moment, while Mahree cast about for words. She was acutely conscious of his intent gaze. Finally, she said, too quickly: "Did *you* have a happy childhood?"

He shrugged. "Not bad."

She gave him a quick, annoyed glance. "I gave *you* a real answer."

Rob's mouth tightened, and he no longer met her eyes, "Okay, truth time. I didn't *have* a childhood—at least, not one that I can remember. I wasn't unhappy while it was happening . . . it was only later, when my sisters were growing up, that I realized *how* different I'd been, and resented what had happened. I blamed my parents for allowing it—though nowadays I realize that they probably couldn't have changed things. I was an awfully stubborn, single-minded kid."

"What did happen?"

"Before I was four I could read. Know what I used to spend my time poring over?"

"*The Prisoner of Zenda,*" Mahree guessed.

He gave a short, ironic chuckle. "No, that came later, when my original interests had flagged a bit."

"What, then?"

"The forty-third edition of Callander's *Surgical Anatomy*. I memorized the whole thing, image by image, and on my eighth birthday, they let me observe an operation. Picture a skinny shrimp of a kid perched on the seat in the holo-vid theater with all those medical and nursing students. My father was doing a heart-lung replacement. I thought I'd died and gone to heaven."

"No wonder you got through medical school so early."

"I had to stand on a box to work on my first cadaver. The table wouldn't go low enough. Luckily, I grew a head taller by sixteen, so when I got to assist on a real operation, I didn't need the box anymore."

She gave him a thoughtful look. "It bothered you, being short, didn't it?"

"Still does"—he smiled wryly—"though I've learned to laugh at short jokes. Self-defense."

"But didn't you ever play games, get into trouble like normal kids?"

"No. Not until organized sports. I was too small for football and basketball, but I was good at soccer. By that time I was in college."

"How old were you when you started?"

"Fourteen."

"That must've been difficult!" Mahree exclaimed.

"Outside the classroom, it was. My social life was nonexistent the first two years."

"Did that bother you?" Mahree asked, remembering her own adolescence.

"At first I was too absorbed in studying to care. Later, yeah, it did."

So you applied yourself to correcting that lack, and excelled at that, too, I'll bet, she thought ruefully. *How many lovers have you had? Have you ever been in love, the way I am with you?*

Aloud she said, "You obviously caught up, somewhere along the way. Nobody could call you a social misfit nowadays."

He chuckled. "My senior year I didn't feel like so much of a freak, because a few freshmen were younger than I was. My grade average dropped into the low nineties, because I even cut classes. Nights I should have been studying, I went out."

"But it was still easy for you?" Mahree guessed.

"Yeah." He frowned. "Too easy. That's why what happened with Simon hit me so hard. That and Jolie. I've finally reached my limit, and sometimes things aren't easy anymore. When you've always excelled without half trying, that really brings you up short, to fail when you were doing the best you could."

"You *didn't* fail on Jolie, Rob! You set yourself unreasonable expectations, there, if you expected to save every patient during the worst plague the human race has encountered in two centuries!"

Rob shook his head uneasily. "Okay, maybe I didn't fail on Jolie. I sure as hell did with Simon, though."

"So, all of us fail at one time or another. You have to learn to accept it, or you freeze up, and then you can't accomplish anything, because you're afraid to try."

"You're right, of course. But I've never been like most people, I guess. I'd better get used to it, since I've got a feeling that it's going to happen more often from now on." He spoke with a hint of sadness, but it was a removed, distant sort of sadness that was, oddly, more painful to witness than his agonized recrimination when Jerry died.

Mahree bit her lip, and did a few stretches, not daring to look at him. "So I'm learning that I'm not completely ordinary, and you're learning that you're not completely extraordinary," she murmured, straightening.

"That's about the size of it," he agreed.

"I guess that's fair," she mused, "but, Rob—your best is always going to be better than most people's."

"So is yours, Mahree," he said. She raised her eyes to find that he was staring at her intently again. Abruptly he cleared his throat, glancing away.

"Rob, what's wr—" she began, but broke off at the sound of Dhurrrkk's voice at the door.

"FriendMahree! HealerGable! I must speak with you!"

"What the hell?" Rob muttered as they hastily grabbed their voders. They bolted out the door.

"What is it?" Mahree demanded.

"Better that you see for yourself," Dhurrrkk' said, his crest quivering with some strong emotion. The Simiu dropped to all fours and loped ahead of them through the corridors so fast that they had to run to keep up. Both humans were panting when they reached the hydroponics section.

"What—" Mahree began, then the inquiry died on her lips as she looked inside. Her breath caught in her throat.

The Simiu vegetation was drooping, its formerly vivid emeralds and cobalts now sickly and pale. Leaves and stems were withering, turning brownish yellow. Only a few species appeared unharmed. "They're dying!" Rob cried.

He started to step into the area, but Dhurrrkk', his crest flattened, quickly barred his way. "No! Do not, HealerGable! Your presence may harm them further!"

"What?" Mahree and Rob obediently backed into the corridor. Dhurrrkk' followed them out, closing the portal behind him. "Further? You don't mean that we caused this," Mahree protested.

Her Simiu friend nodded slowly. "I am afraid so," he said, his crest still trembling with agitation.

"But—*how*? We haven't been in there! We haven't touched them. Rob?" She turned to her companion.

"Not I," he denied. "I haven't been in there."

"I did not mean to imply that the damage was caused by anything you humans have willfully done," Dhurrrkk' told them. "But we are in a small, closed environment. The air circulates throughout the ship, and it is constantly freshened by the hydroponics garden, where oxygen is produced by the plants. The water also recycles. I have checked the plants thoroughly, and everything is correct—the water, the nutrient solutions, the airmix, the lighting. Only one factor has been added to their environment—you two. And that must be what is now poisoning the most numerous species."

The doctor was staring at Dhurrrkk', comprehension dawning in his eyes. "It's possible," he said slowly. "Some trace element that we exhale . . . maybe something in the detritus from our skins that's contaminating the water . . . something about us is killing them. It took a while, but it's showing up, now. Oh, *shit.*"

Mahree turned back to the Simiu. "But . . . but we *need* those plants to replace the oxygen we use!" she protested.

Dhurrrkk' nodded silently, his violet eyes full of despair.

"How far are we from Shassiszss?" she demanded.

"Even if I were to boost our speed so that we have no auxiliary fuel supplies left, we face at least another ten days' journey," Dhurrrkk' told them.

"Well, we can close off unnecessary portions of the ship, leave only the bridge and galley," Rob suggested. "We can sleep on the floor of the bridge, you can sleep on the floor of the galley, Dhurrrkk'. If we do that, how long can we last?" he wondered.

"Don't forget that we brought all those breathing paks with us," Mahree said. "We can tap them for extra oxygen. And you must have some auxiliary air paks for your spacesuits, right, FriendDhurrrkk'?"

The Simiu nodded. "Yes, we must not forget them. How many breathing paks did you bring?"

"I think it was ten." Mahree glanced at Rob for confirmation. "And each has three hours' worth of air."

Dhurrrkk' nodded as he began muttering into his computer link. Mahree and Rob waited tensely.

Finally, the alien looked back up at them, his violet eyes bleak, his crest drooping low. "Calculations show that even with minimum oxygen usage on our part, it will not be enough," he said slowly. "At best, we have only enough air to last six days. If we do not locate another source of oxygen within that time, we will all surely die."

CHAPTER 12

♦

Countdown to Oblivion

Twenty-four hours of air left, now.

I'm considering casting caution to the winds and washing my hair. It won't be easy, but I really hate the thought of dying with an itchy scalp and dirty hair. Rob says we shouldn't move around much, so as to use as little air as possible, but if I sit still and do nothing, I start to hyperventilate. I don't even dare watch holo-vids, because I get too emotional.

Yesterday I watched Rob's film *Casablanca* (for the tenth time) and broke down completely. Fortunately, Rob and Dhurrrkk' were in the control room, so they didn't see. Concentrating on how yucky my hair feels is much safer than sitting here thinking about today being my last day alive . . .

Just reread those sentences, and they sound more than a little mad. Maybe I am. Every time I try to swallow, a big lump in my throat nearly chokes me. It's a sour, evil-tasting lump, and its name is FEAR. I'm terribly afraid . . .

Of what?

Death, of course. I never thought much about what, if anything, might happen After. One doesn't, at seventeen.

(Funny to think that I had a birthday those last days aboard *Désirée,* and nobody noticed. I didn't even remember myself, till the next day, and then what was the point in saying anything about it?)

I have to stop thinking, or I'll start screaming, and not be able to stop. If Rob and Dhurrrkk' can stay calm, so can I.

Actually, that twenty-four-hour figure isn't really the bottom line. We have about twenty-four hours until the last of the breathing paks Rob and I brought is exhausted. We can live off the air in these few compartments for several more hours. I suppose, at the end, we'll even break down and use the breathing paks on our suits, though at the moment we're committed to saving them, in case the alarm goes off.

It was Dhurrrkk's idea to plot a course that would bring us in and out of S.V. drive (wasteful of fuel, but fuel consumption is a secondary consideration in this extremity) long enough to take a spectroscopic reading of each system we reach. If the instruments detect a world with usable oxygen in its atmosphere, the alarm will sound.

We've been taking turns standing watch over the alarm, though the thing is so loud we'd hear it, even asleep. (Though none of us has been sleeping much. It's cramped on the bridge, where Rob and I sleep, and worse in the galley, where Dhurrrkk's been bunking. And, when you've only got a limited amount of time left, you're understandably reluctant to waste it sleeping. I've barely slept at all, these past two "nights.")

You may ask why we don't just pop into the nearest system's Oort Cloud (they all have them) and scoop up a few good-sized chunks of embryonic comets. They're made up mostly of ice, remember? Frozen H_2O?

We thought of that—but we're not aboard a mining ship. We have no grapples, no way of "scooping" up ice short of sending someone out in a suit. And none of the suits aboard have jet-paks. Even if they did, I doubt that any of us could maneuver around well enough in no-weight to accomplish anything worthwhile. Managing a jet-pak in space requires practice.

But that's beside the point. Rob remembered how one extracts oxygen from water through electrolysis, but we don't have the equipment, materials, or expertise to do it. We'd need to melt the ice, purify the water, then either salt the water, or (better) add an acid or a base to it, then run an electrical current through the resulting ionized solution. Then we'd have to collect the hydrogen (and do what with it? Pump it out into space, I guess). The other product of the process is oxygen.

If we were aboard *Désirée* and had Paul or Ray around, it

would be a cinch. But we don't. Believe me, the notion was tempting enough that we spent a whole day ransacking *Rosinante* to see what we might be able to cobble together.

Unfortunately, *Rosinante* is the Simiu equivalent of a luxury yacht, made for relatively short hops. It doesn't have *Désirée*'s labs and machine shops. And none of us is an engineer.

Shit.

I feel so guilty for dragging Rob along on this ill-fated voyage. At least Dhurrrkk' and I *chose* to risk our necks—but I shanghaied Rob.

It's a measure of Rob's unusual decency as a human being that he hasn't—by look or word—implied or said one thing to indicate that he blames me. In a way, it would be easier if he'd lose his temper and scream at me.

But we're all trying to stay calm. Hysteria increases respiration, which wastes oxygen.

This won't be my last entry. I'm going to do an official one, in lieu of a nonexistent log, so that anyone who finds *Rosinante* drifting will know what happened to us. I'll edit this journal and remove all the angst. I can't stand the thought of being laughed at for a lovesick adolescent, even if I won't be around to care.

But right now, I've made up my mind what I'm going to do. I'm going to go pour a cup of water over my head again. At least then I won't have to die with an itchy scalp.

"Rob, can I borrow your surgical scissors?"

The doctor looked up as Mahree entered the control room, where he and the Simiu sat staring morosely at the silent alarm.

"My scissors? What for?" he asked warily

"Don't worry, I'm not considering anything rash," she reassured him with a grim smile. "One of the hair bands on my braids is twisted. I want to cut it free."

Rob stared at her blankly. "Huh? Why?"

"Because I'm going to pour some water over my head. I can't stand it any longer, it's so itchy. My hair's so long that I can't wash it in that little basin . . . I wouldn't feel right using that much water anyway."

He located the scissors in his medical bag, then handed them to her. Mahree stood staring down at them, frowning. "What I really ought to do is cut it, then I could manage to wash it."

She turned on her heel and headed resolutely for the galley.

Cut off all that hair? Just to save water? Rob thought. *When we're going to die tomorrow, no matter what?* "Hey, Mahree!" he called, getting up and going after her. "Wait a minute."

She stopped at the entrance to the galley. "What?"

"Do you *want* your hair short?"

"Nooooo," she admitted, in a tone of reluctant honesty. "But it's silly to try and keep it long under these circumstances. I wouldn't feel right using the water it would take to wash it. Not to mention that it would be hard as hell to manage in that tiny basin."

"Not if you let me help," he pointed out. "I can use a minimum amount of water, and do it a section at a time. It won't take that much. Our *water* reserve is holding out fine. I hate to see you cut your hair off. It's so pretty, long."

Mahree blinked at him. "Really?" She blushed. "I mean, do you really think I should use the water?"

He smiled at her. "Everyone's entitled to one last fling, honey. Clean hair isn't much to ask. And I promise I'll use an absolute minimum."

She smiled back, gratefully. "Well . . . thanks. I really didn't want to hack it all off."

She unplaited her braids, grimacing at their lank, oily feel, then, as Rob located shampoo and a towel, she stooped over the little basin. The doctor filled a cup with icy water, then poured it over her head. She gasped. "Watch that," he said, mock-severely. "You used up three extra breaths."

Briskly, he began lathering her scalp, enjoying the way the soft strands slid through his fingers. "That feels soooo good . . ." She sighed with genuine pleasure. "This is awfully nice of you, Rob."

"Self-preservation," he said, pouring another cup of water. "If I'd stared at that damned alarm for another minute, I was going to lose it completely."

A hand-span at a time, he washed her heavy mass of brown hair, until it lay, a lank, tangled rope, between her shoulder blades, reaching past her waist. "There you go," he said. "All clean."

Mahree grinned at him as she wrapped the towel around her head, turban fashion. "It feels great. Thanks again."

Rob sat down on Dhurrrkk's bedding cross-legged, idly watching as she toweled the hair. When the moisture was squeezed out, she began combing it, pulling the thick rope over her shoulder and working up from the bottom, carefully separating the strands with her fingers before she combed them.

"How long?" she asked casually, after a while.

He checked his watch. "Twenty-three and a half hours."

"Exactly?"

Rob grinned at her. "Hardly. I'm not down to counting seconds."

"Yet."

"Yet," he agreed, sobering.

"Rob . . ." she began, then stopped.

"Yes?" he prompted gently. "What is it?"

Mahree couldn't look at him. She picked blindly at the last knot, obviously fighting tears. "If it weren't for me," she said thickly, "you wouldn't be in this mess."

"I asked to come," he reminded her, his voice even.

"I know," she said, finally running the comb the length of her hair without encountering any tangles. She tossed it back over her shoulder defiantly, then looked up at him. "But you ought to hate me. Oh, God, you ought to. I . . . deserve . . . it." Her voice broke, and she took a deep, gasping breath, covering her face with her hands.

Rob's heart went out to her. "Mahree . . ." Quickly he scrambled over to put an arm around her shaking shoulders. "You know I don't hate you. I could never hate you, kiddo."

She stiffened, then jerked away. When she looked at him, her eyes flashed angrily. "Dammit, Rob, will you *stop* calling me *'kiddo'*? You of all people should have some idea of what it's like to be talked down to because you're young! I'm an *adult*, not your kid sister! I have to fight to be treated with respect!"

Rob felt as shocked as if she had slapped him. "I didn't—" he began, then hesitated . . . thinking, remembering. "You're right," he muttered, finally. "I've been patronizing you right along, haven't I? I'm sorry. You have to believe me, Mahree, I didn't do it deliberately to hurt you."

Mahree ran the comb through her hair again, dividing the thick strands into three parts. "I'm sorry, too," she said in a muffled voice. "I shouldn't have let it get to me like this." She smiled wanly. "I guess I'm feeling the effects of having only twenty-three hours and whatever odd minutes to live."

"Come to think of it, they will be pretty odd," Rob agreed, but the attempted humor fell very flat.

She bit her lip. "At the risk of being morbid, what's in store for us? Honestly, will . . . will it be painful?" Her voice was almost steady.

"Not really," he said slowly. "Uncomfortable, but by the time it gets really bad, we won't care anymore. As the oxygen in here gets used up, hypoxia will set in, and we'll feel pretty good, actually . . . like we'd had a few too many. Then we'll just pass out and . . ." He shrugged, snapping his fingers. "In maybe five minutes, it'll all be over."

"I suppose that's reassuring," she said dryly, then she sobered. "Rob . . . can I ask you a favor?"

"Sure."

"Would you mind if I . . . hold your hand? At the end, I mean?" Hearing her own words, she gave a disgusted snort. "God, I sound like that cringing little seamstress at the end of *Tale of Two Cities*! Forget I asked."

"Hey, that's okay, I wouldn't—won't—mind," Rob said, and now *his* voice cracked. "It'd be comforting to me, too. But . . . Mahree . . . you told me to be honest. If you're thinking that you'll succumb first, you're almost certainly wrong."

She shivered, despite *Rosinante*'s heat. "Why?"

"Because Jolie has a lower oxygen content than Earth, and you've grown up used to breathing less O_2 than Terrans. Also, you're smaller than I am. The less body mass, the less oxygen required, generally. So hypoxia—that's oxygen deprivation, the stage where people get to feeling high—won't hit you nearly as quickly as it will me or Dhurrrkk'. The same for apoxia, oxygen starvation."

"Oh," she whispered. "Are you talking about just a few minutes difference?"

"Maybe," he said, carefully not looking at her. "Or it could be more . . . ten, fifteen minutes, perhaps."

"I couldn't take that," Mahree whispered. "I've seen friends of mine die before, during the Lotis epidemic. I nursed a couple of them, even, but . . . watching you and Dhurrrkk'—I just couldn't. Can you give me something when things get bad that will knock me out? Make me sleep?"

He nodded. "Yeah, I can. I will. Don't worry."

He yawned suddenly, then smiled. "Speaking of sleep, that's

the best suggestion I've heard so far. Best way to conserve our oxygen. C'mon.'' He held out his hand.

Mahree finished braiding her hair, then let him pull her up. Together, they went into the control room. "Time to sleep, FriendDhurrrkk'," Rob said, dimming the lights. "Conserve air."

The Simiu nodded. "I will see you soon, my friends."

In the cramped space beside the pilot's couch, Rob knelt, pulling their sleeping mats close together. "C'mon," he said again, stretching out himself, "lie down. You're worn out."

Reluctantly, Mahree lay down beside him. "It seems stupid to waste the time we've got left."

"We'll be *extending* the time we've got left," he pointed out. He reached over and took her hand, his grip firm and comforting. "We've hardly slept at all for the past forty-eight hours, so close your eyes . . ." He watched her face in the dimness. "That's it . . . relax . . ." Lowering his voice to just above a whisper, he kept up a soothing monotone. "Good . . . just let yourself drift . . . relax your legs, your shoulders . . . that's good, very good. Now you're floating, and that's good, too . . ." Her fingers slackened in his, her breathing slowed. "Good . . . relax . . . relax . . ."

He continued murmuring, watching her drift off.

Rob let his own eyes close. Her hand in his was the last thing he was aware off, as slumber claimed him . . .

Dhurrrkk' wailed, clutching his chest as it heaved, seeking air—but there was none. Mahree's face was contorted and purple as she, too, shrilled a high, keening scream. Both of them tumbled to the deck, thrashing convulsively, their mouths opening and closing, emitting that never-ending shrieking wail—

Rob jerked awake, carrying that last hideous dream-image before his eyes so vividly that it took him a moment to realize that it was, indeed, only a nightmare. And still the wailing shrilled, that insistent, nerve-wracking wail of—

—of Dhurrrkk's alarm!

He sat up, eyes wide. "Whatthe*hell*?"

Mahree was staring at him. "The alarm," she whispered, finally, in an agony of hope. "That's Dhurrrkk's alarm!"

He blinked at her uncertainly for several seconds. "Then that means . . ." he trailed off and grimaced. "I'm afraid to say it out loud, for fear I'm dreaming," he admitted.

"It means that we've found a world with an oxy-nitrogen atmosphere! It means that maybe we've got a chance!"

A slow smile spread across his face. "If I'm still dreaming, please don't wake me up."

"We're both awake," she said. "It's real . . . oh, Rob!" Impulsively, she flung her arms around him and hugged him hard. He returned her embrace so violently that the breath *whoosh*ed out of her lungs.

"Air!" he whooped, kissing her face ecstatically, forehead, cheeks, left eyelid, nose, then hugging her again. "Thank you, God—*air!*"

Her cheeks red with excitement, Mahree pulled herself out of his arms. "C'mon, let's turn off that thing, then wake Dhurrrkk'!"

"*That* rinky-dink little thing?" Rob exclaimed a few minutes later, as he took in the red dwarf occupying the middle of *Rosinante*'s main viewscreen. "Good grief, it's only 170,000 kilometers in diameter—barely bigger than Jupiter! I could pi—" He stopped abruptly at a look from Mahree. "I mean, I could *spit* on that star and put it out!"

Dhurrrkk' nodded. "It is indeed very small," he admitted.

"It's all we've got, so be nice," Mahree said absently, reading a translation of the Simiu characters on her computer link. "It's got two planets—one a frozen hunk not even big enough to be spherical, the other about six-tenths the size of Earth. That's the one with the atmosphere. It orbits the star at a distance of about four million kilometers, and it does not rotate, so it always keeps the same face toward its sun. Its year is a whopping fourteen hours."

"But I *am* getting definite readings of oxygen in its atmosphere," Dhurrrkk' pointed out, in defense of his discovery. "Not as high a content as we could have wished, perhaps, but at this point, we have no alternative."

"Can we breathe the air?" Rob asked.

"Unknown. We are still too far away to judge."

"When we get there, we'll have to land," Mahree said, still speaking Simiu. She had brought her voder along, but so far hadn't bothered to strap it on. "Can this ship perform an atmosphere landing, FriendDhurrrkk'?"

"It has belly-jets for landing. Whether I can pilot it to a safe set-down is another matter," the Simiu said, his expression rueful. "I have performed many docking maneuvers at space stations, and have landed at spaceports, but I have never set down on anything but artificial terrain."

"Won't the computers help?" Rob asked, watching Dhurrrkk's face. Ever since this trip had begun, he'd practiced making himself watch the Simiu when he spoke, rather than relying solely on his voder screen.

"Yes," Dhurrrkk' replied, "they will, but it will be my responsibility to locate a suitable spot for our landing."

"How soon will we achieve orbit?"

"Four hours," Dhurrrkk' told him. "That will not leave us much time, but that cannot be helped."

The doctor nodded. *I really am getting better,* he thought, pleased. *I can understand him pretty well now, when he speaks slowly and simply. Now if I can just get so I can **pronounce** the damned language . . .*

"I'm trying to hold myself back from getting excited," Mahree said quietly. "There's still so much that could go wrong. This planet's atmosphere could contain poisonous trace elements. The air may be so thin that it can't sustain us. The plants may not be something we can transplant to *Rosinante*'s hydroponics area. Hell, there may not even *be* any plant life."

Rob put an arm around her shoulders and gave her a quick, hard squeeze and a peck on the forehead. "Think positive, honey. This place represents our last chance."

He felt her body tense, then she relaxed within the circle of his arm. "It's not as though it can hear us, Rob," she said, with a wry smile.

"You never know," he said. "In one of my films there was this planet that was a huge sentient life-form, and when these hapless astronauts landed on it, it—"

"Spare me," she said, laughing. "You and your films—!"

Rob dropped his arm from Mahree's shoulders as he noticed that Dhurrrkk' was regarding both of them, his violet eyes thoughtful. "I am conscious of a change, here," he observed, at length. "I believe that I am detecting patterns of human pre-mating behavior I have viewed in your holo-vids. First the embrace, then the kiss, correct? If so, is this one of the occasions in which that activity is a precursor to mating?"

Rob opened his mouth to answer, choked instead, and hastily

put a hand over his mouth so he wouldn't laugh. He felt his face reddening.

Mahree colored, too, but handled herself with comparative aplomb. "No, I'm afraid not, FriendDhurrrkk'," she replied. "But it was extremely perceptive of you to notice when Rob hugged and kissed me. You are undoubtedly becoming your world's foremost expert on human behavior patterns."

Dhurrrkk's crest rose to its highest elevation. "You do me great honor, FriendMahree. Will you require privacy for any eventual activities, or are they, like your holo-vids, available for public viewing?"

Rob couldn't look at Mahree as she replied, with serene dignity, "In real life, privacy is the social rule, Dhurrrkk'."

"I understand," the Simiu said aloud in English, with, Rob thought, just a hint of regret.

"Not to change the subject," the doctor announced loudly, to extricate Mahree from any further discussion along such lines, "but I just realized I'm very hungry. Since we have several hours to wait, we might as well eat."

"But he *did* change the subject," he could hear Dhurrrkk' saying plaintively to Mahree as they left the control room. "When he said that he would not. Why would he say that?"

"It's an idiomatic expression, FriendDhurrrkk'," Mahree said, also in English, and Rob could hear her struggling not to break down and laugh. "I can't think of a way to explain it."

"A dirty joke?" Dhurrrkk' suggested, hopefully.

"Sort of," Mahree gasped, losing the battle and dissolving completely.

CHAPTER 13

♦

Twilight World

This is probably my last entry. Dhurrrkk' set us down fifteen minutes ago, and at the moment he and Rob are in the control room, checking the data from the flyovers. I'm waiting until it's time to suit up. There's not much oxygen out there. But we have to try, don't we?

I'm scared.

I'll be leaving my computer link and these journal cassettes in the airlock, which is the first place anyone who discovers *Rosinante* will enter. Unless they're Jerry's energy beings, of course . . .

That's assuming that this ship will ever be found, which is not a bet I'd care to cover. Instead, *Rosinante* will probably crumble into dust or rust away thousands or millions of years from now . . .

I'm leaving this account just the way I wrote it. Sometime in these past hours I came to realize that love is never something to be ashamed of feeling.

The sole UNIVERSAL TRUTH that I've learned in seventeen years is that truthful and accurate Communication is the MOST IMPORTANT thing in the cosmos. I used to think it was Love, but you can love someone and not understand them. Understanding (not necessarily acceptance) is *vital* in dealing with other people, whether those people are human, Simiu, Mizari, or energy beings.

Well, I'm out of time. To whoever finds this, in whatever language you speak, I extend a warm "Hello!"

And—
Good-bye.

Mahree stood in the control room door, wearing her spacesuit, its helmet tucked under her arm. She listened intently as Rob and Dhurrrkk' completed the atmospheric analysis of the chill little worldlet where *Rosinante* now rested.

"That's all very well and good," she broke in, interrupting their jargon-laden exchange impatiently after a few minutes, "but what's the bottom line? Can we *breathe* out there?"

Rob scowled at his link, considering. "Doubtful," he concluded. "At least, not for more than a minute or so. Nothing in the air can *hurt* us to breathe it, but the overall oxy level is like being on top of a high mountain, Earthside. The slightest exertion, and we'd pass out in short order."

"Could we breathe it while we're resting? Sit down and take off our helmets to conserve our breathing paks?"

"*You* might—and I stress *might*—be able to, for a short time, but I wouldn't risk either Dhurrrkk' or me trying it."

Mahree bit her lip. "What about the plants?" she said.

Rob shook his head, obviously bewildered. "I just don't know," he said. "It's an extremely peculiar situation out there. Certain locations have significantly higher concentrations of O_2 than others—but there's no consistent correlation between those oxy concentrations and the patches we identified as vegetation during our low-level sweep. Sometimes they coincide, sometimes they don't. We're not too far from one of the higher concentrations of oxygen, so we'll just have to take a look."

"How can there be higher concentrations of oxygen? Doesn't the gas dissipate into the atmosphere?"

"Sure—some. But this place has no tides, no weather. The temperature is a constant four degrees, just above freezing, and that doesn't vary, because there's no night. So there's no wind to move the atmosphere around. And oxygen is a comparatively heavy gas, so that when it's emitted under these circumstances, it tends to stay in one place, at least for a while." He glanced at his watch. "We'd better get going. Air's awasting."

Within minutes, the three explorers were ready. The doctor carried a sensing device to help them locate and analyze the local vegetation in their search for the O_2 concentrations.

"The gravity is low," he warned Mahree as Dhurrrkk' began

cycling the air out of the airlock into storage, where it could be reused. "About half a gee. Be careful."

"Does Dhurrrkk' know that?" she asked. The two humans could talk to each other, but there had been no time to adjust their suit radios to the Simiu wavelength. They could communicate sketchily by touching helmets and shouting, but that form of conversation had obvious limits.

"Yeah, he knows."

The outer doors split apart, then opened wide. Mahree stepped cautiously down the ramp, watching her footing, because the ramp was steep, and her feet had an alarming tendency to slip in the low gravity—gravity which felt doubly light, because she'd spent days now living at one and a half gee.

Finally she was standing safely on solid ground, free to look around. Mahree caught her breath with excitement, thrilled despite their desperate situation to actually be standing on an alien world. *I'm the first human to ever tread here,* she realized. *One giant step, and all that stuff.*

Slowly, searching for any patches of the vegetation that had so puzzled Rob, she rotated 360 degrees, staring avidly.

It was a bleak vista that met her eyes—cold, yet washed everywhere with a hellish scarlet illumination from the red dwarf overhead. The ground beneath her feet was hard, black-brown rock, with a thin, damp layer of dark grayish brown soil overlaying it. A dank red mist lay close along the ground, pooling deeper in any depressions. Mahree could see for a long way in most directions, because the ground, though rock-strewn and broken, was relatively flat.

She lifted her face to the sun, and her faceplate's polarizing ability automatically cut in—but the protection was hardly necessary. The light level was dim, about that of a cloudy twilight. *Dhurrrkk's going to be nearly blind,* she realized, and said as much to Rob.

"We'll have to keep him right with us," he agreed. "Will you *look* at that sun!"

"I'm looking," she said, awed. "It doesn't look small from here, does it?"

Overhead, the unnamed red dwarf dominated the cloudless sky, appearing five times the diameter of Sol or Jolie's sun, Nekkar (Beta Boötes). As it flamed dully in the deep purply red sky, it appeared almost close enough to touch; Mahree and

Rob could clearly make out solar prominences lashing outward from its disk.

"It probably flares every so often," Mahree said, remembering one of Professor Morrissey's astronomy lectures. "Let's hope it doesn't decide to belch out a heavy concentration of X rays while we're here."

"Let's hope it doesn't," Rob agreed fervently.

After a minute, Dhurrrkk' touched her arm, and Mahree came out of her reverie with a start. "We'd better go," she said. "We can't waste air just standing here gawking."

The three set off across the rocky ground, Rob in the lead, Dhurrrkk' and Mahree close behind him. Once the girl caught the toe of her boot on one of the multitudes of small, jagged outcrops, and stumbled badly, but her fall was slow enough that she was able to catch herself on her hands. *"Easy,"* Rob said, pulling her up one-handed in the light gravity. "One of these volcanic ridges could rip your suit. You okay?"

"Fine," she said, trying not to gasp with reaction to her near disaster. "You'd think walking in gravity this low would be easy, but it's not, the ground's so broken."

The explorers halted when they reached the little lake they'd charted during the flyby. Crimson mist obscured its surface, reflecting the light of the red sun. "How deep is that water? Any vegetation down there?" Mahree asked Rob, stepping cautiously onto the dark rocks of the "shore."

He examined his scanning device. "Not very deep. About two meters in the middle. And yes, there's plant life down there."

"Is it giving off oxygen?"

"Yes, but we can't use these plants, because the Simiu hydroponics lab, unlike *Désirée*'s, is set up for land-based vegetation. The tanks are way too shallow. Not to mention that I can't envision any way of hauling enough of this water aboard to support a significant amount of plant life. Even at one-half gee, water's *heavy.*"

They walked on, frequently having to detour around patches of the mist that were thick enough to obscure their footing, and skirting an occasional head-high upthrust of the black rock.

Finally, they reached the closest large patch of vegetation. The alien plants filled an entire shallow "basin" in the rocky surface, and were clumped together so closely they resembled thick moss. Each plant stood only a few centimeters above the soil that nourished its roots. The moss-plants were a dull dark green in color, with tiny, fleshy-thick "leaves."

His boots hidden by a knee-high patch of mist, Rob bent over to carefully scan the plants. After a moment, he shook his head.

"No O_2?" Mahree asked numbly.

"Some, but not enough. These plants photosynthesize, but . . ." he trailed off, then burst out, "they *can't* be the source of those higher O_2 levels I was reading!"

"How many of these moss-plants would we need to keep us going?"

"Half an acre of them," Rob said disgustedly. "Forget it."

Dhurrrkk' tugged on Mahree's arm, and she leaned over to touch helmets. After conveying the bad news, she straightened. "Okay, where's that higher O_2 concentration you mentioned, Rob?"

He consulted the instrument and pointed. "Thataway."

"Let's get going."

They trudged toward the area he had indicated. Mahree checked the homing grid displayed just above eye level in her helmet, and discovered that they were now well over a straight-line kilometer away from *Rosinante*. The strangely close horizon made estimating distances by eye difficult. She cast a swift, nervous glance at the gauge showing the status of her breathing pak. *Just about two hours left. The walking's so difficult that I'm using more air than I realized.*

The thought made her want to stride faster, but she forced herself to move deliberately, fighting off the sensation of a cold hand slowly tightening around her throat. *Fear uses up oxygen,* she told herself sternly. *Calm down.*

A few minutes later, as though he had read her thoughts, Rob said, "How's your air holding out?"

"One hundred and sixteen minutes," she said. "How about yours?"

"One hundred and eight," he said. "As we predicted, I'm burning my O_2 supply faster than you are."

"That means that Dhurrrkk' has a little more than ninety minutes left," Mahree calculated, her mouth going dry. "The Simiu breathing paks hold less than ours do, and Simiu lungs require more oxygen than human lungs. And we can't share our air with him, because our paks won't fit his suit couplings!"

"I know," Rob agreed bleakly. "Nearly half his air's gone.

Maybe we ought to tell him to go back to the ship and wait for us there, while we continue searching.''

Mahree shook her head. "Dhurrrkk' won't do it. We'd just be wasting time and air trying to convince him. He'd regard leaving us out here as being cowardly and dishonorable. I know that without even asking.''

"Well, then, we'll just have to allow enough air for all of us to make it back to *Rosinante*."

She licked her lips, trying unsuccessfully to moisten them. "What for, Rob?" Resisting the urge to slam her gloved hand against the nearest rock in frustration, she managed to keep her voice calm. "What's the point of that? We'd just be postponing the inevitable for a few hours. I'd rather spend our last minutes out here *trying*, than lying around the ship watching those final seconds tick by. I don't think I have enough courage to face that. Do you?''

Rob did not reply.

A few minutes later he abruptly halted, announcing, "Right in front of us are the O_2 coordinates I pinpointed earlier.''

Both of them hurried forward, then Mahree let out a low cry of disappointment. There was nothing to see.

Nothing.

Nothing but the bare, upthrust ridges of blackish rock, small, tumbled boulders, pebbles that lay nearly buried in a comparatively deep layer of the soil, and a growth of the fleshy-leaved moss-plants. The ubiquitous mist drifted as their feet displaced it, eddying away from them, then settled again.

Rob's voice filled her helmet, harsh with dismay. "But . . . but these are the right coordinates, I *swear* I didn't make a mistake! This is crazy! These are the same plants as before, but there aren't nearly enough of them to cause the O_2 concentration I measured just a couple of hours ago!''

"Is the oxygen level any higher, here?''

He consulted the instrument again. "The overall oxygen level is a little higher, but it's dropped considerably from what I saw earlier. I just don't understand it!''

Mahree felt sick with defeat. She bent over, staring intently at the ground. "These plants look funny," she observed, after a moment. "They're shinier than the ones we saw earlier, though they appear to be the same species.''

"You're right," he said. "That's odd.''

She walked slowly around, peering down at all the plants in the area. "They're all the same," she reported. "Could there be some kind of natural process going on that causes the change from dull to shiny, producing oxygen as it does so?"

Rob shook his head dubiously. "Maybe. That makes as much sense as anything on this crazy planet. But I don't see any agent that could be the cause of such a change. No other vegetation, nothing. It's also possible you know that these plants represent a different variety of the basic species. You know, like long- and short-stemmed roses—one type is naturally shiny, and the other is naturally dull."

"I've never seen a rose, except on a holo-vid," Mahree reminded him. *And it looks like I'm never going to see one, now.* Resolutely, she squelched that train of thought. "Look, Rob, we *have* to discover one of those patches that's still emitting O_2, so we can find out where the oxygen readings are coming from. I think we should search this entire area. Maybe your coordinates were just a little off?"

"Not a chance," he replied grimly. "I checked those readings four times, and then Dhurrrkk' verified them after me. But we might as well do as you suggest—there's nothing else we *can* do, except keep trying."

Mahree leaned over to touch her helmet to Dhurrrkk's, and explained what had happened. The Simiu nodded silently.

"I'll go first from now on. You watch the scanner, Rob," she said, beckoning them to follow her. Trying to choose the clearest path, she increased her pace until she was traveling at the fastest walk possible, given the broken ground.

The three explorers began circling around the area Rob's coordinates had indicated, searching for any sign of the mysterious higher-oxygen pockets. Dhurrrkk' gamely followed the two humans' lead, but Mahree knew that her Simiu friend was nearly blind in the dim light, and thus would be of little help.

Ninety minutes of air left, she noted, reading from her gauge, and had to clench her jaw against panic.

They kept going as the minutes slipped by, Mahree in the forefront, picking the smoothest path possible, Rob behind her, scarcely taking his eyes off his sensing device, and Dhurrrkk' bringing up the rear.

Eighty-two minutes.

Grimly, Mahree fought the urge to glance constantly at her air gauge; avoiding obstacles on the rocky ground required all her concentration. But every so often, she just *had* to look up.

Seventy-one minutes.

Rob's breathing sounded harsh in her ears. Mahree thought of what it would be like to have to helplessly listen to that sound falter and cease, and fought the desire to ask him how much air he had left. *You're better off not knowing,* she thought. *Keep your mind on your job.*

Fifty-four minutes.

Now there was no question of trying to head back for *Rosinante* and the few hours of air remaining aboard the ship. *Rob's taken me at my word,* she realized, grimly. *We're going to keep going until we drop in our tracks.*

She swallowed as she realized that Dhurrrkk' had little more than a half hour of air remaining. *Exactly how many minutes?* she wondered, mentally comparing the ratio, but losing track of the numbers in her growing panic. She tried to fight the fear, but it was like a live creature writhing inside her, gnawing at her mind, until she wanted to shriek and run away.

Calm, calm. You have to stay calm! Dhurrrkk's life may depend on you not losing your head! Breathe slowly . . . slowly. In . . . out . . . in . . . out . . . Gradually, her fear ebbed; she was able to control her breathing.

Seconds later, Mahree turned a corner around a low outcrop of rock, then halted so abruptly that Rob bumped into her. "Look! What are those things?"

"Damned if I know," he said, staring.

The ground before them was covered with the moss-plants, but lying among them, obscuring them in patches, were five large, thick, phosphorescent shapes. They shone white-violet in the red dimness and were roughly rectangular.

Each faintly glowing growth was a meter or so long by three-quarters of a meter wide. They were entirely featureless. The moment she saw them, Mahree found herself irresistibly reminded of a fuzzy white baby blanket her brother Steven had dragged around with him until it fell apart—these things were exactly the same size and shape, and even their edges were ragged, just like Steven's security blanket.

She turned eagerly to regard Rob as he scanned the patch. "Have we found the O_2 emitters?" she asked.

He shook his head, and even in the vacuum suit she could see his shoulders sag. "Negative," he said, in a voice that betrayed the fact that *he'd* experienced a flash of hope, too. "The oxy level's a little higher, here, true enough, just like in the shiny-leaved place, but these things aren't emitting anything. I scan no photosynthesizing capability at all—which fits. Look at their color."

Mahree walked out into the midst of the moss-plants, whips of red mist swirling around her boots. Feeling a strange reluctance to get too near any of them, she placed her boots with exaggerated care. "Are they plants?"

"No. More like fungi." Rob checked his readings again. "Actually, they share some kinship with lichens, too. They must derive nourishment from the moss-plants as they decay."

Mahree glanced at her air gauge and squared her shoulders. *Forty-nine minutes.* "We'd better keep going," she said.

Rob raised his hand to halt her. "Wait. I want Dhurrrkk' to stay here. This place is easily recognizable, and I've got its coordinates. You and I can circle around and wind up back here in fifteen or twenty minutes. Tell him to lie down and conserve his air. That'll increase his time by five minutes or so. Otherwise, he doesn't have a prayer."

"He'll never agree, Rob!"

"Try, dammit!" he insisted. "Tell him that if he insists on accompanying us until he drops, we'll just end up using the last of our air carrying him."

"That's a good point," she admitted. Kneeling beside the Simiu, Mahree touched her helmet to his, repeating Rob's plea.

The Simiu looked uncertain, then, slowly, he nodded and deliberately lay down in the midst of the plants, also being careful not to touch any of the phosphorescent growths.

Surprised, because she hadn't expected him to give in so easily, Mahree peered down into Dhurrrkk's helmet, trying to make out his features in the dim light. *He looks kind of funny,* she thought, worried. *Abstracted. Glassy-eyed. Could the Simiu equivalent of hypoxia be hitting him already? Or is he praying or something like that?*

Once more, she touched helmets. "Dhurrrkk', are you okay?"

"I feel fine, FriendMahree," the alien said remotely, as though he was listening to her with only part of his mind. "I promise that I will wait for you here."

• • •

As he followed Mahree away from the recumbent Simiu, Robert Gable couldn't resist a last glance back at the alien. *He's got about twenty-five minutes to live,* he thought, *give or take five minutes. And I've got twenty-eight minutes and forty seconds.*

"How you fixed for air?" he asked Mahree.

"Forty-five minutes and thirty seconds. You?"

"I'm okay," he replied. "Thirty-nine minutes, here."

Her voice was puzzled and suspicious in his radio. "But before, you were *eight* minutes less than me," she said. "You *gained* a couple of minutes?"

"It takes a lot more effort to lead out here than to follow," he said, using his most reasonable tone. "You're burning O_2 much faster now that you're going first."

She started to say something else, but Rob snapped, "Watch out! You nearly snagged your leg on that rock!"

"I did not!" She increased her pace a bit, and Rob struggled to match it without stumbling. "I hope Dhurrrkk' is okay," she muttered. "He looked sort of odd."

"If there's something wrong with him, there's not a damned thing either of us can do about it," Rob pointed out. "The only chance any of us has, now, is for us to locate the source of the oxygen emissions—pronto."

"And if we do?"

"Then you can take off your helmet, lie down, and wait there, while I use the last air in both our breathing paks to carry Dhurrrkk' back to the ship. Then he can take off and pilot *Rosinante* closer to the oxygen emissions source, and I'll come back and get you—then we'll both collect the plants."

"Why do I have to be the one that stays, while you go rescue Dhurrrkk'? Why not the other way around?" Mahree demanded irritably.

"Because you need less O_2 to breathe, and I'm stronger than you are," Rob replied calmly, forcing himself not to glance at his air gauge. "Dhurrrkk's no lightweight, even at a half gee."

"Oh. But how will you come back to get me if you use up the last of our breathing paks carrying Dhurrrkk' back to the ship?"

"I've got a two-hour supply of pure oxygen in the oxy pak in my medical kit. I can use it to recharge two breathing paks. Pure oxygen will last us longer than standard airmix. That'll give us each slightly more than an hour's worth of air."

"Oh," Mahree said again. After a moment, she asked hesitantly, "Rob . . . do you really think that plan will work?"

"No," the doctor said tightly. "I don't think it has a snowball's chance in hell of really working. But if you can think of anything better, I'm all ears."

Mahree had no response. Rob was relieved, because his powers of invention were drying up. He glanced at his air gauge. *Twenty-one minutes.*

Knowing full well that he would use up his air faster than Mahree, the doctor had decided before they left *Rosinante* that their only hope might lie in keeping her going as long as possible, so he had surreptitiously disabled the emergency broadcast unit in his suit. Otherwise, as his breathing pak ran out, she would have been warned as to his status. *Worrying about me running out of air would only make her use her own supply faster,* he thought, repressing a twinge of guilt. *But if by some miracle we both survive this, she's going to be **pissed** . . .*

Struggling to keep up the swift pace Mahree set, while checking the sensing device he carried, Rob had little time to note his surroundings. He knew from the location grid in his helmet that Mahree was leading them in a wide circle, gradually taking them back to the spot where Dhurrrkk' waited.

A flat, computer-generated voice suddenly spoke inside the doctor's helmet. "Automatic reminder to the occupant of this suit. You have fifteen minutes of air remaining. Fifteen minutes of air."

Fifteen minutes to live. I feel like Dorothy when the witch turns over that big hourglass. Fifteen minutes . . .

Rob found himself remembering how he'd arrived at this moment. Memories of his parents, his sisters, of medical school, and the Lotis Plague flicked through his mind like flat, grainy images from one of his antique black-and-white films. He grinned wryly as he followed Mahree, careful to keep glancing at his sensing device every few seconds. *So it's true, what they say—your life **does** flash before your eyes . . .*

"Automatic reminder to the occupant of this suit. You have ten minutes of air remaining. Ten minutes of air. You are advised to change breathing paks within the next five minutes."

Rob listened to Mahree's breathing over the radio, remembering the first day they'd met, the nearly instantaneous rapport between them; only she, of all the people aboard *Désirée*, had matched his own eagerness for making the First Contact—not because doing so would make them famous or rich, but because she, too, had an abiding belief that contact with extraterrestrial beings would be a Good Thing for the human race.

And then his own belief had wavered and nearly toppled . . . along with Raoul's and the rest of the human crew—and, to hear Dhurrrkk' tell it, the Simiu had lost faith, too. Only Mahree and Dhurrrkk' had managed to retain their belief in each other's continuing goodwill. Was that because they were so young that they hadn't had as much opportunity to have their hopes and ideals trampled?

"Rob, how much air do you have left?"

The doctor sneaked a glance at his readout. *Seven minutes.* "Seventeen minutes," he lied glibly. *There's nothing she can do about it,* he rationalized, repressing a stab of guilt for lying to her, *and worrying will just make her use air even faster. Our only chance is for Mahree to stay on her feet and locate those oxygen concentrations.* "How about you?" he asked.

"Twenty-seven minutes," she replied. "How far are we from Dhurrrkk'? He must be almost out of air by now."

"We're close," Rob said, checking the location grid. "Here, you carry this." *So I won't drop it or damage it when I fall . . .*

She took the instrument without question, and they pressed on. Rob watched her stride forward, forcing herself onward, though he knew she must be at least as tired as he was. *Not one complaint,* he thought. *Not even the suggestion of a whimper. I wonder if she'd concede that this counts as courage . . .*

The doctor experienced a sudden rush of affection for Mahree; they'd grown to know each other so well during this strange odyssey. Comrades, friends . . . in some ways, Rob mused, Mahree had become one of the closest friends he'd ever had. *Too bad I won't get to see her all grown up . . . she'd have been something, I'd bet.*

"Automatic reminder to the occupant of this suit. You have five minutes of air remaining. Five minutes of air. If breathing pak is not replaced within four minutes, hypoxia will commence."

Oh, shut up, he thought irritably. *There's not a goddamned thing I can do about it.* Acting on a sudden impulse, he twisted his head around and deliberately tongued the two manual controls that would shut off his suit readouts. The air gauge and location grid went dark. *There, that's better.*

Rob found himself thinking back over his relationships with women. He'd had liaisons with several while he'd been in school (and was proud that, after the affairs had ended, he'd remained friends with all of them)—but he'd never been *in love*.

If there's anything I regret, Rob thought, pushing himself after Mahree with dogged persistence, and realizing with a sinking feeling that he was beginning to gasp a little, and not from exertion, *it's that I never felt that way about—*

"There he is!" Mahree cried, as they caught sight of the moss-plant hollow and the phosphorescent growths. Dhurrrkk' lay sprawled among them, hands clutching his helmet.

"Is he breathing?" Rob asked, coming to a halt on the edge of the hollow. His voice sounded strange in his own ears, tinny and far away. *But I'm not far away, I'm right here,* he thought fuzzily. He tried to move forward, staggered a little, then recovered by bracing himself on a low outcrop of rock. He let himself slide down until he was sitting atop it. All his limbs felt pleasantly heavy, and his mind was beginning to float.

Like drifting off to sleep after a few beers, he realized detachedly. Somewhere a portion of his brain was shrieking "hypoxia!" but the word meant nothing. His head nodded, and his eyelids began to close.

"He's still alive!" Mahree's voice reached him, and Rob had to think hard to remember whom she was talking about. "But he's barely breathing!"

He forced his eyes open, saw Mahree crouched on the ground beside Dhurrrkk'. *I should get up,* he thought. *Go help . . .*

But his body would not obey him. Black spots danced before his eyes, and he closed them again because they were making him so terribly dizzy.

"*Rob!*" screamed a voice over his radio. The doctor opened his eyes again as he felt himself being shaken violently. He saw Mahree bent over him, her own eyes wide and terrified behind the faceplate of her helmet. "Rob, how much air do you have left? Don't lie to me this time, goddammit!"

He tried to tell her that he had turned off his readouts, that it was okay, it didn't hurt, but his tongue moved sluggishly, and no sound emerged. All the black spots coalesced suddenly into an all-encompassing darkness that swooped toward him like a live creature, enfolding him past all struggle.

With a sigh, Rob gave in and let it carry him away.

• • •

"Oh, God!" Mahree sobbed, catching her companion as he tumbled over bonelessly. "God, help me! Somebody please, please help me, someone—anyone!"

How much air does he have left?

She lowered Rob onto the moss-plants, beside Dhurrrkk', then turned him half over so she could read his breathing pak's outside gauge, located on his right hip.

The first thing she saw was the flash of the red "Low Oxygen Level—Condition Critical" reading on the indicator as it pulsed steadily in the dimness, then before her eyes it changed.

ZERO O_2, it read, in double-size letters. *APOXIA IMMINENT— CHANGE PAK IMMEDIATELY.*

Reflexively, then, Mahree looked up at her own display.

Eighteen minutes.

Eighteen long minutes . . .

I cannot sit here for eighteen minutes and watch them die, Mahree realized, feeling a calm that went beyond despair. *No way.*

Moving as quickly and surely as if she'd rehearsed the procedure hundreds of times, she detached Rob's used breathing pak in a matter of moments, and just as quickly replaced it with her own. *I'm sorry, Rob,* she thought, hearing the sounds of his gasping breaths ease as his oxygen-starved lungs took in the new air. *This is a rotten thing to do to you, love, but I just don't have the courage to let you go first. If we're both lucky, you won't even wake up.*

Then she sat back between the two prone figures, and, picking up Rob's gloved hand, held it in her lap between her own two. *I've got maybe ninety seconds' worth of air left in my suit,* she thought, still calm. *How should I spend them?*

Her early religious training argued that she ought to pray, but the only prayer Mahree could remember at the moment was the one with the line about, "If I should die before I wake."

Talk about stating the obvious, she thought, with grim amusement. *No, I guess praying is out . . .*

As she sat there, waiting, Mahree found that she was fighting a growing urge to take off her helmet.

It's the hypoxia, she thought dazedly. *It must be. The first thing to go is judgment.*

A conviction that if she would just remove her helmet, everything would be all right filled her mind. Mahree glanced around, seeing the phosphorescent growths gleaming weirdly in the sanguine light. *What's happening to me? My mind feels as though it's not mine anymore!* By now she was panting, suffocating, her lungs laboring as they strained frantically to gasp in the last vestiges of oxygen her suit air contained.

Darkness crouched on the edges of her vision, an expanding, hungry darkness without end. But the darkness would go away if she would just get rid of her helmet . . .

Mahree blinked, dazed, and realized that, without being aware of her actions, she'd released the fastenings of her helmet, and now had both hands on its sides, preparatory to twisting it, then lifting it free of her shoulders. The urge to remove it was a driving imperative within her, now, a command that she had no strength left to fight.

What am I doing? she wondered frantically as she twisted, breaking the helmet's seal. She was in agony now, her lungs stabbing fire as they rebelled against the surfeit of carbon dioxide. *Oxygen!* something deep within her mind was insisting. *There will be oxygen! Take the helmet off!*

With a final, lung-tearing gasp, Mahree tore her helmet free, dropping it onto the moss-plants beside her. Cold, moist atmosphere smote her sweaty face like a blow. As blackness flowed across her vision, she inhaled deeply . . .

Slowly, the blackness began to recede.

Moments later, Mahree realized that she was crouched on hands and knees between Rob and Dhurrrkk', her head hanging down, and that she was *breathing*.

Oxygen! she thought, hardly able to believe this wasn't some dying hallucination. *Something here is emitting oxygen!*

A strong sense of affirmation filled her, affirmation mixed with concern. Mahree hastily groped for the fastenings of Dhurrrkk's helmet. Her gloved fingers couldn't grasp the alien shapes, and, with a sob of impatience, she unsealed her gloves, ripping them off. She fumbled again at the Simiu's helmet, and found, to her astonishment, that the seals had already been released. But the helmet was stuck; she had to use all her strength and leverage to twist it free. Finally it gave.

Seconds later, she had rolled the Simiu onto his back. She could not tell whether he was breathing, or whether his heart was still beating.

"Dhurrrkk'!" she yelled, then slapped his face.

When he did not respond, Mahree hastily scuttled around him until she was kneeling facing his feet, then she grasped his chin and pulled the alien's head toward her, tilting it back. His jaw opened, and she peered into his mouth to check the location of his tongue. It was hard to tell in the dimness, but she *thought* she now had a clear airway.

Cupping both hands hard around his muzzle to seal his mouth shut, Mahree inhaled a deep breath of the blessedly oxygenated air, then she bent, placed her own mouth tightly over his nostrils, and blew as hard as she could.

First she gave him four quick, hard breaths to deliver an initial jolt of oxygen, then she tried to settle into a regular rhythm. Mahree *thought* she felt the sense of resistance that meant she'd achieved a proper airway and seal, but she couldn't be sure.

Darkness gathered again at the fringes of her vision as she continued to suck in air, then blow it hard into the unmoving alien's nostrils.

Come on, Dhurrrkk'! she thought, *I'll pass out if I keep this up much longer, so come* **on!**

As Mahree dizzily raised her head for the next gulp of air, she started and barely prevented herself from recoiling violently. A hand-span away from Dhurrrkk's head lay a spectrally glowing, faintly pulsing mass.

My God, it's the baby blanket! It **moved!**

She missed half a beat, then resolutely inhaled again and blew. Her dizziness returned, but as she snatched a quick gasp for her own lungs, it abated. *That fungus* **has** *to be what's giving off the oxygen,* she thought, with sudden certainty. *And right now it's giving off extra oxygen, as if it knows how much I really need it! But that would mean that it's—*

Beneath her fingers, Dhurrrkk's muzzle twitched. *Right! That's it!* she cheered him on, drawing in another lungful of oxygen-rich air. She blew again, and this time when she turned toward the blanket to gulp air, she unmistakably felt a faint tickle of warm exhalation against her cheek.

Another breath. This time she *saw* his exhaled breath steam in the cold, damp air. Another breath . . . and yet another . . .

Dhurrrkk' abruptly gasped, twitched, then gasped again. *He's breathing!*

Mahree hovered, ready to resume the artificial respiration if necessary, but the Simiu no longer needed her help. Soon Dhurrkk's violet eyes opened and focused on her.

"Do not try to move, FriendDhurrrkk'. You passed out, but now that we have air, you will be fine," Mahree managed to say, though her abused throat rebelled more than usual at the Simiu syllables. "Just lie still, please. I must check on Rob."

She turned around to regard the doctor, then glanced at the breathing pak's external gauge. *Fourteen minutes.* She shook her head and looked again. *Fourteen minutes? I don't believe it! All that, and it's only been **four** minutes?*

Hastily, she pulled off his helmet, then disconnected the airflow from the breathing pak to conserve the remainder. Rob did not stir. Mahree pulled up an eyelid, then touched her fingers to the pulse in his throat. *He's okay . . . just out cold.*

She smiled as an idea occurred to her, then, after making sure Dhurrrkk' wasn't watching, she bent over and kissed her unconscious companion lingeringly on the mouth. "Call it my fee for saving your ass, you oh-so-noble bastard," she muttered, remembering how he'd lied to her about how much air he had left.

Then, grasping his limp form beneath the arms, she dragged him over the moss-plants until he, too, was lying with his face close to the phosphorescent growth. "Here, Blanket," she gasped, "you can give *him* some oxygen, too. Please."

Then she sat down, gazing wonderingly at the fungus-creature. Their savior.

*When Rob scanned them earlier, they weren't emitting any oxygen. But when we were in danger of dying, they—or this one at least—started to emit it. And, just when I was getting ready to pass out, the creature moved closer, and gave off additional oxygen. That **has** to mean that—*

Mahree wiped cold sweat off her forehead, then licked her lips nervously. *That's impossible! This is a **fungus,** one of the simplest forms of life around! Don't be crazy, Mahree!*

She bent over, peering closely at the faintly shining growth. It was completely featureless, except for millions of short, threadlike cilla on its top-side. She lay down on her side amid the moss-plants, then squinted up at the fungus's underside. *It moved, it must have. How the hell can it move?*

The blanket's bottom side was covered with tiny appendages nearly the length of her little finger. They moved constantly, rippling over the moss-plants like minuscule tentacles. "So *that's* how you get around," Mahree muttered.

Scrambling back up to hands and knees, she cautiously inched closer to the phosphorescent creature, until her nose was only a hand-span away. "Hi, Blanket," she said, feeling ridiculous—*I'm talking to a fungus? I must have cleared my jets!*—"My name is Mahree Burroughs. I really appreciate your helping us out, just now. We desperately needed that oxygen. I hope you folks don't suddenly stop emitting it." She shook her head. "I don't know why I'm talking. You don't have ears, so you can't possibly hear or understand me, can you?"

Slowly, the edge of the phosphorescent growth lifted clear of the moss-plants, extending itself toward her face.

Mahree couldn't help it—she let out a startled yelp and jerked back. Her heart slammed in her chest. Biting her lip savagely, she steadied her breathing, forcing herself to inhale and exhale lightly and evenly. There wasn't sufficient oxygen in the hollow to sustain her if she hyperventilated.

Maybe it was just exhibiting some kind of involuntary reflex in response to movement? she thought, watching the baby blanket settle back down onto the moss-plants.

Slowly, she leaned forward again. "If you can understand me, Blanket, *don't* move. Stay still, okay?"

Mahree moved so close that her nose nearly brushed the blanket's side, but the phosphorescence did not stir.

"Ohhh-kay," she muttered. "If you can understand me, Blanket, please move *now*."

The edge of the creature rippled, then rose until it was a full hand-span above the moss-plants.

"Holy shit," Mahree gulped. "I was right. You're *sentient*."

Again the sense of affirmation filled her mind.

"And telepathic, right? You can make what you're thinking and feeling go from your 'mind'—or whatever equivalent you've got—into mine?"

Affirmation.

A human groan interrupted her "conversation." Mahree turned to see that Dhurrrkk' was sitting up, holding Rob's hands, and that the doctor was stirring. "Excuse me a moment, please, Blanket," she said. "I must check on my friend. I will return."

Affirmation.

Mahree hastily crawled over to put a hand on Dhurrrkk's shoulder. "FriendDhurrrkk'," she said. "How do you feel?"

The Simiu put a hand on his forehead. "There is pain here," he said. "But otherwise I am fine."

"Just promise me you'll take it easy for a while. You were pretty far gone."

"I promise, FriendMahree." The Simiu's violet eyes were full of emotion. Slowly, minus his customary ease and grace, he reached over to grasp her hand. "You gave me your own breath, so that I could live," he said, switching to her own language. "I will be forever grateful, my friend. We are honor-bound, you and I. For as long as I may live, your honor and your life will be as important to me as my own."

"Dhurrrkk' . . . " Mahree tried to think of something to say, but words failed her. Instead, she gripped his six-fingered hand hard, nodding.

He motioned to Rob. "Honored HealerGable is awakening."

Mahree hastily turned around, to find the doctor lying there with his eyes open. "Hi," she said softly, bending over him. "How are you feeling?"

"I'm *breathing,*" he whispered, his eyes filled with profound bewilderment. "Why am I still alive?"

"Because we've found the source of the oxygen emissions, Rob," she told him. "And a lot more besides."

"Huh? You located one of the O_2 sources?"

"Yes," she said, seeing that he was still weak and disoriented. The rest of her news could wait.

He put out a hand. "Are you *sure* you're really here?" he mumbled, uncertainly. "I'm not hallucinating?"

For answer, Mahree took his gloved hand, unsealed it, pulled off the covering, then grasped his bare fingers tightly. "I'm really here," she said. "Feel."

"Feels good," he mumbled, smiling. "Squeeze tight." After a moment, he shakily sat up, then looked at the Simiu. "Honored Dhurrrkk', I'm glad to see that you're all right."

The alien made the formal greeting gesture of his people. "Honored Healer Gable," he said in English, with a twinkle, "I am pleased to observe the same about you."

The doctor shook his head, confusion filling his eyes. "But I don't understand how we got here—wherever we are. I was out of air. I must've passed out." He glanced down at his side.

"*Waitaminit!* This says I've got twelve minutes left on this pak." He looked back up, glaring at Mahree. "You switched breathing paks, didn't you? Gave me the last of your air?"

"It was the least I could do, after you lied to me," she said acerbically. "One dirty trick deserves another." She returned his glare with interest. "And if you dare to tell me that it was for my own good, you're going to find yourself stretched out on these damned moss-plants again."

"I knew you'd be pissed," he mumbled, obviously deeply touched by his discovery of the switched breathing pak. "But I didn't figure I'd live to hear about it. Forgive me?"

Rob sounded so uncharacteristically meek that Mahree had to laugh. "Let's call it even."

The doctor glanced around him, and his eyes widened as he recognized their location. "Hey, this is the same place as we left Dhurrrkk'!" He scratched his head. "Now, let me get this straight. We came back here to get Dhurrrkk', only this time there was oxygen in this hollow? But how?"

"Thank *them*," Mahree said, pointing to the blanket-creatures. "They're the things that have been emitting the O_2."

"*Them?* The fungi?" He blinked. "That's impossible . . . Crazy. They can't even photosynthesize."

"You ain't *seen* crazy, yet. Brace yourself, Rob. They're *sentient*. We've just made a First Contact."

He stared at her in silence, no expression on his face. "Sentient," he repeated, finally.

"They *are*," Mahree insisted. "They knew we needed oxygen, so they convinced me to take off my helmet, so I could breathe. And when I'd taken off, this one"—she pointed to the closest blanket-creature—"crawled over just so it could give me extra O_2 when I was giving Dhurrrkk' artificial respiration."

He hesitated. "Uhhhhh . . . that's hard to believe," he said, finally, using a carefully neutral tone. "Are you *sure?*"

"Honored Mahree is correct," Dhurrrkk' interjected, in English. "Before I lost my awareness of my surroundings, I was conscious of something contacting my mind, something that touched and questioned with intelligent purpose. It instructed me to take off my helmet, but I was unable to comply."

"That's because it was stuck," she told him.

Rob stared at both of them. Then he looked down at the blanket. "You're telling me this *thing* is sentient," he said, in a this-can't-be-happening-to-me tone of voice. "*This* thing"— he pointed—"this phosphorescent patch of fungus?"

"It's not a *thing*, it's a *person*, Rob. Mind your manners," Mahree admonished. "Watch, I'll prove it."

Turning back to "her" blanket, Mahree ran through the same demonstration that she had earlier. Finally, she said to the being, "This is my friend, Robert Gable—Rob, as he's called. This is what he looks like." She glanced at the doctor's face. "And this is my friend Honored Dhurrrkk'." She looked at the Simiu. "Now, if you don't mind, Blanket, I'd like you to move over and stop in front of Rob, so he'll know for sure that you can understand me."

With surprising speed, the alien creature crawled unhesitatingly over to Rob, stopped, then raised one edge into the air and waved at him.

The doctor paled as he stared at the being, eyes wide, then suddenly he bent forward until his forehead rested on the moss-plants before him. "Good grief, Rob," Mahree exclaimed, "you don't have to *pray* to it! Just say 'hello'!"

He drew several long breaths. "I'm not praying, you idiot," he said crossly in a muffled voice. "If I hadn't gotten my head down, I would've fainted. Give me a break, sweetheart. It's been a long, hard day."

After a minute Rob sat back up, his color much improved. "I'll be damned," he whispered softly, eyeing the fungus-being. He cleared his throat. "How do you do, uh, Blanket? It's a real pleasure."

Mahree concentrated, and received a clear sense of inquiry. "It's telepathic—or something—" she said. "Right now, it wants to know about us. How we got here."

"It is asking me the same thing," Dhurrrkk' said.

Trying to be as clear and simple as she could, Mahree thought slowly, deliberately, of how they had come to this world, aboard *Rosinante,* and why. She tried to make her images of the ship as vivid as possible, knowing instinctively that the creature before her could have no concept of technology or artificial constructions.

Finally, she turned to Dhurrrkk'. "Did you tell it?"

"Yes," he said. "As clearly as I could. Communication with the being is growing easier for me, the more I do it."

Mahree felt a prickle of envy. "It's still pretty hard for me," she admitted.

Rob was watching them. "I can feel it now, too," he said. "A sense of inquiry, and curiosity, right?" When they nodded, he continued, "But it's sure nothing like what Great-Aunt Louise used to do. She spoke in words, except they were silent."

"Maybe Blanket can learn words, eventually," Mahree said. "At first it just communicated faint impressions. Now they're getting stronger."

"It would like to help us," Dhurrrkk' announced suddenly.

"It already *has* helped us," Rob said. "Though I have to admit that it might have been kinder if it hadn't interfered when we passed out. Spending the rest of my life here in this hollow, while we slowly die of thirst, isn't a very appealing prospect."

"No," Dhurrrkk' said. "It is giving me images, now. It thinks it knows a way."

Mahree felt an absurd sense of abandonment as she realized that "her" blanket was now communicating most effectively with the Simiu. *Don't be stupid,* she thought sternly. *It obviously has discovered that a Simiu brain is easier for it to reach.*

She and Rob waited as the Simiu sat there, an abstracted expression on his face. Finally, he raised his violet eyes to theirs. "I have learned something about these beings. Each of these creatures is very, very old, and each is intelligent. Mostly, they are not greatly interested in much outside of pursuing their own obscure musings, mental games, and philosophical reflections. However, the one that Mahree calls 'Blanket' is different. For one thing, it is younger—perhaps only a million or so of my years old."

Mahree and Rob gasped sharply. "A *million* years old?" she repeated, and the Simiu nodded soberly.

"Blanket is far more interested in external stimuli and events than its companions. It is intrigued by the notion of our ship, and traveling through space. It likes us. It does not want us to perish, and it is willing to help us safely reach our destination. If we would like it to, Blanket has volunteered to join us aboard *Rosinante,* and provide us with oxygen. In return, we must promise to bring it back here, when it asks to be returned to its own world."

"Can it give off that much oxygen?" Rob said skeptically, after he'd spent a moment assimilating the Simiu's words. "Doesn't it need its oxygen for itself?"

"No, the blankets themselves require very little oxygen. It is a by-product they produce during digestion. It has no part in their breathing process."

They fart oxygen? Mahree thought, wildly, and giggled shrilly before she could stop herself. Rob reached over to put a steadying hand on her shoulder.

"We will need to provide Blanket with native rock and moss-plants, sufficient to allow it ample nourishment for the duration of our journey," Dhurrrkk' concluded.

"Well, if it tells us how much it needs, we'll be happy to do that," Rob said. "But there's just one thing. How the hell do we get out of this hollow, and back to *Rosinante?*"

"Blanket has asked its companions to assist, and they have agreed. They think their companion foolish for wishing to depart this world in order to aid us," the Simiu paused, then continued, as he evidently received additional information, "but none of them wish to see us perish. As long as they can remain here, the others are willing to help us reach the ship."

"How do they propose to help us?"

"You will see. Please remain still. They mean no harm."

Rob started as two more of the creatures stirred, then began moving across the moss-plants toward them.

Mahree's "Blanket" began crawling back toward her. She felt a moment of pleased satisfaction that it had evidently elected to return to her instead of staying with Dhurrrkk', then the creature moved past her, out of her line of sight unless she turned her head. *What is it going to do?*

Mahree swallowed hard as she both heard and felt something brush against the material of her vacuum suit, then the front collar of the suit was pressed against her throat as something heavy begin pulling itself up her back. She clenched her fists, squeezing her eyes shut, as Blanket slowly inched its way up. *It's saving your life,* she thought, repeatedly. *That's not a fungus crawling up your body, it's a* **person**. *A good, kind person. It's saving your life . . .*

Finally, the creature lay over her shoulders and down her back like a phosphorescent cape. At the extreme edge of her peripheral vision, she caught movement, then two glowing narrow "fingers" appeared as Blanket extruded two corners across her cheeks.

Mahree shivered, forcing herself to sit quietly. She closed her eyes as she felt the cold, admittedly damp substance of the alien being creep across her skin, until both pseudopods met, linking together across her upper lip.

She opened her eyes to find Rob staring down at the phosphorescent mass moving toward him. The doctor was chalky pale, and runnels of sweat coursed down his face. He was trembling violently.

"Rob!" she said sharply. *"Rob!"*

Slowly, he looked up. "Don't pull a Simon Viorst on us, Rob! They're helping us, just keep telling yourself that."

The doctor took several deep breaths, then finally nodded. A touch of color reappeared in his lips. "Okay. Don't worry about me, honey. I'm okay now."

He sat still as the phosphorescent mass crept slowly up his back. "I just wish," he said, and the control he was exerting over himself was palpable, "that I hadn't watched that nineties version of *The Puppet Masters* so many times. Remind me to show it to you if we ever get home."

Mahree drew a deep breath of relief, then picked up her helmet and gloves. "Everybody ready?" she said, standing up. She discovered that, even with her head above the level of the hollow, she was breathing easily—the O_2 level was no thinner than what she'd experienced camping in the mountains on Jolie.

"Ready," Dhurrrkk' said, handing Rob his helmet to carry. His blanket-creature was draped over his neck and back like a second, glowing mane.

"Ready," Rob said. "Let's rock."

"Rock?" echoed Dhurrrkk', as the three blanket-caped explorers picked their way out of the moss-plant hollow. "We must gather a number of rocks, true, along with harvesting the plants, but don't you believe, FriendRob, that we would be better served to do that closer to our ship? Rocks are heavy to carry."

"Uh . . . yeah," Rob said, giving Mahree a wink, and speaking with some difficulty because of the pseudopods linked across his upper lip, "you're right, FriendDhurrrkk'. Rocks *are* heavy."

CHAPTER 14

◆

Doctor Blanket's Miracle Cure

People are strange.

Here it is, almost exactly one week since I sat there on Avernus (that's what we named the little planet; it's a classical name for one of the gateways to the underworld), thinking that I was going to die within the next minute. After an experience like that, one could reasonably expect that I'd spend all my subsequent minutes just being grateful to be alive, *n'est-ce pas?*

WRONG. Instead I'm so teeth-grindingly jealous of my best friend that I can hardy think straight!

Why? Because Dhurrrkk' can "talk" easily with Doctor Blanket, and I can't.

Until last week I thought I'd discovered my "something special." Out of all the humans aboard *Désirée*, I was the best at communicating with the aliens. For the first time in my life, I excelled, I was *unique*.

Not anymore.

The blanket-creature (whom Rob dubbed "Doctor Blanket" because just "Blanket" sounded disrespectful) is safely ensconced in the Avernus-adapted portion of the hydroponics lab, contentedly undulating its way amid clumps of the dull-leaved moss-plants we transplanted, and piles of its native rock, absorbing nutrients and "flatulating" a marginal level of oxygen—enough to keep us alive, but we can't exert ourselves.

It turns out from Rob's tests that Avernians derive most of

their nourishment from a non-sentient variety of fungus that grows on the leaves of the moss-plants, which they cultivate for food. In addition, they also require certain trace elements that they get from breaking down minute amounts of the native rocks. One by-product of this particular digestive process is oxygen!

Rob's been having a wonderful time trying to figure out the Avernians' physiology. He says that in some ways they resemble both Ascomycetes (bread molds, truffles, and such) and Basidiomycetes (mushrooms, bracket fungi, and their ilk). They're multinucleate and without internal cell boundaries, and their bodies are covered with a semi-rigid wall composed of a cellulose-akin material. He also told me that the blankets could be regarded as "the culmination of the coccine state in protistan evolution," but I didn't have the energy to ask him to translate that into English.

He says that each of multitudes of "nuclei" within the creature contain huge numbers of tiny interlocked "threads" of some kind of organic material he'd never encountered in that molecular arrangement before. He thinks that these millions of subnucleic "threads" serve the creature in the same way our brain cells serve us.

Apparently the blankets reproduce (extremely rarely because they're so long-lived) by consciously releasing spores as they cultivate their moss-plant patches. They really *are* asexual, though it bothers me to call Doctor Blanket "it." Seems rather flippant to address such a wise, kind being as though it were an inanimate object.

We've had to make environmental changes to accommodate our Avernian benefactor. White light could literally burn it, so we creep around in a dim reddish twilight, except when we're in the control room with the door tightly sealed. Doctor Blanket is uncomfortable in warm air (in contrast to many types of terrestrial fungi), and the extra gravity bothered it, so Dhurrrkk' turned the ship's temperature way down, and reduced the gravity to one-half gee.

So now, instead of being too hot all the time, I'm *cold*. We wasted so much fuel during our search that we can't afford to use the extra power it would require to maintain different temperature levels on the ship. Besides, we can't expect Doctor Blanket to spend all its time cooped up in the lab.

Incidentally, my dream has come true . . . I'm finally sleeping with Rob. Only problem is, I'm sleeping with Dhurrrkk', too!

We all cuddle together for warmth each "night"—isn't that cozy? We make a snug heap of flesh and fur on the deck of the control room. Rob calls us the S.P.W.S.P.—the Society to Preserve Warmth among Somnolent Primates.

It's so cold that Rob and I can barely stand to wash our hands and faces, much less sponge ourselves off with that icy water. Hypothermia is a constant threat—especially for Dhurrrkk', who's used to a warm climate.

Fortunately, *Rosinante* carried lots of the woven comforter mats in its small crew dormitory, so we pressurized that area long enough to drag the things out. Then, using Rob's surgical scissors and some resin-like material Simiu use in emergencies to "solder" electronic equipment into place, we fashioned garments for each of us, topping them off with long, hooded robes.

Rob says we look like elderly medieval monks as we totter around in the red-tinged darkness, gasping if we exert ourselves too much—except, of course, that in normal light our "robes" would resemble an accident in a paint factory.

Which would *you* rather do, freeze or suffocate? And, to top it all off, we're running short on human food, since we have to eat more to keep our body temperatures up. Dhurrrkk' assures us that the Mizari, with their advanced bio-sciences, will be able to duplicate human food if presented with some samples, and I hope to hell he's right.

This has been such a *fun* trip!

At least we only have about six days' journey left to Shassiszss. We're going slowly, to conserve fuel.

Maybe if I work harder on "listening" to Doctor Blanket, I can communicate with it better. The Avernian is very wise. It could teach me a *lot* if I can only learn to *talk* to it!

Mahree stopped short when she saw Dhurrrkk', bundled in his crude "robes," squatting outside the hydroponics lab. He looked up, saw her, and an anticipatory twinkle brightened his violet eyes. Beneath his hood, his crest rose straight up. "Hello, Mahree. We were just going up to the control room, so Doctor Blanket can 'see' the stars, using the eyes within my mind."

It took Mahree a second to understand the reason for the alien's expression of pleased expectation, then she did a double-take. "Dhurrrkk'!" she gasped. "Your English! It was so . . . so *fluent!* How did you manage that?"

"It was Doctor Blanket," Dhurrrkk' said, no longer trying to conceal his excitement. "When I was practicing my English and my Mizari this morning, it was 'listening in.' It asked me why I was not utilizing all the speech-knowledge areas of my brain, so my thoughts could travel more rapidly between different languages. I replied that I was not aware that I had *not* been using all my language capability. Then Doctor Blanket asked me if I would like to be able to fully utilize those areas—so of course I said 'yes.' "

Dhurrrkk' paused, then switched effortlessly to the sibilants of the Mizari language. "One moment I was sitting there, then it was as though a tingling darkness crept across my mind. I blinked, and when I could see again, I found that I could now *think* in English! And in Mizari! Somehow, the Avernian must have altered the neural paths between my memory and my speech centers!"

The Simiu's new fluency was little short of miraculous. He still had problems with pronouncing certain words, difficulties that were caused by his facial structure and tongue placement, and his accent when he spoke English remained thick and lisping, but the hesitations caused by his having to translate from one language to another were gone.

"What about talking with the blanket?" Mahree demanded.

"Doctor Blanket's thoughts also became easier to grasp—images, words, everything!"

"Oh, Dhurrrkk'! I'm so *glad* for you!" Mahree reached over to hug her friend. His powerful arms tightened around her as gently as if she were fragile porcelain.

When they drew apart, she sat for a moment, thinking, then her brown eyes narrowed with decision. "Dhurrrkk', I want you to ask Doctor Blanket if it can do the same thing for *me*."

Together, they went into the hydroponics lab.

The Avernian was spread atop its rock pile, undulating gently. Dhurrrkk' faced it, his expression taking on that "listening" aspect he wore when he was conversing with the telepathic being.

After several moments, he blinked, his eyes regaining their awareness. "Doctor Blanket responds that although there are language areas in your brain that you are not utilizing—even more areas than the ones in my brain, apparently—it does not think that opening new 'channels' between them would be a wise thing for it to attempt."

Mahree fought back a wail of disappointment. "Ask Doctor Blanket why not?"

The seconds seemed endless before the Simiu spoke again. "It says that my brain is younger than yours, therefore more . . ." For the first time in many conversations he had to signal his computer link for a translation. "More malleable. It says that your brain, while not rigid like Rob's, is much less flexible than mine. It says this 'hardening' is caused by your comparatively greater age."

Mahree stared at him in shock, then her lips tightened. *Shit, that makes me feel like I'm ninety!* "Does that mean it *can't* alter the channels?"

Again Dhurrrkk' "listened."

"Doctor Blanket says that while it could do the same thing to your mind as it did to mine, your brain might not find the process comfortable. It might prove painful."

"So what do I care if I get a headache?" she said, scowling. "Come on, Dhurrrkk', convince it to give me the treatment! Think how helpful it will be if I could become as fluent in Mizari and Simiu as you now are in English and Mizari. You wouldn't have to stand alone to face your people when we reach Shassiszss! We could both explain the situation to the Mizari."

Dhurrrkk' nodded. "That *would* be helpful," he conceded. "I will tell it you are not afraid of pain."

After a moment, the Simiu said, "It responds that it cannot be sure that the 'treatment' will not prove injurious. It would be as careful as possible, of course, but . . ." He shook his head. "Friend Mahree, I do not think you should attempt this . . ."

Mahree sensed that the blanket was weakening. Dropping to her knees, so the Avernian was on her eye level, she "spoke," hoping the creature would comprehend her thoughts: *Doctor Blanket, please! I don't care about the risk! This mission is vital! Please, please—it would mean so much to me!*

She waited, scarcely daring to breathe, then, slowly, reluctantly, the creature's response filled her mind:

Affirmation.

Mahree cast the obviously worried Dhurrrkk' a triumphant glance as she sat down, leaning her back against the lab's bulkhead. "Go ahead, Doctor Blanket," she said, aloud, and held her breath.

The young woman felt nothing at first, nothing except a hint of Dhurrrkk's "tingling darkness." And then, between one heart-beat and the next, it was as though some modern-day Atlas had lifted an entire world and slammed it down onto her head.

Mahree had only an instant to realize that something was terribly wrong, that her mind was being torn, ripped, *shredded*— before she lost consciousness.

Dhurrrkk's agonized howl woke Rob from a nap. He leaped up, nearly falling over one of the bridge consoles, just as the frantic Simiu rushed through the door. "FriendRob! Friend-Mahree has been hurt! I think—I think she may be almost dead!"

Rob's heart seemed to stop, and for one terrible instant he could not move. Then his paralysis broke. Grabbing his medical bag, he raced to keep up with Dhurrrkk's four-footed bounds, his lungs laboring in the thin air.

Gasping, on the verge of blacking out, he skidded to a halt at the entrance to the hydroponics lab. Mahree lay sprawled half in and half out of the door, arms and legs twisted carelessly, as though she'd been picked up and flung by a giant hand. She wasn't breathing, and, when Rob touched her throat, there was no pulse.

Mahree was, at least for the moment, dead.

God, please, don't let me fail this time . . . let me save her, please, please . . .

Rob pressed a sensor patch into place on her temple. When it registered brain activity, he felt a surge of relief, but his elation was short-lived; a moment's glance revealed that the brainwave patterns were abnormal, scrambled, as though neurons were misfiring.

Not a stroke, not a heart attack—what the hell happened? Somewhere in the back of his mind a timer was running, ticking off seconds. *Questions later. First, get her heart beating, get her breathing again.* Rob took a deep, steadying breath, clearing his mind, then set to work.

Placing the oxy-pak over her mouth and nose, he verified that the nasal tubes positioned themselves properly.

The cardio-pacer could not operate through many layers of cloth, so he slit her heavy robes and shirt open, then positioned the unit on her bare chest, setting it for cardio-pulmonary stimulation. Within seconds, Mahree began to gasp.

Rob rechecked the brain sensor. Involuntary brain activity was returning to normal as the pacer unit regulated heartbeat and respiration.

As Mahree's heartbeat became stronger, evening out, and her breathing grew regular, Rob scanned the sensor for her body temperature. He frowned. *Shock . . . hypothermia . . . must prevent them by getting her warm.* He found his sheet, and unfolded it in the corridor. "Help me slide her out here, onto this," he told Dhurrrkk'. Once his patient was lying on top of it, he pulled the transparent length over her, sealed it, then slipped its hood up over her head to conserve body heat. After setting the temperature controls, Rob checked the sensor patch again.

The doctor had seen only one case resembling this one; that of a man who'd been struck by lightning. Some of the patient's brainwaves had produced readings like this. The man had survived . . . but with permanent brain damage.

"Dhurrrkk', her brain activity is not right," he said. "What the hell happened to her?"

"Doctor Blanket," the Simiu said. He glanced at the Avernian, visible through the open door. "FriendMahree asked it to alter the language channels in her mind, as it did for me. When it finally did so, she shook all over, then fell down."

"Doctor Blanket altered her *brain*?"

"It did not wish to, FriendRob. It warned her—*I* warned her—but she insisted. She wished to achieve better communication skills."

Recalling Mahree's depression of the past week, when she'd discovered that, try as she might, she could barely "talk" to the Avernian, Rob had no trouble believing Dhurrrkk''s account.

Allowing sixty seconds for him to fetch me, she was "dead" for less than three minutes, Rob calculated, checking the "time-elapsed" reading on the sensor. *Not enough time for oxygen deprivation to impair the brain . . . under normal circumstances, that is.*

"Doctor Blanket is very sorry," Dhurrrkk' was continuing, after "listening" to the Avernian. "It tells me that it is doing everything it can to restore normal brain functioning."

Rob glanced again at the Avernian, tempted to tell the fungus-creature to keep its "alterations" to itself, but there was no doubt that Mahree's brain scans were showing increasingly normal activity, so he kept quiet. *How could a telepath manage something like this?* he wondered. *Great-Aunt Louise sure couldn't . . .*

Now that Mahree was out of immediate danger, Rob found that reaction to what had almost happened was setting in. Cold sweat slicked his forehead, and his hands began trembling so violently that he could barely adjust the temperature setting on the medical sheet. *I almost lost her. I could still lose her.*

"Will she be all right?" Dhurrrkk' asked, hovering over Mahree like an anxious mother.

"I don't know yet," Rob said. "She's breathing, and her heart is beating normally again, but her brain activity, while it's steadily improving, is *not* normal."

After a half hour, Rob unsealed the sheet to remove the oxy-pak and pacer. He administered electrolytes and Vita-stim, and watched her color improve. The sensor was reporting normal brainwaves again. *She's going to live,* Rob thought. *I didn't fail—unless she has some kind of mental trauma the sensor can't measure.*

A few minutes later, Mahree's eyelids fluttered suddenly; she began to stir. But when her eyes opened, she stared up at the doctor blankly, as though she'd never seen him before. Rob's heart sank.

"Mahree," he said, touching her cheek, "you're all right. Don't try to talk yet." She rolled her eyes so she was staring at Dhurrrkk'.

"Mahree," Rob called, and felt his heart leap when she turned her head to regard him. "Honey . . ." he had to forcibly steady his voice, "if you can understand me, blink three times. Blink slowly, three times."

Her eyes closed, then opened. *One . . . two . . . three . . .* Her lips moved, shaped words he could barely hear. "Rob . . . it hurt . . . it was dark . . ."

"I know," he said softly. "I want you to rest, okay? Sleep. You're going to be fine. I'm right here."

Moments later, her eyes closed. Rob checked the sensor again. Normal sleep.

"Thank you, thank you," he whispered, feeling hot tears break free and slide down his face. He wiped them off on his sleeve, then began repacking his medical bag. *I almost didn't bring it,* he remembered. *And if I hadn't . . . she'd be dead, and my life would be . . . dark. Like a star that's burned itself out . . . dark and cold and lifeless . . .*

The truth had been staring him in the face for some time, he realized . . . but it had taken a near tragedy to bring it home to him. "Dhurrrkk'," he said, standing up, "I'm going to take her back to the control room. Can you carry my bag?"

"Certainly, FriendRob."

Rob scooped Mahree's limp form into his arms, and, gasping, straightened up. "Do you need help, FriendRob?" Dhurrrkk' asked anxiously. "The air is thin, and she must be heavy."

"No," Rob said, holding Mahree tightly, savoring her warm, *living* weight. "She doesn't feel heavy at all."

There had been pain, that she knew. Then darkness. With the darkness had come peace, the cessation of pain. She had not wanted to come back, because the pain might be waiting.

This much Mahree remembered, before she opened her eyes.

She was lying in her sleeping place on *Rosinante*'s bridge, and she was warm. Her body felt stiff, rather strange, but there was no pain, and that was reassuring.

She realized that she was wearing nothing but shorts. Clutching one of the Simiu coverings to her chest, she sat up.

The moment she stirred, there was a sound from the other side of the pilot's seat, then Rob appeared.

Mahree wet her lips. "Hi," she managed.

Silently, he ran his bio-scanner over her, then nodded. He reached out and pulled loose something that had been sticking to her temple. She saw that it was a sensor patch.

"Am I okay?" she asked.

"Apparently," he said, his voice quiet and over-controlled.

"Uh, can I get up? I have to go to the bathroom."

"I'll walk you down there," he said. "Get dressed."

He turned his back as she stood up and slipped her arms into the robe, pulling it tightly around her. "Where's Dhurrrkk'?"

"I sent him to the galley to get you some food," Rob replied. "I want you to eat something as soon as possible."

When they got back from the head, Mahree slipped on a shirt, then pulled her robes back on. She noticed that they had been slit down the chest, then clumsily repaired with the Simiu resin.

By then she was so ravenous that even the tasteless concentrate was almost palatable. All the while she ate and drank, Rob and Dhurrrkk' sat watching her intently, as though they were afraid she might disappear.

Finally, when the silence was more than she could stand, Mahree took a deep breath. "What happened to me?" she demanded. "I don't remember anything. I was trying to—"

"I know what you were trying to do," Rob said tightly. "Dhurrrkk' told me. You owe Doctor Blanket a sincere apology—you nearly scared it into cardiac arrest, too. Not that it has a heart. But it was devastated by what happened."

"Oh, no," Mahree muttered, thinking of the fungus-being's gentle nature. Then something else that he'd said penetrated. "I was in cardiac arrest?" she asked, in a quavering voice. "Don't you mean fibrillation?"

Rob's dark eyes did not waver. "Mahree," he said, still speaking in that ominous, too-quiet tone, "your heart was in arrest. No pulse. No heartbeat. You were *dead*."

"What happened?" she whispered, frightened. *Dead? Oh, my God!* "Why did my heart stop?"

"Whatever it was Doctor Blanket did to your brain, it affected you like being hit by a massive electric shock."

Mahree swallowed, hard. "I really almost died?"

"There almost was no 'almost' about it," he said, and this time the too-even voice faltered slightly. "When I think of how close I came to forgetting to bring my medical kit along on this little jaunt—" He broke off, shaking his head.

"You saved me," she whispered. "Thank you, Rob."

Dhurrrkk' spoke for the first time. "I just informed Doctor Blanket that you are recovered. It is extremely relieved. Perhaps from now on you will believe it when it tells you that something you want is potentially dangerous."

Mahree gave her friend a rueful grimace. "In other words, 'I told you so.' I guess I deserve that."

Dhurrrkk' and Rob were staring at her, plainly astonished. Mahree blinked back at them. "What is it?" she said slowly.

"FriendMahree," Dhurrrkk' said slowly, "what language did you use just now when you were speaking to me?"

She frowned. "Uh . . . English?"

Dhurrrkk' shook his head slowly. "No," he said solemnly. "You addressed me in the same language that I used when I spoke to you—my own."

"But . . . but . . ." she stammered, staring from him to Rob, who only nodded silent confirmation. "But that means that I *thought* in Simiu! That at least part of Doctor Blanket's treatment was successful, if I could respond to you in the same tongue you used, without even having to think about it!"

"Yes," said Dhurrrkk'. "I am . . . pleased . . . for you, FriendMahree. But I still feel that what almost happened to you was too great a price to pay. When I thought you had . . . if you had . . ." the Simiu trailed off, eyes lowered, his crest flattening with remembered misery.

"FriendDhurrrkk'—" Mahree began, but the Simiu only turned around and left the bridge. "I guess he's pretty upset."

"Yes, he is," Rob agreed, still in the neutral, toneless voice. "He felt that he had somehow failed to effectively translate Doctor Blanket's warnings to you." His mouth tightened. "I reminded him that you can't be stopped when you set your mind on something, but I don't think it helped much."

Mahree swallowed. "It was my own fault, and I'll tell him so, and ask him to forgive me," she said in a small voice. *I owe Rob an apology, too. Not to mention poor Doctor Blanket.*

<Do not be too severe with yourself, young friend,> spoke a voice inside her head. <I, too, did foolish things when I was but a small one, barely past sporehood.>

Doctor Blanket? Mahree thought, scarcely believing what she was "hearing." *Is that you?*

<It is,> the Avernian replied. <But there will be time enough for us to "talk" later, when both of us are rested.>

The entire interchange had taken place in seconds. Rob was still looking at her, and saying, "I agree that an apology is in order. Where are you going?" he asked as she started to rise.

"To find Dhurrrkk' and say I'm sorry."

Rob raised a hand, forestalling her. "You can talk to him later. I want you to rest today."

"I feel okay," Mahree said. "Almost back to normal."

"Almost," Rob repeated, still in that unnaturally calm voice that reminded Mahree of distant thunder. It had the same ominous overtones. "Well, when you feel one hundred percent recovered, please be sure and tell me."

"Why?" she said, unable to stop herself from asking.

His unnervingly calm mask vanished between one breath and the next. "Because when you're fully recovered, I am going to *kill* you!" Rob cried, face flushing with anger, voice rising with every word. "How *could* you do something so dumb! That was the most idiotic—the *craziest* stunt you've ever pulled! I thought you had brains! Well, you damn near got them permanently scrambled!"

Now I've done it, she thought, bowing her head before the onslaught. "I don't blame you for being angry," she said meekly, "it was a stupid thing to do, and I'm sorry, Rob."

He wasn't appeased. "If you'd wound up dead, what the hell were Dhurrrkk' and I supposed to do when we reached Shassiszss? Without you, we'd be up shit creek. *You're* the human who can talk to these people without stopping for a translation every other sentence, not me, don't forget!"

"I saw a chance to get even better—" she began.

"It was too damned big a risk to take!" he interrupted. After a moment, he said quickly, "I thought we were a team. I thought you cared about us."

"I do," she said, tears flooding her eyes. "I care. I guess maybe I'd gotten through so many dangers safely that I was getting careless about taking risks. Maybe I needed to be reminded that I'm as mortal as anyone."

"Yeah, 'mortal' was almost the word, all right," he said bitterly. "And Dhurrrkk' and I almost paid the price for your recklessness."

Mahree felt a flare of indignation. "I *said* I was sorry, Rob! I think you're overreacting. I *could* have died, but the fact is, I didn't. Why are you going on like this?"

He sat perfectly still, head bowed, shoulders taut, for long seconds, then he looked up. "Because I love you, dammit," he said softly. "And if you had died . . ." he trailed off, unable to finish.

Mahree gazed at him numbly. Her heart felt as though it needed a jolt from the pacer to get it started again. *Don't be stupid,* she thought, finally. *He just means "love" in the way I love Dhurrrkk'. Don't make a fool of yourself . . .*

She had to wet her lips before she could produce any sound. "Love?" she said faintly. "What do you mean, 'love'?"

Rob's expression was a study in mingled exasperation and affection. "Love as in, 'I've fallen in love with you,' what else?"

This can't be happening. Not to me. "You're kidding."

"Would I kid about that? Hell no, I'm not kidding."

She stared at him, stunned. Her shock must have been evident, for he crawled over to put an arm around her. "Hey, I guess I shouldn't have dropped it on you like that. Actually, I've felt that way for some time, but I only realized it yesterday, when I thought about what losing you would mean."

He peered at her face in the dimness. "This was a helluva shock, wasn't it? Maybe I shouldn't have said anything," he muttered, sounding increasingly nervous. "Uh, listen, Mahree, I don't expect . . . uh . . ." He cleared his throat. "What I'm trying to say, is . . . oh, damn . . . that . . . I know you don't . . . well, that . . ."

Mahree began to shake all over. "Rob," she managed to say between chattering teeth, "Be *quiet!!*"

He dropped his arm. "Look, I'm sorry. Are you okay?"

"I'm dazed . . . or something," Mahree managed to whisper. "Oh, Rob . . . can too much happiness be fatal?" Summoning up all her courage, she slid her arms around his neck and leaned her forehead against his shoulder, enunciating each word precisely: "I love you, too. I have loved you since the first moment I saw you, when I bypassed security and watched your personnel interview vid-record."

"Oh," he said, sounding surprised, then his chest heaved with a long sigh of relief. He gathered her into his arms, holding her.

"Look at me," he ordered, minutes later, his breath warm on her cheek. "I want to see your face when you say it."

Mahree raised her head. "I . . . I love you, Rob," she whispered, then she smiled incredulously. "It was hard, saying it out loud, after concentrating all this time on not saying it."

"Why didn't you?"

She chuckled. "What do you think I am? Crazy? You treated me like a kid sister, remember?"

He smiled. "Oh, yeah. I forgot. What an asshole I was." His smile broadened into a grin. "I think that's when I first began to fall in love with you."

"When?"

"When you called me an asshole. Even though I tried not to, I couldn't help seeing you as a woman from that moment on . . ."

Mahree began to laugh. "Don't laugh," he said dryly.

"Why not?"

"Because I want to kiss you, and it's difficult getting up the nerve to kiss a woman who's laughing at you."

Mahree stopped immediately.

Rob turned his head, and their lips met. His mouth was warm and gentle against hers, and after a moment she relaxed and closed her eyes. Gradually, he become more demanding, parting her lips, softly at first, then more insistently. Mahree made a small, inarticulate sound as his tongue touched hers, sending a jolt of pleasure through her body.

By the time he drew away, they were both breathing heavily, only partly because of the thin air. "I didn't know . . ." she murmured. "I didn't know it would be like that. I didn't know I could feel like this."

His dark eyes never left her face as his fingertips traced the line of her jaw, then her lips, using the lightest of touches. Mahree closed her eyes again as he stroked the contours of her throat. "Are you going to make love to me?" she whispered. "I want you to."

She heard Rob suck in an exasperated breath, then he abruptly pulled away. Mahree opened her eyes to find him sitting at arm's length from her, wearing a most peculiar expression—rueful and resigned and tender, all at the same time. "I wish I could," he muttered. "Nothing would please me more."

"Then why not?" she demanded, puzzled and a little indignant. "You've got an implant, don't you?"

"Of course," he said. "But . . . Mahree . . . sex requires a fair amount of physical exertion. Even if I thought I could . . . uh . . . perform . . . here"—he waved an arm at *Rosinante*'s cramped bridge—"which I'm not sure I could, worrying about whether Dhurrrkk' would walk in at any moment, delighted to have the chance to observe human mating practices . . ." He gave a gasp of choked laughter. "The bottom line, my love, is that we don't have enough damned oxygen. We can't afford to waste that much air!"

CHAPTER 15

♦

Diplomatic Immunity and Other Creature Comforts

I'm nervous as a cat and dirty as a pig—but none of that matters, because Rob loves me! I can't believe how lucky I am! And soon, we'll be at our destination. Dhurrrkk' says we'll be in visual range of Shassiszss in about thirty minutes.

The suspense is terrible! Will the Mizari welcome us? Or will they decide it's in their best interest to side with the Simiu? What will the other CLS members think of the human race?

Could we be in danger? All of a sudden, I'm scared . . .

By its own request, Doctor Blanket is locked in the hydroponics lab. The Avernian wanted to enter what it calls a "resting state" for the next four or five days, so it could assimilate its new knowledge. From the moment that it crawled up onto its plants, it became completely unresponsive to thoughts or touches. Its glow faded away. If it hadn't warned us ahead of time, I'd have thought it was dead.

Even though it's been long, hard, and painful, I wouldn't have missed this trip. I've learned a lot.

Before I left Jolie, I was always trying to act adult, and I fretted constantly that people wouldn't think I was grown-up. But now that *I* know that I'm a fully mature human being, I've quit worrying about it.

(When I expressed some of this to Rob, he said that was a tremendous relief to him. If I weren't an adult, he announced, too solemnly, he'd have to give me up because aboard *Rosinante* he feels like he's eighty—always short of breath, chilled, and peering at things.)

Mizari verb conjugations keep running through my head like a litany.

Only minutes to go, now . . .

"Holy shit!" Rob exclaimed. "*That's* a space station? It makes Station One look like a postage stamp, Dhurrrkk'!"

Both the Simiu and Mahree turned to regard him, puzzled. "Postage stamp?" they said, together.

The doctor shrugged. "Sorry. An ancient method of mail delivery. My father's got a collection handed down from before the First Martian Colony."

Dhurrrkk' was still puzzled. "But what does your father need with a collection of elderly males?" he asked, clearly baffled.

Mahree snickered loudly, and Rob gave her a disgusted glance. "I was referring to something about *this* big." He measured off a space between thumb and forefinger.

"Most interesting," Dhurrrkk' murmured, giving Mahree a sometimes-humans-are-*weird!* look.

"At any rate," she said, before Rob could dig himself in deeper, "you're right. That station is really *huge*."

The structure was a gigantic circular blot against the pale yellow-green disk of Shassiszss. It consisted of two vast, spoked wheel-within-wheel-within-wheel shapes, each placed at right angles to the other. "Like a tremendous gyroscope," Mahree breathed.

From the amount of the planet it obscured, it was obvious the station was gargantuan, but it wasn't until Mahree noticed one of the amber, hammerheaded Simiu craft approaching it that she got any true perspective on its size. *Thousands and thousands of people could live on that thing,* she thought. *Maybe hundreds of thousands.*

"It is indeed very large," Dhurrrkk' was saying. "Holo-vids do not convey the true scale. But, as the headquarters of the CLS, that station houses many different representatives, their staffs, and their vehicles. As well as the headquarters for all CLS functions, such as the League Irenics—those who safeguard the peace and the laws that are made by the member worlds."

"*That* structure is the actual headquarters?" Rob asked. "But I thought it would be on the planet."

"Oh, no," Dhurrrkk' told them. "It is much more practical to employ an orbiting body as CLS headquarters. Many races require lesser gravity, and such conditions are easier to create in space, as you know, than on the surface of a world."

"Yes," said Rob, "and there's always fear of a possible mutation of an alien microbe. Quarantines are easier in space."

The Simiu glanced again at the space station, steadily looming closer. "Also, there is a symbolic value in having the fundamental structure of the headquarters sunk into the soil of no world, but floating free in space."

"I just can't believe the *size* of it," Rob said. "Was it deliberately designed and built to be this large?"

"Oh, no," Dhurrrkk' said. "Originally, there was only that central disk that now forms the innermost hub of the station. When the CLS was formed, the Mizari donated their station as a base from which to begin League headquarters. Financial support from many worlds gradually built this structure you see now."

The Simiu swung himself into his pilot's cradle, preparatory to overseeing and assisting the functioning of the computers that were bringing *Rosinante* closer and closer to her assigned berth.

The tension in the little control room mounted as their vessel was allowed to proceed to her designated docking cradle without escort or hindrance.

When they were safely docked, Dhurrrkk' crawled out of his cradle with a sigh.

"Dhurrrkk'," Mahree said, speaking Simiu slowly, so that Rob could follow her words, "do you think we might be in any danger?"

"I very much doubt it," Dhurrrkk' said. "You two are representatives of a hitherto undiscovered sentient species—as such, you and your world represent a potential treasure trove of new talent, resources, technology, and ideas to the CLS. They will safeguard your lives with extreme care."

"Dhurrrkk'," Mahree said, around a cold lump that seemed to have congealed in her throat, "I was talking about all three of us, and you knew it. Give me a straight answer."

"I do not know, FriendMahree. I am now a criminal—a thief and a liar. Those are serious offenses, for which I might spend several years serving the public good, until I could regain my

honor. Being dishonored and outcast by my family would be bad
enough, but also . . .'' he hesitated, ''the Council will regard me
as a traitor, and the penalties for treason are much more severe.''

''How severe?''

Dhurrrkk' was silent.

''He might have to face a professional gladiator in the Arena,''
Rob said, in halting Simiu. He switched to English. ''Rhrrrkkeet'
mentioned that might happen to her.'' He ran a hand through his
hair, frowning. ''But it might never come to that . . .''

''What do you mean?'' Mahree asked.

''Dhurrrkk' is the only CLS citizen who has sided openly with
us . . . who knows the full truth of what has happened. It might
be in the best interests of the Simiu Council for him to meet with
an unfortunate accident. Or simply disappear.''

Fear enclosed Mahree's heart like a cage of ice. ''Simiu
wouldn't do that,'' she protested. ''It would be too dishonorable.''

''There are Simiu, like that gladiator Hekkk'eesh, who act as
little more than professional assassins, remember?''

''Dhurrrkk', is what he's suggesting possible?''

''I honestly do not know, FriendMahree,'' the Simiu said.

Mahree envisioned a contingent of Simiu waiting outside
Rosinante's airlock, and her throat tightened. ''Dhurrrkk','' she
said impulsively, her mind racing, ''why don't you just let Rob
and me go out there by ourselves? You can just take off again as
soon as we're gone! You've got plenty of food, and Doctor
Blanket can provide you with oxygen indefinitely. Why don't
you just get away while you can?''

''You are forgetting fuel, FriendMahree,'' the Simiu said, his
violet eyes bleak.

''But surely you could get fuel in some other nearby system.
You told us that the Mizari S.V. drive is standard for most CLS
worlds! Have you got any League currency?''

''Some,'' Dhurrrkk' said, ''but what you are suggesting is
impossible, my friend. We do not have enough fuel left to allow
even one transition from realspace to metaspace. There is no way
around that lack.''

Mahree sighed. ''Oh. That's that, then, isn't it?'' she muttered. ''But, FriendDhurrrkk', I'm afraid for you!''

Dhurrrkk' nodded. ''I knew what consequences I might face.''
He stripped off his makeshift robe. ''Come, let's go.''

The alien turned and left the control room, his four-footed

strides somehow shortened and tentative, leaving the two humans to stare after him. Mahree shook her head as she pulled off her own robe and straightened her travel-worn clothing. "Dammit, Rob," she burst out, "if they're out there waiting for Dhurrrkk', they'll just *take* him! We may never see him again!"

"I know," he agreed, picking up his bag.

"Can't we . . . fight, or something?"

"Simiu are the wrong height for a fistfight," Rob pointed out as they walked down the corridor toward the airlock.

"I've never hit anyone anyway," she admitted miserably. "Have you?"

"I boxed in college. Welterweight. But a real fight? No." He shook his head. "We can't, Mahree. Remember how strong they are."

As Dhurrrkk' ushered them into *Rosinante*'s airlock, Mahree's heart was pounding. Rob was pale, but his jaw was set and his eyes were steady and resolute.

When the doors split apart, Mahree and her friends peered tensely out, then relaxed slightly as they saw that there was no one waiting for them. They emerged into a rounded tunnel that blazed brightly with white light. The gravity was approximately Jolie-normal. The air was quite warm, rather dry, and rich with oxygen. *It's a good thing we didn't bring Doctor Blanket*, Mahree thought, squinting in the brightness after so many days in the near-darkness aboard *Rosinante*. The walls of the tunnel were a reflective white; the floor was shiny and black.

As they stood crowded together outside the airlock, blinking and staring, enjoying the welcome warmth of their surroundings while wondering what to do, a thick layer of blue mist began issuing from the walls. Soon the entire corridor was obscured by a sapphire fog.

A voice spoke echoingly in sibilant Simiu: "Please step through the decontamination vapor. We regret the necessity for this procedure, and request your patience. Do not inhale as you move through the vapor. Thank you for helping us."

The three travelers looked at one another. "What did it say?" Rob asked. "I caught only the first part."

Mahree repeated the message. Rob shrugged. "What the hell," he muttered, and strode into the mist. Moments later, Mahree heard his voice magnified by the curving walls. "Tell Dhurrrkk' it's okay!" he yelled. "Come on through, there's someone waiting for us. A Mizari. No Simiu."

Quickly, Mahree plunged into the decontamination vapor. The stuff felt warm and damp on her skin, and made her eyes prickle, so she shut them as she moved forward. Midway through she was conscious of a soft hum, and a bright light flashed. Three more steps, and she was past the light and out of the vapor. She could hear Dhurrrkk' behind her, his nails clicking softly against the polished black material of the floor.

Mahree opened her eyes as she felt air against her skin again. The featureless corridor was filled with a golden light that radiated from the being awaiting them.

So that's a Mizari. Mahree examined the sinuous form of the alien, eyes widening. *But the holo-vids never conveyed that they were so utterly* **gorgeous!**

The alien who faced them was a female. Mahree recognized that fact immediately because of the being's lack of the vestigial dorsal ridge. Beneath the aurulent glow (some kind of protective field), the Mizari's scales shimmered silvery white, with brilliant diamonds of scarlet, black, and orange patterning her back. She had lifted the first third of her body, and the humans could see the tiny gripping appendages that roughened the scales of her underside.

The being's eyes were black, unblinking and pupilless, and nearly on a level with Mahree's head. The head itself was wedge-shaped, blunt-nosed, and surrounded by the thick cloud of moving "tentacles" that were the Mizari equivalent of hands and fingers. The sensitive appendages waved outward, surrounding the being's head and continuing down her "neck," many over half a meter in length. The "tentacles" were black, scarlet, and orange, and each was tipped with the silvery white. They moved so constantly that Mahree could not see whether they were scaled or not.

The alien's overall length was impressive, well over five meters. Her body lay stretched behind her as a counterbalance to her raised head, but, as the three travelers stopped before her, she slowly, deliberately, coiled her lower length, scales sliding over one another with a sinuous whisper.

"God, she's beautiful!" Rob whispered, grinning with unconcealed delight. Then he gave a half-smothered laugh, and muttered something that sounded like, "Snakes . . . why'd they have to be *snakes*?"

Mahree jabbed him with her elbow, wanting to hush him, but

"shhhhh!" in Mizari meant "I itch from shedding," and she didn't think that would be an appropriate first comment. Instead, she placed her steepled hands together over her head and bowed from the waist, as Dhurrrkk' had shown them. "Greetings," she said, in Mizari. (What the ancient phrase literally meant was "good hunting," but Mizari no longer devoured live prey. For hundreds of centuries they had existed on synthetic forms of protein.)

The being raised all her tentacles over her head and then gracefully dipped the first meter of her body. "Greetings," she said, in her own language. Her needlelike fangs were even longer than Dhurrrkk's, though they were now folded back into her mouth so they were barely visible as she spoke. "In my own name, and the name of my people, the"—she hissed the Mizari name for themselves—"and as a duly authorized representative of the Cooperative League of Systems, it is my honor and pleasure to welcome you to this place representing the spirit of our unity. I am Shirazz, the Guest Liaison for the League. I deeply regret that I must remain encased within this bio-protection field, but that is as much for your safety as it is my own."

"We understand, Esteemed Shirazz," Mahree said, still speaking Mizari. "I am Mahree Burroughs, and these are my companions and friends, Doctor Robert Gable, and Honored Dhurrrkk' of the clan"—she voiced the low, breathy growl of the Simiu's extended house. "We have come to ask your aid on a matter concerning interstellar peace. If misunderstandings between my people and Honored Dhurrrkk's are not resolved, there may be physical conflict between our species."

Shirazz had ceased her faint undulations and was poised very still. Even her tentacles stopped moving for a moment as she listened. "You speak our language," she said. "I am pleased and honored—and, I must confess, surprised. Surely you have not met our kind before?"

"No, I have not. I learned your speech aboard Honored Dhurrrkk's vessel. And, while Honored Dhurrrkk' can speak your language, my friend Doctor Gable cannot."

"Does Doctor-Robert-Gable speak—" and the being breathed the low grunt and click that was the Simiu name for their tongue.

"Yes, he does."

"Then," said the Mizari in her excellent Simiu, "let us

converse in that language. Honored HealerGable''—she bowed
to Rob—''and Honored Dhurrrkk' ''—she bowed to the Simiu.

Both males bowed, in turn.

"Also," Mahree said, "I have prepared cassettes that can be
used with Simiu equipment that will provide translations from
simple Mizari into Simiu, thence into English, which is our
standard language. There is also a Simiu/English dictionary we
have developed. I thought they might prove useful." She took
the little cassettes out of her pocket, and held them up.

"Most impressive indeed," Shirazz said. "We thank you.
You may place them on that ledge over there." She touched a
tentacle to the wall at shoulder height for a human, and the
featureless white expanse suddenly extruded the promised ledge.

Mahree hastily complied.

When she had returned to her spot between her companions,
Shirazz said, "And do you have voders that will allow you to
translate?"

"Yes, at least from Simiu into English," Mahree told her.

"Excellent. For three who made such a precipitate departure,
you have arrived very well prepared to communicate."

"Communication with your species and the rest of the CLS
worlds is our dearest wish," Mahree told her.

"We have spoken to Honored Rhrrrkkeet'," Shirazz said. "She
has told us of the situation there. The representatives from Hurrreeah
will be offering their testimony at a meeting of the Planetary
Councillors, tomorrow. But we are also eager to hear your
testimony."

Mahree closed her eyes for a second and breathed an inaudible
sigh of relief. "We will be happy to oblige," she said.
"Tomorrow?"

"No, at the following Planetary Councillors' meeting, three
Simiu days from now. The Councillors will wish to see you, to
hear you speak, and then to have an opportunity to speak to
you . . . question you, about yourselves and your worlds. Will
that be acceptable?"

"That will be fine. We are very interested in meeting the
assorted member races of the League."

"Such meetings will be arranged," Shirazz said, "but first,
you must endure a brief quarantine. You were scanned as you
walked through the decontamination vapor. Soon we will know
whether it is safe for you to have contact with us. If not, we will
provide you with environmental protection fields, like mine."

"We would welcome a chance to rest," Mahree said warmly. "Our journey has not been easy."

"We have put through a request to the Simiu First Councillor, Honored Ahkk'eerrr, for permission for you to speak with Rhrrrkkeet', and also with your human friends," the Guest Liaison said. "You should be able to do so by the time your quarantine is ended. And now, will you humans follow me to your quarters?"

"But what about FriendDhurrrkk', Esteemed Shirazz?" Rob spoke up for the first time, his Simiu pronunciation mangled, but understandable. "Where will he be lodged?"

"Honored Dhurrrkk' is not under quarantine," Shirazz said. "He will stay in the Simiu section of this station. Honored Ahkk'eerrr wishes to speak with him."

I'll just bet she does! Mahree thought. "Esteemed Shirazz," she began, speaking politely but firmly, "Doctor Gable and I wish Dhurrrkk' assigned to our quarters. The three of us do not wish to be separated."

The being uncoiled herself, her scales whispering softly over one another. "I am most regretful that I cannot accede to your request," she said, "but Honored Dhurrrkk' must accompany *them*." Her tentacles gestured at the corridor behind her. Mahree saw two burly Simiu males approaching. "Honored Councillor Ahkk'eerrr insisted."

Mahree turned to her friend in despair. "Dhurrrkk'!" she whispered, squatting down to face him.

"Do not upset yourself, FriendMahree," he said, reaching out to gently hug her. His fur was warm and spicy against her cheek. "I will go with them. I will be fine."

"Bullshit you're going with them!" Rob snarled, in English. He plunked himself down cross-legged on the floor of the tunnel and grasped Dhurrrkk' around the waist, locking each wrist in the opposite hand. His astonished Simiu friend gaped at him, too stunned to protest. "They'll have to drag me off to get you away," the doctor vowed. "Mahree, grab on!"

She stared at him openmouthed for a second, then grinned wickedly as she sat down and wrapped her arms around Dhurrrkk's chest, locking her wrists, just as Rob had. "Esteemed One," she addressed the Mizari, "we will not be separated! It is *essential* that Dhurrrkk' stay with us!"

Shirazz was staring at them, motionless, as the two other

Simiu reached their group. The aliens solemnly made the greeting gesture to the Guest Liaison, then they squatted down on their haunches and stared at the linked threesome, nonplussed.

The Guest Liaison seemed completely taken aback by the humans' action. "I am at a loss to comprehend," she said slowly. "What is wrong? Is there cause for alarm?"

"There is indeed, Esteemed One!" Mahree cried. "*Please* listen and believe! Honored Dhurrrkk' *must* be there to speak beside us at the Council meeting, he *must*! Otherwise, our story will not be complete! And to ensure that he attends, he must remain here, with us!"

Shirazz glanced at the two Simiu. "Perhaps you did not understand, when I said that Honored Dhurrrkk' would be sent to his people—I meant the Simiu contingent *here,* on this station, not on his homeworld," she said, and Mahree could tell she was also speaking for the benefit of Dhurrrkk's would-be "escorts."

"Yes, but does Honored Councillor *Ahkk'eerrr* understand that?" Rob put in, enunciating the Simiu words with dogged precision. "Honored Dhurrrkk' could be on his way to Hurrreeah by the time of the Councillors' meeting. We cannot risk that." The doctor had to clear his throat when he was finished, but he flashed a triumphant glance at his companions.

That's the longest thing he ever said! Mahree thought. *Shirazz understood him, too!* She gave him a proud smile. "We will not be separated from Honored Dhurrrkk'. Our friend must be with us at the meeting of the Councillors, to speak for himself." She glanced at the other Simiu. "He must be protected until then," she finished quietly.

For the first time, one of the Simiu spoke. "We have our orders, Esteemed and Honored Shirazz," the larger one said. He was a fully mature male, taller than Dhurrrkk' by half a head. The other was nearly as big. "This is a matter concerning the internal security of our homeworld. Dhurrrkk'—" (Mahree noticed with a stab of fear that he did not use the term "honored") "Dhurrrkk' must come with us. Ahkk'eerrr has said so. We will escort him to her . . . by any means we must."

"Please, Esteemed and Honored Shirazz," the other put in, "we do not want any unpleasantness. Order the humans away, or we will have to . . ." he trailed off uncertainly. "Do as we must," he finished, finally.

Hearing the implied threat, Dhurrrkk' tried gently to pull

away. "My friends, I cannot allow you to risk your own safety," he murmured, in English. "Let me go! After what Shirazz has witnessed, they will not dare to harm me."

"No!" Mahree told him, and tightened her grip until her friend would have to hurt her to free himself. She addressed the two would-be "escorts" angrily, "You cannot threaten us into letting him go!" Fury was erasing her fear. "How *dare* you?"

The Simiu guards' eyes narrowed, and their powerful hands flexed, as though they were barely maintaining control. "Let him go," the biggest one said, addressing Mahree directly for the first time. "You have no right to do this."

Mahree lost her temper. Furious, she glared hard at the two Simiu, then deliberately bared her teeth. "Yes, I do! We are honor-bound!" she snarled. "His honor is mine! If you take him, you must take me, too, because I will *not* let go! If you try to separate us, I will challenge you myself!"

"So will I!" growled Rob.

Mahree didn't take her eyes off their possible opponents. As she watched, the first Simiu's crest flared, stiffening into the flame-colored halo heralding battle-readiness.

"I am sure," Shirazz announced calmly, "that no challenges will prove necessary." In a quick blur of motion, she slithered her massive length between the two parties.

For a moment the Simiu's huge muscles bunched, then his comrade grabbed his arm and grumbled something inaudible. Slowly, the big male's crest relaxed.

Shirazz looked at the three. "You shared one voyage, and thus one story," she said. "And, it is established League policy to give equal hearing to all sides of a story."

Turning back to the two Simiu, she said: "Our human guests have—rather dramatically—pointed out the necessity of Honored Dhurrrkk's attending the Councillors' meeting. It is my *official* duty to ensure that League policy is upheld."

The two Simiu stirred uneasily. "We will bring him to the meeting," the larger one said grudgingly, after a glance at his companion.

"I am sure you would," Shirazz said blandly, 'but I am equally sure that Honored Ahkk'eerrr will agree with me that there is no harm in acceding to the humans' request. I thereby take it on myself to quarter Honored Dhurrrkk' as I see fit. You need have no fears as to our security, as you know. I trust that will be acceptable?"

The two Simiu shuffled slightly and glanced at each other again. "Tell First Councillor Ahkk'eerrr that I will speak to her personally as soon as I have finished my duties in seeing to the comfort of these guests," Shirazz finished.

The guards' crests drooped, then they managed to recover some of their aplomb. "Certainly, Honored Esteemed Shirazz," the biggest one said graciously. "Honored Councillor Ahkk'eerrr will be awaiting your communication with honored pleasure."

Oh, I'm sure she will, Mahree thought, concealing a triumphant grin. She gave her friend a delighted squeeze, but did not release her hold until the would-be "escorts" left, with no word of parting, in typical Simiu fashion.

Rob got to his feet and heaved a long sigh of relief. "That," he muttered, giving Mahree a hand up, "'was a close one.'"

For answer, she grabbed him and hugged him, giving him a noisy kiss on the cheek. *"Je t'aime, M'sieu le docteur! Tu es magnifique!"*

"Oh, baby," he said, and his laughter had a slightly hysterical edge. "I love it when you talk dirty to me."

Mahree grinned. "I just said that I love you, and that you're wonderful, Rob."

He sobered. "I love you, too."

"How much?" she asked teasingly.

Rob made a sweeping gesture. "To the ends of the universe and beyond the bounds of death." He cocked an eyebrow at her. "Is that enough?"

Mahree pretended to consider, then nodded thoughtfully. "Yeah, that ought to do it."

"Honored Dhurrrkk'," Shirazz was saying, when the humans turned back to their alien friend, "will you allow me to escort you to your quarters?" When Mahree made an involuntary move toward the Simiu, the Mizari waved her tentacles gently. "I will quarter him next to you," she promised. "I guarantee his safety."

Mahree hesitated, then blurted, "Does the door lock?"

Shirazz's tentacles twitched, whether with amusement or irritation, the young woman couldn't guess. "Yes, there is a lock," the Guest Liaison said. "And I will show him how to activate the privacy field, also."

"FriendMahree," Dhurrrkk' said, patiently, "I will be fine.

Please do not fear for me further. Now that I have been placed under official League protection, I am as safe as if I were in my mother's house. Safer.''

Mahree looked over to Rob, who gave her a reassuring nod. "Okay," she said. "We'll visit you as soon as we get settled."

Dhurrrkk' hesitated. "I do not wish to seem unwelcoming," he said, finally, in English, "but I believe I would like to take a nap. A long nap."

Mahree laughed. "Okay, I can take a hint. We'll see you tomorrow, then." She glanced at the Mizari. "Can we talk to each other somehow?"

"Of course," the alien replied. "Now, will you excuse me while I accompany your friend?"

Mahree watched the Simiu as he accompanied the Guest Liaison down the corridor, noting with relieved pleasure that her friend had regained his customary bold swagger.

Minutes later, Shirazz returned. "Now, in order to attend to your comfort," the Mizari said, "I must know your preferences for gravity and airmix, sanitary arrangements, sleeping, hygiene, nourishment, and so forth. Will you help me by detailing them?"

Mahree looked helplessly at Rob. Her mind seemed to have deserted her. She was exhausted. The doctor stepped forward and took her arm, supporting her unobtrusively, then said, "Are you equipped with a voder that will allow you to read Simiu or hear it translated into your own language, Esteemed One?"

One of the tentacles flashed something shiny at him. "Yes, I am, Doctor-Robert-Gable. And I have Honored Dhurrrkk's and Honored Mahree's translation program."

"Good." Rob hastily strapped his own voder onto his wrist and activated his computer link. "This gravity is fine, Esteemed Shirazz," he said, in English. "We are accustomed to Simiu sanitary and sleeping arrangements. This atmosphere mix is fine. Both of us require pure liquid H_2O slightly above its freezing point for drinking. We have little remaining food, but we can provide you with samples that will nourish us, so that you may duplicate them, if possible."

"Certainly," Shirazz said. "Please place your samples over there, on the ledge with the other material. What quantities of these food products will you require daily?"

Rob hastily produced two small wrapped parcels, then placed

them beside Mahree's dictionary cassettes. "Each of us requires five times this amount, each day."

"I understand," the Mizari said. "And personal hygiene?"

"Could we have a *bath*?" Mahree blurted, in English, so Rob would understand, then in Mizari, since the Simiu language had no word for "bath." "A real *bath*?"

Shirazz was unperturbed. "Of course. Sand or mud? Or, if another cleansing medium, please provide its chemical composition."

Mahree stared at Rob, dismayed, but he gave her a reassuring grin, and put in, smoothly, "Liquid H_2O, Esteemed One. A quantity deep enough for immersion."

"To what extent do you wish to immerse yourselves?" The Guest Liaison's tentacles were moving quickly, and Mahree guessed that she was taking notes.

"Deep enough to sit down in," the young woman interposed before Rob could answer, hastily sitting down on her bag so the alien would comprehend what that meant, "and have the water come up to *here*." She held a hand up to her collarbones. "If that's not too much trouble, Esteemed One."

"Assuredly not," the being said briskly. "Our bathing receptacles are designed to accommodate creatures the size of our own race. Adapting one for humans will present no difficulty. What temperature?"

Rob and Mahree stared at each other, blankly. Precise Simiu temperature measurements were still foreign to them. "This air," Rob said, finally, "is approximately ten of our temperature units less than our body temperatures, which you no doubt determined when you scanned us. We would like our liquid H_2O eight of those units *higher* than our body temperatures, if that is possible."

"Entirely possible," the CLS Liaison said. "It shall be as you have requested."

"Oh, and can we please have several lengths of that Simiu woven material they use to cover their sleeping mats?" Mahree put in, thinking of the filthy towels currently occupying her bag.

"Of course."

Rob looked over at Mahree and shrugged, then back at the Mizari. "I think that's all." He gave the alien a rueful grin. "I hope we haven't asked for anything that will be hard to furnish."

Shirazz gazed serenely at them with something approaching amusement in the way she held her slender form. "Not at all,

HealerGable. I have arranged lodging for the Ri, who are aquatic dwellers so large that they would nearly fill up this section of tunnel we are standing in, and so timid that they have been known to die of fear if suddenly confronted with a being of another species. I have housed creatures that require atmospheres of methane and cyanide, baths in liquid ammonia, living creatures for nourishment, and gravity up to five times what we are experiencing here. Your requirements are comparatively simple and modest. Now, if you will wait for just a moment, I will conduct you to your quarters.''

Her tentacles waved gracefully for several minutes, while she communicated their lodging requirements to her staff. Finally Shirazz bowed again. "Your quarters are prepared," she said. "Will you please accompany me?"

Gracefully, she uncoiled and slithered off down the corridor, moving rapidly enough so that she had to adjust her speed downward to suit the two humans' walk.

"By the time we get to Earth," Rob said to Mahree, in English, "we'll be so blasé about First Contacts that nobody will be able to stand us."

She giggled. "I can picture it now. 'And then there was the time I spent the afternoon with that creature from the ammonia ocean—now what *was* its name?' "

Ahead of them, Shirazz halted before a spot in the tunnel wall. "Here are your quarters," she said, and a discernible opening appeared in the previously featureless surface. "And your comrade is there." She indicated another door not far away.

The doorway slid open. "Please," Shirazz murmured, ushering them in. The humans preceded her into an apartment half the size of *Rosinante,* consisting of a sitting room, furnished in typical Simiu fashion, a small galley, a bedroom, and beyond it, in the head, something that made Mahree gasp with anticipation. "The *bath*! Thank you so much, Esteemed Shirazz!"

"Is there any way to adjust the lighting level downward?" Rob asked the Mizari. "Simiu light is too white for our eyes. We prefer a lower level, and more yellow than white light."

"I will show you how to adjust the light levels and reach your friend on the intercom, HealerGable," Shirazz said, and bowed to Mahree, who returned the salutation. "Enjoy your bath, Honored Mahree," she said, and the young woman thought she detected a hint of kind amusement. Shirazz then undulated back out to the other room, Rob trailing behind her.

Mahree looked at the deep, circular depression in the floor that was filled with water, the liquid bubbling slightly from the circulating jets near the bottom of the small pool. The "tub" was easily three meters across, and had one side that sloped upward in a ramp. *Of course,* she thought. *So the Mazari can get in and out easily.* A narrow ledge ran around its inside, about halfway up.

The young woman opened her bag and pulled out her soap and shampoo. Then she stepped out of her clothing, and, with a disdainful grimace, tossed it over to the other side of the room. Hanging on cautiously to the edge, in case the bottom was slippery, Mahree lowered herself into the warm water with a sigh of pure happiness.

For a few minutes she just basked, allowing the dirt to loosen up, then she began scrubbing herself briskly.

Mahree had just dunked her head to rinse it of its first lathering and then raised it again when she heard Rob's voice. "How's the water?"

Holding her nose, she tipped her head backward, submerging it so the long strands wouldn't blind her, then she wiped the water from her eyes. He was leaning in the doorway, not quite looking at her. "Fine," she said, absurdly glad that her hair floated around her, covering her exposed shoulders. "It could be a little hotter, but, under the circumstances, you managed wonderfully. I would never have thought of describing temperatures the way you did."

"Desperation is the mother of invention," he said cheerfully. "Shirazz had to call her staff and remind them to bring the lengths of Simiu cloth for toweling." He hefted several scarlet and blue thicknesses lying across his arms. "I got the feeling heads are going to roll. Conrad Hilton could've learned a lot from her."

"Conrad who?"

"Never mind," he said. "Where do you want me to leave your towel?"

Mahree hesitated for a long moment, then suddenly grinned sheepishly. "Oh, Rob, don't be silly! I'm not going to make you wait while I soak, and I don't intend to climb out in a hurry just so you can get in! Come on in, the water's fine."

When he hesitated, she beckoned with a soapy arm, reaching for her shampoo again. *"C'mon!"*

She was bent over scrubbing her scalp when she felt the water surge higher as his body displaced it. And, despite her brave words, she didn't look up until she was certain that he was fully immersed.

When she glanced up, she saw that he was sitting a little more than arm's length away. Balancing on the narrow ledge, slumped far down on his spine so the water rose chin-deep, he had his head tilted back, and wore an expression of utter beatitude. "Don't anyone disturb me for about a hundred years," he sighed. "I may never move again."

Mahree smiled as she soaped her hands and arms yet again. "It almost makes up for the whole trip, doesn't it? *Désirée* doesn't have anything to match this!"

Finally he stirred and sat up straight. "Now for those layers of grime," he said. She noticed that he was careful to look her directly in the eyes. The water was cloudy, but the circulating jets kept it from being completely opaque. "Lend me your soap?"

"Sure," she said, and held it out to him. His hand brushed hers as he took it, and Mahree blushed. She turned away and briskly began squeezing de-tangler through her hair, then rinsed it again. Not looking up, she began finger-combing out the knots, wondering how the hell she was going to get herself out of the tub and into a towel. *You're being ridiculous,* she thought, *You've been sleeping next to this man for days, this is silly . . .*

But she felt the way she had the time she'd stood on the edge of *Désirée*'s airlock, looking out into space. A quivery, fluttery feeling, as though someone had turned the gravity off.

Water sloshed over her shoulders as Rob submerged himself, then came up streaming. For a moment he was staring directly at her, and there was something in his eyes that caused Mahree to color again—a male awareness of herself as a female. She gulped nervously. "Want some help with that?" he said, moving close enough to pick up a strand of the hair that lay plastered against her shoulder, half its length floating like some kind of exotic seaweed. "Need your back washed?"

"Uh . . ." she stammered, hastily backing away. "I . . . no, not really. I mean, I already did that . . ."

"Okay," he said, amiably, but something flickered in his

eyes that might have been disappointment, "guess I'd better go
see if Shirazz had that food delivered yet. You think Dhurrrkk's
okay? Should we check on him?"

Mahree shook her head. "He's fine, but he was definite about
wanting to be by himself," she said, then hastily glanced away
as Rob pulled himself out of the tub. She heard him slosh over to
the "towels," then the soft whisper of the woven material as he
dried himself off. Then his footsteps receded into the sleeping room.

She shook herself, then put both hands on the edge of the pool
behind her and pulled herself up out of the bath water. Sitting on
the edge of the pool, she hastily squeezed the water out of her
hair, then blotted it with the Simiu towel. *You idiot,* she thought,
a painful lump in her throat, her stomach in knots. *What's wrong
with you? Why did you back off like that?*

Paradoxically, she was also furious with Rob, for not making
more of a move, for not pursuing the issue. *Why did he have to
drop it? Why couldn't he have* . . . She frowned as insight
flooded her. *Because he's a decent guy, dummy.*

Mahree took a deep breath and swung her legs out of the tub.
Hastily, she dried herself with the scarlet length of Simiu fabric,
then wrapped it around her body, loosely knotting it over her
breasts. Her knees felt weak and shaky as she walked quietly
into the room with the sleeping mats. Rob was there, his makeshift towel wrapped around his waist, his back to her.

As she approached soundlessly, he held up a shirt, sniffed
cautiously, then called out, pitching his voice to carry into the
bathroom, "Whew! The next thing on the agenda had better be
laundry. Everything I have smells worse than a locker room.
How much soap do you have left?"

Mahree's heart felt as though it were trying to burst its way
out of her throat. She swallowed it back down, then put a hand
on his shoulder. He started violently, but then, realizing who
was behind him, he stood still, muscles tense beneath her fingers. Mahree had to wet her lips before she could whisper,
"Nearly a whole container. But can't the laundry wait?"

Rob did not reply, only remained unmoving as she slowly,
deliberately, trailed her fingers and palm across the width of his
back to his other shoulder, then ran them downward, spiraling
back and forth along his spine. "You know, Rob," she murmured softly, "I've been thinking about how big this station is.
And almost all of it, apparently, has an oxy-nitrogen atmo-

sphere. That means there's lots and lots and *lots* of air here. Air to burn . . . air to waste.''

Her fingers had reached the edge of the blue fabric at his waist by now, and, taking a deep breath, Mahree slid them beneath it, running her hand over his buttock. Sparse, soft hairs tickled her palm. ''Want to waste some air, Rob?''

Without warning, he whirled to face her, his hands closing on her shoulders, his eyes holding hers. The sudden motion of his body had pulled the blue towel loose, but he ignored that as he stared at her intently. ''Are you sure, Mahree?'' he said, and she saw the pulse leap beneath his jaw. ''Really *sure*?''

She nodded. ''I'm sure,'' she whispered, though again she had to moisten her lips before she could speak. Her teeth wanted to chatter, and she clenched them to control the urge.

Rob leaned a little closer, his eyes searching her features, concerned. His hands tightened on her shoulders. ''You scared?'' he demanded. ''Tell me the truth.''

Mahree shook her head. ''Not scared,'' she corrected, her voice emerging with more strength. ''Just nervous. But I know what I want.''

He gave her a wry grin. ''I'm nervous, too.'' Slowly, his fingers moved up to tenderly caress her throat, the line of her jaw. He slid his arms around her, at first gently, then they tightened, pulling her against him hungrily.

This kiss was different from their first, less tentative, more sensual. More deliberately arousing. For endless moments Rob's lips lightly brushed hers, tracing, nibbling, tantalizing, until Mahree could stand it no more. Opening her mouth wide against his, she captured his tongue with her own. She felt him pull away slightly, then felt him stroking her nipples, her back, her buttocks, and realized with a faraway part of her mind that her towel had gone the way of his.

She clung to him, dizzy from the feel of his body against hers. Finally, when she was gasping and trembling, he lowered her onto the bed.

CHAPTER 16

◆

Something Special?

Yesterday Rob and I became lovers, but that's by no means the most important thing that's happened in the last two days. (Though it certainly has been the most enjoyable!)

It all started tonight, when Dhurrrkk', Rob, Shirazz, and I ate dinner together in Dhurrrkk's suite. Not surprisingly, the Guest Liaison was lovely company, urbane, witty, and entertaining. She and Rob had a lot to talk about, because she's a physician, as well as a diplomat. (Being a Mizari healer means that you treat the entire person—body, mind, and spirit.)

We wound up telling her the entire story of how we'd come to be aboard *Désirée*, and of the Human/Simiu contact. Dhurrrkk', Rob, and I took turns relating our adventures—with one important exception. Before we docked at Shassiszss Station, the three of us decided that it would be best not to mention Doctor Blanket and Avernus until we discovered how things stood with the CLS. So we left all that out.

(When it was my turn, I made sure that I filled in all the gaps in Rob's story, because he tends to downplay his achievements. But Rob repaid me, in kind. Some of the things he and Dhurrrkk' said about me had me blushing.)

Even though I enjoyed speaking Mizari with a native, Shirazz was also careful to have both Rob and me talk to her in English, so she could test out the translation program the Mizari had adapted from the one Dhurrrkk' and I put together aboard

Rosinante. Not surprisingly, we found a few bugs, the most notable of which was the substitution of the definition of "pubic" for "public." Good thing we caught that!

Apparently the story of our dramatic entrance has spread around the station. Dhurrrkk' said the First Councillor referred to it when she called him this morning. I gather she wasn't pleased. At least the publicity makes it impossible for the Simiu to simply "disappear" Dhurrrkk'. I wish I had a holo-vid of that scene in the corridor. We must've looked like something out of one of Rob's Marx Brothers films.

Anyway, after the "party" broke up last night, Rob and Dhurrrkk' came back here so Dhurrrkk' could see our bathtub. I lingered in Dhurrrkk's suite, talking to Shirazz. When I told her that I was worried about Dhurrrkk', she explained to me that the CLS would do everything in their power to keep him safe while he was here on Shassiszss Station, but that it was against League policy for them to interfere with the Simiu legal process.

Then she fixed me with her onyx-like eyes and told me she had something very important to discuss with me, and a great favor to ask.

She wanted this journal! Seems Dhurrrkk' told her that I'd kept a written record of everything we'd been discussing, and she asked to see it for two reasons: (1) She wanted to use it to test the new translation program the Mizari are developing, and, (2) The journal will help them make a decision about an extremely vital project the League has been considering for a long time.

She didn't tell me just what the project is, but it was obvious that Shirazz considered it essential to the future of the Five Founding Worlds and their six affiliate member worlds (Hurrreeah and its colonies are included in the latter category).

The CLS has been looking nearly as long for a very special person to run this endeavor. Someone who comes from a world that is politically and economically independent of CLS interactions and involvements.

In Rob, they think they may have found that person. They were impressed with him from the first, Shirazz told me.

I have to admit that when she first spoke of finding someone to run this project, a sudden, wild hope blossomed in *me*. When she said it was Rob they were interested in, my heart sank for a moment. Then I felt a thrill of vicarious pride and joy.

She wanted to know whether Rob seemed to like what he'd seen of the CLS so far. I told her he did.

"Your journal," she said, then, "will help us to know him better, know whether he is indeed the person we seek. It would be cruel to disappoint him if he is not that person, so I will ask that you say nothing of our discussion to him."

Of course I agreed, though the idea of Rob staying here on Shassiszss, while I went on to Earth, was like a knife in my heart. I don't know if I could bear to lose him, now that we're finally together . . .

So now I've got those cassettes burning a hole in my pocket, until I can hand them over to Shirazz. She's taking us on a tour of this station, now that quarantine's over. I left everything in, all the angst and anguish, except for those references to Doctor Blanket as an intelligent being.

Now you see why losing my virginity got "second billing," as Rob calls it.

But speaking personally . . .

WOW. I had no idea.

Rob is a terrific lover—passionate, remarkably attuned to what I'm feeling, what gives me pleasure. I didn't realize that love-making could be so much *fun*. When you watch the couples in a clinch on the holo-vids, it's all so deadly serious—all groans and gasps and writhings. Well, that's true enough, but you also *play* and that's great! For two people who've been living "on the edge of death" (that's melodramatic, but true), the sheer cathartic *release* of playing, of laughing and making terrible jokes and hideous puns, of acting adolescently moonstruck and *silly*—it's wonderful.

The CLS Guest Liaison led the two humans and their Simiu friend on a tour that left their heads spinning with new sights, sounds, and smells—a long ramble that didn't cover a third of the massive station.

Mizari architecture was based on circles and spheres. The polished white walls with black floors gave a sense of cool purity, enlivened by isolated touches of vibrant color—a piece of pottery here, an abstract mural there.

Growing things flourished. Mizari were enthusiastic garden-ers. Plants from Shassiszss were so dark a green they appeared black in some lights, and many had exotically shaped and colored blossoms. Trellises arched overhead, ground-level plots surrounded exotic fountains composed of water and crystal. These water sculptures created a sibilant sussuration throughout the Mizari portions of the station, muffling the sounds of alien voices and means of locomotion.

Other "spokes" of the six enormous wheels reflected different architectures and environments. For some of the environments, guide and visitors had to don the glowing protective "fields" that protected their bodies from poisonous atmospheres or crushing gravities, while supplying them with breathable air.

Rob, Dhurrrkk', and Mahree saw the "cliff-dwellings" of the symbiotic race called the Shadgui, from a star located near Procyon. The "Shad" portion of the alien was a huge, black-haired shambling creature that looked vaguely like one of the enormous ground sloths that have long been extinct on Earth. The "Gui" were small, red-skinned toadlike creatures the aliens carried on their shoulders. The "Shad" were eyeless, but "saw" perfectly through their symbionts, while the "Gui," in their turn, needed their massive partners to speak for them. Both creatures shared a powerful telepathic and metabolic bond. Shirazz explained that separation of either life-form from the other for more than ten hours inevitably resulted in the death of both.

Next came the Ri, the beings that Shirazz had mentioned as being so shy that the sight of an alien could be a fatal shock. Accordingly, the three visitors could only observe their area on a one-way holo-screen. Ri were an aquatic species that resembled huge, shelled lavender octopi. Each individual was the size of a small room. The Ri Councillor, Shirazz explained, would not attend tomorrow's meeting in person, but would observe and participate via holo-screen.

Then the travelers met the Chhhh-kk-tu. These small, furred creatures came from a star near Sirius, and they resembled wallabies.

Chhhh-kk-tu stood upright. They came no higher than the middle of Rob's chest, and had small, bright eyes, pointed noses, rounded ears on the top of their heads, and four-digited fingers. They had pouches in their cheeks and small, marsupial-like pouches on their fronts that Dhurrrkk' quietly explained had nothing to do with carrying young, but were part of their sexual equipment. The aliens' fur was soft and shining, and varied in colors from a deep seal brown to a pale blue. Many had bandit-masks like Terran raccoons.

The creatures were very friendly and curious about the new-comers. The Chhhh-kk-tu Councillor invited them for dinner the evening of the Councillors' meeting.

"I'm not quite sure how long we'll be staying," Mahree demurred, "but would it be acceptable to let you know after the meeting?"

After that came the beings from the brilliant star humans called Rigel. Mahree shuddered as she gazed into an evil-smelling brackish aquarium at three creatures about the size of large dogs. Rob couldn't blame her; these beings were so alien that he found them disturbing, in a way that transcended their slimy, oozing, constantly changing forms.

Dhurrrkk's sensitive nostrils twitched as he stood on his hind legs, bracing himself with his hands on the protective barrier. "I mean no offense," he muttered, in English, "but it smells to me as though those people badly need a decent grooming. Or perhaps one of your baths."

"They look like a cross between oysters and green garden slugs," Rob observed, pitching his voice low.

"I could have nightmares about those things," Mahree whispered back. "I'm sure they're nice people, but they're . . . I can't describe it, but they look just *awful*."

"No worse than what I've pored over during autopsies," Rob pointed out. "But it goes beyond their physical appearance. Now I know how Steve McQueen felt when he saw 'The Blob.' "

"Remind me to skip that one," Mahree said dryly.

Rob nerved himself up to greet the creatures politely, but, to everyone's relief, Shirazz informed them that communication with Rigellians was a skill currently mastered only by a few special Chhhh-kk-tu. The creatures "spoke" only by means of body pulses. They were unable to use voders or artificial com-munication aids.

"So how do the Chhhh-kk-tu speak with them?" Mahree asked.

"They enter the tanks and the Rigellians wrap themselves around their bodies. It is extremely difficult and exhausting work, translating for the Rigellian Councillor and its aides," Shirazz explained.

Dhurrrkk's crest drooped as he considered that prospect. "The

Chhhh-kk-tu are beings of great honor and remarkable courage," he said gravely.

"We are currently honored to have one of Rigel's foremost artists here for an exhibition," Shirazz told them. "Would you care to see its works?"

"Sure," Mahree said, forcing enthusiasm. "What kind of art could something that looked like *that* produce?" she whispered to Rob as they followed the Guest Liaison.

In a gallery adjoining the aquarium, a series of pedestals displayed a variety of shapes that made the humans stare wide-eyed.

The "sculptures" were airy, spun marvels—iridescent swirls of color, about the size of a human hand. The rippling, rainbow-hued material they were composed of looked like a cross between natural pearls and opals.

Each graceful shape had a predominant color—powder blue, lilac, rose, palest yellow, mint green. But, even more than their exquisite shapes and colors, each creation's delicate symmetry and balance of design captured and delighted the eye.

"They're wonderful!" Mahree breathed. "How are they made?"

"The Rigellians excrete the iridescent substance from their bodies," Shirazz explained. "It is an ability they all have, but not all of them are artists. Most produce lumps of the substance, which are cut, then used in jewelry or as inlay work for mosaics. But this particular Rigellian—they do not have names, so we call it simply 'Master'—is different. It produces works of intrinsic beauty."

"The Rigellians sell this substance they produce?" Rob asked, wishing he had some way to buy a piece for Mahree.

"Yes. It is in great demand."

"Does Master sell its works?" Dhurrrkk' asked. "They seem . . . beyond price."

"Yes, each of these pieces will be sold. We are fortunate to have them displayed here, before they take up residence in the homes of the wealthy."

"I wish I could afford one," Mahree said softly, still enthralled. "I'd look at it for hours each day. And each time I looked at it, I'd learn something new . . . about myself, and about the transcendence of true art, true beauty." She gave Rob a rueful glance. "I've already learned something, from seeing the creator, then seeing its creations."

• • •

"Rob . . ." Mahree began, then trailed off.

On the verge of falling asleep, he opened his eyes in the dim light of their sleeping room. "What, sweetheart?"

"Do you ever wish you could stay here, and not go back?"

"To the *Désirée*?"

"Or Earth."

The doctor stretched, then rolled over and propped his head on his hand, looking down at her. He could see the pale oval of her face, surrounded by the dark masses of her hair, but could not make out her expression. "You mean, assuming that Dhurrrkk' was safe and all?"

"Yeah. Does Shassiszss strike you as a place where you could be happy?"

He shrugged. "I wouldn't want to stay here and never see home again. But this place *is* wonderful." He thought about it for a moment. "Yeah, I could live here . . . especially when I think of how much the Mizari bio-sciences have to offer."

"I could stay here, too," she whispered.

Rob grinned. "No need to ask *you* why. Your eyes light up brighter with every new alien species you see." He yawned suddenly, widely. It had been a long day. "Why the question, anyway? You planning to ask the Mizari to let us stay?"

"I might," she said half seriously.

"Go to sleep," he said, smothering another yawn. "We've got a busy day tomorrow."

He had nearly drifted off again, when she suddenly nestled against him. "Rob? Hold me, okay?"

"What's wrong?" he asked, settling her head against his shoulder. "You aren't still having nightmares about what happened when Doctor Blanket rearranged your mind, are you?"

"No . . ."

"Then what is it?"

"Nothing . . . I just want to be close to you, that's all."

He smiled. "If you keep me talking, I'm going to wake all the way up, and *then* you'll see what 'close' is."

He could hear an answering smile in her voice. "Don't make threats unless you plan to follow through."

Rob rolled over until she was lying within the circle of his arms. "Okay. Don't say I didn't warn you."

• • •

Mahree and Rob crowded uncomfortably into the Simiu lounge seat before the communications equipment, as the "screen" flickered, and Rhrrrkkeet's features emerged. Both humans made the greeting gesture. "Honored MahreeBurroughs! Honored HealerGable!" the First Ambassador exclaimed. "I am so relieved to see that you are safe!"

Mahree said, in Simiu, "We are well, Honored Rhrrrkkeet'."

The Simiu Ambassador gave an almost-human start of surprise to hear the young woman speaking her language, but she quickly recovered. "I have just spoken with my cousin-son, and yesterday I talked with First Councillor Ahkk'eerrr. You three miscreants have had many adventures aboard my vessel, and at Shassiszss Station." There was a wry twinkle in her violet eyes.

"We did, Honored Rhrrrkkeet'," Mahree agreed. "But your vessel is undamaged." She ducked her head, a little abashed. "We apologize for taking it without asking."

"I commend your courage, if not your actions." The Simiu Ambassador's expression was rueful; her maned crest stood at half mast.

"Please, Honored Rhrrrkkeet'," Mahree began. "Do not judge your cousin-son harshly. I demanded his help because we shared an honor-bond. He had little choice, if he wished to keep his honor."

"That is not what Honored Dhurrrkk' told me," the F.A. said. "He offered no excuses and no regrets." Her pale eyelids drooped as she paused thoughtfully. "Frankly, I am impressed with his initiative. Before you humans came, my cousin-son lacked this. Now, it appears, he has more than enough."

"Will . . . will Dhurrrkk' be punished? Will he have to meet a professional gladiator in the Arena?"

"I do not know," the Simiu told her. "The answer to that question will depend on the decision of the League Members tomorrow—whether our world is granted full membership because of our contact with your people. I do not consider that fair, and am doing all that I can to point out that my cousin-son cannot be expected to bear the responsibility for unwise choices made by our Council. I have supporters, but it is too early to tell whether our side will prevail."

"I am glad you are defending Honored Dhurrrkk', Honored Rhrrrkkeet'," Mahree said gratefully. "I was afraid that no one would stand up for him."

"My cousin-son acted with the impetuosity of youth, but in accordance with his personal honor," the F.A. said. "Others agree with me. This communication," Rhrrrkkeet' added, "has been authorized so that you may speak with your people. I will transfer you to them."

Her image flicked out—immediately replaced by Raoul Lamont's broad, good-natured features, his mouth smiling beneath the thick moustache, the glare of Simiu lighting gleaming off his balding forehead. "Mahree!" he exclaimed. "Honey, how are you? And Doc! Are you both okay?"

"We're fine, Uncle Raoul!"

"We're fine, Captain," Rob said. Deliberately, he put an arm around Mahree and pulled her tightly against him. "We've been through a lot, but we're managing."

Raoul's eyebrows went up. "*We?*" was all he said, but the intonation was enough. He looked directly at his niece. She nodded at his unspoken question, and he hesitated, then smiled uncertainly. "Congratulations," he said, with a touch of irony. "You're happy, Mahree?"

"Oh, *yes,* Uncle Raoul!" she said, her eyes meeting his across the parsecs. "I've never been so happy!" She took a deep breath. "If I weren't so worried about that hearing tomorrow, that is," she amended, her smile vanishing. "Dhurrrkk' may be in real trouble."

"So I hear," Raoul said.

"Tell me, Captain, how is Joan? Any trouble with that arm?"

Lamont's expression turned grim. "Joan's arm is healed," he said, "but things aren't the same around here." He took a deep breath. "We . . . aren't together anymore, if you get my drift."

"Oh, Uncle Raoul . . ." Mahree said, in French, "when I heard how she talked to you during that meeting, I was afraid of that."

"Thanks for your discretion," he said, in the same language. "But Rhrrrkkeet' knows about that meeting. She and I are old buddies, by now. Still, it's not nice to wash dirty linen in the presence of strangers."

"You *told* Rhrrrkkeet' what happened in that meeting?" Mahree was aghast. *"Mon Dieu!"*

"I told her, yes. And the lady stuck up for us, even so. The Council was already on the verge of firing her for defending us.

Now she thinks her defense of Dhurrrkk' will constitute the last straw. But she doesn't give a damn.''

"Oh, *mon oncle* . . .'' she said, thinking of all that had happened, how things had changed, ''did I mess things up, coming here? At the time, I thought I was doing the right thing, but now . . .''

Raoul gave her a smile that was meant to be reassuring. ''It took strength to do what you did. I'm sorry that you didn't come to me before taking off—but I understand why you didn't. Nobody was communicating very well about that time.'' He sighed.

"But tell me how things are now!'' Mahree said, to change the subject. She couldn't bear to see her normally cheerful uncle like this.

"Your departure really brought things to a head. When the story of what you and Dhurrrkk' had done hit the Simiu news media, they knew that it was only a matter of time until the CLS found out about us. So the High Council started falling all over themselves to tell us that *of course* we were free to leave.''

"Is Khrekk's family still demanding satisfaction?''

"I understand Khrekk's family resigned their positions in protest when diplomatic relations with us were resumed. One good thing . . . they're screening the people they allow to meet us a bit more carefully these days,'' he said, with a touch to irony. ''Things are still rather strained, but I think any danger to *Désirée* is definitely past.''

"I can't tell you how relieved I am to hear that,'' Mahree said. ''And, *mon oncle,* if there's any way you can manage to let the Simiu Council know that humans will take it very ill if they try to punish Dhurrrkk' for helping us, you owe that to him.''

"I agree,'' Lamont said. ''And I will. When are you two coming back?''

Oh, God, Mahree thought, with a stab of anguish. *What if only I return? What if Rob stays here!* But she schooled her face. ''I'm not sure. The Mizari will tell Rhrrrkkeet', so you'll know. It'll take about a month to get back from here. We've got to stay through tomorrow, because that's when the CLS Councillors are meeting, and we have to testify.''

"Rhrrrkkeet' explained all that to me,'' Raoul said, then switched back to English. ''I wish you both the best of luck tomorrow. Doc, I think you ought to let her make the closing

remarks . . . I'll never forget how she spoke that day we decided
to pursue that crazy frequency. She convinced *me* . . . maybe
she can convince a bunch of aliens.'' He gave his niece a proud
smile. ''Wait until the Terran government finds out that our best
and brightest hope for the biggest event in history was a seventeen-
year-old,'' he said. ''I hope I'm the one that tells them. I want to
see the President's face.'' He chuckled, then sobered. ''I guess
that's it, except to tell you both to take care of yourselves.''

Rob cleared his throat. ''One more thing, Raoul—how's
Sekhmet?''

Lamont grinned. ''Thought you might ask that,'' he said.
''Yoki?'' He beckoned, and a second later a pair of hands
deposited a sleek, purring black bundle into his arms. ''She
sleeps on my bunk at night.''

CHAPTER 17

✦

The Councillors

I feel as though I'm suspended in a cube of transparent plas-steel—I can't think about anything but that hearing. Everything else seems muffled and distant . . . unreal. Rob and Dhurrrkk' aren't here; Dhurrrkk' is in his room, grooming himself nervously, and Rob went to talk to Shirazz, get her advice on how best to conduct ourselves at the meeting.

Will she take this opportunity to tell him about the job? Will I have to return to *Désirée* by myself? Maybe the Mizari could find something for *me* to do—translating, maybe, so I could stay with him? I can't imagine settling down as a university student on Earth after all this. There's no career they can teach me at the Sorbonne that I have any interest in pursuing. Rob was right—what I want to do is learn about aliens, and there's no college degree for *that*.

In a way it was easier when all I had to worry about was whether I'd be alive to wake up each morning.

Four hours to go until the meeting. I wish I could stop counting the minutes.

Rob and Shirazz were in the Mizari's office, talking. The doctor sat on the floor, cross-legged; the Guest Liaison was draped over a series of brackets fastened to the wall. There were walled, padded cubicles surrounding him that served the aliens as places to support their coils should they decide to rest in one place—the Mizari equivalent of chairs.

But Shirazz was like a human who paced as she thought; she kept adjusting the draping of her coils over the brackets, resulting in a slow, steady progress around the room.

Rob discreetly edged around on his backside to follow her restless movements. "It was Raoul's last comment that made me begin thinking about it," he admitted.

"Raoul-Lamont? The Captain of your vessel?"

"Yes. Do *you* think I'm doing the right thing?"

Shirazz hung poised on her brackets for a moment, evidently considering. Even her halo of scarlet, orange, and black tentacles barely moved. Then her wedge-shaped head turned, and she regarded him with her pupilless unblinking eyes. "Yes, I agree with your decision," she said. "I believe you will be doing the best thing. But I can recognize that this was a most difficult conclusion to reach, Doctor-Gable."

"Please, call me Rob. Yes, it was a hard decision," he admitted, "but now that I've made it, I feel much better. Thanks for your advice, it helped a lot."

"Feeling better after coming to a difficult decision appears to be a trait our peoples share," she said. "Now, if I may, Rob, I would like to ask you a personal question."

He glanced up at her, startled, then shrugged inwardly. Mizari were extremely curious beings and, notwithstanding their customarily diplomatic patterns of speech, were capable of bluntness when the occasion warranted. "Go ahead," he told her. "What do you want to know?"

"Do you like children, Rob?"

Completely taken aback, the doctor wondered for one wild moment whether he was about to become the recipient of the first interspecies proposal, then he gave himself a mental shake. *Don't be silly, Shirazz is married, and Mizari are monogamous.* "Children?" he repeated, considering the question. "Yes, I like children. As a matter of fact, I considered specializing in pediatrics—the treatment of children—before deciding to take up colonial medicine."

"All ages of children?" she persisted.

What's this about? Rob wondered, completely mystified. "Yes, all ages," he said. "Having had younger sisters, I can change diapers with the best of them."

A brief exchange concerning the meaning of "diapers" occurred, then she inquired, "What about young people of approximately Dhurrrkk's age? Those who are poised on the edge of adulthood?''

"That's one of my favorite age groups," he replied. "I enjoyed working with adolescents and teenagers very much."

"You have had experience dealing with this age group, then?"

"Yes, I did quite a bit of counseling with young people when I was taking my psychology degrees. I was younger than the other counselors, so many of the kids seemed able to relate to me better than they could the older therapists."

Don't pat yourself on the back too hard, Rob, he thought. *Remember how insensitive you were with Mahree.* He sighed. *But she wasn't a patient, either. Be fair to yourself. There were other considerations operating when you were with her, even if you weren't consciously aware of them at the time.*

"I am very gratified to hear that, Rob," Shirazz said, sliding down off the brackets, coil by coil, and gliding over to face him. "I know you are wondering why I wished to know, but I cannot tell you at this time. If, later, I become able to do so, I promise that I will."

Rob nodded. "I'll be content with that, then," he said. Glancing at his watch, he said, "I must get back, Shirazz. We've talked far longer than I'd realized. I ought to eat something before I give my testimony." He smiled wryly.

She inclined her head in one of her people's graceful gestures—almost a nod of acquiescence. "You have my respect, Rob," she said formally. "I will come to escort you to the hearing in two of your hours."

He stood up. "We'll be ready."

"How disgusting—a pimple! Of all the rotten things to happen when we're about to be presented to the CLS as prime specimens of humanity . . . I have to get a damn *zit*!" Mahree muttered in a furious undertone, gingerly probing her chin. She and Rob were standing outside the door to their quarters, waiting for Shirazz and Dhurrrkk'.

He inspected the afflicted area narrowly. "It's not that bad. Quit touching it, you'll make it worse."

"I thought having sex was supposed to clear up your face," she grumbled, giving him a sidelong glance.

"Good grief, is that ancient fable still hanging around?"

"Sure," she said, straight-faced. "You mean it isn't *true*?

Those guys who told me that were *lying*? I'm shocked!" She sobered. "Be honest, do I look awful?"

"No, you look great. It looks like a beauty mark."

"Now *you're* lying, but I love you for it." She paced, tugging her dark blue pants and pale blue tunic straight, pushing the rippling fall of her hair back off her shoulders. "Maybe I should've put my hair up. I'd look older."

Rob chuckled. "Most of these people have never seen a human before, so how do you expect them to judge your age? Quit fretting! You're making me nervous."

"Good. You perform admirably under stress."

He grimaced. "You're the one who speaks their language."

"They've got the translation program," Mahree pointed out, making a herculean effort not to finger her chin.

Rob shifted restlessly, jamming his hands in his pockets. "Yeah, the translation program," he muttered sourly.

The doctor paced the width of the corridor, then turned back again. "Look, now you've got me doing it. I wish I had something better to wear than an ordinary ship's coverall. You should've made me bring something."

"You're lucky I brought *you*."

He gave her a strained smile. "I am, aren't I?"

The door beside them opened, and Dhurrrkk' joined them. "Hello, my friends," he said. His grooming efforts had paid off; every hair in his mane was in place, and his dappled flanks gleamed under the bright lights as though they'd been polished.

"Dhurrrkk', you look very nice," Mahree said.

"Thank you, FriendMahree," he said. "I was nervous, and grooming is soothing."

Hearing the faint whisper of scales sliding over polished flooring, they turned to see Shirazz, and gave her the Mizari greeting, which the CLS Liaison returned.

"Shall we go?" the alien said, gesturing with half her tentacles.

Via walkway and lift, the travelers were guided deeper into the gigantic station than they had ever been before, until they had reached the innermost hub of the gyroscope.

"The Council chamber is directly above us," Shirazz said, signaling open the portal to a bare, circular room and waving them past her. "We will be occupying the center section. In addition to ourselves, and the Simiu Councillors, there will be the Secretary-General, as I believe the term would translate. She is a Drnian named Fys, and you may address her as 'Most Esteemed Fys.' Also present will be the League's Chief Mediator, Esteemed Ssoriszs. The Councillors from each world will be seated around us.''

"This Ssoriszs . . . he's a Mizari?'' Rob asked.

"Yes,'' Shirazz said. "He conducts the proceedings, and renders judgment, when needed.''

"First Councillor Ahkk'eerrr will be in the center with us?'' Dhurrrkk' asked, sounding apprehensive.

'Yes, along with the entire Simiu delegation. You may choose to join them, or you may remain with the humans.''

Dhurrrkk' glanced up at Rob and Mahree. "I will stand with my friends,'' he said, without hesitation.

"Very well,'' Shirazz said. "Each of you will be given a chance to speak. If you humans prefer to use your native language, the translation program is enabled.''

"And after the Councillors hear our testimony?'' Rob asked, in careful Simiu. "What then?''

"They will decide whether Honored Dhurrrkk's people will be permitted full membership status, and the increased representation in the League that accompanies that privilege.''

She dipped her head to Rob and Mahree slightly. "Then, after your testimony, you will be officially welcomed as a new sentient species. Many of the Councillors may wish to extend good wishes and ask questions. Feel free to reply as fully or as briefly as you choose. The Councillors know that you are here informally, as our guests, not as official representatives.''

"After the meeting is adjourned,'' Shirazz continued, "there will be a . . . reception, a social gathering. The Councillors who are comfortable in your environment will attend. They may ask whether your people are interested in joining the League.''

"There are obvious benefits,'' Rob said.

"For our peoples as well as yours. Are you ready?''

Mahree moved closer to Rob's side, and he took her hand. When she extended her other hand to Dhurrrkk', her friend sat back on his haunches and gripped her fingers with his own. She could feel the silky brush of the flame-colored hairs on the back of his broad, leathery palmed hand. "We're ready.''

The floor quivered, then rose slowly, as the ceiling irised open.

They were rising into an arena, a dome, that was the largest enclosed space she had ever seen. The topmost part of the huge half sphere was transparent, revealing the profusion of stars and portions of Shassiszss station outside. The vista was breathtaking.

The curved walls were opaque. There were seats, though none humans could have occupied comfortably. There were also cubicles filled with the glowing field that indicated the presence of different atmospheric conditions, concealing whatever was inside.

Shadgui and Chhhh-kk-tu were visible, and several winged, vaguely insectile-appearing beings, looking like pictures Mahree had seen of Terran bees, though they were larger—perhaps the length of her arm. Another section was filled with tall aliens shaped for all the world like clumps of broccoli—and they were shiny dark green with purplish undertones, which added to the impression of huge walking vegetables.

"*Day of the Triffids*," muttered Rob when she unobtrusively drew his attention to the broccoli-creatures. "You suppose they're really *plants*?"

"Those are the Vardi," Dhurrrkk' told them softly. "A race who share characteristics with both plants and animals. They absorb nutrients from certain species of algae, but also produce chlorophyll through photosynthesis. They communicate by scents. The 'clumps' on their heads are olfactory-sensing and scent-releasing organs."

"Doctor Blanket's a *fungus*," Mahree reminded Rob, in a whisper. "That's even stranger than sentient plants."

As the platform and its occupants became visible to the beings waiting in the arena, Mahree saw that all the aliens who possessed identifiable optical organs were now gazing avidly at her and Rob. She caught sight of a creature that reminded her of a holo-vid of "Little Red Riding Hood." The being fixed her with hot yellow eyes in a furred silver-gray face. Its muzzle was pointed, and so were its many teeth.

As the platform neared the top, Rob suddenly glanced from her to Dhurrrkk', then back again, a grin spreading over his face—the wide, reckless grin that Mahree had always found irresistible. "I can hardly believe I'm actually here!" he exclaimed, glancing around at the assembled aliens. "There ought to be a John Williams score blaring in the background."

Mahree gave him a look that was both fond and exasperated. "John *who*?"

As the massive platform drew level with the floor of the

Council chamber, Mahree saw that it was a fifth of the entire floor area of the arena. There were no tables or chairs, only Simiu loungers, one bench, and a podium behind which a Mizari, probably the Esteemed Mediator Ssoriszs, coiled.

Ssoriszs was brilliantly colored, his pale green iridescent scales patterned with diamonds of emerald green and amber. His pupilless eyes were golden. As he saw Mahree's gaze on him, the being graciously bowed. Mahree poked Rob, who was busy not-staring at the sharp-toothed canisform, and squeezed Dhurrrkk's hand warningly, then all three travelers bowed to the Mizari.

Another alien stepped over to join the Mediator. Mahree decided this one must be the Secretary-General. Fys the Drnian was a tall, skinny, two-armed biped with dry, shiny, sable-colored skin. She was the first alien the humans had seen who wore clothing. A short, sleeveless green tunic was belted around an improbably tiny waist, and below the sticklike legs, her long-toed feet were shod with matching sandals. She also wore a necklace, wristlets, and earrings of the iridescent Rigellian exudate.

Humanoid as the Drnian's body appeared, the faint resemblance ended with her face. Beneath coils of fine, wirelike hair as dark as her skin, the Drnian's forehead bulged out, a bulge matched by the one at the back of her skull, so that the top of her head was flattened. Her eyes were huge and red, half-covered with nicitating membranes, and below them, instead of a nose, she had a sunken depression with two slits that Mahree assumed were nostils. Fys' mouth was small, round, and wet-looking, and, as she watched the Drnian, trying not to stare openly, the young woman saw a tongue emerge—a pale pink tube of a tongue.

Remember the lesson the Rigellian Master taught you, she thought.

The Secretary-General slowly, ceremoniously, made the Mizari greeting-bow, following it with a complicated gesture with her elongated fingers that Mahree guessed must be her native greeting. The three friends bowed together, then they walked over to the Drnian.

Fys towered over both humans by half a meter. "How do you do, Most Esteemed Fys?" Mahree said in Mizari, holding out her hand. "It is a pleasure and an honor."

The Drnian barely hesitated. "I do well, most well, Mahree Burroughs. I thank you," she said, in heavily accented but understandable English, while extending her own hand. Surprised and touched, Mahree took the Drnian's hand gently and carefully shook the dry, sticklike fingers. The Secretary-General lapsed back into Mizari. "Thank you for attending our meeting. We are eager to hear your story."

Dhurrrkk', at Mahree's side, made the Simiu greeting gesture, and Fys returned it, greeting him in accented Simiu.

"Most Esteemed One," Dhurrrkk' said.

The Drnian hesitated again as she turned to Rob, but his hand was already out. "A pleasure and an honor to meet you, Most Esteemed Fys," he said, carefully, in Mizari, bowing over her hand.

"How do you do, Doctor Robert Gable," Fys said, enunciating the English words carefully.

"Very well, thank you," he responded, smiling.

The humans and Dhurrrkk' stepped back as the Drnian turned away. Ssoriszs bowed, first to them, then to the Secretary-General, and finally, ceremoniously, to the assembly. "We are begun," he said formally, in Mizari.

Rob, Mahree, and Dhurrrkk' walked over to the bench Shirazz indicated. It appeared to have been constructed especially for humans. Dhurrrkk' squatted beside them on the floor, and Shirazz coiled herself at the opposite end.

Mahree took out her computer link to record the proceedings, while Rob reserved his to translate, since Shirazz had warned them that Mizari was the official CLS language.

While she waited for the hearing to start, Mahree glanced around, seeing the Simiu contingent sitting tensely atop their padded lounges. One elderly female she tentatively identified as First Councillor Ahkk'eerrr. There were also three other females and a male representing the Simiu worlds.

Not far from their bench a complicated sling-type arrangement supported a single Shadgui. Mahree wondered what the symbiont was doing there, but she was distracted as Ssoriszs began to speak: "Friends, we are gathered on this occasion to meet two individuals from a hitherto unknown species, an occasion which is always one of great celebration for our League. Allow me to present the humans, Mahree-Burroughs . . . and Doctor-Robert-Gable."

As he spoke her name, the young woman stood up and made the Mizari greeting, as did Rob.

A ripple of murmurs ran throughout the amphitheater.

"We meet today in special session, to hear the stories of these humans, and a young Simiu, Honored Dhurrrkk'." Mahree's friend made the greeting gesture. "The Simiu Councillor has testified that the actions of these three in coming here was unwarranted and capricious, since no League intervention was needed or desired by their world or the humans in authority. The Simiu contend that their First Contact with the humans has been entirely successful, and thus qualifies them for full League membership and representation."

Ssoriszs' thin tongue lashed out for a second, then withdrew as the Mediator went on. "Since ascension to full membership is dependent on establishing a successful First Contact with a previously unknown people, it is vital that we discover the truth. We therefore ask our visitors to tell their story."

The Mizari turned to Dhurrrkk'. "Honored Dhurrrkk', as a member of a League-affiliated species, will you speak first?"

Dhurrrkk' straightened up onto his haunches. "With all due honor and respect, Esteemed One, I will not speak."

The Mizari stood very still, in what Mahree now recognized as the way his species expressed surprise or distress. First Councillor Ahkk'eerrr growled wordlessly, in the silence.

"May we know the reason why, Honored Dhurrrkk'?" the Secretary-General asked.

Dhurrrkk' nodded. "I am honor-bound to Mahree-Burroughs. We braved danger together, we have shared the prospect of imminent death as well as the breath of new life. Her honor is thus mine to defend and uphold. Because we share many honor-bonds of silence, I wish her to speak for us. I place full trust in her judgment. Also, I hereby release her from all constraints occasioned by our honor-bonds, so that she may speak as freely as necessary, in relating our stories."

Mahree stared at her friend in dismay. "Dhurrrkk'!" she whispered. "You have to defend yourself! It's your only chance!"

He shook his head, calmly. "It is my right to ask that you speak for me. Speak truthfully and well, my friend, and you will do us both honor."

Ssoriszs then turned to Rob. "Very well. Doctor-Robert-Gable, will it please you to speak first?"

Rob rose to his feet and faced the Mizari, his eyes steady.

"Esteemed One," he said, in slow, careful Mizari, as though reciting something he had memorized, "I respectfully decline."

"Rob!" Mahree blurted.

"Shut up," he whispered, in English. "This is the way it has to be. Don't make it any harder."

Again the Mediator seemed distressed. "May we know why, Doctor-Robert-Gable?"

"Yes," Rob said, in that slow, precise manner, "I would prefer that Mahree-Burroughs speak for me, since my ability to speak League-recognized languages is inferior to hers. Effective communication is essential in a situation of this magnitude, too essential to be entrusted to mechanized—and possibly faulty—translation programs." He bowed and sat back down.

Ssoriszs hissed quietly to Fys, evidently concerned, then turned back to the humans. "Mahree-Burroughs, will *you* speak?"

Mahree rose to her feet, trembling. "One moment, please, Esteemed Ones."

"Certainly," the Mediator said. "Begin when you wish."

Still shaking, she managed to bend her knees and sink back onto the bench. She looked at Rob's set, determined face. *"Why?"* she demanded, her mouth so dry she could barely speak.

"You heard why," he said fiercely, his voice low and bitter. "You think I like bowing out of the most important event in human history? Shit, no! But this is too important. Remember the 'pubic awareness' translation the other night? We can't risk any misunderstandings!"

"But I *can't*—" she began. *It's too much to have the whole thing depend on me! It's too much!*

"Yes, you can!" he snapped. "Now stand up and *do* it!"

Mahree's mind seized on one inconsequential matter out of all the questions and protests jumbling within her. "But you—where . . . how did you learn the Mizari?"

"Take deep breaths," he ordered, reaching over to grip her hands. "Relax. You'll do fine. What do you think Shirazz and I were doing all morning? I told her that I had decided to let you speak for both of us, and she agreed. Hell, Raoul knew it too, remember what he said? So I told her what I wanted to say, she translated it, and I memorized it."

As he spoke, he absently chafed her hands, eyeing her closely. Mahree forced herself to breathe slowly and, though she was still shaky, that helped. "Are you *sure*?" she pleaded. "What if I screw up?"

"I'm *positive*," he said, his eyes holding hers.

Mahree stood up.

"Most Esteemed Fys, Esteemed Ssoriszs, Esteemed Shirazz . . . Honored Ahkk'eerrr and her staff, Honored Friend-Dhurrrkk', my esteemed companion, Doctor Robert-Gable . . . and members of this most admirable and beneficial League," she spoke Mizari, feeling as if her voice were coming from someplace light-years away. "I am grateful for your invitation to speak."

She glimpsed First Councillor Ahkk'eerrr's reaction as the Simiu heard her speaking fluently in the official CLS language . . . saw her flame-colored crest suddenly droop, then flatten completely. *Surprised you? You deserve it, for what you tried to do to Dhurrrkk'!* she thought triumphantly.

Mahree had memorized a prepared speech earlier, but little of it now applied, since it was up to her to relate both sides of the story.

What should I say? she wondered frantically.

Suddenly her mother's words from when she was a child in the third grade flashed into her mind. "Honesty is the best policy, Mahree," Renee Lamont had told her little girl. "Not only because it's morally and ethically right, but because trying to remember lies is chancy. But you'll always *know* the truth."

Okay, Maman, she thought. *Here goes.*

Mahree took a deep breath. "I am young, the daughter of a builder and a healer. I was traveling between the stars so that I could attend a place of higher education when our ship picked up a radio frequency . . ."

She recounted what had happened as she had witnessed it, sparing neither her own people nor the Simiu. The misunderstandings and evasions that had mounted up between them, then Simon's insanity, and Khrekk's wounding. Her voice faltered as she spoke of Jerry's death, then of Khrekk's tragic suicide, resulting from Raoul's refusal to allow his people to enter the Arena. She related her panic when she'd overheard the frightened crew making plans to escape, no matter what the cost . . . then proudly told of Dhurrrkk's decision to seek CLS aid, knowing that he might be punished for helping the humans. Then, briefly, she summed up their voyage and its perils.

She left out only two things: how she had held Rob at gunpoint, and the truth about Doctor Blanket's sentience. But even as she characterized the blanket as simply an oxygen-emitting fungus, a plan was crystallizing in the back of her mind concerning the Avernian.

As she spoke, Mahree lost her self-consciousness, and her voice grew in conviction. "My people want only honor and good to come to the Simiu, who have been our gracious hosts. We regret the misunderstandings that occurred and would not want our voyage here to stand in the way of their full League membership."

She took a deep breath. "Our actions were impulsive, I know that. It is possible that we did the wrong thing, Dhurrrkk' and I, in not appealing to our elders. But we were two young people who faced a situation whose possible consequences seemed to us too dire to risk.

"So we acted. For me, the decision to act was easy, because my people stood to lose the most by inaction. My friend Honored Dhurrrkk' is the one who demonstrated not only nobility of spirit and great courage, but also a true commitment to interstellar peace. He could have related to his people what I had told him, but he chose instead to stand by his personal honor and the bonds of our friendship. It is my greatest hope"—she looked straight at Councillor Ahkk'eerrr—"that he will not be made to suffer for helping my people."

Mahree paused to wet her lips. "The Simiu goal of CLS membership is one I can fully understand, one that I believe humans will share. I am not officially authorized to speak for the leaders of our worlds, but I believe that Earth and its colonies will be very interested in becoming CLS members. Your organization seems to be the embodiment of all that is best and noblest in human dreams coming true—and if my words have helped in any measure to advance that day, then my life has been given lasting meaning."

She paused, then said, "Thank you for listening."

And sat down.

Again the rippling murmur, much louder now, ran through the vast auditorium. Mahree closed her eyes, then turned to Rob, a silent question on her face.

"You were *wonderful*," he whispered hoarsely, giving her a lopsided grin.

Mahree heard a sound from the Drnian. She faced the Secretary-General, then, at a gesture from Shirazz rose to her feet again.

"We thank you, Esteemed Mahree-Burroughs," the Drnian said. "Your story is one we will not soon forget." The Drnian glanced over at the Simiu contingent. "Most importantly, it was *true*."

Ahkk'eerrr did not move, but seemed to wince inwardly.

The Secretary-General gestured at the lone Shadgui, whom Mahree had forgotten, hanging there, silent and still. "Though you did not know it, our Esteemed Truth-Searcher touched your feelings to evaluate the truth of your words."

That Shadgui's some kind of living lie detector! Mahree glanced at Rob, with a can-you-beat-that? expression. Wondering whether Dhurrrkk' had known the Shadgui's function, she gazed inquiringly at him. Interpreting her look, he nodded, proudly. "Ahkk'eerrr refused monitoring," he said softly. "That is not unusual among my people, for we are renowned for our honesty. But it makes her look very bad in light of your testimony."

Dhurrrkk's got more faith in me than I deserve, Mahree thought, feeling wrung out. She returned the Drnian's bow, then sat down again.

Ssoriszs now spoke: "Assembled members," he said. "You have heard the human's story. You have also heard the testimony of First Councillor Ahkk'eerrr during our previous session. What is your decision? Shall the Simiu receive credit for a First Contact, and thus full League membership, or not? Please indicate your decision at this time."

A heartbeat's worth of silence fell over the massive dome, then the Mediator glanced down at his podium. "The decision is rendered," he said. "The Simiu did not handle their contact with this new species successfully enough to qualify them for full League membership."

Mahree gasped. Somehow, she'd never really believed that the Simiu would lose the vote. *Dhurrrkk's in a world of trouble. What'll they do to him? What will they do to the Désirée?*

First Councillor Ahkk'eerrr sat up on her haunches, only her diplomat's training keeping her from snarling openly. "I appeal the decision!"

"I regret that the voting has gone against your people," the Mediator said. "But the decision of the assembled members is well reasoned and just. Evasions, untruths, and lack of tolerance for other customs are not the way to forge bonds of trust and friendship. Your appeal is denied.''

With a glare at Dhurrrkk', Ahkk'eerrr subsided.

The Secretary-General spoke up. "Contact with the humans will be pursued, through a joint Mizari-Simiu mission to their homeworld, Earth. We will conduct the humans back to Hurrreeah, where CLS contact will be initiated with the *Désirée*. Esteemed Ssoriszs will lead the contact specialists.''

Rob nudged Mahree's arm, whispering, "The Simiu won't dare act up if they're under Mizari observation!''

"Yeah, but this is going to mean a tremendous loss of face for the Simiu. The Council may blame it all on Dhurrrkk','' she pointed out grimly.

His face fell. "You're right.''

With an air of decision, Mahree stood up and waited to be recognized. When Fys looked at her, she said: "There is one piece of evidence pertaining to the Simiu ability at initiating a successful First Contact that I did not tell this assembly. That was because, rightly speaking, it was not my information to offer. But Honored Dhurrrkk' has declined to speak, so I must do it for him. I know this assembly wishes to act as fairly as possible. I ask permission to present this evidence now.''

The Drnian glanced at the Mediator, who said something softly. Then Fys warned, "The decision of the assembly will not be overturned in regard to the Simiu/Human First Contact, Esteemed Mahree-Burroughs.''

"I understand that, Most Esteemed Fys,'' she said. "What I wish you to know concerns a different matter.''

"You may offer your evidence, then.''

Mahree knelt beside Dhurrrkk' and whispered three English words into his small, furry ear. Then she turned to the Guest Liaison. "Esteemed Shirazz, will you please assist Honored Dhurrrkk'? Without your help, this would be difficult, but I know you will provide for all contingencies.''

The Guest Liaison, though visibly surprised, agreed.

Together, Shirazz and Dhurrrkk' left, via the sinking platform.

Time went by as the murmuring assembly waited. Mahree sat hunched on the bench. Rob held her hand. They didn't look at one another as the minutes dragged by.

Finally, thirty minutes later, the lights suddenly dimmed and took on a reddish hue as the white light was leached away. The murmurs from the assembled League members grew louder.

Mahree glanced over at Rob; he gave her a thumbs-up.

The surface beneath her feet vibrated slightly as the platform began to rise; the floor irised open again.

Dhurrrkk' and Shirazz came into view as the platform drew level with the floor. The Simiu was draped in a glowing phosphorescent "cape" that shone a ghostly blue-white in the dimness.

Mahree and Rob walked over to stand on either side of their friend. Together, they faced the Secretary-General. "Most Esteemed Fys, Esteemed Ssoriszs, Councillor Ahkk'eerrr," Mahree said. "May I present Doctor Blanket, the *second*—and eminently successful—Simiu First Contact. The first person to successfully speak with Doctor Blanket was my friend, Honored Dhurrrkk'."

The Avernian's edges rippled as it lay atop Dhurrrkk's mane; warmth and a gentle amusement brushed Mahree's mind with the most delicate of mental touches. <You have done well, my young friends,> the creature remarked. <Truly, this gathering contains many wonders! I will learn much here.>

Then the Avernian's mental "voice" filled the amphitheater as the creature formed thought-words in perfect Mizari. <Greetings to the Cooperative League of Systems from an inhabitant of the planet these humans have named Avernus. My three young friends have also given me a personal designation—the name of Doctor Blanket. I am extremely pleased and honored to meet all of you!>

CHAPTER 18

✦

Troubled Homecoming

Dhurrrkk' is too damn honorable for his own good. If he'd kept his muzzle shut about who was the *first* person to communicate with Doctor Blanket, the Simiu might have received full credit for the Avernian Contact. But that honorable so-and-so told the truth, so the Simiu, in a precedent-setting decision, wound up getting only *half* the increased CLS representation they wanted so badly.

Since they fully expected to get no additional representatives at all, getting half mollified them somewhat, and Dhurrrkk' is now a planetary hero!

How ironic!

The Esteemed Mediator told me that the human share in the Avernian Contact will count very favorably toward Earth being invited to join the CLS . . . it may even give our worlds increased representation if we do join. How 'bout that?

He also said that the CLS will place Avernus under protection, whether or not the Blankets join the League. The discovery of a species with such powerful telepathy is a momentous one. The coordinates of the Avernian system are to be considered TOP SECRET.

Doctor Blanket is fine. Shirazz and Ssoriszs seem captivated by the Avernian's wise, kind nature, and its gentle but whimsical sense of humor. It accepted Ahkk'eerrr's invitation to meet the members of the Simiu Council, on the condition that Dhurrrkk' will "interpret" for it, since it's still difficult for it to "speak" to new minds.

But the news of the Avernian Contact came too late to save Rhrrrkkeet'—the Simiu Council, spurred on by members who supported Khrekk's "aunt," had already given her her walking papers. However, that turned out favorably, too, because Esteemed Ssoriszs was so impressed by what Uncle Raoul told him that he asked her to serve as the CLS liaison between the Simiu and Mizari during their mission to Earth. She accepted, and, I hope, thumbed her nose at her former bosses.

So here we are, aboard the Mizari vessel *Dawn Wind*, enroute back to Hurrreeah and *Désirée*. We've been traveling for ten days, and we'll be there in ten more. Mizari ships are *fast*.

And *big*—so big that *Rosinante* is crowded onto the lifeboat deck. Rob and I have a suite all to ourselves, with a *bathtub* in it. What luxury!

I've gotten to know Ssoriszs during the voyage, and he's a real treasure. He always calls me "Esteemed Mahree," in his charming, formal manner. He's teaching me about the CLS member species and their cultures.

When he gave me back my journal cassettes, I asked him straight out if Rob was going to be offered that CLS position. He told me he didn't know, but that he planned to recommend him for it. He wouldn't give me even a hint as to what kind of job it is, though.

I'm having second thoughts about begging the Mizari to let me stay with Rob. I don't think I could stand watching *him* work with the CLS, and not doing it myself. I feel petty admitting that, but it's true.

Maybe they want him to be the Earth/CLS liaison. That makes sense. They're going to need one.

It's hard, knowing what I know, especially after we're lying there after making love, and Rob talks happily about us being together, what we'll do on Earth, the places we'll go, the things we'll see.

The other night we watched *Casablanca* together, and I had to excuse myself when M'sieu Rick tells Ilsa, "We'll always have Paris."

At least Rick and Ilsa were still going to be on the same *planet* . . .

Mahree activated the portal and stepped through into her little cabin aboard *Désirée*. She leaned against the plas-steel bulkhead, wiping tears from her eyes. The jubilant greetings of her friends still echoed in her ears, and her shoulders tingled from all the bear hugs and back slappings.

It was blessedly quiet in her quarters, and she sighed with relief. She was happy to see everyone, she truly was, but . . . her ears were ringing from the loudness of their voices. Human speech seemed so *noisy* compared to the soft, sibilant hissing of the Mizari! And she'd never realized that human beings moved so jerkily!

These are your people, she chided herself. *You've been gone for two months, that's all. No wonder it seems strange to be among humans again. You'll get used to it.*

But the thought of her room aboard the *Dawn Wind* still made her swallow, and she wished she could go back there.

Exhausted, Mahree sank down onto her bunk, looking around her wonderingly. *So much has changed,* she thought. *And yet it still looks exactly the way it did the day I left.*

The big Mizari ship had docked at Station Three, not far from *Désirée*'s new docking location. The Simiu had asked the humans to move their vessel to one of the berths in their "interstellar" station—part of their new open policy.

Mahree and Rob, escorted by Dhurrrkk' and Rhrrrkkeet', had toted their bags down the brilliantly colored corridors with their now-familiar flat-topped pyramid shapes, until they'd reached one of the featureless white connecting tubes they all had such cause to remember. Then Dhurrrkk' had activated the outer lock and waved them through. "I will see you soon, FriendMahree, FriendRob," he'd said. "Enjoy your homecoming."

Clutching their bags, the returning wayfarers started down the overly bright tunnel. They hadn't gotten halfway before *Désirée*'s airlock had opened, and the crew, Raoul foremost among them, had come pouring out in a wave of yelling, exuberant humanity . . .

Well, I can't just sit here, Mahree thought, giving herself a mental shake. *Raoul said we'd all meet in the galley so we could tell everyone about our adventures. But first, a change of clothes and a wash . . .*

Minutes later, she came out of the head, clad in a fresh ship's jumpsuit. "Mirror," she commanded absently, reaching for her hairbrush—

—and froze.

Who is that? she wondered for a fleeting moment, before she realized that she was looking at herself.

The woman who stared back at her from the mirror was almost a stranger—a lean, wiry stranger, with a confident set to her shoulders. Her cheekbones showed prominently, and her brown eyes seemed larger, because the face in the mirror had lost the last traces of rounded, unmarked girlhood. Stepping closer, Mahree could make out tiny shadowings in the skin around her eyes and mouth that would someday be lines. *Mon Dieu,* she thought, blankly, *I look as though I've aged **years** instead of a few months!*

Hastily, she checked her hair for gray, but was relieved to find only the same brown.

Mahree tilted her head, studying her reflected features, and decided that she liked what she saw. *I don't look ordinary anymore,* she realized. *I look like a person who has been places, done things. Distinctive. That's better than being pretty.*

At a sudden thought, she hastily turned sideways to examine her breasts. *Oh, well. I guess that was too much to hope for,* she thought, and the woman in the mirror gave her a wry grin.

She heard a tap on the door. "Mahree?"

"Come in, Rob!"

Hair freshly cropped and clean-shaven again (his beard repressor had worn off before they'd left Shassiszss), he walked into the cabin, Sekhmet in his arms. "Hi."

"Sekhmet!" Mahree exclaimed, going over to pet the cat. "How are you, honey?"

"I'm fine," Rob said. "Felt good to get rid of that beard," He handed her the little animal.

"Not you," she corrected, "I was talking to the cat." She rubbed Sekhmet beneath her chin, crooning to her, and finally elicited a tiny purr. "How does she seem"

"Well, I'm not sure whether she knew me or not. Now I don't think she can decide whether to fall all over me with welcome or give me the cold shoulder."

"We'd better head for the galley," Mahree said reluctantly. "We're going to be the center of attention for a while, there's no getting around it."

"Guess so," Rob agreed, giving her a concerned look. Then he gently took the cat out of her arms and put the animal down on the bunk. He put a finger beneath her chin, holding her so she had to look straight at him. "Hang on a second . . . what's wrong?"

She sighed. "I don't know . . . doesn't it feel strange to you to be back with humans?"

"Hadn't thought about it. Does it feel strange to you?"

She glanced away. "Some. It all seems so . . . crowded. Noisy. And rather . . . petty. I feel awful saying that, but I can't help it."

He smiled. "That's because you've been seeing aliens at their best, doing Great Things, making Profound Decisions. You haven't had to see the equivalent of Esteemed Ssoriszs bumping into the furniture before he's had his morning coffee."

She managed to smile at the image. "I suppose you're right. I'll get used to it. But now humans seem so . . . tame. Rather a letdown."

Rob grinned at her. "How you going to keep 'em down on the farm, once they've seen Shassiszss, eh? C'mon, cheer up. Let's go tell everyone *everything* we've been doing—in lewd, lurid detail." He wiggled his eyebrows suggestively.

She grinned. "Even the time we turned the gravity off to see what it was like in no-weight—but forgot to drain the bathtub first?"

"Sure," he said, straight-faced. His eyes searched her features. "Feeling better?" When she nodded, he smiled. "Good. After our recitation, we can get some real food and have time to ourselves later tonight. Anything you'll need to move over to my quarters?"

She blinked at him, surprised. "Move?"

"I've got the double bed."

Mahree glanced over at her own small bunk. "Oh. I hadn't thought about that."

"Did you envision us sneaking back and forth in the wee hours, like kids in a co-ed dorm?" He gave her shoulders a little shake. "Hey, I want you beside me when I wake up each morning. I've gotten used to you being there."

Mahree thought of Ssoriszs saying, *"The decision is not final, but he has my recommendation . . ."* and had to bite her lip. She forced a smile. "Okay. If you want me, I'll be there."

"Of *course* I want you," he said, his dark eyes very intent. "Matter of fact, I . . . uh . . . well, this isn't the time . . . but we'll talk about it later, okay?"

Puzzled, she shrugged. "Sure. Whatever you say."

"That's what I love, a complaisant female who always says 'yes,' " he said teasingly.

• • •

"Real food!" Rob said contentedly, raising his mug of beer to Mahree in salute. "Did you approve of my selections?"

She nodded, and clinked her mug against his. "It was great. And using the processor in the infirmary and eating in your office was a terrific idea. We haven't had a moment to ourselves all day."

"I know. Tomorrow's going to be busy, too." He frowned, sorted desultorily through the greens in the bottom of his salad bowl, then pushed the dish away and stood up. "Another beer?"

"No, two is plenty for me," she said, wondering at his sudden change of mood. He seemed uneasy and tense, which was unlike him.

He went into the infirmary, and a moment later came back into his office with another beer. But he didn't sit down; instead he began restlessly pacing the small confines of his office, sipping the beer as he went. Finally he paused, seeming to study the old-fashioned diplomas and certificates hanging on the bulkhead over his desk. "Have you made up your mind about what you'll be doing when we reach Earth?" he asked, the question so abrupt that it sounded brusque.

Mahree shrugged uncertainly. "I don't know. The thought of college doesn't excite me the way it used to."

"Yeah, I know what you mean." He was standing half turned away from her, so that she could only see him in profile. The rigid set to his shoulders reminded her sharply of the day he'd first told her that he loved her. "What do you think you'll be doing?" she asked, trying to keep the question casual. *Does he suspect about the CLS job? Did Ssoriszs talk to him? Is that what he's leading up to?*

"I'm not sure," he said. "In the normal course of things, I'd go back to school for a couple of catch-up courses. Then I was planning on going to NewAm, which is where I'd originally figured on practicing."

He frowned. "But all that's changed, now. I don't know what I'll do. I suppose there will be media hoopla, and government debriefings, that kind of thing. We'll be famous, I guess." He sighed and shook his head. "What a depressing thought. I may be a glory hound, but I'm not a publicity hound."

Mahree nodded, understanding exactly what he meant. "Maybe something will present itself," she suggested offhandedly. "Something . . . really special."

He finally turned to look at her. "I've got that already. *You're* special, Mahree."

She forced a smile. *Soon, I won't be able to hear him say that anymore.* "You're special, too," she said, sitting back and finishing the last of her beer.

"Mahree?" he said, and she glanced up. His dark gaze held hers, and there was something in it that made her uncomfortable. "Love me?" he asked softly.

" 'To the ends of the universe and beyond the bounds of death,' " she said, repeating their now-ritual phrase.

'You're so good at languages, surely you know what that translates to, don't you?" he asked, staring straight at her.

Mahree's heart began to pound, and she had a sudden impulse to run out of the room. But she forced herself to meet his eyes. "What translation?" she asked, her voice sounding distant and tinny in her own ears.

"Till death do us part," he said seriously. "As in, will you marry me?"

She gaped at him, wondering whether she could possibly have heard him correctly. Rob drew a long breath, then ran a shaking hand through his hair. "Whew! I had no idea it'd be so hard to get that out," he muttered, half to himself. "Thought I'd be much more suave than that. They make it look so easy in films."

Mahree was still speechless.

"What's the matter, honey?" he said, taking in her stunned expression, and beginning to smile again. He came over and sat down on the edge of his desk. Reaching down, he picked up her hands and held them, his grip warm and strong. "The way you look, you'd think I'd proposed boiling you in oil, instead of honorable marriage."

Mahree's eyes suddenly flooded with tears, and she tightened her fingers around his. "Rob, I don't know what to say," she whispered brokenly.

"Say 'yes,' " he suggested cheerfully.

"And I don't know *how* to say it, either," she continued, as though he hadn't spoken.

"It's easy," he insisted, his insouciant confidence slowly ebbing as he took in her grave expression. "You can say it in English, or French, or Simiu, or Mizari—hell, say it in Hindustani, for all I care. It's a nice, short syllable. 'Yes.' Y-E-S. Try it."

"No," Mahree said, in a choked voice. One of the tears broke free and slid down her cheek. "I love you, Rob, but no. I don't want to marry you. I'm sorry."

His breath caught in his throat, as though she'd struck him. Mahree forced herself not to look away from his face; looking away would have been cowardly. But leaping at Simon Viorst's gun or sitting down to die on Avernus had been easier than watching first the bewilderment, then the baffled hurt, and finally the undisguised pain that slowly took shape on his features. It made her want to sob aloud.

"Mahree," he said, finally, "if you're kidding, it's not funny." He spoke loudly, as if by suggesting she were joking, he could make her agree with him, and thus make her stop.

Mahree swallowed. Pulling a hand free, she wiped her eyes. "Rob, I wouldn't kid you about this, believe me."

He took a deep breath. "Oh . . . kay. Let's talk about this. Why . . . or, rather, why not? You say you love me."

"I *do*!"

"Then what's wrong with marrying me?"

She sighed. "I'm too young."

"Wait a minute. You can't have it both ways—*you* convinced me that you're a grown woman. You say that on your world, women your age get married all the time."

"They do," she agreed. "But with all that's happened . . . Rob, you might have to . . . well, both of us have a lot to do before we should think about making a commitment like that. Things are too up in the air now."

His expression lightened a little. "Okay, it doesn't have to be today, Mahree—even though nothing would please me more than to get your uncle to perform the ceremony tomorrow." He ran a hand through his hair again.

When she didn't respond, he put a finger beneath her chin and tilted her face up. "Okay. Not tomorrow, then. I'm patient, honey, I'll wait. A long engagement is fine by me. A year, or even two . . ."

"I'd still only be nineteen," she whispered.

"Hell, three years, or five, then! Just as long as I know it'll happen—that we'll always be together, that'll be okay."

Mahree hesitated, tempted to tell him "yes." *You can always break an engagement,* she thought. But finally, she said, "Saying that I'm worth waiting for is the biggest compliment anyone has ever paid me, Rob."

He was watching her, eyes narrowed in thought. "There's a bottom line, here, and you still haven't told me what it is. C'mon, be truthful. Is it that you don't love me enough?"

She swallowed painfully. *I should be overjoyed to discover that he loves me enough to compromise so he can be with me on a permanent basis, but instead I just feel cornered. What in hell is wrong with me?*

Mahree bit her lip, trying desperately to think of the right thing to say, but no words came.

Rob was staring at her, his face drawn. As she continued to hesitate, he released her hands, then stood up and walked away. "Can't we just be together for now, with no formalities, no binding commitments?" she blurted, afraid that he might just keep going.

He stopped in the middle of his office and stood there for a long time, then spoke without turning around. "I don't know," he said bleakly. "You're making me wonder if you really mean it when you tell me you love me."

"Please believe me," she said, fighting back fresh tears, "I really *do*!" *And if you knew what's probably going to happen for you soon, you'd know that now isn't the time for this conversation, damn you, Rob! And you say I'm pigheaded!*

Mahree leaned her forehead in her hands, feeling slightly woozy from the alcohol. *We shouldn't be having a discussion this serious when we've both been drinking,* she thought miserably. "Rob, I'm so tired that I can't think straight. *Please . . .*" she faltered, and could not continue.

"All right," he said remotely. He walked over to pick up his beer and stood sipping it, not looking at her.

"All right, what?" she asked, looking up and wiping her eyes. When she saw his face, Mahree was frightened by his total lack of expression, sensing that behind his calm mask lay anger, frustration, and bitter disappointment. She would've rather he'd yelled at her—anything was better than watching him just *go away* like this.

"All right, we'll do it your way. No commitments, no promises. Just today, and maybe tomorrow, but who knows after that?" He spoke sardonically, in a cool, distant voice she'd never heard him use before. Mahree wanted to put her hands over her ears to shut out the sound of it. "If you ever want to talk about it again, it's up to you to bring the subject up."

Would it be so awful to say "yes" to being engaged, just to make him happy? "Rob," she whispered, then took a deep breath. *No. I can't waver. Marriage is something both people have to want, and I don't **want** to get married. I love Rob, but this isn't the time.*

He'd already raised a hand to forestall her. "No, I don't want to talk about it anymore. I don't want you to agree to something you don't want, because you feel sorry for me." He was pale, but his voice was steady, and so was his hand when he reached down to pull her up out of her seat. "It's late," he said, glancing at his watch. "Time for bed. You run along and I'll be there shortly."

Mahree felt numb with weariness and liquor as she stumbled into his adjoining cabin and through her customary bedtime routine. She dragged off her clothes, then crawled into the bunk, wondering where Rob was.

Nearly an hour later, she awoke from a restless doze, hearing his footsteps. Softly, he ordered down the lights, then the bunk shifted as he settled beside her in the darkness. He did not touch her or speak. Gradually, his breathing deepened and became more regular, then he began snoring lightly.

He's drunk, Mahree realized. *Dammit, he didn't ask so much . . . I wish I could have said, "yes, someday," I wish I could have promised, "always."*

She sighed, realizing that it could be easier dealing with people from a totally different species than one of her own. I'll make it up to him, she promised herself, feeling sleep stealing over her again. *I'll think of a way . . . somehow I'll . . .*

Turning over, Mahree draped an arm over him and snuggled against his warmth, spoon-fashion . . . Finally, she relaxed enough to drift off.

CHAPTER 19

♦

Death-Challenge

It's been two days since we came back.

Two *miserable* days.

We've got to get through this, somehow. I want things to be fixed, not broken; mended, not torn; whole, not ripped apart.

Somehow I have to come to terms with myself, so I can come to terms with Rob. I'm terrified that this is going to utterly wreck what we have together.

He was gone when I woke up yesterday morning. And last night, he was polite . . . not cold, but still he was *gone*, if you know what I mean. His body was there, but his emotions and his . . . *essence* . . . was closed up tight. I couldn't even glimpse it, much less touch it.

He was busy all day, catching up on work, so he had a perfect excuse for turning in early. I wanted to try and reopen the subject, but I didn't know what to say, or how to say it. I sat up, trying to think things through, without much success. And, by the time I came to bed, he was asleep, so I didn't disturb him.

Later, though, as I lay there staring at the ceiling, wishing that I dared to touch him—thinking that the hand-span of distance between us might as well be a parsec of empty space—I realized suddenly that he was awake, and also lying there, staring wide-eyed at the dark.

There was nothing I could do. I wanted to talk; there was nothing to say. I wanted to weep; the tears wouldn't come. I wanted things to be the way they were—and I knew then that they never will be.

Even if we get through this, somehow, I know instinctively that this is the kind of situation that changes things . . . relationships, people. It will never be the same again.

It wrenched Mahree's heart to see Joan. Her aunt sat in her cabin, hands resting listlessly in her lap, her shoulders bowed; she looked terrible, like a puppet with half its stuffing missing.

Mahree realized that Joan's auburn hair now had gray scattered through it, and the lines in her face made the younger woman want to cry. Joan looked as though she had aged decades since her niece had left.

When Mahree had entered the small, single cabin, she found Joan lying on her bunk, staring at the ceiling. She turned her head to see who her visitor was, then silently looked away. Mahree hesitated, but then, when her aunt didn't order her to leave, she sat down on the room's only chair and waited, quietly.

Finally Joan sat up, her eyes studying her niece's face. After a time she said quietly, "I heard that you were back. Hello, Mahree."

"Hello, Aunt Joan," Mahree said. She didn't ask how Joan was, because the answer was evident.

"Yoki told me where you went," the First Mate said. "What happened out there, honey?"

Mahree told her the whole story, even the part where she'd pointed a gun at Rob, threatening to shoot him. Somehow she wanted Joan to know that she wasn't the only person who had been driven to desperation during the crisis.

When Mahree finished, her aunt was silent for several minutes, then she said, "And these snake-people, the Mizari, they brought you home?"

"Yes, aboard the *Dawn Wind*."

Joan sighed. "I made a royal mess of things, Mahree. I flew off the handle and nearly wrecked this First Contact, and I *did* wreck things with Raoul. I came damn close to forcing him to do something that would've been disastrous . . . it would've been as bad as mutiny."

"I know, Uncle Raoul told me. I don't think he plans on filing any formal reprimands for insubordination," Mahree said. That was the only thing she could think of to say that might comfort the elder woman.

"That's what Doctor Gable said, when he came to see me this morning," Joan muttered.

"Did he?"

Rob had been gone when Mahree woke up; she hadn't seen him all day. Even though she tried to keep her voice even and noncommittal, something must've shown on her face. Joan's eyes narrowed. "You two were out there alone for a long time," she observed mildly.

Mahree nodded. "Yeah, we were."

Joan nodded, as though she'd had her speculations confirmed. "Growing up, aren't you?" she said, with a faint smile.

Her niece smiled back. "I didn't have much choice about it. Now if I can just get the rest of the way there."

Her aunt's smile widened, but her eyes were so sad, they broke Mahree's heart. "There is no 'rest of the way,' honey. You keep trying to get there all your life, until one day you realize it's too late to try anymore."

She looked down at her hands, hard, capable, short-fingered, ridged with prominent veins on their backs—working hands. Not pretty to look at, but good for getting things done. "Raoul . . ." she began, then stopped. "He hasn't spoken to me, since that day, except ship's orders. I tried to tell him I was sorry . . ."

"I know," Mahree said, remembering her talk with the Captain the day of their return. "I know he's unhappy with the situation, but it's going to take more time." She hesitated, then took the plunge. "He still loves you, Aunt Joan."

"I know he does," she said. "And I love him . . . no matter what happens, part of me always will." She gave her niece a look filled with bitterness. "I don't think we're going to make it through this one, Mahree. Sometimes love just isn't enough."

"I'm finding that out," the younger woman said, her throat aching. "Aunt Joan—when he does come to talk . . . please, don't just sit there. *Talk* to him. You two have got to communicate, so you can try to understand and accept what's happened. One way or another, you can't go on like this."

"Talk to him," Joan repeated softly. "Easier said than done," she said, with a touch of her old asperity.

She took a deep breath, then straightened, giving her niece a proud smile. "I still can't believe you can actually talk to those aliens. Tell me a sentence in Mizari."

Mahree complied.

"What did that mean?" the older woman asked.

"I said, 'Hold onto your courage with all your grasping appendages, for there is no night that does not end in dawn, my esteemed and dear female blood-kin.' "

Sudden tears glistened in Joan's eyes. Mahree reached out and laid a hand over hers. Joan covered it with her free hand, and the two women sat in silence for a while.

Finally Joan stirred. "You'd better go," she said. "Didn't you say something about going on a tour of Station Three?"

Mahree nodded. "Dhurrrkk' and Rhrrrkkeet' are taking Rob and Uncle Raoul and Esteemed Ssoriszs and me on a tour of this station. I can hardly wait to have Uncle Raoul meet a Mizari—they're such nice people!"

"You run along, then," Joan said, and her niece stood up. "You don't want to be late. Will you . . ." she hesitated. "Will you tell Raoul that I said hello?"

"Sure," Mahree said, around a lump in her throat. "And I'll come back to see you again . . . if you don't mind."

"I don't mind," she said. "You can tell me all about your tour. Have fun, Mahree."

Mahree glanced at Dhurrrkk' unbelievingly. "You mean the whole Council came up to this station just so they could meet Doctor Blanket?"

Her friend nodded. They were standing in the connecting tunnel, outside *Désirée*'s airlock, waiting for the others to join them for the scheduled tour of Station Three. "Several of the oldest members had never been off-planet before, FriendMahree. You should have seen them trying to make the greeting gesture in the low gravity the Avernian requires! One of them overbalanced and fell over!"

She smiled at the image his words conjured up. "So, how did you do, 'interpreting' for Doctor Blanket?"

Dhurrrkk' gave her a sideways glance. "I honestly believe that the Blanket was able to pick up their thoughts for itself, FriendMahree, and did not need me for that. But it is still difficult for the creature to project thoughts into an unfamiliar mind. When it 'spoke' to the assembly on Shassiszss, it was a tremendous effort for the Avernian."

"Did Doctor Blanket say how long it wants to stay here?" she asked. "The way its plants are growing, it could stay for a while longer. And Rob told me about you bringing it over to the infirmary for a nice X ray 'bath.' ''

Dhurrrkk' nodded. ''Such a concentration of X rays would kill one of your people or mine,'' he said. ''But our friend found it as refreshing as a thorough grooming!''

Mahree chuckled. ''All the comforts of home!''

Her Simiu friend nodded. ''I am glad to see you have not totally lost your ability to smile, FriendMahree. I sensed when we first met today that you are not your usual self. Your good spirits seem lacking. It was the same yesterday with FriendRob. Has something happened between you two?''

She sighed. ''It's hard to explain, Dhurrrkk'. We had a . . . disagreement. I guess you could call it a fight.''

''He struck you?'' Dhurrrkk' bristled indignantly. ''He is my friend, but I cannot in honor allow—''

''Oh, no, no!'' she interrupted hastily. ''This was a word fight, only, please believe me! And it was my fault, as much as Rob's. We disagreed over something very important to him.''

''What is that?''

''This hard to explain . . . you know how my people take permanent mates?''

''Yes,'' the Simiu said. ''For companionship, as well as offspring, correct?''

''Correct. Well, Rob wants me to become his wife—for us to be permanent mates.''

''And you do not want him?''

She made a helpless gesture with her hands. ''It's not that, exactly. I think someday I *will* want him. But I don't want him *right now*. I'm just too young to get married—mated permanently.''

Dhurrrkk's violet eyes were sympathetic. ''I understand. You are too young, just as I am too young to mate, still. No wonder you have not yet conceived. These things should not be rushed, FriendMahree. You need to allow your body time to mature.''

Mahree rolled her eyes at the ceiling. ''Uh . . . yeah. It's not quite like that, FriendDhurrrkk', but the end result is the same. But FriendRob is hurt by what he sees as my rejection of him.''

''You will just have to explain it to him,'' Dhurrrkk' said, reasonably. ''He is a good person. He will understand, eventually.''

''I hope so,'' she said, with a sigh. ''If he doesn't, I—''

She broke off as the Simiu airlock opened, and Rhrrrkkeet' and the CLS Mediator entered the tunnel.

Even as the four of them were exchanging greetings, *Désirée*'s airlock cycled, and Raoul Lamont and Rob Gable joined them.

Mahree introduced her uncle to Esteemed Ssoriszs, and was proud of the way the Captain remembered the greeting-bow and "a pleasure and an honor to meet you" in the Mizari language.

Raoul was wearing his voder, so the group, by mutual consent, conversed in Simiu so Lamont and Rhrrrkkeet' could both understand what was said. As the human Captain and the CLS representative exchanged pleasantries with each other and with Rhrrrkkeet', Mahree glanced cautiously over at Rob, only to find him looking at her. When their gazes met, he looked away.

She sighed, wishing she could skip this tour; it was torture to spend time with Rob when things were so strained between them. A hand touched hers, comfortingly, and she looked down to see Dhurrrkk's sympathetic eyes on her face. A wave of affection for her Simiu companion made her swallow. *He's the best friend anyone ever had,* she thought, touched.

After a few minutes of conversation, the party set off on its tour. Mahree walked beside Dhurrrkk', listening to Rhrrrkkeet' describing the sights as they encountered them.

Station Three was even larger than Station One, although constructed along the same "abacus" design, and the group spotted various signs of the interstellar trade currently docked there—they passed several Chhhh-kk-tu from a vessel carrying ore, and one of the Vardi from the *Dawn Wind* greeted them via voder, simultaneously filling the corridor with scents reminiscent of hothouse flowers, frying bacon, and a beach at low tide.

Mizari ships, Chhhh-kk-tu ships, and a ship belonging to the insectoid people Rob and Mahree had dubbed the "Apis" were in port, and several times they stood by huge viewports, exclaiming over the different designs of the assorted space freighters.

Raoul and Esteemed Ssoriszs, Mahree noted, seemed to be getting along famously. She kept an ear cocked in case either of them needed help with translations, but they appeared to be managing well. Ssoriszs spoke tolerable Simiu, and while Mahree and Rob had been gone, Paul Monteleon and Ray Drummond had refined and expanded the translation program.

Once she found herself walking beside Rob, and had to fight the urge to slide her fingers into his. He was the same as he'd been for the past two days—polite, even friendly, but impersonal. He still refused to meet her eyes.

Tonight, Mahree thought, with grim determination. *If we can't get this resolved tonight, I'm moving out. I can't go on like this.*

"Where's *Rosinante*, Dhurrrkk'?" Rob asked. "I'd like to pay my respects."

"I'd like to see that ship, too," Raoul said. "After all the adventures you had aboard it, it's a famous vessel."

"*Rosinante*?" Rhrrrkkeet' said. "What is that?"

"Your ship, Honored Rhrrrkkeet'," Dhurrrkk' said, with a sidelong glance. "The one we . . . borrowed."

"My vessel is currently having its engines overhauled," the former First Ambassador said, with a twinkle.

"*Rosinante* is in . . ." Dhurrrkk' paused. "Inside. When a ship is taken into a structure so workers do not have to suit up to work in vacuum . . . what is that called?"

"Drydock?" Mahree suggested.

"Yes, drydock," Dhurrrkk' said. "Bay 29. We are not far from there."

The group followed the Simiu down the corridors, until they reached an area in the outer "frame" of the abacus. The cavernous, pressurized area had movable raised platforms and catwalks for the convenience of workers, and could be depressurized when a ship was cradled and brought in for work. It was accessed by means of an airlock, just as the connecting tubes were.

After cycling the lock, the visitors stepped into the docking bay.

There sat hammerheaded little *Rosinante*, deserted now that the workers were off-shift, her engine housings opened. A spidery lattice that was the Simiu version of a ladder trailed up her side to a small, raised platform placed over the top part of the hull, so workers could reach all parts of the vessel easily.

"There she is," Rob said. "Hard to believe something that small could make FTL voyages."

"Poor thing, it looks like a beached bloat-fish," Mahree said. "Not in its proper element at all."

"The Council has already asked me whether I would relinquish ownership," Rhrrrkkeet' said. "They would like to display the ship in which Honored Dhurrrkk' and Honored Mahree-Burroughs and Honored HealerGable made the Avernian Contact."

Rob grimaced. "Give them the credit, Honored Rhrrrkkeet'," he said, in his careful, labored Simiu. "If it had been left up to me to discover that the Blankets were sentient, we still wouldn't know they were anything but patches of fungi."

"Do not be too sure, Robert," Ssoriszs said. "From what Esteemed Mahree tells me, you—"

"Stand and face death like a civilized person, human, if you would prove your honor!" a snarling Simiu voice rang out from behind them, followed by the soft *thud* of the airlock door cycling. There was a fizzing sound, then the smell of ozone as something shorted out.

Mahree whirled around to see two Simiu, a huge, scarred male and a smaller, middle-aged female, confronting them. Totally taken aback, she gaped at them as they paced slowly forward across the deck of the drydock bay. "Who?" she gasped. "What?"

"It is Kk'arrrsht'!" Dhurrrkk' muttered, horrified. "And with her—that is Hekkk'eesh!"

Khrekk's aunt! Mahree recognized both names. *And the famous gladiator, the one who maimed Dhurrrkk's teacher so horribly!*

"What are you doing here?" Rhrrrkkeet' was demanding. "You must both leave immediately!"

The former Council member ignored her. "RaoulLamont!" The human name sounded nearly unrecognizable as she spoke it. "I challenge you in the name of my clan and sept, so that we may regain our honor! Prepare to do battle with our honor-vessel, Honored Hekkk'eesh!"

"Kk'arrrsht'!" Rhrrrkkeet's voice cut through the resulting stillness like a laser as she stepped out to face the other Simiu female. "You are creating a grave diplomatic crisis here—you must leave immediately! Your actions are contrary to all honor and law! Leave! Now! Or I will summon security personnel!"

"I have shorted out the locks and the intercom system," Khrekk's relative replied, gesturing at the airlock door. "So do not waste your time trying to leave or call for help. No one will depart this place until our business with this human is concluded. Stand aside, Rhrrrkkeet', because this does not concern you. It concerns the human only." She looked past the Simiu/Mizari liaison to *Désirée*'s Captain. "Step forth, RaoulLamont, to meet our honor-vessel! Or run, and be hunted down as the coward you are."

"You cannot do this!" Rob protested, speaking Simiu as he moved to a position between Lamont and the two Simiu. Then he addressed the Captain in English. "Raoul, get the hell out of here. There must be another exit!"

"He's right, Uncle Raoul!" Mahree said. "Dhurrrkk', is there another way out of here?"

"I am sorry, FriendMahree, but I do not know," her friend said.

Mahree turned in a dizzy circle, blinking in the overly bright Simiu illumination, trying to spot another exit. "You've got to get out of here, Uncle Raoul! He'll kill you!"

"I'd be happy to run, *chérie*," her uncle said tightly. He was sweating, not only from the humid Simiu heat, but from fear. "But I only see the one exit."

"Honored Kk'arrrsht'," Ssoriszs said, in his most persuasive tones, "let us discuss ways in which your injured honor may be restored without resorting to lawless acts. Perhaps I can act as mediator—"

"Keep silent, scaled one!" Kk'arrrsht' snapped. "It is you and your kind that are weakening my people, making them doubt the honor-codes we have lived by for centuries! Stay out of what does not concern you!" She beckoned with one hand at the gladiator, and he slowly approached Raoul, ignoring the doctor, his muscles rippling beneath his flame-colored fur, his violet eyes blazing with excited eagerness.

"As honor-vessel for the clan"—and he voiced the growl of Khrekk's family name—"I, Hekkk'eesh, challenge you. I demand reparation for the injuries you have given—you will pay in blood, in bone, with life itself. I voice death-challenge!"

Raising himself onto his haunches, he snarled, his mane bristling out in a stiffened flame-colored halo, his enormous fangs gleaming as he offered the ritual threat-display. "Come to meet me, RaoulLamont, or continue to hide behind your underling, it makes no difference. Stay, or run—it will be the same. I am Hekkk'eesh, and you are the path I will take to restore my honor, as well as the honor of my client."

Rob bent his knees slightly, assuming a boxer's stance, fists up and ready. He was pale, but resolute. Behind him, Raoul also clenched his fists as he braced his body for the anticipated rush.

The Simiu gladiator's dappled hindquarters quivered as he tensed for the leap designed to carry him into battle with his chosen opponent.

"No!" Mahree cried desperately. "No, *don't*!" She moved to throw herself at Hekkk'eesh.

"No!" A flash of flame blurred by her, slamming into Mahree's calves, sending her stumbling back. Her feet flew out from under her, and she sat down hard on the deck. The impact was doubly jarring in the high gravity, and her breath *whoosh*ed from her lungs.

"*I* challenge!" Dhurrrkk' skidded to a halt before Hekkk'eesh, his mane bristling nearly as full as the larger, mature male's. "In the name of my friend, MahreeBurroughs, I challenge! She and I are honor-bound, and nobody touches her or her kin while I live!" he growled, then yawned his own threat-display full in the other's face, his fighting fangs nearly brushing the astonished gladiator's nose.

"Stand aside, youngling," Hekkk'eesh rumbled, putting out a hand to push the smaller male aside. "My fight is not with you."

"I say it is! In the name of my friend, MahreeBurroughs, and in the name of my teacher, K't'eerrr—he whom you so dishonorably maimed—I say that before you will touch any human, you will first kill me!"

At the mention of K't'eerrr's name, the gladiator's violet eyes narrowed angrily, but still he hesitated. Dhurrrkk' gestured at the platform over top of *Rosinante*'s hull. "If you ingested even the smallest measure of true courage or honor with your mother's milk, you will meet me on that platform, so we may settle this between ourselves, without interruption. Follow me, if you have any honor left you, Hekkk'eesh—or be forever named Hekkk'eesh the coward!"

Then, without a backward look, Dhurrrkk' loped straight over to the lattice-ladder and swarmed effortlessly up it. Hekkk'eesh, despite Kk'arrrsht's rumbled protest, followed him, his strides quick and furious, his mane bristling with indignation at Dhurrrkk's insults.

With Rob's help, Mahree stumbled to her feet, barely aware of the doctor's steadying hand on her arm. "My God!" she gasped, half sobbing with fear. "He'll be killed! He can't face a professional fighter like Hekkk'eesh!"

Frozen with shock, the observers watched as the two Simiu squared off to face each other atop the platform. Both combatants made the greeting gesture, formal as a martial arts expert's bow, then began the ritualized movements so familiar to her from the holo-vids she'd watched aboard *Rosinante*.

"We have to stop them!" Rob muttered, gripping her arm.

But how? Mahree thought, watching the two maned figures. *Hekkk'eesh is determined to regain his honor by killing Uncle Raoul, and Dhurrrkk' is determined that he'll die trying to prevent that! I know he won't declare ritual hence this time, no matter how badly he's injured! I know it! He'll keep fighting until he's too maimed to continue . . . or until he's dead.*

She wrung her hands, thinking furiously, her mind grappling with the problem even as the two fighters eased into the ritual circling that would end with a mutual rush and the true beginning of the battle. *Hekkk'eesh sees this as his return path to true honor, he said so . . . but Kk'arrrsht' and her clan are really using him as a dupe, because this fight won't restore their honor, and they must know it . . . the whole planet will turn against them. They're just seeking revenge . . .*

Her mind cleared as she managed to push aside her terror, her fear for Dhurrrkk', the emotions that were clouding and slowing her thinking. Mahree constructed the problem again, searching for a solution.

Searching—

Turning, she grabbed Rob's arm. "I think I know how to stop them!" she hissed, in a tense undertone. "But I've *got* to get up there with them, so Hekkk'eesh can hear me! Don't let anybody stop me from climbing up there, Rob, understand?"

"But you could be—"

"No buts!" she insisted. "This may be Dhurrrkk's only chance! Don't let anybody stop me, no matter what!"

Reluctantly, he nodded, then Mahree dashed toward the platform, before anyone realized she'd left the stunned little group of observers. She heard her uncle shout for her to stop, heard the pound of human footsteps, but she forced her aching legs to cover the hard deck in record time.

In seconds, she was at the lattice, her hands going out to grasp the curved sections, her feet feeling for the first steps in her upward climb.

"Mahree!" she heard Lamont's yell.

She swarmed up the lattice like a pirate going up rigging, thankful that she'd never been bothered by heights. The platform was at least fifteen meters high.

"Mahree!" Raoul bellowed, from below her, and a hand snagged her ankle. She clung frantically to the lattice, trying to jerk her foot away.

Raoul tightened his grip, just as Rob's full weight slammed against the Captain's side, breaking her uncle's hold. Mahree scrambled a little higher, then glanced down, seeing Rob dart in front of Lamont as he recovered himself. Looking dangerously slender and boyish in comparison to the Captain's height and bulk, the doctor braced himself against the lattice. "Raoul—no!"

"Get out of my way!" Lamont roared, sweeping the younger man aside as effortlessly as a bull would bat a sparrow. But Rob skidded, regained his balance, then came in again, yelling wordlessly.

Absently, Raoul reached out to thrust him away again, and the doctor ducked under his arm, slamming a vicious left into the Captain's stomach. Lamont's breath went out in a *whoosh* and he grunted, doubling over. In a blur of motion Rob punched him again, a hard right to the jaw, wringing cries of pain from both men as the doctor's knuckles impacted on bone. Raoul staggered, and Rob gave him a short, sharp left in the eye. The bigger man buckled at the knees and went down.

Gasping with pain and exertion, Rob looked up, cradling his right hand. "Get *going!*"

Whimpering with shock and terror, Mahree climbed.

When she reached the platform and swung herself up, Dhurrrkk' and Hekkk'eesh were already locked in a straining, grunting mass of flame-colored fur. It took her dazzled eyes a moment to sort out which of them was which as they grappled, biting viciously at each other's heads and necks, their canines flashing in the overhead lights.

Oh, God, I'm too late! she thought, watching helplessly as they rolled over and over, snapping and clutching, dangerously close to the edge of the platform. Both were bleeding from jagged rips on their muzzles and shoulders. Dhurrrkk' had given a good account of himself—the gladiator was streaming blood from a slash on his forearm, and his ear was torn.

But Hekkk'eesh was strong, and seasoned, and he knew every trick. Slowly, inexorably, he forced his opponent down, onto his back, as his hands wormed themselves past Dhurrrkk's muzzle, burying themselves in the thick mane, groping for a stranglehold on the younger Simiu's throat.

Seconds later he found it, and the muscles in his arms bulged as he slowly, inexorably, tightened his grip. Dhurrrkk' struggled without success to free himself.

Mahree flung herself down beside the gladiator, knowing full well that physically she could do nothing. "Hekkk'eesh!" she demanded. "Listen to me! You have been played false by Khrekk's family! If you kill Dhurrrkk', or me, or RaoulLamont, your honor will be forever gone! Listen!"

Without releasing his pressure on Dhurrrkk's throat, he glanced sideways at her, and the ripped ear nearest her twitched. Mahree plunged on, speaking in rapid Simiu. "Your path to honor does not lie with killing this youngling—what honor is there in that? You are so far above him that everyone will know how easily you could have conquered him—or all of us! True honor only lies in *not* killing! In being wise enough not to allow yourself to be used, as Kk'arrrsht' would use you!"

Dhurrrkk' was gasping, now, thrashing helplessly.

"Listen to me, Hekkk'eesh!" she pleaded. "I speak the truth, may my mother die in misery if I lie—they will use you and discard you, as they have discarded their own honor . . . you must know that the Council has decided against them! Since the Avernian Contact their clan has no public support—and Dhurrrkk', whose throat is between your hands, is the hero who *made* that contact! Tell me, will your world honor the person responsible for his death?"

The grasping fingers grew no tighter, but there was no need to—by now Dhurrrkk's violet eyes were glazing, and his frantic struggles grew weaker. "You know me!" Mahree said. "I am MahreeBurroughs, and my name is spoken of with honor among your people, is it not?"

Hekkk'eesh did not answer, but she thought she saw acquiescence to her statement in his eyes. "Then consider!" she said. "I have seen your holo-vids, watched you fight and admired you for your grace and ability! Before you tarnished your honor with K't'eerrr, you were the best—the best! I do not want you to throw away your honor this way, and so I care enough for your honor that I have been willing to compromise my own! Have I not broken the rule of silence, to speak during the battle? No person of honor would do that except to prevent a greater wrong! I speak truth!"

The gladiator's hands slackened a little as he turned his head to regard her, full-on. Mahree dared to put out her hand, touch that bloody forearm, her arm only a handbreadth from Hekkk'eesh's muzzle, from the canines that could slash her open as a human would rip frayed fabric. "Trust my honor," she said. "I beg of you. Do not make my sacrifice in breaking silence be in vain. Let us both regain our honor. Release him."

For a heartbeat longer, the Simiu hesitated, then his fingers loosened, and slipped away. Dhurrrkk' slumped bonelessly to the top of the platform and lay inert—

—but still breathing.

Mahree watched his nostrils move, saw his chest rise and fall, and tears of relief flooded her eyes. *He's not dead! He's just unconscious! He'll be all right!*

She turned back to Hekkk'eesh, who was staring at her. Slowly, ceremoniously, the gladiator made the sign for ritual hence—formally conceding the battle to Dhurrrkk'.

"You have gained great honor by this, Honored Hekkk'eesh!" she cried, her throat tight with emotion at the Simiu's gesture. "I will tell everyone of your actions, by my mother's honor, I swear it!"

There came an enraged shriek from below. "No! Kill them! You must *kill* them!"

Both Mahree and Hekkk'eesh scrambled to the side of the platform to look down. Kk'arrrsht' and the others were standing on the deck, looking up at them. The former Council member was nearly foaming as she glared at her erstwhile champion. "Kill RaoulLamont!"

Hekkk'eesh regarded her steadily. "No," he said, finally. "I will not."

"Then *I* will!"

The former Council member leaped at Raoul's throat. Kk'arrrsht' did not have the formidable fighting fangs of the Simiu males, but she still posed a grave threat, lost as she was in a berserker rage. Lamont went down with a crash, arms stiff and braced, trying to hold her off.

"No!" Rhrrrkkeet' grunted, and charged full into the other Simiu, knocking her away from the Captain. The two female aliens struggled, gasping and snarling, ripping at each other's flesh.

"We have to stop them! You must carry Dhurrrkk'! Come on!" With desperate haste, Mahree swung herself over the side of the lattice and began climbing down. Hekkk'eesh, Dhurrrkk's limp body slung over his shoulder, passed her before she was halfway down.

When Mahree reached the deck, she saw that Rhrrrkkeet' lay helpless, while Raoul and Rob were trying desperately to pull Kk'arrrsht' off her. Esteemed Ssoriszs was beside the airlock, the Mizari's tentacles flying as he tried to release the fused and jammed controls so he could open it and summon help.

Mahree bent over Dhurrrkk' for a second, saw that her friend was beginning to stir back into consciousness, then she raced toward the struggle. Hekkk'eesh loped ahead of her.

When she reached the former ambassador's side, Mahree cried out in dismay. The visible portion of Rhrrrkkeet's face was a mask of blood, ripped fur, and pulped flesh. Khrekk's aunt had her teeth fastened in her opponent's throat.

"Let me!" the gladiator demanded, pushing Rob and Raoul roughly aside. Hekkk'eesh grabbed his employer's clenched jaws, exerting his full strength to prise them apart. Dragging Kk'arrrsht' up and away, the gladiator prisoned the former Council member in an unbreakable grip, despite her frantic struggles to escape.

Even as the pressure on Rhrrrkkeet's throat was released, a spurt of magenta blood fountained up. Mahree clamped her hands across her mouth to keep from screaming in horror.

Swearing at the uselessness of his swollen, broken-knuckled right hand, Rob groped desperately with his left, searching for a pressure point amid the tangle of fur and open wound.

Raoul flung an arm around Mahree, as much to steady himself as her, as the three humans knelt beside Rhrrrkkeet'. Praying, Mahree watched tensely, hardly daring to breathe as blood jetted upward with every beat of the Simiu's heart.

"Oh, God!" Rob gasped, trying to guard his eyes from the hot splashes. "Got to—can't remember where—*got* it!" he muttered, in triumph, closing his left fingers hard. The deadly spurting faltered, then stopped. He looked up at Mahree, his face a gory mask. "For God's sake, somebody get a doctor!"

CHAPTER 20

✦

Opportunity Knocks

Dhurrrkk' just called. Rhrrrkkeet' is definitely out of the woods.

Uncle Raoul and Rob are recovering. Both spent time on the regen unit yesterday and today—Uncle Raoul for his black and swollen eye and jaw, and Rob for his hand. He broke two knuckles when he punched Uncle Raoul.

They decided to call it even.

Uncle Raoul was really undone by Rhrrrkkeet's defense of him, nearly at the cost of her own life, and when he learned that they couldn't save her right eye, he wept unashamedly before pulling himself together and going to wait outside the operating room. They wouldn't let him see her, but he waited anyway.

Dhurrrkk' will be stiff and sore for a few days, but he's fine. When I saw him last night in the Simiu hospital on Station Three, he was even getting a little cocky about the fact that he'd scored "first blood" in battle with the fearsome Hekkk'eesh. (Rob acted much the same about decking my uncle, who's a third again his size. Males, I swear—!)

And it was *Hekkk'eesh* who declared ritual hence, not Dhurrrkk', remember. As Yoki says, he'll gain much "face" from this.

Kk'arrrsht' is in custody, along with the other family members who plotted to kill Uncle Raoul. I expect the Council will deal severely with them.

Uncle Raoul went to see Joan last night, when we staggered back from the hospital, still splashed as he was with

287

Rhrrrkkeet's blood. I don't know what they said to each other; but he was with her for nearly half an hour, and then she came out and helped him get cleaned up and put something on his eye.

I don't know whether they can patch up their marriage . . . but I think maybe now they'll at least try to be partners again.

And last night, I finally talked to Rob . . .

Mahree sat on the bed, braiding her hair. "Rob . . . I want to talk to you."

He dropped his undershirt over the back of a chair with a sigh, then gave her a wary yet resigned look. "All right."

"You caught me flat-footed the other night," she said, fastening the end of her braid. "It never occurred to me that you would want to marry me. After all, when I first met you"—she gave him a sideways glance—"you didn't seem like the kind of man who was interested in marriage."

He sat down opposite her in the chair to kick off his shoes. He shrugged. "I wasn't," he admitted. "I never thought it would happen to me like this, but it has." He smiled thinly. "I guess I've changed."

"So have I," Mahree said. "Probably more than you have, since I had a lot more growing up to do in the first place. I'm going to be honest with you, Rob. I love you, more than I can say. I want us to be together, I want to sleep beside you each night. I've even found myself"—despite her resolve, she faltered, and blushed—"I've even found myself imagining you as the father of my baby . . . someday. I think we could be happy together."

His expression brightened, and he put out his good hand and clasped hers. His grasp was so warm and strong and familiar that Mahree's eyes filled with tears. She kissed the back of his hand, and her throat ached from loving him, and also from what she still had to say.

"But try to understand, Rob . . . I'm just not ready to marry anyone. In six months I may feel different. Or six years—I can't say. I need time to adjust to all that's happened—between you and me, between us and the Simiu . . . the Mizari and the CLS . . . everything. Can you understand what I'm trying to say?"

He nodded, though she saw disappointment in his eyes. "I'm afraid I can," he said. "I pushed you the other night, didn't I?"

She nodded. "Frankly, you scared me half to death," she

confessed. "I felt . . . like my horizons were closing in. I don't know what I want, or what I'm going to do, but I'm sure of one thing, which is that it would be wrong for me to marry you now."

Pain shadowed his features, and his mouth tightened. She continued, hastily, "If it were a question of losing you . . . I'd probably give in and agree to marriage. But that's not the way you want it, is it?"

He considered for a moment, then silently shook his head. "That wouldn't be right," he said, finally. "Though for a second there I was tempted, I have to admit. I want you that badly." He bit his lip, not meeting her eyes. "It scares me, how much I want you."

She wanted to put her arms around him, but she made herself sit still. "I know this isn't easy for you, either. But never think that I don't love you. I do."

Things were different between them, and Mahree knew that, as she watched him nod, silently. *It won't ever be quite the same again* . . . Where before it had been all joy, now there was sadness that came from the knowledge that they could hurt each other.

Raoul Lamont postponed *Désirée*'s departure until they were sure Rhrrrkkeet' would be recovered enough to assume her duties aboard the *Dawn Wind* as the Mizari/Simiu liaison. During those three weeks, the Simiu Council officially appointed Dhurrrkk' as the First Ambassador to Avernus, though, as he told Mahree, his duties would probably consist mostly of returning Doctor Blanket to its home, and ensuring that the fungus-beings were disturbed no more than they wished to be.

Dhurrrkk' also told his friend that as soon as *Désirée* departed for Earth, he was planning to leave for Avernus, and from there, he'd be traveling on to Shassiszss. Mahree struggled against envy for her friend, imagining Dhurrrkk' free to shuttle between Shassiszss and Hurrreeah in his work with the Avernians. She gained a new respect for the Simiu Council, knowing that they'd truly selected the best person for the job.

Rob caught up on his work, and he and Mahree spent most evenings watching his old films, or talking with Joan, Raoul, and Dhurrrkk'. The doctor managed to spend some time each day with Ssoriszs, continuing his Mizari lessons. He could now understand and speak Mizari better than he could Simiu, though he knew his accent was far from good.

A few days before *Désirée*'s and *Dawn Wind*'s scheduled departures, the Simiu Council came up to Station Three en masse and hosted an official reception to honor the humans. The entire crew was invited.

At Esteemed Ssoriszs' request Rob went over to the station early to talk to the Mizari. He was curious as to the Mizari Mediator's reason for the meeting; Shirazz had been extremely evasive when Rob asked her why the CLS official wanted to see him.

When he reached the corridor outside the big meeting room, Rob found the alien waiting for him. Ssoriszs seemed both pleased and excited about something. The doctor greeted the Mizari. "You asked to see me?"

"There is something I would like to speak to you about, Robert. Something important." He gestured with his tentacles.

Puzzled, the doctor followed the Mediator into the small chamber, and sat down cross-legged on floor cushions, as the Mizari coiled himself.

"This morning one of our vessels, the *Twilight Blossom*, docked here at Station Three, Robert. It bore a messenger from the CLS Council, saying that my recommendation on a certain matter has been discussed and affirmed. Thus I am now free to speak to you about something that has been under consideration since first you came to Shassiszss."

Rob blinked. "I'm dying of curiosity. What's going on?"

"For years we Mizari have watched the CLS grow, and known that accurate and truthful communication among our member species was becoming increasingly difficult. The more member species we garner, the more difficult it becomes for all of us to speak together. There are inherent problems, as you know, with mechanical translation devices.

"We have long sought for a way to bridge the ever-widening gap we perceived. For some time now, we have thought that the key to what we desire lies in the young people of our member species—those who are flexible and energetic enough to learn other languages, and adapt to alien ways."

"Like Dhurrrkk' and Mahree," Rob said.

"Exactly. They have provided a most shining example of

what we would like to accomplish on a far larger scale. After much consideration, we Mizari came to believe that bringing young people of different species together, so that they may learn one another's languages and customs, would be the best way to ensure understanding and communication in the future. We would like to establish a school to train such young people."

Rob suddenly remembered Shirazz asking him whether he liked kids, and a few pieces of the puzzle began to click into place. He waited silently for the Mizari to continue.

"However, there was a major stumbling block," Ssoriszs said. "We Mizari are only too often accused of trying to run the CLS to suit ourselves. We did not want to take the lead in proposing and promoting this school, and we do not want to be chief among those who direct and administer it."

The alien's scales whispered gently as the being cocked his golden-eyed head at the doctor. "But when we met you humans, we began to think our problem has been solved. You are a strong, intelligent people, with a great deal of vitality and enthusiasm. And, most important of all, you are not yet enmeshed in CLS politics—you are independent of such intrigues and wranglings, and will be, for some time to come."

When the Mizari paused, Rob said, "I see what you mean. But how do I come into it?"

"We want you to propose the idea for the school to your people, then to join with us in finding support and funding for it, on Earth, and the CLS member worlds. And after the school is built, we would like you to work there, directing it, helping to counsel and advise the students. We admire the way you have adapted to Dhurrrkk' and Mahree's friendship, helped to foster it. She gives you much of the credit for establishing good relations between the humans and the Simiu at the onset of contact between your peoples."

Rob ran a hand through his hair, thinking it over. "That's a lot of faith to put in someone you hardly know," he muttered, trying to take in the idea.

"Ah, but I *do* know you, Robert. I learned about you from one who knows you very well."

The doctor grinned, beginning to experience a rush of excitement as he thought about what this job offer could mean to him—and also to Mahree. *A chance to work for the CLS! It's her dream come true! She'd jump at the chance to be associated with that!*

During the past three weeks, Rob had become increasingly confident that before too long—perhaps by next year—Mahree would agree to marry him, and he felt, instinctively, that this job would only advance his cause.

Hell, she loves aliens—she'd like nothing better than to be at a school filled with them, he thought. *And she'd be a big help. Maybe she could teach—or be my assistant. Mizari mate for life, so they'd be bound to let us stay together.*

He thought about what it would be like to live among aliens. *It would mean giving up medicine, I suppose. Could I do that? Of course, I'd still be counseling, and I really liked that . . .*

He thought about a school filled with young people of different species, about what it would be like to counsel them, to guide them, then to watch them go off into positions of power in the galactic community. Young humans, young Mizari, young Simiu . . . young Chhhh-kk-tu—hell, even young Rigellians, he supposed. *They'll be training to be ambassadors and diplomats. Councillors to the CLS . . . interpreters . . .*

And I'd be a sort of dean, he thought. *Hardly the job for a glory hound—who ever notices a dean? An important job, but . . . strictly a backstage one.*

"Where would the school be located?" he asked Ssoriszs.

"There is a section of space about three of your Terran months' journey from most of the inhabited worlds—including your Earth. It is comparatively free of stars, so it is frequently used for a transition point for ships changing their headings— they drop out of metaspace into realspace, then activate their S.V. drives again. Captain Lamont says your human ships know it. We Mizari have a station nearby. We call this sector—" and the Mizari used a phrase that took Rob a moment to puzzle out.

The link . . . connection? . . . between stars? No, that word means "across"—the bridge across stars? Something like that.

"StarBridge?" Rob asked, in English.

The Mizari dipped his iridescent head gracefully. "That is a good translation," he said. "We think it would be best if the school were to be located not on any world, or too near any world, but in space, truly *between* the Twelve Known Worlds. We Mizari have a large asteroid we would be willing to donate. There is a rich vein of the material that powers starships—

your Paul Monteleon says you humans call it 'radonium'—that could be used to provide power for the school. This small world could be brought to that location, and placed where it would be out of the paths of space-going vessels, but convenient to the shipping lanes.''

Rob nodded. ''I'm extremely flattered by this offer, Esteemed One,'' he said, in Mizari. ''But can I have a little while to think it over? There's someone I want to discuss it with, before I give you my answer.''

''Of course,'' Ssoriszs said. ''If you agree to take the position, I would like you to return to Earth with me, abroad the *Dawn Wind*, so that we may spend the voyage time planning our strategy. I will also be talking to others whom I would like to enlist—the Chhhh-kk-tu messenger who arrived today, Kkintha ch'aait, for one. I am going to ask her to accompany us to Earth. Kkintha is a most efficient administrator. I also wish to speak with Doctor Blanket before it leaves to return to Avernus. I believe the Avernian would prove a most excellent instructor for telepathic students. You have telepaths on Earth, yes?''

''We do,'' Rob agreed. ''And I agree with you about Doctor Blanket. It would certainly be a good person for the job.'' *Have to do something about calling Doctor Blanket "it,"* he thought. *That always rubs me the wrong way. It would be too easy for kids to be disrespectful of something that's called an "it."*

He realized then that he was already thinking about ways to organize the school, and shook his head slightly. *Whoa, slow down. Talk to Mahree. Think this over carefully.*

As though his thought had summoned her, she poked her head into the room. *''There* you two are! Dhurrrkk' and I have been looking for you. The Council members are gathering.''

Rob got up and went out into the corridor, greeting Dhurrrkk' as he went. The Mizari slithered ahead of them into the meeting chamber, just behind their Simiu friend, but when Mahree would have followed them, Rob stopped her with a hand on her arm. ''Wait, honey. I have to tell you something.''

She turned back to him, let him draw her a few paces down the hall. ''What is it?''

''Esteemed Ssoriszs just offered me a job working for the CLS.''

Mahree's face lighted up, then she flung her arms around his neck and kissed him excitedly. "He *did*! Oh, I *knew* you'd get it! What kind of job?"

"Waitaminit—" Rob held her still, staring at her intently. "You *knew* about this?"

"Just that you were under consideration for some kind of CLS position. I didn't—don't—know what."

"They want to start a school for kids of different species to study alien languages and cultures. They've decided that young people are the ticket—at least partly from observing you and Dhurrrkk', apparently. They want me to try and get support for it on Earth, and then to work with the kids after it's founded."

"That sounds wonderful!" she cried excitedly. "Young people from all the different worlds in one place!"

"I knew you'd say that," he said. He frowned suddenly. "Hold on, here. If you knew about this, was the possibility of my getting this job the reason you said 'no' to my proposal? Figuring that you'd leave me free so I could take it?"

Mahree shook her head. "That was one consideration, yes, but that wasn't why I said 'no.' I told you the reason."

"Okay," he said, relieved. "Although this is the best argument yet for us getting married eventually, honey. If I decide to do this, I'll be going back aboard *Dawn Wind*, not *Désirée*, and I'll want you with me. You'd be a lot of help during the planning stages, and, after the school's built, you could help me run it—or maybe you'd rather teach."

She shrugged thoughtfully. "Maybe. I don't know whether I have any aptitude for teaching. I guess I could manage human students, at least. There *will* be human students, right?"

"Of course."

"Do you think you'll take it?" she asked.

Rob shook his head. "It's tempting," he said. "Not quite the 'something special' I had in mind, but I must admit I'm really flattered by Ssoriszs' faith in me. I don't know if I'm the person they want, frankly."

"Of course you are!" Mahree said. "You're smart, and capable, and good with people—all kinds of people. And you like kids."

He grinned at her. "Some of my best friends are kids," he agreed.

"I guess we ought to go in," Mahree said, glancing at Raoul, Paul, and Joan as they went past. "Do I look okay?"

For the first time since he'd seen her, Rob really *looked* at her, and his eyes widened in surprise. "Good grief, I didn't even know you *owned* a dress. What are those things down there?" he demanded, in mock disbelief. "Legs? Real *legs*?"

She laughed, smoothing the aqua-colored fabric. "C'mon, you've seen my legs before. And this is my one and only dress. Shirazz dropped a hint that I might want to look my best. My guess is that the Council members are planning to formally thank us for saving Dhurrrkk's and Rhrrrkkeet's lives."

"That's strange . . ." Rob said, frowning. "Nobody gave *me* any hints." He indicated his own everyday ship's coverall.

"It's probably just that Shirazz didn't get a chance to tell you in time," she said, and turned a pirouette. "Anyway, how do I look?"

He shook his head admiringly. "You look great. Good enough to make me want to skip this party . . ." he trailed off suggestively. "C'mon," he said, catching her arm and pretending to drag her off down the corridor. "The Council can tell Raoul how grateful they are."

Mahree planted her heels, laughing. "Come on inside, you idiot!"

Rob shrugged, then ceremoniously crooked his arm at her. "I should've worn my suit."

Mahree smiled as she took his arm. "I can't picture you in a suit!"

"Hey . . ." he muttered, sotto voce, as they moved toward the door, the sounds of alien and human conversations growing louder, "baby, at home I have a velvet *tux*. You should see me. I love formal parties."

Her reply was lost in the noise as they entered the large chamber.

For Rob, the following hour went by in a blur of greeting the Council members, of feeling his throat grow raw with the effort of making polite conversation in Simiu, or, occasionally, translating an unfamiliar word for one of *Désirée*'s crew members. From time to time he searched the crowd for a glimpse of aqua and flowing brown hair, and found Mahree chattering effortlessly, bright-eyed and animated among the assorted aliens.

Rob shook his head slightly as he watched her, thinking that she was as much in her element as a bird in the air.

Not only Mizari and Simiu were present, but also the Chhhh-kk-tu messenger Ssoriszs had spoken of, Kkintha ch'aait, plus a Vardi from the *Dawn Wind*. Even Doctor Blanket was there, covered against the Simiu lighting with something the Mizari engineers had come up with—a *light nullifier*. Shrouded in protective darkness, the Avernian had spread itself over one of the Simiu loungers, and was "talking" to well-wishers with Dhurrrkk's help.

The Simiu Council members extended formal thanks to Mahree, Rob, and Raoul Lamont for their help in saving Rhrrrkkeet's life, and the Simiu/Mizari liaison made a brief appearance herself, her ravaged eye socket uncovered and still so newly healed that it looked raw. Simiu never covered or removed scars gained in honorable battle.

Rhrrrkkeet' made a brief speech, thanking all of them, and concluded her remarks with the wish that humans and Simiu would continue to grow in understanding throughout the long voyage ahead of them. Since the two ships would be traveling comparatively close, radio communication would prove possible for both of them.

The humans applauded when Rhrrrkkeet' was through, earning themselves startled glances from several of the Simiu Councillors. Then Ssoriszs took Rhrrrkkeet's place at the head of the room.

"On this occasion of celebration and goodwill," the Mizari Mediator began, "I would like to speak of an extraordinary person. This morning I received a message from Shassiszss that the CLS Councillors have approved an unprecedented honor for a member of a new species."

Rob felt his cheeks grow warm. *Oh, shit,* he thought. *Am I going to have to go up there?*

"This human," Ssoriszs continued, "has demonstrated such courage, loyalty, and devotion to the cause of peace and good relations between peoples that we would like to honor her today."

Her? Rob thought blankly, thinking that the Mizari had made a mistake, then blushed again as he realized his error. *Oh—of course!*

"Esteemed MahreeBurroughs, will you please join me?" Ssoriszs said.

Flushed and excited, smiling nervously, Mahree walked forward to stand beside the Mizari.

"Esteemed Mahree," Ssoriszs said, "if it were not for you,

this day . . . this gathering . . . might never have come about.
The CLS Councillors were already most impressed with you, and
your actions during the crisis in Bay 29 merely added to their
admiration. The League values talent for communication, and
the courage to be truthful. You have amply demonstrated both
those attributes, plus a steadfast devotion to the cause of interstellar peace. You are truly a remarkable individual, and I feel
honored to know you.''

Slowly, formally, the old Mizari bowed deeply, then straightened. ''The CLS Councillors, in a unanimous decision, have
chosen to extend CLS membership to you, Esteemed Mahree-
Burroughs. This membership is given to you as an individual,
apart from any planetary membership your people may receive.
Membership for an individual is something that has never been
granted before.''

Ssoriszs looked out across the assembled gathering. ''This
gesture is being bestowed by the League in the hopes that
Esteemed Mahree will stay among us as a CLS Councillor. We
always have need of courageous, truthful individuals who are
devoted to the cause of peace and good relations among the
worlds. It is also our hope that, through her, we may begin to
know and understand you humans better.''

The Mizari turned back to Mahree. ''Esteemed Mahree, you
will be accorded one vote in our councils, a vote which will be
yours alone, and not contingent upon the number of representatives your world is granted, should it apply for membership in
the League.''

Mahree stood there speechless as Raoul and the rest of *Désirée*'s
crew began applauding wildly. Rob's breath caught in his throat,
and he shut his eyes, even as he, too, clapped. *That's it,* he was
thinking, with a sudden, cold certainty. *I've lost her. Dear God,
I've lost her. I can't compete with this.*

Finally, the Mizari waved his tentacles for silence, and the
humans slowly quieted down. ''Esteemed Mahree, I have for
you a gift,'' he said. ''One created for you by an individual who
belongs to a member species of the CLS. This person made this
gift in the hopes that you will consent to visit their world.'' The
Mizari turned to the little Chhhh-kk-tu messenger, and took from
her a small package.

After stripping the outer wrapping off it with his topmost
tentacles, Ssoriszs bent and placed the small, opalescent Rigellian

sculpture in Mahree's hands. "When the Rigellian Master heard the story of your adventures," the Mizari explained, "it was so touched by your courage that it created this sculpture specifically for you, that you might know that courage—and the appreciation of courage—is just one of many admirable qualities that transcends the boundaries of physical shape and form. Please accept this work of art, from Master—and from all the CLS members."

Mahree looked down at the beautiful, delicate little shape, and touched it with reverent fingers. Rob saw her eyes glitter, but she blinked back the tears. "Thank you," she said, in Mizari. "From the bottom of my heart, I thank you. I have never been so touched. I will treasure this always." She repeated her words in Simiu, then in English.

The presentation ceremony over, Raoul and the others rushed forward to congratulate Mahree. Jostled by the crowd, dazed with the realization he'd be going back to Earth alone, Rob hung back, numb with shock and grief. *She hasn't even realized yet that this means good-bye,* he thought, watching her laughing, flushed face. He pictured her taking her place among the Councillors on Shassiszss, wrestling with the problems of trade agreements and keeping the peace between the stars.

Rob wished he could leave, but he knew he had to stay. He forced himself to smile and act as normal as possible. He'd finished exchanging polite inanities with one of the Simiu Council members when Raoul Lamont touched his arm and whispered, "You okay, son?"

Rob managed to nod. "Yeah."

Lamont gave him a doubtful glance. "You sure?"

"Yeah."

Raoul glanced at his niece. "Maybe they'd let you stay, too."

"I haven't been invited," Rob pointed out, bluntly.

"Maybe, when she realizes what this means, she'll decide against it."

The doctor just looked at the Captain, then he shook his head.

Raoul patted the younger man on the shoulder sympathetically before moving away.

As soon as the initial rush of congratulations had slowed and calmed, Rob moved up until he was only a few paces from Mahree's side, standing half hidden behind Raoul's bulk. He watched as she bowed to Ssoriszs and said, "Please tell Master and the other Rigellians that I would be honored and delighted to visit their world.''

"Not just their world," the Mizari official told her. "Invitations to visit have been extended from each of the Twelve Known Worlds, including my own. If it is acceptable to you, you will first travel to Shassiszss aboard the *Twilight Blossom*. The ship is scheduled to leave this world about the same time as *Dawn Wind* and *Désirée* depart for Earth.''

Mahree blinked. "Oh! I guess I hadn't realized—you mean immediately, almost—''

Ssoriszs dipped his tentacles in agreement. "I only wish that I could be the one to show you my world. We could converse together among the gardens, and see the patterns the moons make as they cross the night sky . . . but, since I must go on to Earth, Esteemed Shirazz"—the Mizari indicated his assistant—"will take my place, and accompany you.''

Mahree smiled. "I would be pleased and honored to have her company.''

Ssoriszs flicked his tentacles at Dhurrrkk', who was sitting quietly on his haunches by Mahree's side. "Your friend, Honored Dhurrrkk', has also asked to accompany you. Since his appointment as First Ambassador to Avernus, he has declared that returning Doctor Blanket to its homeworld and pursuing the Avernian Contact is his first priority. Avernus will be your first stop.'' The CLS Mediator gestured in the direction of the Avernian, where the being lay beneath the shelter of its light-nullifier.

"Dhurrrkk'!" Mahree exclaimed. "You'll be going with me?''

"Yes, FriendMahree," the Simiu said. "Then we can travel on to Shassiszss together, so that I may make my report to Ahkk'eerrr and the other CLS Councillors.''

"Oh, I'm so glad!" Hastily handing her sculpture to Shirazz, Mahree stooped down to hug her friend. "It's going to be wonderful!" she exclaimed. "Traveling in space, all of us together again—''

She broke off, and Rob knew that it had finally hit her. He watched her expression, seeing the dismay as the truth slowly sank in. Mahree straightened up, biting her lip. "Where's Rob?'' she said, looking around her. "Rob?'' she called.

Guess that's my cue, the doctor thought, and stepped around Raoul into view. "Congratulations, sweetheart," he said unsteadily, holding out his hand.

Pale and shaken, she clutched his arm. "Rob! Oh . . . *Rob!*"

"Yeah," he said. "I know."

Mahree took a deep breath, struggling visibly to control herself, then turned to the Mizari. "Esteemed One, will you excuse me for now? I . . . need a little while to assimilate all this."

The Mizari bowed. "Certainly. We will speak again tomorrow."

Rob headed out the door, with Mahree beside him. He saw Dhurrrkk' start after them, then hesitate, and he shook his head quickly at the Simiu.

Outside, in the corridor, he put an arm around Mahree's shoulders and guided her back to *Désirée*. She walked like an automaton, her expression stricken. He took her straight to his office, displacing Sekhmet from the nearest seat. "You'd better sit down," he said.

She obeyed him mechanically, then sat with shoulders bowed, twisting her hands in her lap. Rob brought back a cup of coffee for each of them. "Coffee," he said. "You look like you could use some." He sat down in his desk chair, opposite her.

Mahree's voice was unsteady, and she did not look up as she spoke. "When Shirazz first told me that you were being considered for that job, I thought that *you* might be staying," she said, dully. "I was all braced to see you go off to Shassiszss. I hoped that they'd let me come with you, as a translator, maybe."

Rob took a sip of his coffee. It burned his tongue and the roof of his mouth, but he scarcely noticed it. "Talk about irony," he remarked, and then he could not stop himself from saying, "You could always turn them down." It was an effort to keep his voice level, but he managed. "You're not shy about saying 'no.' "

She looked up at him wordlessly, her eyes wide and haunted in her pale, drawn face. "I'm sorry, that was a cheap shot," Rob said. He took another sip of the coffee. "Why can't spaceships ever have decent coffee?" he wondered aloud, and was dismayed to hear his voice crack. He cleared his throat.

"Rob . . ." Mahree put her hands to her cheeks and shook her head distractedly. "Now I know what it feels like to be pulled apart, like that ancient execution they used to do with the teams of horses!"

"I know," he said. "I understand."

"If only there were some way . . ." she trailed off.

"Maybe you could . . . delay . . . this for a while," Rob suggested. "Go to Earth first, then we could both come back to

Shasssiszss together." He swallowed. *Don't beg,* he thought. ***Don't.***

But she ought to realize what she's giving up, he decided. *If you don't speak up now, you'll spend the entire voyage back to Earth cussing yourself for not trying, at least.* He took a deep breath. "What about your college, Mahree? Your education?"

"Think of all the things the Mizari could teach me, Rob! Their science is more advanced than ours. I could probably earn the equivalent of a Ph.D. in bio-sciences from studying with Shirazz!"

"And there's Earth itself," he said, continuing in the same vein. "If you're going to be representing humanity, don't you think you ought to get a look at your homeworld?" He leaned toward her. "There's lots we could do on Earth, sweetheart. Paris—shit, you've never seen *Paris,* and that's half your human heritage! The Louvre, the Arc de Triomphe."

He leaned over and took her hands in his. "Mahree . . . the Rockies are gorgeous. The Grand Canyon is breathtaking. So is the Great Wall! There's Tokyo, Moscow, New York! Honey, do you realize we've never even been on a *date*? We've never had any *fun*?"

She glanced at the door to their sleeping cabin, then looked at him sideways. He sighed, rolling his eyes. "Okay, we've had fun, right. But we haven't had a chance just to be together, two people in love, without the fate of worlds to worry about."

Slowly, she nodded. "You're right, we haven't."

"Dancing," he said. "Have you ever been dancing?"

"I don't know how," she admitted, in a small voice.

"I could teach you. I could teach you to ski, too, in the Rockies. Or the Alps."

She sighed. "I'm a good skier."

"Terrific. So am I. Can you ice skate?"

"Sure."

"I can't. *You* could teach *me.* Mahree . . ." He tightened his grip on her hands. "We could hike . . . go horseback riding . . . lie on the beach. You could find out what it's like on Earth. And *then*—in a year or two—you could come back here. And I'd come with you."

She was already shaking her head. "No, Rob . . . in the first place, saying 'not now, later' would be rude to the League. In the second place, what would you do if you stayed with me—

follow me around as my personal physician, maybe? Sit back while you watch me in the spotlight? I don't think you could stand that—any more than I could be happy being a faithful faculty wife. And that reminds me—what about Ssoriszs' plans for that school?''

Rob had forgotten all about the school at StarBridge. He let go of her hands and got up to pace around the little office, stopping to stroke Sekhmet as she sat on the edge of his desk. Her throaty purr was loud in the stillness.

Finally Rob squared his shoulders and looked back up. "*Shit*. You're right, babe . . . I couldn't hack trailing around after you like some supportive politician's spouse. The envy would get to me—sooner or later, damn it, it'd get to me.''

Mahree broke down, burying her face in her hands. Rob wanted to comfort her, but he hurt too badly himself at the moment. He stood there, fighting with the pain in his chest, taking deep breaths, trying to swallow the tightness in his throat.

Finally he was able to control himself enough to walk over and grasp her shaking shoulders, pull her up into his arms.

"Hey . . . it'll be all right," he whispered, stroking her hair. "It will, you'll see. You've got the most magnificent opportunity in the history of mankind. You'd be an idiot to turn it down. I was being selfish, but it's only because I love you too much to let you go without a fight. But I'll shut up, I promise. It won't be the end. We'll see each other, we'll manage somehow. Take it easy, baby . . . shhhhh . . . c'mon now . . . easy . . .''

Finally her sobbing died down into sniffles and hiccups. "Go wash your face,'' Rob said, giving her a gentle push toward the lavatory. "It'll make you feel better.''

When she came back, her eyes were still red, but she was outwardly composed. "Hey, cheer up, it won't be forever,'' Rob told her. "I'll be back on the *Dawn Wind*. That'll only be six months or so.'

"*Six months!*'' She gave him a despairing glance. "I can't live without you for six months!''

"Yeah, you can,'' he said, unable to keep the anguished edge out of his voice. "And you will. You'll be busy, honey. And you'll have Dhurrrkk' and Shirazz.'' He glanced down and shrugged. "You'll make out better without me than I will without you.''

Mahree stared at him bleakly. "I don't know what to do.''

Rob gazed back, his dark eyes holding hers. "Yes you do. Don't bullshit yourself, and don't bullshit me," he said. "This is going to be hard enough as it is. You're going to stay, Mahree, you know that." He paused for a beat, then said gently, "Don't you?"

She took a deep, ragged breath. "You're right. I'm going to stay."

CHAPTER 21

◆

Wishes, Stars, and Promises

He's gone.

They're all gone.

I'm the only human for parsecs, by now.

Dawn Wind left yesterday, two days after *Désirée*. The Mizari ships are faster, so they won't have any problem catching up.

I can still hardly believe it. A hundred times today I thought, *I'll have to tell Rob* . . . only to realize—*again*—that he's not here, and that he won't be back for a long time. That six-month estimate he mentioned may well be conservative. Who knows how long it will take the ruling powers back on Earth to pull themselves together when *Désirée* and *Dawn Wind* show up?

My parents won't even know what's happened for at least eighteen months.

They've given me a nice apartment here on Station Three, though I've now been cleared to go down to the surface of Hurrreeah. (Dhurrrkk' wants me to come home with him and spend some time in his mother's house the next time we're here. I think I'd like that.)

Last night, after Rob left, I broke down completely. I felt so alone. My little apartment was so *quiet*!

I finally just lay there, hurting all over, wishing I could sleep, but knowing I wouldn't. Then Dhurrrkk' signaled the door and came in. We didn't talk much; he just held my hands in his hard, leather-palmed ones, then stroked my hair as gently as he would

Sekhmet's fur, and gradually I felt better. We finally curled up together, the way we had on *Rosinante*, and then I was able to sleep.

Shirazz has been a big help, too. She's my personal physician, can you believe it? Rob spent a week coaching her, and gave her copies of all his medical texts, plus a whole pharmacopoeia of medicines designed to get me through just about any crisis. He also instructed me on what to take, if I get sick.

Uncle Raoul left me with all kinds of supplies. My own food-processing unit, textbooks, holo-vids—everything I'm likely to need. I'm going to design myself a little study curriculum, with Shirazz's help, and the next ship back is going to bring me a complete correspondence course. It may take me a while, with my other responsibilities, but I'm going to get that college degree. And someday, I hope, I'll see Earth.

Rob left me a bunch of his old films. He put one on the top of the stack. It was his beloved copy of *Casablanca*. The note accompanying it said:

> *Until we can have Paris, too—*
>
> > *Love,*
> > *Rob*

And then there was a little sketch—a very clever caricature of Rob and Ssoriszs, wearing those funny old trenchcoats, walking and slithering away together, with a background of an old-time airfield in the fog. And the Rob-figure is saying, "You know, Ssoriszs, I think this is going to be the start of a beautiful friendship."

I had no idea that Rob could draw.

This will be my last entry in this journal. I'm going to leave it behind when we depart on the *Twilight Blossom* day after tomorrow. I've gotten in the habit now, so I daresay I'll start a new one. But in that journal I'll record the present, and my plans for the future, and try not to think about the past.

"Be careful what you wish for, you might get it," goes the old saying.

Before I go to bed, I think I'll walk up to the observation deck, and look at the stars. They always comfort me. I think about the planets and the people that may be orbiting them, and I smile.

I'll watch the stars, for a while, clear and steady here where there's no atmosphere to make them twinkle, beautiful in their myriad hues . . . blue, white, yellow, red, and orange . . .

I'll watch them . . . but, believe me, it'll be a long time before I do any more wishing.

AUTHOR'S AFTERWORD

One day when I was in the third grade, I went to my local library and discovered something terrifying: *I had read all the horse books!*

Horrors! A lifetime of desolate boredom stretched before me.

Desperately I scanned the shelves, searching frantically for something new to read. My tracing fingers halted on a volume with a rocket on its spine. I pulled it out, began turning pages, and within a minute or two, laid the book beside me instead of putting it back on the shelf. *Rocket to Luna*, by Richard Marsden, I believe it was. And within minutes, another joined it . . . *Star Rangers*, by Andre Norton.

I don't remember which one I read first, but by the time I'd finished both, I was *hooked*. Science fiction was my passion. I read all the books with the rocket on the spine, and all the books by Andre Norton . . . and, as the years went by, books by Robert Heinlein, Isaac Asimov, Theodore Sturgeon, Samuel R. Delaney, Harlan Ellison, Roger Zelazny, Anne McCaffrey, Ursula K. LeGuin . . . the list goes on and on.

In the early days of my science fiction reading, though I continued to devour space adventures eagerly, I began to feel that *something* was missing. It wasn't until I was fourteen and read Andre Norton's *Ordeal in Otherwhere* that I finally figured out what the missing "something" was. Females. Girls. *Women*.

I wanted space adventures featuring female protagonists!

Not just girls who got rescued once in a while, but women who had adventures—the kind of adventures the male protagonists had. Why couldn't there be female space pilots, or traders, or explorers, I wondered. It wasn't fair for the guys to have all the fun!

Of course, nowadays we have Cirocco Jones, Ellen Ripley, Kate Harlin (from Anne Moroz's *No Safe Place*) and dozens of other great female protagonists. Heroines abound in science fiction and fantasy. But in those days, until Andre wrote about Charis Nordholm (her heroine in *Ordeal*), women were conspicuous only by their absence.

Even in *Star Trek*, which I loved and watched from its inception, most of the females did little more than swoon over James T. Kirk. (You'll note I said *most*. There were a few notable exceptions, such as "Number One." Gene Roddenberry has stated that the network moguls turned pale at the idea of having a woman second-in-command. "Get rid of her," they commanded. "And while you're at it, get rid of that guy with the ears, too." Oh, well. These were the same people who cancelled the show after its third season, on the grounds that it wasn't popular enough, so that shows how in touch with reality *they* were.)

More years went by. I became a writer myself, and enjoyed having my female protagonists explore, lead, fight, spy—and even rescue the guys, from time to time.

Then, in 1985, my agent said that she thought the time was ripe for a series of space adventure books—and she suggested that I invent one. Thus *StarBridge* was born. I knew what I liked to read, and I knew from the popularity of my *Star Trek* books that other people liked to read the same kinds of stories. So I sat down to invent a universe where those kinds of stories could be set; books about adventure in space, featuring lots of interesting aliens, with the emphasis on character interaction rather than hardware.

Books like those old space-adventure tales that I'd loved as a kid—with one difference. You guessed it—the heroes of these stories could be either male *or* female.

You'll note that the book you're holding in your hands is labeled "Book One." Currently, there are four more books under contract in the StarBridge series, with the possibility of additional books in the future. For the next volume, *Shadow*

World, I teamed up with a talented newcomer, Jannean Elliott. *Shadow World* is set about fifteen years after the events chronicled in this book.

Even though the five books are a series, they are basically independent stories, and can be read in any order. (No cliffhanger endings to make you grind your teeth waiting until the next book comes out, I promise!) ACE tells me they'll be issuing the books at approximately half-year intervals.

Here's hoping you enjoy *StarBridge* . . .

—Ann Crispin
April 1989